# The men and women who tamed the west

*Bledsoe*—The aged hunter who took in two orphan boys and raised them as his own.

*Ellen Harnett*—as tough as she was tender, she taught young Santee what a woman really was.

*Alcey Martin*—The sensitive British girl whose marriage made her yearn for freedom—and a man who could never possess her.

*Aimee*—The half-caste beauty who crossed the barriers of hate to claim the man she truly loved.

*Santee and Jubal Collier*—two brothers, one a skillful hunter and dedicated soldier, the other a ruthless businessman, an empire builder. Two men linked by blood and the quest for independence and identity in a bold, untamed land.

# They ignited the . . . FRONTIER FIRES

# FRONTIER FIRES

## by
## Aaron Fletcher

A Dell/Bryans Book

Published by
Dell Publishing Co., Inc.
1 Dag Hammarskjold Plaza
New York, New York 10017

Dell ® TM 681510, Dell Publishing Co., Inc.

ISBN: 0-440-12805-6

Printed in the United States of America

First printing—March 1980

# Part One

# CAPE FEAR

# Chapter One

Frieda woke slowly, her mind emerging reluctantly from the oblivion of sleep. She shrank from the growing awareness of her surroundings, trying to cling to the fleeting escape of sleep as sensations returned and nausea began stirring in her stomach again from the constant heaving motion of the ship. Noise dinned in her ears—the agonized groaning and creaking of heavy timbers, the wild shrieking of the wind outside, and the furious pounding of waves flinging themselves against the hull. She cringed from the fetid stench, a foul odor of unwashed bodies and clothes coming from the mass of people crowded into the tiny bunks lining each wall of the narrow compartment, and an acrid affluvium rising from the slimy mixture of vomit, urine, and seawater washing about on the floor as the ship rolled.

Then she was fully awake, her contact with her surroundings complete. And she recoiled from the meaning of the waxy, lifeless feel of Gerhart's hand in hers.

Terror exploded within her, bursting from the recesses of her mind where she had buried it during the past days. His appetite had waned, and he had been feverish and listless, so much like the others who had wasted away. The ship had been in a storm for days, and the only food had been biscuits and cold, gray, odorous chunks of meat. He hadn't eaten. The day before, his blue eyes had been shadowed with a cloud of fear. His booming voice had been only a husky whisper. She had tried to keep her smile brave and confident, both for him and to bury the gnawing fear building within her.

She clutched his hand between hers, kneading it frantically as she moved closer to him and tried to see him in the darkness. Then she felt his face, moving the tips of her fingers over his lips and nose. His skin was clammy. There was no warmth of breath against her fingers. She pulled herself closer and put her arm around him, trying to warm his body with hers and fighting the awful finality of his slipping beyond her reach. An agony of sorrow swelled within her, becoming excruciating as it cut and clawed through the numbing detachment built up during the past weeks of hardship.

Warnings had come early, during the first weeks of the voyage. But the ones who had sickened and died then had been the old and weak, the ill and infirm gambling their last dregs of strength on the possibility of finding a new life and new purpose for clinging to life. Frieda had been confident of her strength, and her only fear had been for the life developing in her womb. There had been no inkling of doubt about Gerhart's ability to shrug off any privation or passing illness. A tall, powerful man, he had always been imbued with a vitality beyond that of others. A man with a hearty, burgeoning enjoyment of life, he had seemed invincible.

Frieda lay with her arms around him and sobbed dryly, her swollen body sagging and swaying against him as the ship pitched and tossed. A gray, dim light slowly crept into the compartment as day broke outside. Gerhart's lips were parted, and his eyes were open slightly. The sparkling life of his rich blue eyes had disappeared into a dull glaze. The weak glimmering of hope that she might be wrong disappeared. She clutched him, moaning with grief.

Voices and the sounds of movement registered dimly on her consciousness as the others began stirring, climbing from the tiers of bunks, moving about in the slime washing across the floor, and talking to each other. After a time, a voice was raised in a shout near her, and several people clustered around her bunk.

Frieda lay with her arms around Gerhart, her back to those gathering around her bunk. Gerhart had understood and spoken a little English, but she spoke only German. She knew they would want to take him away and was determined to resist them. During the burials at sea she had witnessed, the canvas-covered bodies had slipped beneath the water and disappeared, leaving only a ripple that was immediately consumed by the waves. The subdued atmosphere over the ship's company had passed quickly. When there had been near relatives, their grief had been almost as transient. During bad weather those who died had been even more unceremoniously taken out and dropped over the side. Each time a human being had gone without leaving a visible trace.

And she fiercely rejected the thought that Gerhart might utterly disappear, as though he had never lived. The cemetery around the small, ancient church where her family had worshiped in Traben Trarbach was crowded with the tombstones and vaults of those who had walked the narrow, cobblestone streets down through the centuries. Level space had always been at a premium between the vineyard-covered bluffs overhanging the Mosel, but it had always been freely relinquished to expand the cemetery. There was always room to erect a monument that would weather the ages so that all who passed by would know that an honored and loved one had died. So she would keep him with her. When the ship arrived at its destination, she would dig a grave with her own hands. There was money sewn in the hem of her dress, and she would buy a monument.

But when the weather was severe, no one went on deck except for the most urgent reasons, and her fight to keep Gerhart would be deferred until the weather moderated. A man's hand reached across her to touch Gerhart, and Frieda knocked it away with her arm. The people talked loudly, and a couple of them laughed. Their nonchalant, uncaring tones and laughter cut deeply, and she felt helpless and forlorn.

Then a woman moved through the people toward Frieda, her voice raised in an angry shout. It was Nellie, a tall, buxom woman several years older than Frieda, who had been kind to her since the beginning of the voyage. The warm, congenial smile on her round, red face and her motherly attitude had bridged the lack of a common language, always providing a more complete communication than the most carefully chosen words. She sat down on the bunk, resting a hand on Frieda's shoulder and snarling at the people. They began moving away, talking and laughing. Nellie moved closer, leaning over Frieda and talking quietly as she patted her. The words were meaningless, but her hands and voice were soothing. And her sympathy brought a wave of renewed grief. Frieda clenched Nellie's hand tightly and began shaking with sobs again.

Gerhart's death was a final, crushing blow, undamming the reservoirs of despondency that had accumulated during the past months. Gerhart's love and her love for him had enabled her to endure the voyage, but the homesickness and sadness had been more intense because the first months of their marriage had been sheer bliss. Her family had continued to express extreme satisfaction over the union with the wealthy Kohler family, owners of the Kohlerhaus Winery. Friends had come to visit and admire her house. Acquaintances who had always been better dressed and snobbish about her father being a carpenter had been envious. The house was magnificent. Money for new clothes, the best of food, and other things had been abundant.

Most of all Gerhart was more perfect than she had dared hope, cheerfully teasing her out of her obligatory pique when he stopped at a gasthaus or lingered to sample the family wares after work, devouring what she cooked and boasting about her housekeeping to anyone who would listen. Tall and handsome in his frock coat and silk hat when they strolled along the sward by the river in the evenings and greeted other strollers, he made her feel beautiful when he looked down at her, his eyes on hers and his smile a silent reference to his intentions when they returned home. Always bringing her small things, a sweetmeat or a flower, Gerhart was kind, gentle, and loving.

Then the time of bliss came to an end. The head of the family, an uncle named Friedrich, had decided to expand the reach of the firm. An uncle and a brother were in France, a brother was in England, and Friedrich had decided to plant a branch of the firm where hordes of emigrants from the Rhine and Mosel valleys were going, in the British colony of Virginia in the New World.

Gerhart hadn't wanted to leave, but the family had a tradition of discipline. Frieda was resentful, because she considered Gerhart's brother Johann the logical choice if someone had to go. He was younger and unmarried, also small and frail, as was Friedrich. The only characteristics they had in common with the rest of the family were the

Kohler black hair and blue eyes; they were small men in a family of exceptionally large men, quiet and withdrawn in a family of more or less outgoing men. But Gerhart had shrugged off her suggestion that Friedrich was showing favoritism, telling her that Johann's health wasn't up to a sea voyage.

In London they stayed with Gerhart's brother Franz during the long delay while Gerhart sought passage on a ship. Many had been going to the colonies; weeks had passed and the only available accommodations were in the general passenger holds of immigrant ships, and the time for her confinement had drawn closer. After discussing it, and against Gerhart's best judgment, they had taken accommodations on the next ship.

Along with the appalling filth, lack of privacy, and inadequate food the ship had been buffeted by storms during the voyage, making Frieda seasick much of the time. But none of the storms had been as severe as the one during the past days. And through the numbing fog of despair gripping her, Frieda was remotely aware that the motion of the ship was becoming even more violent. Nellie made a startled sound and braced herself as the rolling of the ship pressed her heavily against Frieda. A man stumbled and fell across the cabin. Others laughed at him.

The ship rolled back to the other side, and Frieda felt herself slipping toward the edge of the bunk, Gerhart's body shifting and pushing her. The ship righted itself again, then there was the staggering, swaying feeling of the ship's changing course. A man shouted, his voice shrill with alarm as the ship began rolling to one side again. Nellie screamed a question at someone, bracing herself to keep from leaning against Frieda too heavily. Any reply was lost in the sudden uproar of shouts and screams, the floundering of people toward the narrow companionway at the rear of the compartment, and the rending crash of heavy timbers breaking and falling on the deck above.

The ship rolled over to an impossible angle and hesitated, shuddering and quivering. A penetrating stab of fear cut through Frieda's daze of despair as people shrieked, stumbling about the compartment. Then the ship began righting itself. The light in the compartment brightened and the sound of the wind was louder as someone opened the hatch at the top of the companionway. Nellie put an arm firmly around Frieda, dragging her off the bunk.

People were stumbling and lurching toward the companionway in a deafening chorus of shouts, their eyes wide and their faces blanched and grotesque with panic. Frieda suddenly realized that she was being dragged away from Gerhart, and she threw herself back toward the bunk, reaching for him. Moving back to the bunk and snatching up the bundle of belongings that Frieda had selected to keep with her during the voyage, Nellie pushed the bundle into Frieda's arm as she kicked and pushed her way toward the companionway, dragging Frieda along.

The ship began tilting back the other way. People fell, rolling and sliding on the floor, their limbs flailing. Frieda tried to get her feet under her, but the hem of her dress and the edges of her petticoats were soaked with water and tangled around her feet. People were clustered in a seething mass on the companionway, beating and pushing at each other as they tried to climb up. A geyser of water burst down the companionway, washing them into a mass of thrashing limbs and bodies at the bottom.

Heavy timbers splintered and crashed to the deck overhead as the ship again heeled far over. Another geyser of seawater boiled down the companionway, and some of those floundering at the bottom were swept into people on the other side of the compartment. As the angle of tilt became more acute Nellie clung to a bunk and held onto Frieda. Blankets and crude mattresses spilled across the floor into the people churning about in the foaming seawater. An older man was farther up the companionway, gripping the rail and pulling himself up, his loose leather breeches black with water, his woolen stockings slipping down his spindly legs, and his heavy shoes slipping on the wet steps. Nellie gripped the back of his breeches, jerked him out of the way, and continued up the companionway as he tumbled back down it.

Frieda slumped under Nellie's arm, numbly looking around. The shrieking wind whipped rain and spray across the deck in stinging droplets. The deck was a scene of destruction. The superstructure at the rear of the ship was a mass of wreckage. The forecastle and rails had been carried away. All three masts had splintered, and a tangle of spars, cordage, and shredded sails littered the deck and trailed in the water. Several sailors and a few passengers stumbled aimlessly about, their faces twisted with panic. The sea was a churning maelstrom. A gigantic wave loomed over the side of the ship like a mountain, an enormous mass of oily green flecked with white.

The wave began collapsing toward the ship. Nellie ran toward the ragged stump of the mainmast, pulling Frieda. The deck began tilting as the ship rode up the base of the wave. They stumbled through the cordage and spars, sliding on the wet deck. The angle on the deck became steeper, and Nellie scrambled the last few steps and snatched at the thick tangle of rope hanging around the broken mast. The ship seemed to hang onto the side of the wave, on the verge of rolling over. She jerked at ropes frantically, pulling them around herself and Frieda. The top of the wave began collapsing onto the ship.

The flood of water roared down onto Frieda with a crushing force. Agonizing pains shot through her stomach. The stinging, choking seawater filled her mouth and nose. Her lungs ached for air. She tried to hold her breath and keep the water out of her nose. The choking sensation became more intense, and her head began swimming.

The water receded, and Frieda sagged limply, gasping for breath and choking and coughing. Her hair had fallen down over her face, and she pawed at it weakly. Nellie jerked at the ropes and pulled at Frieda, shouting something. Frieda looked up at her, trying to get her feet under her. Her legs were rubbery, and she collapsed. Nellie released her and let her fall to the deck.

Time slowed to a crawl as an instant passed, seeming to take an age. When Frieda looked up, the friendly, smiling Nellie of before was gone. She was an animal intent on survival. Her face was a mask behind the lank, sodden strings of hair, her lips a thin line drawn back over her long, yellow teeth, her nostrils flared, and her eyes glaring. She made a gesture of dismissal and started to turn away, her coarse linen dress swaying limply. Then she turned back, leaning over Frieda and snatching her up, pushing her toward the rear of the ship. Frieda's shoes slid along the deck, her bundle a heavy weight on her arm.

Several men were clustered in the lee side of the wreckage

of the superstructure, throwing things into the water and leaping after them. A boat came into view at the side of the ship. Nellie leaped over splintered timbers from the superstructure, and Frieda's legs slammed into them painfully as Nellie dragged her across them. The deck began tilting again. Nellie hesitated, bending and digging in a jumble of broken wood, rope, and other debris that had washed into a pile. She jerked a marlinespike from the rubble and pushed it under her belt as she pulled Frieda around the ruins of the superstructure and toward the edge of the deck.

Frieda stiffened and resisted instinctively, but the deck was tilting again and the rail along the side of the superstructure had washed away. Nellie gripped Frieda tighter as they went off the edge of the deck and plummeted through the air. Excruciating pains shot through Frieda's stomach as she slammed into the water. The water closed over her, blinding, stinging, and choking. She tried to hold her breath, but the water rushed into her throat. The suffocating pressure crushed in around her, and she struggled frantically. Her head broke out of the water, then went under again. She surged upward, gasping for air.

A stunning, stinging blow struck the side of her face. Nellie glared into Frieda's eyes, slapping her again. Frieda went limp, her head reeling. Nellie turned and began swimming awkwardly, pulling Frieda. A wave washed over Frieda's face, and she held her breath. Her head broke out of the water again, and she choked and gagged weakly, then gasped heavily, breathing in precious air.

The ship loomed over them, breaking the force of the waves, but the spray and foam splashed across Frieda's face and waves continued washing across, submerging her. Then the boat came into sight. It was small and riding low in the water. Four men were in it, and other people were in the water around it. Two of the men were fumbling with oars, another bailing water with a canvas bucket, and the fourth pushing people away as they tried to climb into the boat.

Wreckage floated in the water, and a man clung to a piece of spar with bits of rope trailing from it. Nellie moved toward the spar, and Frieda lost sight of it as the waves continued breaking over her face, crushing her under. It seemed to last for an eternity, then her face was out of the water again. Nellie stopped, pulled at the marline-spike, and lunged with a sudden jerk. There was a meaty thud over the sound of the wind. Nellie pulled Frieda to the spar, pushing the marlinespike back under her belt. The man who had been on the spar floated away, spread-eagled in the water, the back of his head covered with blood.

The spar rode to the top of the waves, and Frieda clung to it numbly, vomiting seawater and gasping for breath. The screams of the people around them were barely audible over the shrieking of the wind and the hissing of the water. The boat came into sight again, tilting precariously as a man tried to clamber aboard and one of the men in the boat struggled with him. They both jerked out knives, grappling and stabbing at each other, then both fell into the water. Another man tried to climb in, and someone in the boat lifted an oar and hit him over the head.

A large wave washed over Frieda, and she held her breath. The pressure subsided, and her head broke out of the water again. She drew in deep breaths. Her hair covered her face, water streaming from it into her mouth, and she pushed at it weakly. Only two men were left in the boat, one of them bailing with the canvas bucket and the other punching an oar at people in the water. Nellie put her arm firmly around Frieda to pull her toward the boat. When Frieda clung to the spar, Nellie slapped her and she released the spar and sank lower in the water, her bundle trailing on her arm as the older woman pulled her toward the boat.

Most of those around the boat were floating face down, water washing over them as they brushed against Frieda. Nellie moved from side to side and dodged the oar as it flailed the water, then she caught the end of the oar and struggled with the man in the boat. Frieda turned in the water and splashed frantically with the arm unburdened by the bundle. The boat was almost within reach, and she lunged toward it. She missed, her fingernails clawing down the side of the rough boards, then she lunged again and gripped the gunwale.

Nellie had the paddle end of the oar and the man held the other end, while the boat tilted and rocked as they pushed and pulled. The other man in the boat continued

bailing with one hand, his other arm limp, seemingly unaware of the struggle a few feet from him. The man released
his end of the oar, bent down, and picked up a knife
from the bottom of the boat. Nellie dropped the oar
and moved toward the boat, pulling out the marlinespike.
The man leaned over and stabbed at Nellie, who seized his
wrist and struck at him with the marlinespike. The man
lost his footing and fell over the gunwale, almost tipping
the boat over.

They splashed and made hoarse, animallike sounds as
they struggled. A wave washed across, but the boat rode up
almost to the crest and Frieda's head was under only momentarily. The man in the boat continued bailing, his eyes
blank and unseeing. One arm flopped limply, the palm
turned forward and his forearm purple and swollen where
the bone was broken. The splashing in the water stopped,
and Nellie pulled herself through the water to the side of
the boat. She dropped the marlinespike into the boat and
clung to the side, panting heavily and gripping her side.
The man in the boat continued bailing, apparently unaware
of Nellie.

Frieda watched as Nellie pulled herself slowly into the
boat with one arm, holding her side with her other hand.
Water streamed from her heavy dress as she slid over the
gunwale. Her face was gray, haggard, and drawn, and her
dress under her hand was soaked with blood as she sat up
in the bottom of the boat. She looked at Frieda, then laboriously dragged herself along the boat toward her. Frieda
pulled herself higher, sliding her arms across the gunwale
and lifting in the sodden bundle hanging on her arm, as she
tried to pull herself into the boat. Nellie reached the end of
the boat and leaned over Frieda, gripping the back of her
dress with her free hand and making small, whimpering
sounds of effort. Frieda's face was pressed against Nellie as
she rolled into the boat on top of her bundle. There was a
strange taste in Frieda's mouth and a sticky feeling on her
lips, and she pawed at her face. It was Nellie's blood.

Stabbing pains lanced through Frieda's stomach, and she
lifted herself and turned onto her side, resting on the bundle. The water was littered with debris and people, most of
them motionless. The man was still bailing. Nellie fumbled
with an oar, fitting it into an oarlock. The pains in Frieda's

stomach became more intense, and she lifted herself and
turned onto her other side.

Fingers were gripping the gunwale inches from her face,
then a man's head slowly came into view. Water streamed
from his face and beard. His red, dull eyes looked at her
numbly. She stared at him, her mind slowly assimilating
what she was seeing. An imperative clamored in her mind,
directing a course of action, and she pondered it for long
seconds. Then she slowly pushed at one of his hands. His
lips pulled back from his teeth in a grimace of a pleading
smile, and he shook his head. The boat began tilting as he
pulled himself higher.

The thick end of the marlinespike slammed down on one
of his hands with a heavy thud, crushing his fingers against
the gunwale. Nellie leaned over Frieda, lifting the marlinespike again. The man slid his arm into the boat to his el-
bow, his fingers shapeless bloody tubes of flesh, and pulled
himself higher. He looked at Nellie with his lips drawn
back in a grotesque rictus of a grin, uttering something in a
quavering, begging wail. The marlinespike thudded down
on his other hand. His voice rose to a shrill shriek as he
began sliding back into the water. The marlinespike
slammed into his face. His face was a mask of blood. He
fell back into the water.

Nellie moved back along the boat, saying something to
the man who continued bailing with the bucket. Then he
slid forward and reached for the other oar.

The wind drove the spray and rain into her face and eyes,
but the waves rarely poured over the gunwale and into the
boat as Nellie and the man worked the oars. The pains in
Frieda's stomach became excruciating again, and she twisted
and turned, trying to find a position that would help ease the
pain. She lifted herself higher on the bundle and leaned
against it. The effort seemed to drain her last reserves of
energy. She slowly sank into a numb daze of pain and
exhaustion.

When Frieda opened her eyes the pain in her stomach
had stopped. And time had passed. Occasional droplets of
spray splattered over the gunwale and against her face, but
the rain had stopped and the wind had abated to an extent.
The waves were smaller. She lifted her head.

The boat was riding the waves smoothly. Debris dotted

the water around the boat, but the ship was gone. There were no people in the water. She turned her head. The man was leaning over his oar and the gunwale, his injured arm trailing in the water. He looked unconscious. Nellie was clutching her side and bailing with the bucket, her face drawn in lines of pain and her movements slow and faltering.

It was cold. A shiver raced through Frieda, then a trembling spasm gripped her. She lay back against the bundle as she began shaking uncontrollably, her teeth chattering.

It had been frigidly cold the first time she met Gerhart. She had seen him countless times before about the city and at various times of the year, quickly ducking her head each time so he wouldn't see her looking at him. But the first time they had actually met it had been one of the winters when the cold spilled down from the north and gripped the valley in an icy clutch, freezing the river all the way across. Her mother had scolded her for wanting to shirk her chores and go skating, but she had relented and let her go. The ice was covered with skaters, black figures against the white in the misty blue twilight spilling down from the snow-covered vineyards. Gerhart skated past, then returned with a dazzling smile to help her adjust her skates. Her skates were old and worn, passed down from her mother, and her coat was old and worn, passed down through two sisters. But he hadn't noticed, looking only at her eyes.

She had shivered from more than cold as they skated together. Gerhart had walked her home. Her mother had been ready to renew the scolding, but then she was beaming with smiles and rushing to prepare hot drinks.

Gerhart asked her not to skate with anyone else. And she never had.

Frieda stopped shivering. She looked up at the gray, featureless sky overhead, smiling.

# Chapter Two

Bledsoe woke, his mind instantly alert, and he lay motionless and looked into the darkness, listening for what had awakened him. Then he relaxed. It was the wind changing and diminishing. And the rain had slackened, dying away to a soft patter of sprinkles on the shingle roof.

Some along the river had taken precautions for a storm, tightly securing window shutters and doors, dragging boats inland, and driving animals to places of safety. But he had known the wind and rain would be moderate. The wind had remained out of the east, signaling that the storm was well out at sea and moving to the north. If the wind had shifted to the south and started gusting, it would have been a warning that the storm would pass near. If it had strengthened further and started shifting to the west, it would have been the harbinger of a storm making landfall.

But more than an analytical assessment of the direction of the wind he'd had an intuitive feeling that there wouldn't be a storm. There had been no feel of tension in the wind, no crackling atmosphere of turbulent forces gathered and poised to unleash themselves. Most of the people who lived along the river had no such intuitive feelings. Most of them had spent their lives in cabins in settlements and towns in the colonies, or in the teeming towns and cities of Europe. And the comfort of houses and cabins dulled the perception. The safety of towns, cities, and settlements enfeebled the senses. Most peple lived in masses, doing as others did. He was a lone hunter, and he walked alone.

The corn-shuck mattress rustled as he pushed the blanket aside and sat up, reaching for his clothes. The rain had stopped completely, and trickles fell from the eaves outside. The ashes in the fireplace in the main room of the cabin settled with a whisper. The dog, curled up outside the wall by the bed, heard Bledsoe moving and he stirred, yawning, stretching, and shaking himself. Bledsoe picked up his buckskin breeches and shook them out to put them on. Hannah woke with a jerk, listened to him moving, then yawned and began getting out of bed.

He put his feet into his breeches and stood up, pulling them on. "Lie abed, if you've a mind to. It's well before daylight."

"I'll not lie abed while you're up and about, Caleb," she replied sleepily, fumbling with her dress. She pulled it on over her head, and tugged at it to straighten it. "And you'll be wanting a bite to eat."

"I can see to myself."

"Not while you're home, you won't. Chance enough for that when you're away."

She went into the other room, feeling her way through the darkness. Bledsoe picked up his wamus, a loose knee-length shirt of buckskin, and pulled it on over his head. Hannah moved around in the main room of the cabin, stirring the ashes in the fireplace and breaking up pieces of wood. The dog whined and trotted around the cabin to the front door. Bledsoe tightened the laces across the opening down the chest of the wamus, turned the wide collar down on his shoulders, then sat down and pulled on his leggings and moccasins. He pulled the leggings up over his tight breeches as he slipped his feet into the moccasins, tied the thongs in the top of the leggings below his knees, and tightened the laces between the moccasins and leggings. A feeble glimmer of light came through the doorway as sticks in the fireplace flamed up, popping and cracking. Hannah tossed larger pieces of wood onto the fire and pulled an iron skillet across the stone hearth. Bledsoe picked up his wide leather belt and put it on as he walked toward the door, gathering in the wamus around his waist.

The cheerful, flickering yellow light from the fireplace filled the front room, playing over the thick, heavy home-made furniture and casting dancing shadows among the clusters of onions, herbs, and strings of dried beans and fruit hanging from the low rafters. Hannah's cat had un-curled from its nest of rags in the corner and was sitting on the edge of the hearth, watching with interest as Hannah knelt in front of the fireplace and moved pans and skillets around. Bledsoe crossed the room to the washstand, poured water from the wooden bucket into the basin, and washed his face and hands.

"There's ample left from what we had last night, the salt pork and all. And a pone of cornbread."

Bledsoe nodded, wiping his face on his sleeve. "That'll do, and more." He pulled the leather thong out of the back of his hair, smoothed his hair back and gathered it in his hands, and retied the thong. "The rain has laid, and the wind seems to be coming about."

"It has, hasn't it?" She put a skillet on the hob in the side of the fireplace and tossed more wood onto the fire, chuckling. "That lot with their wind up about a storm would have done well to mind you, wouldn't they?"

He smiled and shrugged, combing his beard with his fingers as he walked toward the door. "I would have told them if they'd asked. I'll go see to my horses."

"This'll be ready when you're through."

Bledsoe nodded, going out. The dog sprang up outside the door, wagging his tail furiously. Bledsoe patted the dog's head as he closed the door and dropped the wooden latch into place, then walked along the front of the cabin toward the corner, the dog following him. The darkness was complete, the sky heavily overcast, but Bledsoe walked with a long, sure stride through the mud at the front of the cabin. He was completely familiar with the surroundings and always mentally cataloged distances and objects around him, unthinkingly and automatically, in case he might have to move quickly in the darkness. He passed the chopping block and woodpile, turned at the corner of the cabin, and walked toward the outbuildings and stock pens behind it.

It was late summer, but the air was almost cold from the wind and rain. Heavy drops from the trees smacked soddenly into the wet ground, and chickens roosting in the lower branches of a tree by the cabin stirred and clucked sleepily. The creek off to one side splashed and gurgled as it rushed toward the river, swollen by the rain. The river below the slope made a quieter, deeper sound, a low rumble more felt than heard. The hearty, earthy barnyard odor of the animals and manure became stronger in the damp air as Bledsoe approached the stock pens and outbuildings.

The horses heard and smelled him and began snorting and stamping. The milk cow stirred and lowed softly. Bledsoe opened the slat door in the front of the corn crib, felt for the large basket, and began filling it with the dried unshucked ears. Mice scampered among the corn. He filled the basket and dumped it into the pen, then climbed through the rails and walked toward the barn. The horses became more impatient, pawing at the front of their stalls. They were Chickasaws, a breed developed by crossing horses from England with those brought from the Spanish territories by Chickasaw Indians in their migrations. They were wiry, hardy animals, capable of traveling long distances without rest and on little food and water. Small but sturdy, and able to trudge for days under loads that would stagger larger horses, still they were large enough to feed a man for days if starvation threatened.

They were also young and dangerously lively when fat from a summer of rest, plenty of corn, and grazing in the thick, lush grass in the pasture, and Bledsoe stood to one side of the doors as he turned the wooden buttons and opened them. The horses charged out, bucking and kicking, then ran to the corn. Bledsoe waited until they began eating, then he circled around them, climbed back through the rails, and walked back toward the cabin.

The rich odor of woodsmoke hung low around the cabin, and a gleam of yellow light came through the crack around the window shutter. It was a comfortable place, a sound cabin, good outbuildings and pens. And it was adequate, less than fifty acres, but had more than enough fertile land to grow vegetables to last through the year and plenty of pasture for the stock. Others acquired huge tracts and imported slaves, but he didn't have the money for large-scale undertakings. And he never would have, because he didn't have the desire to invest his life in accumulating possessions and wealth. His summers were spent in planting and harvesting, repairing the buildings, taking care of the animals, and preparing for winter. His winters were spent in the remote, deep forests by himself, hunting and trapping. It was the life his father had lived before him, and the life his father had taught him. And he was satisfied.

But reasons for dissatisfaction were materializing and multiplying. He had moved to the Cape Fear River ten years before, in 1730, fleeing the rapid growth of the population in South Carolina. Farms and plantations had been spreading across the land where he had hunted and trapped with his father in his youth, the forest and game had disappeared, and the autumn treks to find good trapping territory had become longer and longer. And most of all, there had been a feeling of being smothered in people.

North Carolina and the Cape Fear River region in particular had seemed a good choice. The overall population was small compared to other colonies, and most of it was centered around Albemarle Sound and the Pamlico River, to the north. The Cape Fear River had been settled relatively late because of continuing hostilities with the Indians in the area, and because of the difficulty in navigating the treacherous Frying Pan Shoals off the Cape of Fear. Those who settled along the river had done so because of the vast stands of longleaf pine along the river, and they had been involved in making and shipping tar, pitch, and resin to England for naval stores. The settlers had still been few in number, because the population involved in producing naval stores was far smaller than the numbers of people required on plantations. Land had been cheap enough, and it had been a short distance to move. The town of Brunswick was nearby for selling hides and furs and buying supplies. The region was settled enough to make Indian forays unlikely, providing safety for his wife during winter, but the population was still scattered and small enough for comfort and relative solitude.

When he had been planning and making the move, he heard that North Carolina was changing from a proprietary charter to a Crown colony, but it had meant nothing to him at the time. After his arrival he heard that George Burrington had arrived as the first Crown governor, which had also meant nothing to him. But things had started changing.

In order to eliminate the British Empire's dependence upon naval stores from the Baltic, bounties had been established for their production in the colonies. Governor Burrington had started an aggressive policy of settlement, particularly on the Cape Fear River region. People had come from other colonies, and Welsh, Highland Scots, English, French, and German settlers had come across the Atlantic.

Farmsteads and plantations had been established all along
Cape Fear River, from the tidal basin to the upper tributar-
ies. Tobacco, rice, indigo, flax, and hemp had become major exports. Many of the settlers carted their produce to
ports in Virginia and South Carolina, and the hinterland
was crisscrossed with trails. Another settlement had been
established up the estuary from Brunswick, called New
Liverpool at first, then Newton, and finally Wilmington,
and it had mushroomed in size. The game had disappeared.
His autumn treks had become longer again, stretching beyond the Cape Fear River valley, then into the Piedmont,
and finally into the foothills of the Blue Ridge.

He had selected land on the low-lying east shore of the
estuary near the mouth of Cape Fear. The shore was heavily forested and had fertile land in a belt, but farther inland
the forest strip thinned out into wind-blasted scrub and finally sand dunes, limiting the potential size of a farm.
When he had come, the area had been used mostly as a
common for swine to roam and feed on the forest mast,
and it had seemed unlikely that others would settle nearby
when other available areas had unlimited backholdings. But
when other available areas had been filled, then people had
settled around him.

It had become too crowded. And it was time to think
about moving again. But Hannah liked the place, liked having neighbors near for visiting back and forth when he was
gone through the winter months. And that was at least a
consideration. He loved her deeply. Around others he had
little to say. But around her he talked freely. He wanted
her comfortable and satisfied. He stopped outside the cabin
door, listening to her humming to herself as she moved
about inside the cabin, then he turned away from the door
and looked into the darkness, thinking.

There were other considerations. The mud had leaked
through the seams in his moccasins and his right foot was
throbbing dully. Two years before he had broken the foot.
It hadn't healed properly, frequently became swollen, and
was sensitive to cold and dampness. As a native of the colonies, he escaped the debilitating illnesses that plagued immigrants, his health was good, and his eyesight and hearing
were keen. But winter cold caused aches and pains he
hadn't suffered in his younger years, and exertion sapped

his strength more rapidly. He was forty, a substantial age for a long hunter. He had been on the Cape Fear River ten years, and after ten years in another place he would be fifty, ancient for a long hunter. All things considered an extra week or two of traveling to find good trapping areas didn't seem too inconvenient. And the aggravation of having people all around him could be borne. He lifted his hand, testing the wind. It had shifted to the north, a drying wind.

The dog looked up at Bledsoe hopefully and wagged his tail, plastered with mud and shaking with the damp chill. Bledsoe snapped his fingers and motioned to the dog. The dog leaped inside and trotted toward the fireplace. The cat arched its back, hissing and spitting, and darted back to its nest of rags in the corner. The dog ignored the cat and curled up in front of the hearth. Hannah carried a pewter plate and wooden cup to the table as Bledsoe closed the door.

"This rain has put paid to digging the potatoes for a while, no doubt."

"That and gathering the fodder," he said, as he sat down at the table. The cup was filled with buttermilk, and the plate was piled with pieces of fried pork, hominy, peas, and beans boiled together into a soft mass, and a large piece of cornbread. He picked up the spoon and took a bite. "But it wasn't a hard rain. And the wind's turning to the north. A north wind and a day or two of sunshine will dry it out."

Hannah nodded as she walked to the fireplace. She picked up a wooden bowl from the floor by the hearth and crumbled cornbread into it as she carried it to the buttermilk urn on a stand in the corner, then dipped buttermilk into it. The dog stood and wagged his tail as she brought the bowl back to the hearth, and he began gulping it down. Hannah tossed another piece of wood onto the fire, looking over her shoulder at Bledsoe. "The treadle on my spinning wheel is coming loose. If you'll be around the cabin today, you might have a look at it."

"I'll be about later, and I'll have a look at it then. I had in mind going down to the spit and gathering a bucket of clams."

"Aye, a pottage of clams would be good, wouldn't it?" She sat down on her stool by the hearth with a sigh, pulling her sewing box closer and rummaging in it. "The roof seems to be sound enough now. I could have done with those new shingles last winter, because I was spending all my time dragging things from under drips and keeping from under them myself."

Bledsoe smiled, sipping the buttermilk. "Aye, it appears it'll shed rain for a while now, as long as we don't have a heavy blow."

Hannah nodded, taking pieces of homespun from the sewing box and arranging them on her lap. The dog moved the wooden bowl around noisily as he licked it, then he curled up again, sighing and licking his lips in satisfaction. Hannah leaned over and tossed another piece of wood onto the fire, then held up a needle to the light to thread it. "When do you think you'll be driving in the hogs for fattening?"

Her tone was too casual, and her round, smooth face was too expressionless as the light of the flames gleamed on it. The last thing he did before leaving each autumn was butcher hogs, so the question was an indirect query on when he would be leaving. She never complained, but her sunny disposition always became progressively more subdued as the time for him to leave approached. "I hadn't thought about it, because there's ample time yet. What are you making there?"

"A kirtle for the oldest Forbes girl down the way. She's a sweet thing, and she puts me in mind of my sister Marcie when she was that age. And her ma doesn't have time to provide her properly with clothes, what with having seven to look after. . . ."

Her voice faded, her eyes dropped, and she cleared her throat diffidently as she looked down at the homespun. Her first husband had been killed by Indians, and there had been no children born to them. And none in the years she had been married to Bledsoe. She regarded her barrenness as a severe deficiency, becoming guiltily apologetic and embarrassed any time their conversation touched on the subject of children. Bledsoe would have liked a son, but children were more important to those with vast acres than they were to him. He would have liked for her to have companionship while he was gone, and he would have liked to see her natural outgoing affection for children satisfied. But other than that he had no regrets about not having children. And he wanted to reassure her, but conversation on delicate subjects was difficult for him, even with her. He took another bite of food and looked at her as he chewed.

"The girl will be glad of it then, won't she?"

Hannah cleared her throat again and nodded. "It won't take much in the way of cotton, and I had these bits of material left over. . . ."

"You don't have to explain yourself to me, Hannah. I'm not worried about a bit of cotton, and your time's your own, as you well know. If it pleases you to make a kirtle for the girl, then I'm pleased to see you do it."

She looked up at him with a wide smile, then looked back down at her sewing. Bledsoe pushed the plate away and drank the last of the buttermilk, then stood and crossed the room to the washstand. He took an oak bucket from under it and snapped his fingers at the dog as he walked to the door. "I'll be on my way, then."

"Aye, I'll see you when you return, Caleb."

The dog followed him out of the cabin and along the path to the creek. The sky had lightened with the first glimmering of dawn, and the dark shadows of the tree trunks along the path were visible. The path ended at the springhouse, a small, squat structure of stones used to keep milk, butter, and eggs cool in summer and to keep them from freezing on the rare days in winter when the temperature fell that low. The boat was nosed up onto the bank by the springhouse, and Bledsoe put the bucket in the boat, untied the bow rope from a sapling, and snapped his fingers. The dog scrambled into the boat, and Bledsoe pushed the boat out into the water and sat down in it, picking up the oars.

The sky was a pale shadow between the overhanging trees on each side of the creek, and Bledsoe moved an oar occasionally to keep the boat in the center of the creek as it drifted toward the river. Then the foliage opened out ahead, and the rushing noise of the creek diminished as it flowed into the river. Bledsoe pulled on the oars, rowing the boat well out into the river, then turned downstream.

Dawn broke. The estuary was some two miles wide and, to a casual glance, the east side remained largely in its original, untouched state. A few stumps and open spots marred the line of thick foliage above the tide shelf, a thin haze of woodsmoke hung in the trees, and there were distant sounds of axes ringing against wood, cows lowing, and dogs barking. But in the quiet half-light of early dawn, signs of habitation weren't glaring.

Brunswick stood on the high west bank, flanked by plantations that lined the river from the Frying Pan to the Forks. The town was a cluster of buildings behind spindly piers built out into the estuary, the streets rigidly parallel to the shoreline in the center, where the original grid had been laid down, and dissolving into twisting disorder on each side of the main roads at the edges of the town. Shacks extended down to the edge of the tide shelf in places, and some of the outlying buildings of the town were ramshackle and flimsy. Some had been damaged by storms and abandoned, and others were collapsing from decay and neglect. Many of the piers were sagging, and some of the warehouses at the end of the piers were abandoned. The bulk of the naval stores for export were still loaded at Brunswick, but the governor had moved the customs and naval offices to Wilmington and made it the port of entry. Much of the growth of Wilmington had been at the expense of Brunswick.

A few of the huge Georgian plantation houses, towering structures of brick, were visible from the estuary, and there were glimpses of others at the end of long driveways flanked by massive live oaks. The mansions were surrounded by landscaped parks carefully maintained by slaves, and the drives were connected by bridle paths and roads. Beyond the mansions stretched the reaches of longleaf pine that had paid for them. They were the homes of the Moores, Allens, Moseleys, Swanns, and others who had pioneered naval stores production on the Cape Fear River.

The east bank curved to the south and became the Hauleover, a narrow finger pointing toward the Frying Pan and separating the estuary from the open Atlantic. The sun rose as Bledsoe approached the Hauleover. It peeked through cracks in the clouds in the east, spreading a ruddy light and glinting brightly on the water. The tide was ebbing, and the rowboat picked up speed along the main channel as the water rushed toward the outlet to the sea. Bledsoe rested on the oars and waited until the boat passed the point where the trees thinned out into scrubby growth on the border of the encroaching sand, then he rowed toward the bank.

The dog leaped out of the boat and trotted around, sniffing, cocking his leg on the scrubby growth, and scraping his feet in the sand. Bledsoe pulled the boat up out of the water, started to take out the bucket, then hesitated and looked around. It would be some time before slack tide, the best time for clams. He dropped the bucket back into the boat, snapped his fingers at the dog, and began walking up the slope.

The sun rose higher as he climbed the slope. The bottom of the clouds in the east glowed with a fiery red, and the color faded to a dull, somber magenta in the west. The dog raced back, barking furiously, and Bledsoe stopped and shaded his eyes with his hand as he scanned the top of the slope. Game was scarce around the estuary, but bears occasionally roamed through. And he didn't have his rifle with him. But the dog's bark was one of excitement rather than warning as he darted back and forth a few paces, indicating the high ground. Bledsoe trotted up the slope, and the dog ran ahead, barking.

The dog waited for him, quivering with excitement. The brilliant crimson from the clouds gleamed on the waves rolling in, blinding Bledsoe as he stopped and shaded his eyes with his hand and looked down at the beach. Flocks of birds swarmed there and objects dotted the sand and rolled back and forth in the lapping waves. It was the debris of a shipwreck. Bledsoe ran down toward the beach.

Timbers, boards, pieces of cloth, and ragged lengths of rope floated on the edge of the water. Birds flew up with outraged screeches and crabs scuttled as Bledsoe approached the body of a man, his features obliterated and parts of his arms and chest eaten. Bledsoe ran on along the beach. There was another body, then another. A large piece of ironwork on a timber caught his eye, and he slid to a stop. All iron had to be imported, and it was a valuable item of barter among settlers for making and repairing tools and implements. Seeing another human form through the glare of the wet sand he ran on.

It appeared there were no survivors, at least none who had come ashore along that point. There were no tracks in the sand, and swarms of birds rose from each human form. He stopped, breathing heavily and looking around. The dog barked on down the beach, and Bledsoe looked closer. It was a boat containing three inert figures. He ran toward it.

The bodies of a man and woman lay in the center and stern of the boat. The man was small and thin. His left arm was swollen, and it was pocked where the birds had been feeding. Birds had been tearing at the woman's dress and feeding on her side, where rib bones were showing. Their eyesockets were hollow, gaping holes. Their features were relatively undamaged, twisted in the ugly grimaces of death.

The smaller woman in the bow of the boat was untouched by the birds. Bledsoe knelt, putting his wrist in front of her lips and nose. A feathery touch of warm breath brushed against his skin as he lifted her head. Her face was caked with salt, and her lips were cracked and swollen. Her tongue moved slightly between her open lips, and her eyelids fluttered. A whisper of sound came from her throat.

As he gathered her into his arms, he noticed that she was heavily pregnant. Her arm was thrust through the top of a heavy bundle which fell out of the boat as he lifted her. He started to kick it aside, then put her down, put the bundle on her stomach, and picked her up again. He ran along the beach with the woman, the dog racing ahead of him and barking.

# Chapter Three

Bledsoe took short, rapid strokes with the oars as he pulled across the current of the outgoing tide. The boat forged through the current, drifting sideward, then passed out of the main channel and into the eddies near the east bank. Bledsoe began taking longer strokes, heaving his weight against the oars.

There was a physician in Brunswick, a dealer in herbals and a drawer of abscessed teeth, and Bledsoe had heard of two more in Wilmington. But they were patronized mostly by the wealthy and by Crown officials. Most settlers doctored themselves or endured until they recovered or died, and Bledsoe automatically had more faith in Hannah and her stock of remedies than in a physician. Also the woman was pregnant. Minute twitches of her features indicated she might be having labor pains, and Hannah had mentioned a midwife who lived somewhere near their cabin.

But the authorities had to be notified about the shipwreck so they could collect whatever washed ashore and search for other survivors. There were several other boats moving about on the estuary, most of them putting out from Brunswick and going upstream, well out of hailing distance. As Bledsoe continued rowing, looking over his shoulder as he heaved against the oars, he saw a movement at the mouth of a creek ahead of him. A boat came out of the creek, and the occupant beached it and began walking up the tide shelf toward the edge of the trees.

Bledsoe took longer strokes with the oars until he came abreast of the man, then he rested the oars, cupped his hands around his mouth, and shouted.

"There's been a shipwreck on the shoals! Go tell the constable in Brunswick!"

The man looked at him, then waved and nodded, run-

ning back to his boat. Bledsoe began pulling on the oars
again. The man pushed his boat into the water, hopped
into it, and began rowing rapidly across the estuary. Bledsoe rowed on along the shore, looking over his shoulder
and glancing between the woman and the mouth of the
creek that ran near his house. He angled out away from the
shore as he approached the creek, then turned straight toward the creek, taking short, rapid strokes as the boat met
the current of the creek.

His breath came in deep pants as he fought the current,
slowly forcing the boat into the mouth of the creek. Then
he reached the slack water along the bank and began taking longer strokes. He turned the boat into the shallow pool
by the springhouse, drove it into the bank, then dropped
the oars and got out, pulling the bow up onto the bank.
The dog ran up the path to the cabin, barking wildly. Bledsoe drew in a deep breath, gathered up the woman in his
arms, and trotted heavily up the path, limping on his right
foot.

Hannah was coming around the corner of the cabin from
milking the cow, the cat following her. She looked at the
dog barking frantically, and her mouth fell open as she saw
Bledsoe running up the path with the woman. She dropped
the pail she was carrying and trotted toward him.

"There's been a shipwreck!" he panted. "I found this
woman on the beach, and she's having a baby!"

Hannah ran back to the cabin and threw the door open,
holding it for him. Bledsoe carried the woman inside, and
Hannah ran into the lean-to bedroom at the rear of the
cabin, straightening the blanket on the bed and looking at
the woman. "Put her right there, Caleb. Why, God bless!
She's only a child. And a pretty little thing, with that salt
all over her little face. . . ."

Bledsoe put the woman on the bed and straightened up,
breathing heavily. "She might be a child, but she's having a
baby."

"Aye, and she looks in a sad way and all," Hannah murmured in a worried tone, leaning over the woman and
pushing her hair back. "I'll fetch some water and wash all
this salt off . . . no, I'd best go for Widow Dobson without delay." She turned away from the bed and walked rap-

idly toward the door. "The baby's on its way, or I'll miss
my guess. I'll be right back, Caleb."

He nodded, following her out. She went out the front
door, gathering her skirt in one hand and lifting it, then ran
down the slope in front of the cabin and disappeared
through the trees. Bledsoe sat down heavily on the split log
bench by the door, catching his breath. The cat was lapping up the milk that had spilled from the bucket, and it
hissed and spat as the dog began lapping noisily at the milk
on the ground. Bledsoe drew in a deep breath as he rose
from the bench and went back inside. From the fireplace
he took a slender length of hickory he had been whittling
on the night before and glanced through the doorway at the
woman on the bed. He sat down on the bench again, turning the piece of wood in his hands and visualizing the ax
head that would go on the end of it, then he took out his
pocketknife and began shaving thin pieces from the end of
the stick.

There was a rustle of movement and a sound of women's
voices in the trees. Hannah came into sight, followed by a
tiny, wizened old woman in a bulky homespun dress too
large for her and an old-fashioned coif with a wide brim
around the front. The woman's features were a maze of
wrinkles in the shadow of the brim, her sharp nose and
chin almost met across her thin, toothless mouth, and her
eyes were sharp, bright, and beady. She nodded frigidly
and silently as she brushed past Bledsoe, following Hannah
into the cabin.

They went into the back room, and Bledsoe could hear
them moving around, murmuring to each other. Hannah's
footsteps came back into the front room and crossed to the
fireplace, where she built up the fire and put on the kettle
to heat, then filled the basin at the washstand and returned
to the back room. After a time she came back out for the
kettle and carried it into the back room. Bledsoe whittled,
listening to them talking quietly. Hannah's footsteps came
back into the front room again, crossing it toward the door.
Bledsoe rose and looked in.

Her face was strained and pale, and tears were standing
in her eyes. She sighed heavily, shaking her head. "Widow
Dobson says she's in a bad way indeed, Caleb. She mightn't
see another dawn."

Bledsoe nodded sympathetically, patting her shoulder. "Well, there it is, Hannah. She was in no condition to suffer through a shipwreck."

"Aye, and she's such a pretty little thing, Caleb. And gentry as well, you know. Her dress and linens are the finest, those of a lady of quality."

"Aye, I noticed her dress was of good stuff. Is there anything I can do here? If not I'll get back to the spit. It could be that there are others needing help."

Hannah pushed at her hair, sighing again and shaking her head. "No, we await God's pleasure, and all we can do is pray."

"I'll be off, then. And whatever happens don't let it plague you. You're doing all you can."

Hannah nodded, turning away from the door. Bledsoe put the stick behind the bench by the door and put his pocketknife away as he walked toward the path to the creek, snapping his fingers at the dog. He walked down the path, and as he started to motion the dog into the boat he noticed the woman's bundle in the bow. He took it out, put it in the springhouse, then motioned the dog into the boat and pushed it out into the creek.

The news had spread rapidly. Several boats were going down the estuary toward the Hauleover, and more were putting out from Brunswick and the east bank. A yawl was approaching the Hauleover, putting about and nosing into the shore, and several boats were pulled up onto the sand. Bledsoe rowed slowly along the east bank, let the current take the boat around the bend, then beached it and walked up the slope.

Several men were standing about, watching what was going on below, and some of them turned and looked at Bledsoe as he climbed the slope. Some were artisans and laborers, in loose shirts, wide leather breeches down to their knees, coarse stockings, and heavy shoes. Others were clerks, merchants, and other businessmen, wearing frock coats with wide cuffs, long waistcoats, silk or linen stockings, linen shirts and cravats, buckle shoes, and wide-brimmed or tricorn hats. Bledsoe's buckskins set him apart from all of them.

And his disposition also set him apart. His solitude in the forests through the years had made it his natural state.

He knew a few of the people by sight who lived along the east bank of the estuary, a few merchants and other people in Brunswick and Wilmington, and he had no particular desire to know any of them better. As a group they talked too much, too loud, and too aimlessly. He angled off to one side as he walked up the slope and stood by himself looking down at the beach as the dog sat down by him, panting.

Constables from both Brunswick and Wilmington were on the beach, and they had brought prisoners from the jails to collect debris and bodies. A man who appeared to be some sort of official was standing halfway down the slope, watching the activity. His long waistcoat was richly embroidered, his cravat and stockings were snowy, he had a cockade on his tricorn, and he wore a sword. He stood with one hand on the pommel of his sword and the other cocked at his wrist, and talked to the tall, blonde-headed man Bledsoe had hailed on the way back up the estuary.

Bledsoe had seen the blonde-headed man several times, once while driving his hogs the year before, and a few times while going up and down the estuary. He looked like some kind of artisan, and he seemed a friendly man, with an open, amiable face and a frank, congenial smile. As he talked to the official, he glanced along the top of the slope, and his eyes stopped on Bledsoe. He lifted his arm and waved. Bledsoe nodded. The official and the blonde man exchanged comments, then the official jerked his head toward Bledsoe and looked back down at the beach. The blonde man climbed up the slope toward Bledsoe.

He smiled affably as he approached, breathing heavily from the climb. "His nibs would like a word with you."

Bledsoe nodded and the two men began walking down the slope. "He's Captain Bixby, in charge of the naval and customs office," the man continued. "And I don't believe we've met properly, have we? I'm Alvah Raines."

"Caleb Bledsoe."

"I'm pleased to meet you. It's coming onto four years that I've lived here and I suppose it's past time that I came by to meet you, but I believe our wives have a word now and then."

"Aye, they probably have."

Bixby turned and looked at Bledsoe as he approached. There was automatic, instinctive antipathy between them as his eyes moved up and down Bledsoe and Bledsoe looked back at him stonily. "Well now, what's this? I have it that you saw the wreckage, then took yourself away without reporting it properly. Flotsam and jetsam are Crown property, you know, not treasure trove for the first one who happens by. What did you find here that you made off with so suddenly?"

"There was a woman here, and I took her to my wife."

"A survivor?" Bixby said, his bored nonchalance changing to quick interest. "What has she had to say?"

"She's said nothing."

"Nothing? She's incapable of talking?"

"Aye."

"Bloody hell!" Bixby snorted impatiently. "Out with it, man! Must I drag the bloody words from you? Is she injured, or what?"

"She's with baby. My woman has the Widow Dobson to her, and Widow Dobson opines she's dying."

Bixby grunted, looking away. He took out a snuffbox and tapped the lid with a forefinger, looking back at Bledsoe. "I'll have a look at her, then. Where do you live?"

"Cooper Creek, the first cabin on the rise to the left."

Bixby nodded, sniffing a pinch of snuff. He put the box away, took out a handkerchief and dusted his nostrils, and flicked at a speck of snuff on his cravat. "I'll be along, then. And you've assumed responsibility for seeing her buried if she dies, you know. It'll be done properly, as well, the same as those down there will be. She'll be buried in her clothes and in a box in the churchyard, not naked in a bloody swine-run or such as that."

"I'll see to her properly, if need be. And I require no bleeding admonitions on how it's to be done."

Bixby flushed, and his eyes narrowed. "That may be, but you could assuredly do with a far greater measure of respect for His Majesty's appointed officials. You may go. And hold yourself in readiness where you live until I arrive there."

Bledsoe turned and walked back up the slope with long strides, his dog following him. He heard Raines and Bixby say something to each other, then Raines came up the slope behind him. As Bledsoe reached the top of the slope,

Raines caught up with him and puffed heavily as they walked down toward the boats.

"I apologize if my long tongue got you mixed up with that lot," he panted, smiling at Bledsoe. "I'd told him that I wasn't the one who first saw the wreck, then when I saw you on the rise there, I let my tongue slip. . . ."

His voice faded expectantly, waiting for a reply. Bledsoe shrugged.

"I am sorry, you know. More than anything else I was searching for a way to be shot of him and be about my affairs. I'd like to know that you don't harbor any resentment on the matter."

"I don't," Bledsoe replied, as they stopped by his boat. He motioned the dog into the boat and began pushing it into the water. "With a bugger like him, it would have been all the same if I'd met him on a path."

Raines chuckled and nodded as he helped Bledsoe push the boat into the water. He stepped back as Bledsoe hopped into the boat, and he made a sound as though he were going to say something else. Then he silently waved. Bledsoe nodded, sliding the oars into the locks, and rowed away.

The overcast was breaking up into high clouds, and the sun gleamed on the water as Bledsoe rowed back along the estuary. Raines followed him in his boat at a distance of two hundred feet and turned in at the mouth of the creek he had come down before. Bledsoe frowned thoughtfully and pondered as he rowed on toward the creek by his cabin. Raines had been friendly to a degree greater than the situation warranted, and Bledsoe felt vaguely suspicious, wondering if Raines wanted something from him. Bledsoe turned in off the estuary at the creek and pulled to the bank by the springhouse. As he got out and tied the rope to a sapling, he thought of the woman's bundle. It wasn't inconceivable that Bixby would look around to assert his authority, and the bundle could cause a lot of trouble. Bledsoe went into the springhouse and pushed the bundle under the shelf of crockery urns and egg baskets, then walked up the path toward the cabin.

A blanket was hung over the door to the back room. Bledsoe stood outside the front door of the cabin for a moment, listening. There were movements and a breath of a whimpering sound in the back room. He called out quietly. "Hannah?"

The blanket stirred, and Hannah came out. Her face was pale and drawn, and she shook her head morosely. "She's the same, Caleb. And Widow Dobson thinks she might have to cut if the child sinks any more."

"Cut?"

"To take the baby. Or babies, because Widow Dobson thinks there might be two. But that poor child seems gone, come whatever, and she'll take the baby with her when she goes if nothing is done."

Bledsoe sighed heavily and nodded. "Well, Widow Dobson knows best. The girl's said nothing, then?"

"Nothing that a body can understand. But Widow Dobson allows that she might be a Dutchman. We just can't understand her, and I believe she might be right."

"Dutchman?" Bledsoe mused, shaking his head doubtfully. "The bodies I saw were proper English, not Dutchmen. But it could be that she is, and took passage on an English vessel."

"It may be," Hannah sighed, moving away from the door. "If Widow Dobson has to cut, she'll ask your leave, as the man of the house."

Bledsoe nodded uncertainly. Hannah went into the back room, dropping the blanket in place behind her. Bledsoe sat down on the bench by the front door and patted the dog absently, thinking about what Hannah had said. There was a sound of footsteps on the path, and the dog stiffened. Bledsoe stood up as Raines came into sight, his blonde hair bright against the foliage. A woman carrying a large kettle and a bucket followed him. The dog snarled and started to charge toward them, but Bledsoe snapped his fingers and called him back.

"My woman thought she would bring some victuals and see if she could be of help," Raines said with his affable smile as he approached. "And I brought her over in my boat so she could keep her feet dry."

"Well, we're much obliged," Bledsoe said cautiously.

"We're pleased to help. Sarah, this is Caleb Bledsoe. Caleb, this is my wife Sarah."

She was a small, pretty woman, wearing a muslin dress rather than homespun in recognition of the occasion of visiting another cabin, with her hair tied up in a colorful kerchief. She smiled and nodded. "I'm pleased to meet you."

"I'm pleased to meet you. Just step on in, if you like. Hannah and Widow Dobson are in the back room."

She went in, and Raines took a bottle from his pocket as he and Bledsoe turned toward the bench by the door. "I brought this along, because I thought a sip might be welcome."

"Aye, I'll have a sip with you, then."

Raines took out his pocketknife and prized at the cork in the bottle as they sat down on the bench. "I understand you're a long hunter."

"Aye."

"I'm a carpenter myself, but these past days of rain have turned me into a loafer. I had some work on a cabin down the way and two clapboard houses going in Brunswick, and now I'm days behind." He smiled and nodded in thanks to his wife as she came out with two cups half filled with water and put them on the bench between them. He poured a splash of rum into each cup. "But I'm sure there'll be ample work left undone when I'm dead and gone. Here's your health."

Bledsoe nodded, taking a sip from his cup and reaching behind the bench for the hickory stick. Raines put his cup down, went to the chopping block, and searched through the wood by it. He picked out a billet of oak and walked back to the bench, taking out his pocketknife.

"How far do you go on your hunting trips?"

"Only as far as I have to. Hunting's not as much problem as trapping, and I've been going over across the Blue Ridge these past years before I've found much beaver."

Raines was silent for a moment, turning the piece of wood in his hand and cutting long slivers to smooth it down, then he glanced at Bledsoe and nodded. "That's a good way away. Well, I've been wanting to meet you properly for some time, because there's something I'd like to discuss with you. My oldest boy Isaac is fifteen, and I've been trying to place him. He doesn't take to carpentry, and I had him with a monger and a cooper in Wilmington for a time, and he didn't take to either of those. The boy likes hunting, fishing, trapping, and things like that. And he's middling good at it, because he brings a lot of food into the house. Now I'd like to ask you . . ." His voice faded as Bledsoe silently shook his head. "Well, could I ask you to meet the boy and talk to him before you turn it down out of hand?"

Bledsoe shrugged, looking down at the hickory stick as he whittled on it. "I'll meet him and talk to him, but it'll still be no."

"I'd be more than willing to pay what I could afford to apprentice him to you."

"That doesn't enter into it, because I wouldn't want anything if I did it. But I won't, because the boy's liable to get killed. I hunt and trap in Indian country."

"I realize that, and Sarah wasn't overly fond of the idea when I talked to her about it. And I've no desire to put my boy into danger. But he's going to go, that much I know, because settlement life isn't for that boy. As I see it, my only choice is between putting him with someone who can teach him and give him a chance, or having him in far greater danger by being by himself or with someone who knows little more about it than he does."

Bledsoe turned the hickory stick over and began whittling on the other end, feeling mildly aggravated over the way Raines had developed the situation for his own purposes. But he could understand a man's concern for his children. And there was reason to be concerned. A lot of men hunted and trapped their way into the border country over a period of a couple of years, gradually becoming more confident, then fell prey to Indians or the natural dangers of the wilderness when they ventured too far. Sometimes they were unlucky, but most of the time they were careless and knew little about the deep forest. Many simply starved or died from exposure. Survival in the wilderness required highly developed skills, and surveyors and others from settlements never went into the wilderness without Indians to guide them and hunt food for them.

But it was something to consider. At various times during the past, he had hunted and trapped with a partner for a year or two at a time. It was far safer to be with a skilled and cautious partner than alone, because there was always the possibility of a disabling injury, losing or damaging a knife, gun, or some other crucially important piece of equipment, or being surprised by a party of Indians that could overcome one but not two. But it was also more dangerous to be with someone who was unskilled than it was to be alone. On the other hand a novice who was cautious, attentive, and had keen senses and a natural aptitude for the wilderness could develop skill in a short time.

The dog stood, growling. Two women carrying kettles and buckets came through the trees in front of the cabin, and Bledsoe snapped his fingers at the dog and called him back. Raines stood up, brushing the wood shavings off himself and smiling and nodding to the two women.

"Good day, Martha, Prudence. Have you met Caleb? Caleb, this is Martha Forbes and Prudence Killion, from down the way."

They nodded and murmured, and Bledsoe nodded to them. "I'm pleased to meet you."

"We thought we'd bring some victuals and see if we could be of help."

"We're much obliged. Just go right on in, if you like. The others are inside."

They went in, and Raines chuckled as he and Bledsoe sat down and began whittling again. "It's like when all of mine were born—they ran me out of my own cabin." He took a drink from his cup and turned the piece of wood in his hand, scraping it with his knife. "Will you talk to the boy and think about it, then?"

"Aye, I'll talk to him and think about it."

"You haven't already turned him down in your own mind, have you?"

Bledsoe shook his head. "No."

Raines looked at him, then nodded in satisfaction as he looked back down at the piece of wood.

The women moved around inside the cabin and talked quietly as Bledsoe and Raines whittled on the pieces of wood. The sun was approaching its zenith, the high clouds had become large, fleecy, and brilliantly white as they moved slowly across the sky, and the air was warm and humid. The dog lay by the bench and snapped drowsily at flies, and chickens came around the corner of the cabin in a loose cluster, scratching and pecking at the ground and clucking.

The conversation between the women in the cabin became louder, and footsteps moved rapidly back and forth.

Hannah said something in a tearful, protesting voice. Widow Dobson's cracked, rasping voice replied in an irritable bark. Raines sat up, looking at Bledsoe and at the door. Footsteps came toward the door.

Widow Dobson stepped into the doorway, and the Forbes woman looked at Bledsoe over the old woman's shoulder, her face pale and apprehensive. The old woman was holding a long, sharp butcher knife, and her beady eyes glared at Bledsoe from the shadow of the brim around her coif. Bledsoe stood up, brushing at the shavings on him. Hannah was sobbing something on the other side of the room, and one of the other women was talking to her quietly.

"She's going. I need to cut."

"Well, do whatever you must."

The old woman turned away from the door, the Forbes woman following her. Bledsoe sat back down. Raines sighed as he took out the bottle, and he poured more rum into the cups. Bledsoe took a drink from his cup, turned the stick in his hands, and began whittling again.

Hannah wept, wailing something in a loud voice. One of the other women prayed. Then there was a thin, mewling sound. It became a baby's thin, wavering cry. A moment later there was a sound of another baby crying, a strong, lusty bellow.

# Chapter Four

Bledsoe knotted the rawhide thong between the horse's fore-legs and released it. The horse stumbled over the hobbles as it turned away, then it recovered its balance and began cropping the deep grass as it moved toward the other horses with cautious, hopping steps. Bledsoe turned and walked back into the trees along the edge of the grassy meadow, the dog following him. A path led through the trees, and the trees opened out into the tilled area, a square of five acres behind his stock pens and outbuildings. He looked at the crops as he walked along the path at the side of the rail fence enclosing the tilled area. The corn had started drying, and it could be gathered after another day or two of sunshine. It would take somewhat longer for the long rows of potato hills to dry enough to dig easily. The rain hadn't made any difference in gathering beets, turnips, onions, cabbages, and carrots. The late peas were mature, ready to pick at any time.

Women's voices were a soft murmur as he passed the outbuildings and approached the rear of the cabin. Widow Dobson had gone to her cabin for walink to brew into tea for the babies, a couple more women had come back with her, and more had come as the news spread. The tone of the women's voices in the cabin was a blend between the subdued, respectful attitude when in the presence of the dead and the excited admiration when in the presence of new life. Hannah's voice was audible among them, sounding both sorrowful and exhilarated. When he found the woman on the beach, he had regarded her pregnancy only as a condition that lessened her chances of recovery. It hadn't occurred to him that a baby might be forthcoming, much less two. And it hadn't occurred to him that Hannah would assert a claim on the babies.

But she had. All the women appeared to acknowledge it, and Bledsoe was pleased for Hannah, as well as apprehensive. He'd had a glimpse of the babies, and one of them looked very sickly and frail. Some women had two or three babies before they kept one past the first year of life. It would be a severe blow for Hannah if they died.

Bledsoe walked along the creek toward the river, watching for snakes as he picked his way through the thickets of briars and undergrowth in the damp, rich soil. The sun glinted brightly on the estuary as he pushed through the undergrowth at the mouth of the creek, and he shaded his eyes with his hand as he scanned the estuary.

Several boats were moving up and down the estuary. One going up the river turned, angling across the river. Bledsoe watched it as it came closer. There were two men in it, and a smaller figure in the stern. One of the men was smaller than the other, and they both had bright blonde hair. It was Raines and his boy. Bledsoe turned and walked back along the creek.

He waited by the springhouse. The boat came up the creek and turned toward the bank, and Bledsoe stepped to the edge of the water to take the bow and pull it onto the bank. The boy looked at Bledsoe, trying not to be obvious about it. Bledsoe pulled the bow onto the bank, and the boy and Raines got out, taking the gunwales and pulling the boat farther onto the bank.

"Caleb, this is my boy Isaac. Isaac, this is Mr. Bledsoe."

The boy was nervous, anxious to make a good impression. He had his father's frank, open face, and he would have his father's large size. His appearance showed a mother's demanding care, because he was neat and clean, his heavy shoes freshly tallowed and blacked, his hair tied back tightly, and his shirt and stockings worn but clean. He nodded and gulped, his right hand moving hesitantly to shake hands. As Bledsoe put out his hand the boy grinned and nodded.

"I'm mightily pleased to meet you, Mr. Bledsoe."

Bledsoe silently nodded, looking at him thoughtfully, then at the Indian woman in the stern of the boat. Raines motioned to the woman and stepped along the side of the boat to help her out.

"Come along, let's have you out of there. I believe she'll

be suitable, Caleb. One of the Indians helping me with the houses over in Brunswick got her for me. She's his aunt, sister, or something like that, from what I could understand."

The woman was young, eighteen or twenty. She was short and stout, wearing a greasy, ragged buckskin dress and shapeless moccasins, and carrying a tiny bundle of belongings in a tattered, dirty blanket. Her hair was short and stringy, her eyes dull and dispirited from abuse. She was dirty and unkempt, her face was bruised, one eye swollen almost closed. She climbed heavily out of the boat and stood motionless, her expression vacant. Her breasts were heavy and sagging, and there were two large, wet milkstains on her buckskin dress.

"Where's her baby?"

"It died. Or perhaps it was born dead—I'm not sure. But it was born only two or three days ago, and she's still full and fresh, as you can see. And she appears healthy enough, doesn't she?"

"Aye, if a bit grimy, but that's soon remedied. Does she understand English?"

"Fair enough, it appears. She's been quick enough to do what I told her."

"Well, let's have her on up to the cabin, then. Come along . . . what's her name?"

"She'll answer to Nina. That's not her proper name, but it's a bit like what the fellow I had her off was calling her."

"Come along, then, Nina. Up this way you go."

Her lifeless eyes moved toward him, then away again. She turned and trudged along the path to the cabin, the dog circling and sniffing at her suspiciously. Bledsoe looked at Raines as they followed her. "I'm more than obliged to you for finding her. What did you have to give for her?"

Raines hesitated, then shrugged. "Nothing that matters, and I'm glad to be of help to you."

"No, I can't allow you to do this, Alvah. I know you had to pay something for her."

"Well, let's see if the nippers take to her. That sod Bixby is on his way over here, by the way. I saw his boat putting out from the dock at Brunswick as we started up the creek."

Bledsoe nodded and shrugged in resignation. "I could do

without him, but the sooner it's done the sooner we're finished with him, I suppose. He has to do his bit of mucking about with people, the same as the rest of those buggers in Wilmington."

Raines grunted affirmatively, nodding. One of the women in the cabin looked out as they came up the path, then Hannah, Sarah Raines, Widow Dobson, and a couple more of the women came out.

"Couldn't you have found one a bit cleaner, Alvah?" his wife said.

"The boat's down at the creek if you'd like to have a go."

"Well, it does seem you could have found one a bit cleaner."

"Her name's Nina, Hannah," Bledsoe said. "Just tell her what you want her to do. She can understand English."

Hannah nodded, beckoning to Nina. "Aye, come along, then."

Nina put her bundle down outside the door and went in with the other women. Bledsoe, Raines, and Isaac waited, watching the doorway. One of the babies began crying, then the other one. Then they stopped. Sarah Raines came to the door, smiled, and Raines nodded with satisfaction.

"Hell, that's done, isn't it? And you can have her for as long as you wish, by the way. She either doesn't have a husband, or he died or something—I'm not sure what the one I had her off was trying to tell me."

"Aye, that's good, and I trust it'll be for a good while. That one baby looks healthy enough, but I'm not so sure about the other one. Let me settle with you now on what you gave for her."

"It's neither here nor there, Caleb, because the fellow does jobs for me and I'll have it out of him in one way or another. Besides that it was nothing to speak of."

"Well, I can't argue with you when I don't know what I'm arguing about, but I'm much obliged."

"I'm glad I could help you. While I was over there, I heard that they'll be burying the others from the shipwreck at St. Philips tomorrow morning. That would be as good a time as any to see what you have to do, wouldn't it?"

"I suppose it would."

"Then Isaac and I can knock together a coffin for you,

and you'll only have to settle with the parson on the plot. And I shouldn't think that would be much."

"No, now I certainly can't allow all this, Alvah. I want to settle with you fair and proper."

Raines smiled and shook his head, starting to reply, when the dog bristled and began barking, trotting toward the path to the creek. Bledsoe called the dog back, looking along the path. Bixby came up the path, followed by four sailors. He walked slowly, one hand resting on the pommel of his sword, an expression of bored disdain on his face, and he stopped a few feet from the three, looking at Bledsoe coldly. Bledsoe looked back stolidly.

"How does the woman fare?"

"She's dead," Bledsoe replied flatly. "Widow Dobson had to cut her to take the babies, and she was dying at the time."

Bixby lifted his eyebrows, pursed his lips, and sighed wearily as he looked away. He glanced at the cabin and the chickens in front of it with distaste, taking out his snuffbox. "Before she died, did she make any mention of the destination of the ship?"

"Hannah?" Bledsoe called, turning to the cabin. "Step to the door, if you would."

Hannah came to the door, a couple of the other women looking out from behind her, and her face paled and became tense as she looked at Bixby and the sailors. She plucked at her skirt and bobbed, smiling nervously.

"This is Captain Bixby of the naval and customs office, Hannah. He wants to know if the woman said anything before she died."

Hannah shook her head rapidly, looking at Bixby apprehensively as she pulled at her skirt and bobbed again. "Not a word, your worship. She didn't say a word. I'll take very good care of the babies, your worship. I'll look after them just as though they were—"

"Foundlings and orphans are a matter for the Church to deal with, not the naval and customs office," Bixby interrupted acidly. "I am interested only in the woman. Did she have anything on her to establish her identity?

"She had naught, your worship," Hannah said quickly, shaking her head. "Naught but the clothes on her, and nothing in her pockets." Her voice faded as she licked her lips and swallowed, and she cleared her throat nervously.

Bixby sighed again, looking away from Hannah as he tapped his snuffbox with a forefinger. He opened it, took a pinch of snuff, and inhaled it.

"Would you like to step in and have a look, your worship?" Hannah said nervously. "We have her properly laid out and—"

"I've seen sufficient corpses for one day, thank you," Bixby said, tucking his snuffbox back into a waistcoat pocket. He took out his handkerchief and dusted his nostrils, glancing over the cabin and at the chickens again with a disparaging expression. "And I've no particular desire to see some dead serving wench."

"Did you identify what vessel it was, Captain Bixby?" Raines asked.

He looked at Raines and nodded. "The brigantine *Lillian*, out of London. And apparently destined for some other port. I had hoped to find out here what port, but . . ." He shrugged and tucked his handkerchief into his cuff as he turned away, looking at Bledsoe. "You shall see to the burial. And in a fitting manner."

"I said I would, so I will."

Bixby hesitated, frowning at him, then looked at the sailors and motioned to them as he began walking along the path to the creek. They turned and followed him. Hannah watched the men as they left, then stepped outside, looking at Bledsoe.

"Am I to keep the babies, then, Caleb?"

"Who's to say no? And whoever does will hold their tongue soon enough when they find they're talking to the end of my rifle."

"I expect they would." Raines laughed, then he looked at Hannah. "I'm sure you'll have no trouble from the parson on that score, Hannah. They've more now than they can feed." He looked back at Bledsoe as Hannah turned and went back into the cabin. "Well, we'll be about the coffin, Caleb. And it occurs to me that you might need another room on your cabin. That's something we can talk about."

"Aye, but if we do, we'll have to talk a proper trade, Alvah. I'm becoming burdened with debt to you."

Raines smiled and shrugged. "It's clear enough what it's for, Caleb. I'm always ready to help a man who needs it, and in addition to that, I'll make no secret of the fact that I'd like to have you favorably consider what we discussed concerning my boy here. But at the same time if those babies don't sicken down and die within the week, then they've a fair chance and you'll need another room for them and that Indian woman. I'm sure you could do it yourself, but you might not have time to do it before you leave, what with all else you've to do. So we'll settle it one way or another, and I'll be fair about it when we do."

Bledsoe nodded, looking at Isaac musingly as he stroked his beard. Isaac flushed and stiffened self-consciously, and he shuffled his feet as he glanced nervously at his father and Bledsoe. "I've been thinking about it," Bledsoe said, looking away. "And I'll probably decide to take him, because I can't tell how he'll do until I have him in the forest. If I take him with me, I'll want you to provide him with two good horses, weapons, equipment, and supplies. If he returns, I'll give you pelts to repay you and to supply him for the next season." He turned his head and looked at Raines warningly. "But if he doesn't return, it won't be on my head. I'll do what I can, and if that isn't enough it's no fault of mine."

A beaming, triumphant smile spread across Isaac's face. Raines smiled, nodding to him and looking at Bledsoe. "I can't ask any more than that, Caleb. We'll go see to the coffin, then. And after the burying tomorrow, I'll send Isaac over with a load of seasoned logs to get the extra room on your cabin started. Then I'll come on over when I can. With the three of us working on it, we'll have it done in no time at all."

"Aye, very well, Alvah. And I'm obliged."

They set out along the path to the creek, Isaac grinning toothily and Raines with his hand on his son's shoulder, smiling with satisfaction. Bledsoe looked at the cabin, musing. The babies were crying again, a thin, wavering blur of sound over the murmur of the women's conversation. An immediate need was some sort of makeshift crib for them, a wooden box padded with unspun flax that would keep them warm. And that would serve as a coffin if one or both of them died. He walked around the cabin toward his toolroom.

The toolroom was at the rear of the barn, with a small

forge in the corner, tools and pieces of scrap iron hanging
on pegs on the wall, and an oak workbench along one side-
wall. Leftover shingles were stacked against the rear wall of
the room, and seasoned boards that had been painfully
rived and smoothed or whipsawed from logs were stacked
on log rafters overhead. Bledsoe selected boards from the
stacks in the rafters, then searched through a pile of scrap
wood for pieces of straight-grained oak to make pegs. The
sun was inclining toward the west and the light in the toolroom was dim as he took the wood, his saw, and a gimlet
for boring holes and carried them outside.

Bledsoe measured and sawed the boards, drilled holes to
fit them together, and began making pegs. As he started
assembling the box, there was a noisy rustling in the underbrush in the trees along the creek. Bledsoe turned and
looked toward the creek, and the dog lifted his head and
cocked his ears. Hannah came out of the trees, her face
flushed and excited. She looked at the cabin and glanced
stealthily around as she trotted heavily toward Bledsoe, a
bundle of wet clothing under one arm and her other hand
clenched tightly.

"What is it, Hannah?"

She shook her head and frowned, looking at the cabin
and hurrying toward him, and she held out her hand as she
approached. "Look what I found, Caleb," she panted
breathlessly. "I took that child's clothes down to wash them
and lay her out properly, and look what I found in the hem
of her dress."

He examined the heavy coins and bit one of them between his front teeth. There were eight foreign coins, all
solid gold.

"How many guineas are they worth, Caleb?" she whispered.

"I've no idea. But many, Hannah, many."

"I was washing the salt out of the dress, and I felt something in the hem. I thought it might be bits of lead that
ladies have in their hems to make their skirts hang properly, then I looked and found those, as well as bits of lead.
What should we do with them, Caleb?"

"We'll keep them to see the babies right in whatever they
wish to do, when the time comes. For now I'll bury them
in a corner of the toolroom for safekeeping. And if some-

thing ever happens to me, you can dig them up and use them to see to yourself and the babies."

"When I saw that money I almost had a spell, Caleb. I've never seen so much money in my life."

"Nor have I. I daresay there's more here than I've earned in all my life. And the woman had a bundle with her as well. I left it down at the springhouse, and when it's dark and everyone has left, I'll bring it up and we'll have a look at it. It appears to be clothing and such, and there might be things in it that you can use for the babies."

"Aye, we can see. What are you doing there?"

"I was making something for the babies to lie in until I have time to make proper cribs."

"That's good, because we only have a pallet for them. Well, I'll take these on down and dry them by the fire so we can finish laying that child out."

"Raines and his boy will have the coffin over here directly. We'll take her over to the churchyard tomorrow and have her buried when they bury the others from the ship."

Hannah sighed heavily and nodded as she turned away, walking toward the cabin with the clothes. Bledsoe looked at the coins again and weighed them in his hand as he walked into the toolroom. He took a shovel from a peg, dug a shallow hole in the corner of the dirt floor, and buried the coins.

It was almost sunset when he finished the box. He took it around to the front of the cabin, put it inside the door, and went to bring in his horses from grazing. Raines and his son had brought the coffin and left when he returned, and most of the women had gone. They had brought bunches of flowers, wild azaleas, columbines, magnolia, and honeysuckle, and the cabin smelled strongly of them. A couple of women moved quietly around in the back room, arranging the flowers on the coffin and talking in hushed tones. Widow Dobson and Hannah hovered over the makeshift crib by the hearth, discussing the babies, and Nina sat on the floor by the crib, her bruised face shiny from being washed, her hair combed back, and one of Hannah's homespun dresses large and bulky on her. Her face was blank and impassive and her eyes were lifeless as she looked down at the floor. Then one of the babies began crying, and her eyes became bright and animated as she took the child out of the crib. She smiled slightly as she rocked back and forth with the baby cuddled in her arms, the tips of her fingers moving over the baby's face.

The rest of the women left as the shadows became longer and the soft, golden sunset faded into twilight. Bledsoe milked and fed the cow, took the milk into the cabin, then walked down to the springhouse for the bundle of belongings he had found in the boat with the woman. Darkness had fallen as he walked back along the path with the bundle, and the open cabin door was a square of bright yellow from the light of the fireplace. Nina still sat by the crib, looking into it, and Hannah moved back and forth in front of the fireplace, moving pans and skillets around. She looked up at him as he carried the bundle in and put it in the corner by the hearth.

"Is that it, then? We'll have a look at it when we've had a bite to eat. They brought us food to last a week, you know. We have some good people living around us here."

"Aye, it was good of them. Still and all I'm partial to the way you fix food."

She smiled at him, turning away from the fireplace. Crossing the room she took pewter plates from a shelf. "It won't hurt us to lie on the floor in here for the night, will it? It seems a small thing for us to give up our room to that child, when she's going to be in the ground on the morrow."

"It's nothing to me. This floor is a better bed than I have all winter."

"It'll only be for tonight. Sarah Raines said her man might talk to you about building more onto the back of the cabin."

"Aye, his boy will be over tomorrow with some seasoned logs, and we'll start on it then. And I'll probably take the boy with me this winter."

Hannah carried the plates back to the hearth, knelt, and began filling the plates from the pans and skillets of food. "Yes, Sarah mentioned that her man might talk to you about that. She doesn't favor the idea."

Bledsoe shrugged as he pulled his stool closer to the hearth and sat down. "If he doesn't go with me he'll probably try going by himself, and I daresay she would favor that idea less."

"I daresay she would," Hannah said, handing him a plate and a spoon. Then she smiled. "It could be there'll come a time when you'll be taking one of your own with you, Caleb."

He smiled and nodded, taking a bite from the plate. "Aye, it could be."

Hannah filled a plate and handed it to Nina, filled a plate for herself, then filled cups with buttermilk from the urn in the corner and brought them to the hearth. One or the other of the babies occasionally stirred and moved in the crib, and Nina stopped eating each time and looked into the crib. Bledsoe drank the last of his buttermilk and put his plate and cup down on the hearth. He stood up, took his pipe and tobacco from the mantel, and stepped over to the crib to look at the babies as he filled his pipe. The small one was lying on his side under the cover, completely motionless. The larger one slept restlessly, his limbs moving and a scowl on his small, wrinkled face. Bledsoe stepped back to his stool, put the tobacco on the mantel, and took a sliver from the pile of wood by the hearth as he sat down.

"That one is twice the size of the other."

Hannah nodded, gathering up the plates and cups. "He is, and he has his fill twice as often as the other. But she has ample milk, so there's plenty for both of them."

Bledsoe leaned over and lit the sliver of wood from the fire, then sat back and lit his pipe, watching Nina as she looked in the crib again. He puffed on the pipe and tossed the sliver of wood into the fire. "She appears to keep her eye on them."

"She does indeed," Hannah replied, carrying the plates and cups to the washstand. "She's missing her own, poor thing. And I don't mind sharing them with her."

Bledsoe puffed on his pipe and nodded as he looked back at Nina peering into the crib. Hannah stacked the dishes on the washstand, fed the dog and cat, then made a pot of tea. She took three pewter cups down from the mantel and filled them, put one on the hearth in front of Bledsoe, and took the other two to the table and stirred spoonfuls of molasses into them. Nina sniffed at hers doubtfully as Hannah gave it to her.

"No, you go ahead and drink it," Hannah said as she sat

down on her stool. "It'll be good for you and the babies both." She nodded with satisfaction as Nina obediently took a sip and grimaced, and she took a drink from her cup and looked at Bledsoe. "We can have a look at that bundle now, if you wish."

Bledsoe took a puff on his pipe and put it down on the hearth, then leaned over and pulled the bundle toward him. It was covered with heavy canvas crusted with salt, the corners tightly knotted. He worked the knots loose and spread the canvas open. A pile of neatly folded clothes was inside, and Hannah picked up the top dress with a sigh of admiration.

"Isn't it lovely, Caleb? That child was truly loved, and I'd wager this dress alone cost an earl's ransom."

Bledsoe took a drink of his tea and puffed on his pipe. "And she had plenty of them, it appears."

Hannah put the dress aside and picked up another. "But this would be only what she had immediately at hand, wouldn't it? No doubt she had boxes stored away for safe-keeping during the voyage. And one can see that she was a Dutchman from her clothes. They all have a foreign look to them, including the dress she has on. Fancy the poor child dying where no one could even understand her and speak her language to comfort her."

"Aye, for whatever comfort anyone can be at such a time."

There were more clothes, shoes, then three bundles of oilskin. Bledsoe picked up one and unfolded it. It was a small oil painting of a young couple, and the woman in the picture was the dead girl. He handed it to Hannah.

"It's her wedding picture, Caleb. Wasn't she the loveliest child? And her man was striking handsome and all, as well he should be. Do you think he might have been on the ship as well?"

"He very well could have been."

"Aye, I daresay he was, wasn't he? No man would let such a child venture off alone, and he looks the sort of man who would protect her."

Bledsoe nodded, unwrapping another oilskin bundle. It was a framed charcoal drawing of a river scene. A bridge with towers on each end connected a city spread along both sides of the river, and towering bluffs covered with cultivated squares overlooked the river. He handed it to Hannah, and she frowned and shook her head as she looked at it.

"Do you think this might be a picture of where she was from? I had it in my mind that Holland was flattish, with dikes, windmills, and such as that."

Bledsoe shrugged and shook his head, unwrapping the last bundle of oilskin. It contained a large, heavy book damp from seawater that had seeped in through the folds of the oilskin, and the book looked like a Bible. He handed it to Hannah.

"Aye, she was a Dutchman, right enough. This is her Bible, and I can't make out a word of it. Or even pick out a letter I know, as far as that goes." She shook her head, holding it to the light and thumbing through the pages as she peered at it closely, then she stiffened. "There's writing here, Caleb! It's her name!"

Bledsoe leaned over and looked at the writing on the front page in the Bible, slightly blurred by the seawater that had seeped into the oilskin. He sat back, pulling a sliver from a stick in the pile of wood, and leaned over to light it from the fire. "Can you make it out?"

Hannah narrowed her eyes and leaned closer to the fire, her lips moving as she looked closely at the writing. "Aye, it's . . ." She hesitated, biting her lip and frowning, then slowly nodded. "Sheila. Sheila Collier. That was her name, Caleb. It was Sheila Collier."

Bledsoe puffed on his pipe, relighting it with the sliver, then tossed the sliver into the fire and smiled whimsically. "She had a proper good English name for a Dutchman, didn't she?"

Hannah looked at him in aggravation and held out the Bible. "Here, you have a go, then."

He chuckled and shook his head. "I'd be like a blind man trying to track a deer, because I can't even read my own name. If you say her name was Sheila Collier, then it was."

"Well, that's what it says here, just as plain as anything. But when you put the names on the registry, you'd be within your rights to give them your own name. And it's a good name, I'll tell the world. Also no one would be asking how it was you found out her name, would they?"

Bledsoe puffed on his pipe and looked into the fire, thinking. Then he slowly shook his head. "No, that's neither here nor there. The clerk at the registry wants his five bob, and he'd put down the king's name if that's what you told him. But that money we have out there is going to see to them, and it came from the ones their blood comes from. I think we should call them Collier."

"Aye, well, I always abide by your wishes, Caleb, and if that's what you think we should do, I'll not question it." She looked down at the Bible, then at him, smiling hesitantly. "If there had been but one, I wouldn't think of anything but to call him Caleb. But as there are two, I'd like to call the small one Jubal, after my youngest brother. He was a sweet child, and I'd like to carry his name on. Then we could call the other one after you."

Bledsoe looked into the fire again, thinking. "Jubal Collier has a good sound to it, so we'll call the small one that, if you wish. As for the other one I'd rather name him after where I'm from instead of after myself. My mother had me on the banks of the Santee, and I'd like to call him Santee."

Hannah nodded, smiling widely. "Aye, I like the sound of that, Caleb. Santee Collier sounds a proper good name to me, so that's what we'll call him, then."

# Part Two

# THE LONG HUNTER

# Chapter Five

Santee stood motionless, his weight balanced on his toes. The buck turned his head from side to side, his massive spread of antlers gleaming in the early morning light pouring down into the glade. His eyes passed across Santee, searching for motion rather than form, his ears cocked to catch any whisper of noise over the natural sounds of the forest, and his nostrils sampling the breeze. Santee watched the buck's tail as it twitched from side to side, a flickering glint of white against the brown of his rump, and he lowered his head and began grazing again. Santee glided forward.

The fallen leaves were damp with dew, and the rustle they made as his toes pushed them aside was lost in the murmur of the breeze in the foliage overhead and in the clamor of the birds trying their voices in the early morning. He felt for twigs with his toes through his moccasins and stepped over them. His eyes were riveted on the buck's tail, watching for the telltale movement that always revealed when the whitetail was going to raise or lower its head. He swung the long, heavy rifle to move between two clumps of brush, and the ends of the brush passed soundlessly across the soft buckskin he wore. The buck's tail flicked from side to side. Santee froze. The buck lifted his head and looked around, chewing rapidly, his ears cocked and his nostrils quivering. The buck's tail flicked again and he lowered his head. Santee glided forward again.

Santee stalked the buck until he was within a hundred feet, an easy shot into a vital spot and a distance at which the ball would still be traveling at full speed for lethal impact. He stopped, planted his feet firmly, and lifted the rifle. The buck flicked his tail from side to side and lifted his head. Santee froze, the barrel of the rifle pointing at the ground just under the buck.

The rifle weighed eleven pounds, most of it in the forty-four-inch barrel and well forward of Santee's left hand under the wooden forearm in which the barrel was mounted. He was large and strong for his age, but he was only fifteen and his muscles had yet to attain the strength and endurance that would come with full manhood. His left arm began cramping from supporting the weight of the rifle.

It was tempting to lift the rifle on through the few degrees that it would take to bring it to bear on the buck's neck. But the risk was unacceptable. The buck's keen eyes might detect the motion. The wary caution of the grass-eater in a carnivorous world might be stirred. The surety of a lethal shot would become the possibility of a disabling shot. He waited.

The twinges of pain in his left arm became agony. After what seemed an eternity the buck's tail twitched again and he lowered his head to crop more grass. Santee sighted down the barrel at the buck's neck. The seething pain in his left arm made the barrel waver, and the bead swam across the soft brown of the buck's neck. It was tempting to lower the rifle and rest his arm, but the buck might decide to move on. At the same time the shot had to be sure. Powder and lead were precious in the wilderness. And each shot was a risk, a sound that carried far and might fall on hostile ears—an acceptable risk but not one to be taken lightly.

He summoned his willpower, stiffening his left arm and steadying the rifle. The pain became excruciating. He ground his teeth together, forcing his left arm to stop trembling. The bead stabilized on the buck's neck. He drew in a deep breath, taking aim. The wind was quartering from the buck to him and would deflect the ball a negligible fraction of an inch over a distance of a hundred feet. No elevation was necessary at a hundred feet. The glade was sloped slightly and the buck was slightly above him, but not far enough to compensate for shooting uphill. For all practical purposes it was a point-blank shot, the strike of the ball at the point of aim. He released his breath, slowly tightening his entire right hand on the grip of the rifle and pulling the trigger back with his forefinger.

The hammer snapped forward, the flint between its jaws striking the lid of the pan and knocking it forward on its hinge as the corrugations on the lid drew sparks and spilled them into the powder in the pan. The buck stiffened convulsively from the snap of the lock. The pan flashed, followed immediately by the splitting crack of the rifle as a billowing cloud of black smoke belched from the barrel. Birds exploded from the trees overhead, shrieking, and squirrels scampered to safety, chattering. Santee knelt and looked under the smoke. The buck's rear quarters were down and it was folding, every muscle in its body rigid and its mouth open and tongue thrust out in its dying efforts to flee. Then it collapsed. The spot of damp crimson on its neck became larger as it twitched, then was still.

Santee walked quietly to a large tree, looking around and listening as he slid the slender hickory ramrod out of the thimbles in the forearm of the rifle and opened the patch box in the stock of the rifle. The first seconds after a shot were the moment of greatest peril, because he was unarmed. If an Indian skillful enough to be undetected had been stalking him, it would be the signal to attack. If Indians were anywhere in the vicinity the sound of the shot would draw them like a magnet.

He took a patch and the cleaning worm out of the patch box, screwed the worm onto the end of the ramrod, then slid it into the barrel and moved it up and down to dislodge burned powder from the lands and grooves in the barrel. He drew the ramrod back out, blew down the end of the barrel to clear the touchhole by the pan, then jerked his powder horn and shot bag around. A hollowed tip of a deer antler hung by a short thong at the end of the powder horn, and he filled it with powder and poured it into the end of the barrel. He pushed the stopper back into the end of the powder horn and dropped it, reached into the buckskin shot bag, and took out a ball and laid the patch across the end of the barrel and put the ball on it. He unscrewed the worm from the end of the ramrod, centered the ball carefully on the patch so its flight would be true when it came out of the barrel, then put the end of the ramrod against the ball and forced it down into the barrel, tapping it to seat it firmly against the powder charge. He lifted the stock of the rifle, looking at the firing pan as he put the cleaning worm back into the patch box and closed it. A few grains of powder had leaked through the touchhole, so it didn't need to be cleaned with the frizzen pin. He took the stopper back out of the powder horn, shook a pinch of powder into the firing pan, then closed the lid on the pan, glancing at the hammer. The flint was still sharp, still firmly anchored in the jaws of the hammer. He was armed again, and he cradled the rifle across his chest and leaned back against the tree, relaxing slightly.

But only slightly. He was armed again, but the sound of the shot carried far, revealing his presence over a wide distance. It could be minutes, hours, or days before he would have to pay the price in peril for having revealed his presence. The year before Isaac Raines had lost two horses and almost his life to Indians. Two years before, the first year Santee had hunted and trapped the deep forest with his foster father and Isaac Raines, he and Caleb had lain in grim, gray-faced, utter silence for hours within yards of a large war party that had abruptly glided through the dense growth toward them and decided to rest just at that spot. Survival in the deep forest took constant, unremitting vigilance, keen senses, and sharply honed skills. Isaac Raines would have lost his life but for his vigilance, senses, and skills. The Indians had been waiting for him, knowing he would return to the horses. But he had detected them lying in wait and had slipped away.

The excitement and fright created among the birds and small animals by the shot began dying away, and the forest around Santee resumed the pulse of small sounds he unthinkingly listened to and classified as normal. The calling of a bobwhite quail held his attention for a moment, because Indians closing in on prey frequently used birdcalls to communicate, most commonly bobwhite during the day and whippoorwill at night. But the call of the bobwhite was a familiar sound from earliest childhood, when he had set traps for them in the belts of forest and meadows around the farm on the Cape Fear River. He had mimicked the call to trick others into setting their traps in the wrong places, and others had tried to do it to him. But the most adept hadn't been able to fool him. The call he heard was a quail, not an Indian. He moved away from the tree and walked toward the buck.

He put his rifle down within easy reach, took his skinning knife from the sheath on the front of his belt, and began skinning the buck, glancing from the buck to the trees around him. The carcass still had its body heat, and the skin came off easily, pulling away at the layer of tissue between the skin and the layers of fat the buck had accumulated for winter. He slit down the inside of the legs, cut the skin loose above the hooves and below the point where he had shot through the neck, then turned the buck over and pulled the skin off the back. Leaves, grass, and dirt adhered to the sticky inside of the skin, and he knelt and brushed most of it off as he rolled the skin up and tied it with a rawhide thong. He slung it over his back, picking up his rifle. A heavy odor of flesh and blood hung in the air, and the carcass gleamed red in the sunlight. Santee moved quietly out of the glade, and birds flew down from the trees to gather around the carcass.

The sun was well above the horizon, rapidly burning off the dew. It was the time of day when deer would seek shelter in deadfalls and thickets to chew their cud and sleep. They could be stalked when bedded down, but the return wasn't worth the effort, because it took hours to stalk a single deer. And he had killed four deer since first light, which was equal to or more than what Caleb or Isaac Raines could do. The other three skins and the choice tenderloin strips from the fat doe he had shot were in a clump of brush two hundred yards from the glade, where he had left them so he would be unencumbered while stalking the buck. He paused by the brush, slung the skins and meat over his back, and turned toward his temporary camp.

It was the first year he had hunted alone, with his own horses and equipment. The previous two years he had hunted alternately with his foster father and Isaac Raines during the early season, when they split up to take deerskins before meeting for the winter's trapping. At thirteen it had been necessary to shoot from a rest, because he was unable to support the weight of a rifle steadily enough to hold it on target. And his foster mother had wept when he left, at thirteen. But while her tears had been sincere, there had been an undertone of relief rather than the despair in her tears at other times.

At ten he had finally become strong enough to turn the

scales and whip a boy of thirteen or so who had been bully-ing him for a couple of years. And the flush of victory had awakened some dark impulse that kept him punching and kicking until the flushed excitement on the faces of the boys gathered around had turned into frightened consterna-tion. The boy's father had come to the Bledsoe cabin, en-raged because his son hadn't been able to work for several days. There had been other fights, and adults had been prone to give him dark, distrustful glances, regarding him as a troublemaker.

Then at twelve there had been a more serious fight. A boy had pulled a knife on him, and he had taken the knife away and cut the boy. A constable had come to the cabin. Shortly after that, while on an errand in Wilmington, a stout and pompous man coming out of the port offices had stopped him and peremptorily ordered him to fetch his horse, then rapped him smartly across the back with a cane when he hesitated and frowned resentfully. Santee had taken the cane and broken it across the man's head. He had been publicly whipped in Wilmington, and there had been a fine.

His foster father's thrashings had been painful, some-thing to endure as the price of having ventured into unfor-tunate circumstances where he lost control over himself and what was going on around him. And they had been less than effective because of Caleb's attitude, one of going through a necessary rote, with more satisfaction and under-standing than disapproval. In particular, after the incident with the cane, the quiet, late-night conversations between his foster parents around the fireplace had consisted of chuckling murmurs from Caleb and indignation from Han-nah.

His foster mother's exasperated, tearful remonstrances to be more like Jubal had only stirred a belligerent, obstinate resentment. Jubal was different, quiet, withdrawn, and frag-ile, a shadow departing early every morning to the offices of the trading and shipping factor where he was appren-ticed, and returning late every night to his solitary meal, to pore over sheaves of papers as Nina and Hannah clucked solicitously around him. Jubal was too weak and too busy to do chores, prone to illnesses, and with a fireplace in his bedroom so he would be warm on cold nights.

At thirteen the burgeoning, seething frustrations of life closing in around Santee had been removed. The cause for angry rebellion over being held at fault for the unexpected, and for things over which he had only indirect control, had disappeared. The constrictions, animosities, bustling, frenzied clamor, and squalid filth of the cabins and town along Cape Fear River had been left behind. Turmoil had been exchanged for peace, the awesome silence of deep avenues of massive trees blotting out daylight overhead, the clean sparkle and ripple of cheerful creeks, the turgid might of massive rivers coming from the unknown and passing into the unknown, the poignant beauty of flowery glades and tiny hidden valleys painted with autumn colors, and endless vistas of wooded mountains stretching for vast distances, fading into a blue, hazy infinity.

His foster mother had wept. Nina had stood in silent, expressionless misery. Caleb had frowned, warning of constant danger, dire perils that could bring instant death. Isaac Raines had been darkly doubtful, shaking his head over the young age of thirteen. But in the deep forests his control over himself and his surroundings had been far more complete. He had watched his foster father and Isaac Raines, and once the skills had been mastered and his senses had been attuned to the environment, he had become one with the deep forest, as much a denizen of the wilderness as the catamounts, wolves, Indians, and other carnivores.

But the spring thaw often revealed scattered bones when the snow melted into trickling rivulets of water, the bones of an aged, unlucky, or careless carnivore. Survival depended on the ability to identify potentially hazardous times and places, alert senses, and immediate reaction to the first indication of danger. The horses were a constant danger, and one that was unavoidable. They were a necessity for packing in supplies and packing out furs and hides, but a trail left by shod horses was evidence of the presence of a white man. Horses were noisy and odorous, and they could be detected from a long distance away. He heard the chink of a horseshoe against a rock when he was well over a hundred yards from his temporary camp, and the breeze carried the musky odor of the horses. He turned and began working his way up the rise at one side of his camp.

Despite all precautions a campsite became more dangerous the longer it was used. Foot trails radiated out from it,
marked by a broken twig here and a depressed clump of
grass there that a keen eye could detect, and the area became saturated with the odor of the horses and their manure as the days passed. He had picked the campsite with
care, knowing that he would spend several days there before rejoining Caleb and Raines. There were no Indian
trails in the vicinity, so it was out of their usual paths of
travel. It was only moderately good deer-hunting country,
deep stands of pine broken with patches of scrub and limestone outcroppings instead of the forests of oak, beech, and
hickory interspersed with grassy glades that deer preferred,
so it was unlikely to draw many Indians hunting deer for
winter stores of pemmican and jerky. It was a narrow valley, with water and sufficient graze so the horses wouldn't
have to be moved, and it contained their odor to an extent.

A rocky bluff overlooked the camp, and the spur behind
the bluff was a relatively safe path of approach to overlook
the valley where the horses were hobbled. Best of all he
had found a small cave halfway up the bluff, its entrance
and the approach concealed by scrub and stunted cedar.
He crawled from one place of concealment to another,
working his way along the spur toward the brow of the
bluff. A rattlesnake sunning itself after the nighttime chill
held him up for a few minutes. It was almost invisible in a
scattering of leaves and twigs and against the mottled color
of the limestone rock where it lay, but his eyes picked out
its characteristic form when he was three feet from it, the
same way he spotted quail huddled in cover or a deer
standing motionless in broken shadows. He backed away,
gathered a handful of pebbles, and began tossing them at
the snake. The snake lifted its head and shook its rattle
irritably, still torpid from the chill of the night before. He
continued tossing the pebbles. When the snake lowered its
head and slithered away, he continued crawling forward.

The horses were grazing quietly. Young, impulsive, and
reckless braves might kill the horses for a feast or lead
them away to a secure place, then lie in wait for him. More
crafty and more dangerous braves would leave them,
knowing they could be taken at will when the more valuable trophy of the scalp had been taken. Santee lay under a

thick clump of brush and searched the valley and opposite slope with his eyes, systematically looking at each shadow and tree, and at the clumps of growth in a brushy opening on the opposite slope. When he finished, he did it again. There were no Indians lying in wait. He backed out of the brush, crawled a short distance back along the spur, then began working his way down through the brush and around to the cave in front of the bluff.

The stone at the mouth of the cave was worn smooth, and his first concern had been that the cave might be a lair for a bear or catamount. After he had crept around the entrance to look for hair and crawled a few feet into the cave to smell, that possibility had been eliminated. But then he had found a fire pit of stones carefully fitted together on one side of the cave, and the roof of the cave was black with smoke for several feet from the entrance, evidence of occupants more deadly than bears or catamounts. But it had been immediately obvious that the signs of occupancy were very old. The last fire in the fire pit had been so long ago that the ashes had long since disappeared, and the soot on the roof of the cave had become a hard patina on the rock from the passage of many years. Bones buried in the dirt and shards of rocks on the floor of the cave dissolved into dust as he handled them. At the back of the cave there were crumbling human skeletons in niches that had been dug into the rock, some covered with facings of rock and others exposed where the facings had collapsed. The implements and weapons in the niches were crude, unlike any Indian artifacts he had ever seen, and any wooden handles they might have had were long since dust. Rough drawings had been scratched into the smoke on the ceiling. On the walls near the niches were patterns drawn on the rock in red clay and charcoal.

It was puzzling and interesting, as were the clearly recognizable seashells buried in the limestone miles from the seashore and far above sea level. But it had nothing to do with survival, food, or deer hunting, so it was only remotely interesting. His buckskin hunting bag was by the fire pit, containing what was left of the essentials he had taken from the supply cache when he, his foster father, and Raines had split up. He took out his flint, steel, and tinderbox, and kindled a small fire in the fire pit. The twigs were seasoned hickory, burning rapidly and settling quickly into a bed of hot coals, and the little smoke that came from the fire was hidden by the screen of brush concealing the mouth of the cave until it was dissipated by the breeze. He put the strips of tenderloin on an iron skewer and hung them over the fire, then took his calendar stick out of his hunting bag. It was an essential for keeping track of the days when alone in the wilderness, because the days began to run together after a short time. He notched the stick, then again counted the notches since the days he had left the others, confirming when he was due to meet them.

The tenderloin hissed and popped over the coals, and the appetizing odor of roasting meat eddied through the cave. He took a handful of dried corn from his hunting bag and put it on a rock at the side of the fire pit to parch, then began unrolling and fleshing out the deerskins he had taken that morning. Deerskins from previous days were rolled in bundles and stacked along the side of the cave, all of them rolled with the hair inward so it would loosen enough to be scraped off with a knife. His foster father and Raines usually buried skins or sank them in a creek for a few days to make the hair slip. It was an easier way of taking off the hair, but it also took a lot of moving around. Places where the ground had been uprooted were left behind, and slipping hair from a deerskin could float far down a creek. Santee preferred the additional work and trouble of scraping off the hair with a knife, instinctively feeling that an added margin of safety was gained by moving about as little as possible and by leaving behind as little sign of his presence as possible.

There were other ways in which he had begun to pull away from the ways his foster father and Raines did things, and it extended to appearance. Their wamuses hung down to their knees, and he wore his only to his thighs to give him more freedom of leg movement and to make it easier to mount and ride a horse. They wore felt hats, but he wore a fur cap with a raccoon tail hanging in back. Their buckskins were plain, but he spent odd moments in decorating his, stitching beads in patterns on his moccasins and wamus, and he had long, heavy fringes around the wide collar and down the outside sleeve seams on his wamus, as well as down the outside seams on his breeches. His foster father and Raines were tolerantly patronizing about his decorating his buckskins, but he was sure the long fringes helped break up the outline of his body and conceal him to an extent when in deep shadows.

The tenderloin was roasted through when he finished with the deerskins. He ate half of it and half of the corn, then lay down at the entrance of the cave and dozed off. The screech of a jay awakened him an hour later, and he was immediately alert and wide awake. He listened to the bird hovering and moving along over some disturbance in the forest, then relaxed. It was moving too rapidly to be an Indian. The sound faded into the distance, and he dozed off again.

It was early afternoon when he woke again, and he left the cave and worked his way down the bluff into the valley. The horses were dozing in the shade, their hobbles secure and not chafing their forelegs. Pawpaw trees clustered in a thicket where the trickle of water running from the upper end of the valley turned into marshy ground at the lower end, and he picked a dozen of the yellow, heavy fruit. He drank at the stream, picked a handful of blackberries, and ate them as he climbed back up to the cave, then sat at the entrance of the cave and munched pawpaws as he waited for sunset.

The autumn colors became richer as the sun touched the horizon, then they faded into hazy, mottled brown as the light began failing. He left the cave again and went across a low hill on the upper end of the valley, the opposite direction from his early morning hunt. The deer were moving, nervously venturing forth in late daylight in response to instincts that warned them to store layers of fat for the approaching winter. He saw two does and passed them by, not wanting to shoot until he was farther from his camp-site, and they grazed peacefully, unaware of his presence.

A few minutes later a rending, crashing noise ahead of him brought him to a standstill in the shadow of a tree. Then he recognized the noise and crept forward. A fat bear was busily ripping apart the rotted trunk of a wind-felled tree and eating the grubs in the pulpy wood. Santee worked his way around the bear until he was downwind, then he began stalking, slipping silently through the underbrush. The whitetail was easier to stalk because of its invariable practice of wriggling its tail before it lowered and lifted its head, but bears were less cautious than deer. And the bear he was stalking was engrossed in its feast on grubs. Santee worked his way to within two hundred feet of the bear, an easy shot to the head. Fifteen minutes later he was trotting silently on through the forest, the bearskin slung over his back.

He killed and skinned a buck as the last light was fading, then worked his way slowly through the dark forest until he came to another brushy opening. The moon was rising and the stars were bright, and he sat down at the edge of the trees on the downwind side of the opening and waited. The chirping of crickets was a constant blur of noise, punctuated by the other sounds of the forest, a shrill scream of a rabbit caught by a fox or other carnivore, the mournful call of a night bird, the distant shriek of a catamount, and the more chilling sound of a wolf howling.

A shadow moved on the edge of the opening in front of him. His eyes became riveted on it. It moved away from the trees and into the blanched light of the moon streaming down into the opening. It was a doe. He started to slowly lift his rifle to bring it to bear, then hesitated. Another doe followed the first one into the opening. Then he waited and watched, his eyes moving between the does and the edge of the opening. Chivalry was an invention of humans, and after long minutes passed a larger form moved at the edge of the trees.

Santee groped in his shot bag, took out three rifle balls and put them in his mouth, then lifted his powder horn and held it in his left hand, loosening the stopper with his thumb and forefinger. The buck moved farther into the opening, hesitating and looking around every two or three steps, ready to break into flight. Santee waited. The buck lowered his head and began grazing. Santee lifted the rifle, bracing it across his left forearm and still holding the powder horn in his left hand. The buck lifted his head, chewing, and looked around. Santee sighted down the barrel at the buck's neck and closed his right hand, pulling the trigger back.

The sharp crack of the rifle shattered the stillness. Insects became silent, roosting birds fled from trees overhead, and small animals scuttled madly through the leaves. The buck went down, his legs thrashing. The does froze in panic-stricken terror, not knowing in which direction the danger lay. Santee rose to his feet, pushing the stopper from the powder horn with his thumb, and he blindly dumped powder into the barrel of the rifle and spat the three rifle balls into it, tamping the butt on the ground to seat the balls in the powder. He lifted the rifle, held the barrel elevated to keep the balls against the powder as he blindly dumped powder into the flash pan, then he closed the flash pan, pushed the stopper back into the powder horn and dropped it, and shouldered the rifle as he pulled the hammer back. The does began darting toward the edge of the trees. He swung the barrel across the nearest one and pulled the trigger, tracking the doe with the barrel. The flash from the overcharged pan was blinding. A long tongue of fire licked from the end of the barrel as the rifle boomed. The doe went down.

The rifle had been heavily overcharged, and it was likely that the touchhole was fouled. It would have to be cleaned out with the frizzen pin, which was difficult to do in the dark. In the meantime he was unarmed. The doe was thrashing about, only wounded. It was possible that the doe would gather sufficient energy to escape into the forest and beyond any hope of tracking in the darkness after the initial shock of the wound passed. At the same time the doe was making enough noise to precisely pinpoint his location for any Indian who might be coming in the direction from which he had heard the shot. Santee hesitated, then put the rifle down and crouched low as he trotted into the opening.

Any wounded animal was dangerous, and a direct blow from a sharp hoof of a deer could be anything from extremely painful to lethal. He circled the doe cautiously, making out the form on the ground, then approached from the back. There was a choice of his tomahawk hanging in the back of his belt or his fighting knife in a buckskin sheath by the tomahawk, and he chose the knife, a heavy, gleaming blade twelve inches long and four inches wide. He eased forward and chopped the knife down on the doe's neck. The razor-sharp blade sank deep, and he stepped back and wiped the blade on the grass. The doe's movements became violent, convulsive throes, then stopped.

Santee put the knife back in the sheath as he crept back across the clearing.

He sat with the rifle across his legs, took the frizzen pin out of the side of his shot bag, and felt for the touchhole by the flash pan with the tip of the pin. The frizzen pin slid into the touchhole, he worked it back and forth until he was sure the touchhole was clear, then he replaced the frizzen pin in the side of his shot bag and stood up. He carefully reloaded the rifle by feel, then went back across the clearing to skin the deer.

It was late, the frosty touch of autumn made the night air chilly, and he was weary and cold by the time he slowly worked his way back through the dark forest to the valley. He climbed up to the cave, built a fire to heat the rest of the venison and parch more corn, and fleshed out the deerskins and bearskin. The fire warmed the cave, and the flickering, cheerful light playing over the inside of the cave gave it an atmosphere of cozy security. He rolled up the deerskins, spread out the bearskin to dry so the hair would hold, then ate the corn and venison, and a couple of the pawpaws. The fire died down, and he filled his pipe and lit it, pulled his blanket around him, and dozed off between puffs on his pipe.

When he woke, he went to the entrance of the cave and looked at the stars, then collected his rifle, powder horn, and shot bag, and left the cave. The moon was down, and the first light of false dawn came as he moved slowly up the hill across the valley from the bluff. He killed a deer at the top of the hill, then another one in the next valley. Full dawn came, and he killed his third deer of the morning as the sun was rising. He returned to the valley, collected all his equipment and skins, loaded the horses, and led them out of the valley to the west.

His senses of direction, distance, and feel of the land over which he was traveling had been honed to a sharp accuracy during the past two years, and although he had never passed across this territory, he had a good grasp of his location and destination. The rendezvous was near a tributary of the Holston, a river they had crossed and re-crossed the previous two years, and he was now in the watershed of the Holston. He worked his way over broken, rocky hills to the west, and he saw mountain peaks in the

distance that he recognized from the year before. When he
changed direction and traveled through a deep valley toward the peaks, he crossed several Indian trails, and immediately left the valley and traveled up a wooded slope to the
south. The landmark peaks were almost directly west of
him, and he recrossed the valley and the Indian trails and
went up a series of shelving ridges on its other side. As he
gained the top of the highest ridge the setting sun gleamed
on the Holston through a gap in the mountain ahead of
him, less than five miles away. He unloaded his horses and
hobbled them, making a cold camp in a deadfall a hundred
yards from them, where he wouldn't be endangered by
their odor and noise, but where he could hear if anything
bothered them. When darkness fell, he rolled up in his
blanket, put his rifle, tomahawk, and fighting knife on the
ground near him, and munched a handful of dried corn
and a piece of jerky from his hunting bag.

He woke well before dawn, caught his horses and loaded
the packsaddles on them, and he reached the Holston by
sunrise. The rendezvous was along a stretch of the river
where it ran almost directly east and west, upriver from a
salt lick they had passed before on the river. There was
some doubt in his mind whether he was upriver or downriver from the rendezvous, but his instincts pointed upriver.
The salt lick was a prime hunting area because of animals
collecting in the area for the salt, and Santee concluded
that he was traveling in the right direction when Indian
trails began joining and showing wear from heavy travel. He made a detour up the side of the mountain overlooking the river to get away from the trails, then saw the salt
lick on the river below him and gradually worked his way
back down. Raines and his foster father had described the
rendezvous, a creek with a large bluff of sandstone at its
mouth, and he found the bluff during late afternoon and
turned up the creek. A few minutes later he smelled woodsmoke.

They usually chose a briar thicket for a campsite, and
there were several in sight up the narrow valley. He led his
horses slowly up the valley and heard and smelled their
horses. The odor of woodsmoke became stronger, eddying
in the breeze sweeping down the valley. He tied his horses
and walked slowly ahead. A dense thicket of briars around

a clump of trees was up the slope to the left, and the horses were only a few yards away on up the valley, hobbled in an opening. He crept softly up to the thicket, listening. A chink of metal against stone came from somewhere in the thicket, and the smell of woodsmoke was almost overpowering. He knelt and began working his way into it.

The briars were almost like a wall, entwined and bristling with thorns. He moved forward at a snail's pace, quietly untangling the briars so he could slip through them, and watching for twigs that would snap and leaves that would rustle. For a time each inch took minutes. Then the thicket became less dense, the individual branches thicker and spaced farther apart. He could hear their voices as they talked quietly.

The briars were a wide ring around the clump of trees, and he worked his way toward a tree. The campsite became visible through the foliage, colors that clashed with the ground, rocks and foliage. Then when he was close to the tree and the foliage in front of him was thin, he could see the packsaddles, the edge of the fire, an ax, a moccasin, and part of a legging. Their voices were clearly audible. His foster father was talking as he slipped past the last clinging branches of the briars and stood behind the tree.

". . . what happened to that boy. I hope he didn't come up against any Indians or run into some other kind of trouble."

"You've no fear of that with Santee," Raines replied in his deep voice. "I'd have the lad with me on a hunt before most men you could name, because he knows what he's about when he's in the forest, lad or no. If he's not here today, he'll be along tomorrow, Caleb."

His foster father mumbled and sighed heavily in reply. Santee cautiously moved to one side, peeking around the edge of the tree. They were lying on the ground with their feet toward the fire, ten feet from the tree. Caleb was looking away from the tree, but Raines was facing it. Raines turned his head, reaching for his hunting bag. Santee silently stepped around the tree, put the butt of his rifle on the ground, and leaned on it as he stood by the tree.

Raines jerked convulsively and snatched at his rifle, seeing Santee on the edge of his vision. Santee's foster father sat up with a jerk, reaching for his rifle. Then they both froze, looking openmouthed at Santee. Raines exploded into laughter, pounding his thigh.

"Did you see that, Caleb?" he howled. "That lad can bloody well out-Indian a flaming Indian! Here he crept through that thicket and walked in on us, and you're concerned about him! Bloody hell, man, be concerned about us!"

"Aye, and well I should," Bledsoe laughed. "I bloody should indeed. How did you fare, then, son?"

Santee smiled and shrugged, moving away from the tree and toward the dead fire. Raines was tall and burly, a tinge of white showing in the blonde hair at his temples and in the moustache and beard he let grow while in the forest. Caleb was a shorter man, his frame thinned by age and hardship to a lean, wiry strength, and his face above the white beard and moustache was dark, leathery, and creased from exposure. Packsaddles, canvas bags of supplies, and other gear were piled along one side of the clearing, and a fire-blackened kettle of stew was on the stones by the ashes of the fire, smelling appetizingly of onions, sage, and peppers. Santee fished a piece of meat out of the kettle and took a bite of it. "Well enough."

"Sit down and eat, son. There's cornbread in that pan, and we opened a bladder of the honey. It's over there."

The path they had cut through the briars was on the other side of the small clearing in the center of the thicket, and Santee rose and walked toward it. "I'll fetch my horses up and settle in."

"How many hides do you have, Santee?" Raines asked.

"Fifty-three, and two bear."

Raines laughed again, slapping Bledsoe's shoulder. "Did you hear that? Another year and we'll be going shares with him, rather than him with us."

Bledsoe chuckled and nodded, his eyes shining with pride as he looked at Santee. Santee pushed the rest of the meat into his mouth and chewed it as he walked toward the path.

# Chapter Six

The blazing colors of full autumn covered the slopes as they traveled west and crossed the Holston, hunting deer along the way. Vast clouds of ducks and honking strings of geese spotted the sky during the day, moving from north to south. They settled into canebrakes, marshy bottoms, and beaver lakes on creeks during late afternoons to rest and feed and burst into clamoring flight at sunrise. Santee carried a bladder of corn soaked in water, and when they stopped to camp and hunt, he baited fishhooks on long cords with the corn, catching fat mallards, teal, widgeon, and an occasional goose. Sometimes he plucked the fowl and roasted them over the fire on a skewer, but more often he drew out the entrails and left them unplucked, filled them with a stuffing of rice, corn, sage, onions, and red peppers, plastered them with a coating of mud that stripped off the feathers when it was removed, and baked them overnight in a fire pit lined with hot stones.

Indian trails became more frequent as they crossed the jagged hills, deep valleys, and innumerable winding, twisting streams west of the Holston, and they traveled slower and more cautiously, hunting less and devoting their attention to safely crossing the area heavily traveled by Indians. The competition between the French and British over settlements along the Ohio had broken into hostilities that had increased, culminating with the defeat of Colonel Washington at Fort Necessity the previous summer. Tribes and factions supported by the warring nations had become more active, and sporadic raids by Indians armed and urged on by the French had spread all along the border country, wiping out many isolated settlers and driving others back into more populated areas.

During the previous two years their direction of travel

had been more to the south in the first weeks of their trek. Santee was unfamiliar with the territory they were crossing, but Bledsoe and Raines had traveled it several times, and they mentioned a nearby major Indian trail in their conversations over the campfires at night. Other Indian trails they crossed began showing more recent signs of parties that had passed along them, and they abandoned hunting entirely and made cold camps, eating corn and jerky from their supplies. A strong odor of woodsmoke became more pronounced as they were working their way across a mountain one afternoon, and they saw several campfires in the valley below them when they reached the top of the mountain. They returned to a steep valley they had crossed in the side of the mountain, where the horses could graze and water in relative safety, and they made camp for the night. At daybreak they went back to the top of the mountain. The campfires were still burning in the valley below.

They moved along a narrow, rocky ridge extending down the side of the mountain, cautiously approaching the valley. The trail was one that had been made by foraging buffalo, stretching through the trees and canebrakes along a wide creek in the valley, and it had been widened by use until sections of it were clearly visible from a long distance away. Indians were camped in openings and trampled spots along the trail, and there was an occasional glimpse of movements of horses and Indians back and forth along the trail. By late morning Santee, Raines, and Bledsoe had crept down rocky outcroppings to less than a mile from the trail, and they crawled into a thicket of brush on a bluff overlooking the trail.

A half dozen Indians raced their horses across an open spot on the trail, waving their rifles. Their whoops and shouts were barely audible, and a distant, muffled crack came over the sound of the breeze as one of them fired a rifle. "Cherokee," Raines murmured. "And getting themselves worked up to no good. I'll stay well away from that lot."

"You will if you want to keep that yellow thatch on your nob," Bledsoe chuckled.

Raines smiled and nodded, then his smile faded. "And they're no doubt armed and supplied by the French on the

Mississippi. The border settlers in Virginia will have their hands full when that pack breaks out of here."

"Aye, they will," Bledsoe murmured. "And we'll all be having a fear for our scalps if this trouble keeps building and that grand mob of peabrains who should be doing something about it keeps on mucking about as they've been doing. The Anson boys joined that regiment Colonel Innes raised, and they got sent home along with most of the rest of the regiment before they were halfway across Virginia. It seems that no sod had given a thought as to what they were to eat."

"It's a bloody pickle, right enough," Raines replied. "But they'll have it unraveled if it gets any worse. We have the Iroquois and others on our side, and no doubt we'll have more regulars in, if it keeps up."

"No doubt. But all that will be of little comfort to those on the North Forks of the Holston and such places, who have only themselves and their rifles."

Raines grunted and nodded, sighing heavily.

"Where does this trail lead?" Santee asked.

"It joins another trail north of here," Raines said. "That one leads over toward Virginia to the east, and in the other direction, I'd say it might cross through the mountains on over to the north and west and go into the place the Indians call *Kenta-ke*. What do you say, Caleb?"

"I'd say you could be right, for all I know. And I'd also say that it makes little difference to me, because I want nothing to do with it. Nor with *Kenta-ke*. From what I've heard, a man's scalp is worth less than a blade of grass in a forest fire in *Kenta-ke*."

"I've heard that also," Raines replied. "But I was talking to Martin Ashe when he came through Wilmington during the summer, and he told me that a Doctor Thomas Walker from Virginia had traveled along some Indian trail into *Kenta-ke*. The trail crossed through the mountains at a place they called Cave Gap, and Walker renamed it Cumberland Gap. That was about five years ago, and the trail Walker traveled could have been the one to the north of here."

"It could have been, and there was a lot less trouble with Indians five years ago," Bledsoe replied, sliding backward.

"Let's go back across the mountain, and we'll have another look tomorrow."

Raines nodded, turning and following Bledsoe out of the brush. Santee looked down at the trail again, then picked up his rifle, squirmed around on the ground, and followed the others.

They went back across the mountain to their campsite, checked on their horses, and spent the rest of the day in a deadfall near the horses, fleshing and scraping the hair from deerskins. The following morning they returned to the top of the mountain. The campfires were fewer, indicating the Indians were leaving. The last of the campfires died away during the afternoon, and there were none the following morning. The three loaded their horses, cautiously went through the valley, and crossed the trail, continuing west.

The autumn colors dipped into the deep valleys, the nights were cold, and the weakening sun took hours to warm the chill from the frosty air during the day. They found scattered buffalo on the trails trampled through the valleys, then they found herds of a hundred as they came out of the mountains and into foothills that gradually changed into rolling tableland covered with meadows and forests. Santee still caught a few ducks and geese, and he caught fat catfish and perch in the rivers. Persimmons and pawpaws were juicy and sweet from the frost that had touched them, and dewberries and gooseberries could still be found on low bushes in the undergrowth. They shot deer and an occasional elk, numbers of buffalo, and bears and turkeys fattened on the beech, chestnut, and acorn mast in the forests.

Falling leaves became thick and the days turned cold as they moved back into the foothills. They retrieved a cache of cooking utensils, tools, and extra traps left the year before, then looked for a place to trap during the winter. Deep in the foothills they stopped to scout a valley where Bledsoe and Raines had trapped several years before. There were few Indian trails, and nearby creeks were dotted with lakes that teemed with beaver and otter. They built a log and sod cabin in the wind-sheltered end of the valley and settled for the winter.

The last of the leaves and the first of the snow fell, the

trees becoming stark black skeletons in the gray overcast of the short, bleak days. The time of the year when Indians were less active had come, and Santee, Bledsoe, and Raines moved about more freely. They put out traplines, made moccasins lined with fur, and wrapped themselves in makeshift coats of buffalo skins to check their traps and hunt. Most of their efforts went into trapping for beaver and otter—the pelts in highest demand—but they also trapped fox, raccoon, and muskrat. Santee set snares for rabbits and built traps for quail and turkey for food. The furs were carefully cased, fleshed, and dried, then tied into bundles by type, and the bundles began to stack up against the walls of the shelter.

Deep winter came, and the snowdrifts piled up against the cabin and across the trails they had made in the snow to check their traplines. The hunting diminished, their presence and the pressure of their activity driving the game out of the area, and there was only an occasional glimpse of a deer, winter-starved and harried by the packs of wolves combing the foothills. The trapping continued to be good, but running the trapline took up only a part of the day; the days were frigidly cold, and much of their time was spent in the shelter.

Santee's buckskins were less than a year old, but they had become uncomfortably tight. He selected four good buckskins, boiled them in tanbark, worked them over a straking board to soften them, and began making himself new breeches, moccasins, and wamus. He cut and sewed them with extra room in event he continued growing as rapidly, working on them for long afternoons and evenings in front of the fire, sewing on beading, cutting long, thick fringes on the seams, and chuckling as he listened to Bledsoe and Raines counting the notches on their calendar sticks and arguing about how long it was until Christmas.

January brought weather far colder than it had been the two previous winters, which had been frigid compared to the more moderate winters of Wilmington. The temperature plummeted far below freezing, the air became deathly still, and the only sound that broke the frozen quiet was the howling of wolves. Trapping became poor, with only one or two beaver in the traps on some days and none on others. Then the frigid grip of the cold relaxed. The trapping became good again, and the air didn't burn in their nostrils and lungs when they crossed the snow to run their traplines. In February the breezes began to come from the south, and it became warmer.

The snow crusted from being warmed by the weak sun during the day and frozen at night. The ground began to show through the trails they had made through the snow to their traps, then the trails became puddled and muddy during the middle of the days. The drifts around the cabin shrank, and icicles hanging from the eaves dribbled and made holes in the snow below. Then the icicles began falling. Dark spots showed through the snow on the beaver lakes, and water began gurgling at their outlets.

They checked the shoes on the horses and began feeding them corn to strengthen them for the return trip. Rivulets gurgled down the hills as the days became longer and the sun stronger, the snow became thinner on protected slopes, then dried grass showed through it and the horses grazed more easily. Some of the beaver pelts began to show signs that the beaver were shedding their winter fur, and Santee, Bledsoe, and Raines took in the traplines and prepared to leave.

The nights and some days were still frigidly cold. Snow still covered many meadows and openings in the forest, and it clogged many narrow valleys. Some streams had thawed, and the ice on others was unsafe to cross, necessitating wide detours. Creeks began turning into rivers, and rivers became wide, swollen torrents, sweeping masses of driftwood along in their strong currents. Some rivers could be forded at spots where they were still wide and shallow, but others had to be forded in narrow valleys, the furs, rifles, and equipment floated over on rafts and the horses forced to swim over. The wood was usually wet and smoked too heavily to build a fire, so they camped cold most of the time, soaked and shivering in their blankets. Bledsoe's right foot pained him constantly, and his shoulders and back became stiff and painful.

The Holston was the last hard crossing, and they camped for two days to dry out, warm themselves, and rest the horses. Buds were showing on the trees in the mountains, and the trees in the valleys were starting to sprout leaves as they traveled on to the east. The pale green haze of new

foliage covered the mountains as they forded the Nolichucky and crossed the Bald Mountains. They turned
north through the lowlands east of the mountains, then east
again and crossed the Blue Ridge. Many of the scattered,
isolated farms they saw were deserted.

A large stockade was being built near a tributary of the
Yadkin, a refuge for families in the area and a mustering
point for launching units of militia against marauding Indians. It was to be called Fort Dobbs in honor of the governor, and it was hurriedly being finished before the anticipated summer raids. Farms and settlements were thick
along the creeks and rivers as they turned to the southeast,
and the trail widened to rough roads stretching out among
the farms around the larger settlements. Preparations were
being made for spring planting, and cabins and outbuildings were being put up at new farmsteads. Men, women,
and children working in fields on the farms stopped what
they were doing and looked as the train of horses passed,
Bledsoe riding in front and leading five heavily laden
horses, Raines leading five, and Santee leading three.

The settlements were clusters of log buildings around a
muddy square, a trading post with its log warehouse and
stock pens, occasionally an office for a sheriff and justice of
the peace, usually a church, and a few cabins, with vegetable gardens and stock pens behind them. Frequently there
were inns in the settlements, dirty and vermin-infested, and
the three camped by creeks and in copses of trees by the
roads. When they stopped at a trading post to exchange a
buckskin for corn and fodder for the horses, loiterers and
farmers in from outlying farms gathered around to ask
about Indians, and children gaped in wide-eyed and openmouthed wonder.

Sometimes entire families had devoted the day to coming
into the settlement. Women and children crowded into
muddy wagons, men and boys trudged through the mud in
their heavy boots. Youths looked at Santee in envy, murmuring among themselves. Pretty red-cheeked daughters in
their teens looked at Santee from the corners of their eyes,
bright and colorful in the calamancoes, shawls, and bonnets
they had donned to come to the settlement, sedate and demure under the watchful scowls of their mothers. Santee
sat on his horse with his rifle cradled in his arms and

looked at them from the corners of his eyes, gratified that he had on his new buckskins.

The trace along Cape Fear River was heavily traveled, wagons loaded with food staples and other goods coming upriver, and wagons loaded with indigo, flax, tobacco, and other produce going down the river to the port at Wilmington. The settlements along the road were large and old, and the farms were well established, with signs of having been tilled for years. Then there were no settlements for a long stretch, and the breeze had the salty odor of the sea.

The trace turned into a road, and the odor of the sea was lost in the smoke and smells of lumber mills and rendering plants for pitch and resin off the sides of the road. Scattered dwellings and other buildings along the road became clusters, and trees disappeared except for isolated, bedraggled survivors that had somehow escaped the ax and that had an almost furtive and apologetic air about them as they put out their leaves in hope of another year of avoiding notice as live wood among masses of dead. There were livestock yards and warehouses smelling of rope and pitch, then there was a processor of foodstuffs, with wagons loaded with hogsheads of salted pork and beef trundling out of the yard and lean, furtive-looking stray dogs prowling among the refuse piles scattered around the building. The gaps between buildings disappeared and they changed from squat log structures to multistoried clapboard, housing taverns, shops, lodgings, and other businesses, and the road changed into a crowded street paved with puncheons and rock and congested with drays, wagons, porters carrying loads, riders, vendors pushing carts and crying their wares, and pedestrians moving cautiously through the melee. Dirty winding streets lined with buildings branched off on each side. Puncheons and rock became cobblestone, and at a wide intersection one fork led into the center of the town where large brick buildings housing government offices and businesses were located, the other leading toward the waterfront.

The bustle of activity increased, and side streets teemed with activity. The street became narrow, muddy, and odorous, large warehouses on each side blotting out the light. Then it widened again and there were ship's chandlers and outfitters, trading and shipping factors, mercantiles, taverns, cheap lodgings, and general merchandise and sundries. The street curved, and Santee saw their destination on a corner ahead, the firm of Eleazer Porter, shipping factor and trader. The building filled the corner of the street, a sprawling structure of weather-darkened clapboard with offices on the main street and a loading dock on the side street. It was where they always brought their furs and hides, and it was also where Santee's brother Jubal was apprenticed.

A wagon was being loaded at the dock, and a clerk saw the horses coming and went inside. Bledsoe turned onto the side street, crossing it toward the dock. The clerk came back out with Porter, a small, portly man in his forties with the appearance of a successful businessman—dark wool coat, waistcoat and breeches, and tidy stockings, cravat, and peruke. Raines crowded his horses to the dock beside Bledsoe's, and Santee reined his horses up by the others, dismounted, and climbed onto the dock with the other men.

"Caleb! Well, well, you're back safe and sound, aren't you? Not that I had a moment's fear of anything else, of course. And still hale and hearty, I see."

"I'd be better off if this one foot would go ahead and rot off, but I'll do. You seem well enough."

"I am. I'd be a wealthy man if my business fared as well as my health. Isaac, it's good to see you again. And with all your hair about you still, I see."

"Aye, there's no Indian foolhardy enough to fight my nitties for my scalp."

Porter laughed too boisterously, with a gushing enthusiasm and a wide smile that didn't reach his small, sharp eyes. His smile moderated as he looked at Santee with the grudging courtesy of a respected businessman compelled to be polite to a youth with something of a reputation as a troublemaker. "I see you're growing yet, Santee."

"I've stretched a bit more, I believe."

"Yes, just so, just so." His effusive smile returned as he looked back at Bledsoe. "Well, let's see if we can't find a drop of cheer, what? And I'm sure you're looking forward to having a word with Jubal. My man can see to the unloading and counting you in, unless you'd care to check his tally as he goes."

"No need of that. And I wouldn't say no to a taste of something to warm my bones. After this past winter it'll take me until August to thaw. How's Jubal faring?"

"Excellently, excellently. And I shall sorely miss him if he decides to leave when his term with me expires this year. As much as he does and as much as he knows, I might be bounden to take him on as a partner to keep him."

Porter continued talking and chuckling as they turned toward the door. The clerk held the door and stood back out of the way, nodding aimlessly and grinning ingratiatingly. The interior of the building was massive, the far corners lost in the dim light, and it was cluttered with stacks of crates and barrels piled to the low ceiling. The air was stale and damp, with a strong, overpowering stench of raw hides and furs blending with the odors of cotton fabric, oily metal, spices, and rum coming from the crates and barrels on each side of the narrow aisle. The aisle ended at a door, which opened into a dark hallway with doors spaced along it. Porter opened a door and waved them in.

"Step right in and make yourselves comfortable. I'll see about a sip of something to drink, and I'll fetch Jubal. Just make yourselves comfortable, and I'll be right back."

The office where he always conducted them when they arrived was a dirty cheerless room, smelling of old sweat and musty paper. A desk with pigeonholes full of papers sat against one wall, and shelves stacked with ledgers and sheaves of papers lined the wall on each side of the desk. The small pane in the window was grimy, the clapboard walls were moldy from dampness, and the floor was covered with old mud turned to dust. There was one chair in front of the desk and two others, so Santee leaned his rifle in a corner and sat on his heels as Bledsoe and Raines took the chairs, talking quietly about what they anticipated the furs and hides would bring.

Porter's footsteps came back along the hallway, and he came in with a bottle and pewter cups, followed by Jubal. Jubal seemed to have aged visibly during the few months, and he had always looked far older than his years, with deep lines around the sides of his mouth and on his forehead, and an air of settled maturity about him. The lines emphasized the unhealthy pallor of his face. He was small and thin, but neat as always, his black hair tied back in a clout, his linen shirt, stockings, and cravat clean, his breeches unwrinkled, and his buckle shoes blacked. And as always he was remote and withdrawn, his eyes hooded.

"Father, it's a pleasure to see you're back safe and sound. Did you fare well?"

"Tolerably well, son. And how are you? Eleazer tells me you're still doing well."

"I'm gratified he thinks so. You seem in good health."

"I am, I am. How's your ma and everyone?"

"Mother and Nina are well, and I'm sure their spirits will be much improved now that you've arrived. Mr. Raines, how are you?"

"I'm fit, Jubal. Have you seen my woman and little ones lately?"

"I spoke with Mistress Raines not three days gone, and she and the children are well."

His tone was courteous and controlled, as was his smile. And he communicated a vague impatience to be done with them and return to his work. Bledsoe looked remotely uneasy and unsure of himself, as he frequently did when dealing with Jubal, wanting to be more demonstratively affectionate but dissuaded by Jubal's reserve. Jubal's blue eyes became cold and thinly veiled with distaste as they turned toward Santee and moved over the fringes and beading on his buckskins.

"How are you, Santee?" His tone was flat and perfunctory.

Santee looked back at him, unsmiling. "I still have my hair. How are you?"

Jubal nodded indifferently in reply, moving back to the door and glancing around. "I'll see you at home, Father. And I'm sure I'll see you again shortly, Mr. Raines."

They murmured and nodded as he left, and Porter poured rum into the cups on the desk. Santee stood up and stepped forward to take his as Porter passed them around, and Porter's smile became expansive again as he lifted his cup.

"Here's your health, and many safe trips like this one past, gentlemen."

Bledsoe grunted as he took a gulp from his cup, and he shook his head as he wiped his mouth with the back of his hand. "With all the Indian trouble starting up on the border, I'll wager there'll be some whose trips won't end as happily."

"I won't argue with that," Porter replied morosely, his smile fading. "Have you heard about General Braddock's defeat?"

Bledsoe and Raines looked at each other then at Porter in consternation. "Braddock was defeated?" Bledsoe said.

"And killed," Porter sighed heavily. "He marched on Fort Duquesne at the forks of the Ohio with two regiments of regulars and a regiment of militia, and he was soundly defeated and killed. The stories I've heard have it that there was an ambush, and the regulars bolted and ran. Our Colonel Washington restored order and the militia fought well, being more familiar with fighting Indians, but it was a devastating defeat. We will probably feel the repercussions of that for some time."

"I know we will," Raines said glumly. "This is some bloody bad news to come back to."

"It is and all," Bledsoe said. "If something's not done soon, the French and their Indians will push us into the Atlantic."

"The Assembly is taking steps," Porter said. "They've authorized the recruitment and funds for the maintenance of two companies of militia to protect our border settlements, and they are raising additional companies to send to the north. And they've also authorized funds to build several forts along the border."

"We saw one of them," Bledsoe said. "And I opine they might be trying to kill a buffalo with a switch. Their two companies and their forts won't last the summer if the brunt of the trouble comes this way."

"Let's hope that it doesn't," Porter sighed worriedly. "I wish no ill on anyone, but when trouble has come before, most of it has been in the north. It could be that—" He broke off as a soft knock came at the door, and he stepped to open it. The clerk from the dock handed him a piece of paper, and he closed the door and walked toward his desk, looking at the paper. "Let's see what we have . . . we make it five hundred and twenty-three deerskins, six hundred and twelve prime beaver, one hundred and sixteen prime otter, and other assorted furs and skins amounting to just under one hundredweight."

Bledsoe and Raines looked at each other. Raines thought for a moment, then nodded. Bledsoe looked at Porter, taking a drink from his cup. "I won't find fault with that."

"Well, it was an excellent season for you, gentlemen," Porter said, sitting down at his desk and reaching for a quill. "An excellent season indeed." He dipped the tip of the quill in an inkwell and jotted numbers on the paper. The room was quiet except for the scratching of the quill against the paper as Bledsoe and Raines looked at Porter intently, waiting. He added the numbers rapidly, then put the quill down and picked up the paper. "And that will amount to . . . oh, odd shillings over three hundred and twelve guineas, so we'll call it three hundred and fifteen guineas."

Raines pursed his lips, thinking, then nodded. Bledsoe looked at Porter. "That sounds fair enough to me."

"Then we'll call it a bargain. If you can come in tomorrow forenoon, I'll have the money in hand."

Bledsoe nodded, draining his cup. "We'll be here. And I'm much obliged for the rum."

"You're more than welcome. It's always a pleasure to have your custom, and yours, Isaac, and I trust that our arrangements will continue to our mutual satisfaction. . . ."

He talked on, and Santee drained his cup and blinked away the tears the fiery rum brought to his eyes as he picked up his rifle. There was a feeling of anticlimax, as there had been the two previous years. While in the wilderness and during the trek back there was a keen anticipation of the return, a feeling that he was coming back to something. But when he arrived, it wasn't there. He put the cup on the desk and followed the others through the warehouse to the dock.

The horses had been moved to one end of the dock to make room for three wagons unloading goods, and Porter's manner was distracted as he shook hands again. Bledsoe doubled back through part of the town, then took a street that led out to the road along the east side of the estuary. The bustle of the town was left behind as they turned onto the road. Raines caught up with Bledsoe and rode by him, and they exchanged waves and greetings with the occa-

sional man in a cart or on horseback or foot. Bledsoe
turned off at the path leading to his cabin, saying good-bye
to Raines and waving. Raines nodded and waved, and
looked back at Santee and waved.

The milk cow and oxen in the pasture lifted their heads
and looked disinterestedly, then continued grazing. The
tilled area was sprouting weeds, the fence on one side
needed mending, and scattered cornstalks missed during
the previous year's harvest of fodder were withered and
crumpled, torn and beaten down by the winter winds.

Smoke trickled from the chimney, and the breeze carried
the smoke and the smell of fresh cornbread along the path.
The dog raced along the path, barking excitedly, leaping
into the air as Bledsoe laughed and snapped his fingers,
and wriggling all over as he wagged his tail furiously. Nina
looked around the front corner of the cabin, uttered a
whoop, and lumbered heavily along the side of the cabin in
an awkward trot. Bledsoe reined his horses around to the
front of the stock pen and dismounted, smiling widely.
Hannah shrieked happily, running along the side of the
cabin. Santee slid off his horse by the stock pen and tossed
the reins over a rail as Nina ran to him, her arms out.

Tears streamed down her wrinkled brown face as she
hugged him with a crushing grip, then she looked up at
him through her tears, moving her hands over his shoulders and arms, touching his face with the tips of her fingers. "You all right, Santee?"

"Aye, I'm well, Nina. Are you?"

She nodded, breathing heavily, and her lips trembling as
she tried to control her sobs, then she embraced him tightly
again.

Bledsoe laughed heartily as he and Hannah embraced.
"What's this, now? What's these tears for, woman? We're
back, and we had a bloody good season and all."

"Aye, but we've been so worried, Caleb. We've heard
there's been a lot of Indian trouble."

"You've no cause to worry about us. We've been coming
and going for a good while now."

"Aye, but we heard . . . Lord have mercy, look at that
boy! Caleb, have you been taking growing biscuits and
feeding them to that boy? He's grown more just this past

winter. Here, let me hug my boy. How did you fare, Santee?"

"I'm well, Ma. Are you?"

"But for worrying myself into my grave before my time,
I am. My, my, another year and you'll be looking down on
Isaac Raines, Santee."

Love shone in her eyes and in the beaming, happy smile
on her wrinkled face, love and relief that he had returned
unharmed. But there was also a fleeting analytical light in
her eyes as they searched his face for guilt over having
done something he shouldn't, or something that would
cause trouble. A probing, penetrating light that had often
been in her eyes. Then she squeezed him again, patted his
face, and turned back to Bledsoe.

"Well, you two come in and sit. We have fresh bread,
and we've been keeping victuals ready to cook for three
days."

"I'm ready, because my stomach thinks my throat's slit.
We'll pen these horses and give them a bite of corn, and
we'll be on in."

"You go ahead, Pa," Santee said. "I'll look after the
horses."

Bledsoe nodded, turning toward the cabin. "There's a
good lad. I won't say no to that, because I want to get off
this foot."

"Has it been plaguing again this past winter, Caleb?"
Hannah said, walking toward the cabin with him.

"Oh, not so much. It'll be all right after a day or two of
rest."

Bledsoe and Hannah walked away, an arm around each
other. Santee started to lean his rifle against the stock pen,
and Nina reached for it. He handed it to her, and she
hugged it to her and watched him with a smile as he began
taking the horses into the pen.

# Chapter Seven

something else ... ... ... ... ... ... ... ... ... at the
place of meat ... ... ... ... ... ... ... ... the dog was
pulling the familiar ... ... with faint ... and ... ... ...
The dog ... to ... ... him, and ... turned toward the
dog, back as ... ... ... around toward the path.
The ... of ... toward the ... ... ... ... ... back and
freeze ... ... ... ... ... ... ... ... ... ... ... children.
... ... ... ... ... ... ... ... ... ... ... ... of ... ... ...
Bond ... ... ... on the road. The light is there ... of the
... ... ... ... ... ... ... ... the ... ... ... ... ... ... because

Santee turned the oxen into the stock pen, put the rails
back in place and hung the halters over the top of a post,
and walked around to the toolroom. The dog was lying in
front of the door, and he rose stiffly and yawned as Santee
stepped across him. Bledsoe was at the forge, his eyes narrowed against the heat as he held a piece of iron in the
glowing charcoal with a long pair of tongs and worked the
bellows with his other hand.

"That last patch is plowed, Pa, but it needs to dry out
for a day or two before it can be harrowed properly."

Bledsoe glanced at him and nodded, turning and lower-
ing the piece of hot metal into a bucket of water. The surface of the water boiled and steamed as he stirred the hot
metal around in it. "Have yourself a rest, then, Santee. I
want to finish this and get the door back on the corn crib
before we start on those rails."

"I thought I'd step into town and get myself some fishhooks. The river's going down, and we should have some
good fishing before long."

Bledsoe was lifting the piece of iron to look at it. He
hesitated and looked at Santee with a calculating, thoughtful expression, then he nodded and lifted the piece of iron,
turning the tongs from side to side as he examined it. "No
reason why not. A lad with coins in his pocket likes to
spread them about a bit, and there's nothing wrong with
that. Your ma would like you to put on proper breeches
and a shirt before you go to town, though, no doubt."

"No doubt," Santee chuckled, glancing down at his
buckskins. "That's why I had in mind leaving from here."

Bledsoe laughed and nodded. "Go ahead, then."

Santee turned, untying the thong at the back of his hair.
Bledsoe glanced at him as though he were going to say

something else, then he changed his mind and looked at the piece of metal again. Santee stepped through the doorway, pulling his hair back with both hands, and retied the thong. The dog began trotting after him, and Santee motioned the dog back as he walked around toward the path.

- The belt of forest along the estuary had been thick and deep during his childhood. There had been quail, squirrels, raccoons, and opossums as well as dozens of hogs rooting about and feeding on the mast. The road at the rear of the forest had been only a path. But the estuary had become more settled, some people subdividing their land and selling portions to others, and fathers giving sons land on which to build.

The trees had thinned, turning into cabins and firewood. Hogs had been penned. Game had disappeared. Carts and wagons had bounced along the path, gradually crushing the larger rocks and chewing stumps down, and a road of sorts had developed. Then the wealthy and Crown officials in Wilmington had discovered the efficacy of the sea breezes for escaping the summer heat, stench, and illnesses of Wilmington. Workmen had widened and smoothed the road, and it became a thoroughfare between Wilmington and the beach on weekends.

The perimeter of Wilmington had spread, gradually absorbing land around it, and the road into Wilmington was much shorter than before, tentacles of the town reaching along the estuary. There were streets and alleys where he had roamed among trees as a child, looking for places to set rabbit snares and quail traps. Shops, taverns, lodgings, and other businesses stood where cabins and vegetable gardens had once been. And things had changed during the past winter. Different signs were on some buildings, and in some places two or three small buildings had been replaced by a single larger one. Activity had also increased during the past months. Streets that had been quiet backwaters the year before were crowded with people, pushcarts, wagons, and riders.

Santee weaved his way through the throng, crossing the town to the dealer in hardwares where Bledsoe usually did his purchasing. And he thought about the taverns in the area of the hardware shop. The day was warm and he was thirsty, and having money in his pocket as well as total freedom to do as he wished for a time was unusual. His foster father was usually more reluctant to release him to his own devices, preferring that they go places together, and the tacit acknowledgment of his increasing maturity made a cup of beer in a tavern seem an appropriate diversion, particularly since he had rarely been in a tavern.

The hardware shop was near Porter's firm, and as he turned onto the street where Porter's business was located, he glimpsed a familiar face on the other side of the street. It was Martha Raines, Isaac's wife, elevated above the other people on the street as she sat in a wagon with her children. Then Santee saw Raines and a clerk coming out of a store, struggling with a large barrel of flour and carrying it toward the wagon. Santee angled across the street and through the traffic, trotting toward them.

"I'll give you a hand, Isaac."

"Aye, we can use it, Santee," Raines panted. "Get a side of this bugger, and mind your fingers when we put it in the wagon."

They were carrying the barrel upright, and Santee pushed between them and gripped the top and bottom of the barrel, straining at it and shuffling toward the wagon with them as they pushed their way through the people between the store and the wagon. The clerk gasped and chuckled weakly in relief.

"By God, there's a husky lad. My guts were starting to pull loose."

"Mine were dragging the ground," Raines puffed. "Now let's lift it just a bit higher. Watch your fingers, Santee."

Santee strained harder as the two men grunted with effort, and the barrel slid into the wagon. They pushed it in past the tailgate, and the clerk stood back and dusted his hands together, heaving a sigh of relief. Then he smiled at Santee.

"By God, he is a sturdy lad and all. He has a good size on him."

"He'll have more yet," Raines said. "This is Caleb Bledsoe's boy, Santee."

"Oh, aye, one of those two . . . God's blood, he's sprouted all of a sudden. It seems no time since he was a tyke, and he'll make two of his brother."

"Or more, and he's a good man in the wilderness as well. Are you running a message, Santee?"

"Aye, my own. I came to get some fishhooks."

"Go get them, then, and you can ride back with us. I'll be through here in a bit, then I'll be on my way back."

"Well, I believe I'll stop in over there and wet my throat."

Raines looked across the street at the tavern, pursing his lips in thought as he frowned slightly, then he looked back at Santee and nodded. "I'll go with you, then. I'll see to the rest of my business here, and then we can—"

"I'll not sit here in the sun while you're rumming in a tavern, Isaac," Martha said. "And have you forgotten your manners, Santee?"

"I beg pardon, Mistress Raines. It's good to see you again."

"And you, Santee, but it's no pleasure to hear you talking about loitering in a tavern."

"There's nothing wrong with Santee having a sip when he does a man's work and has a man's money in his pocket," Raines said. "And we won't keep you waiting long. We'll have a sip, go see to Santee's business, and you can have a chat with him while he rides back with us." He looked back at Santee. "I'll be through here in a moment, Santee, and we'll go on over."

"Well, I'll go over and wait for you, then."

Raines hesitated, then nodded and turned toward the store. "Go ahead, then. I'll be there in a bit."

The clerk nodded to Santee as he and Raines walked back toward the store. Martha looked at Santee in stern disapproval, then averted her face with a sniff. The three children in the wagon looked at Santee with owlish gazes. Santee turned and weaved through the traffic as he crossed the street.

The tavern was in the lower floor of a narrow three-story clapboard building, with lodgings on the floors above, its dark doorway a step down from the street and crowded in between the lodgings and the doorway of the business in the adjacent building, a dealer in fabrics. It was dim, crowded, and noisy inside, smelling strongly of stale beer, spirits, vomit, and the sawdust and borings on the floor. Men stood at the long deal counter along the left side of the room, and at most of the tables scattered across the rest of the room men were talking and laughing noisily, some playing cards and throwing dice.

A short, burly man sat on a stool behind the counter, with kegs and barrels on a trestle and bottles and cups on shelves behind him. He slid off his stool as Santee moved up to the counter. "What's your pleasure?"

"I'll have a cup of beer."

Santee put sixpence on the counter, and the man rattled coins in the pocket on the front of his leather apron, put threepence down and took the sixpence, and went back to his stool. The beer was thin and bitter, but it tasted better because of the atmosphere, the laughter and conversation around him, the slap of cards and rattle of dice.

Two apprentices at the counter on Santee's right were discussing their masters in laughing, disparaging voices. There were also men who looked like tradesmen, laborers, and artisans at the counter and among the tables, as well as a number of men like those always loitering about trading posts. On Santee's left was a fat man in his thirties, wearing woolen breeches and stockings, heavy shoes, and a linen shirt open at the throat. His coarse, heavy features were drawn in a surly scowl as he talked to the man beside him, his conversation indicating that he was a foreman or overseer at one of the naval stores' plantations. He was balding, his thin hair pulled back into a stringy, greasy swatch and tied with a string. A stubble of beard covered his cheeks and chin, and his right ear was almost gone, only a mutilated stump of scar tissue remaining.

A serving girl, laughing and talking with the men, moved among the tables. Her dress was very tight, hugging the lines of her full breasts and hips. Her arms were bare, the hem of her dress barely reaching the middle of her calves, and the top of her dress gave a tantalizing glimpse of the cleavage between her breasts. She was pretty in the dim light, and there was an alluring suggestiveness to the way she moved around the room, swinging her hips as she weaved between the tables, and tossing her hair as she laughed, her white teeth shining.

A glowing, throbbing warmth stirred in him. Serving girls in taverns were reputed to be readily available. He had once overheard a conversation between two apprentices, one telling the other that he had paid a tavern serving girl to go to her room with him. Apprentices were notoriously penniless, so it was likely that Santee had more than enough money in his pocket, if only he knew how to approach the transaction. The fact that he didn't know precisely the nature of the services he would be buying did nothing to diminish his fascination with the thought.

She stepped to the counter between Santee and the fat man on his left, putting a cup and several coins down. "More geneva here, Tom. And he says he'll have less vinegar in it this time."

The man behind the counter slid off his stool and took a bottle from a shelf. "It's not my doing if it has vinegar in it. And if he doesn't fancy what he gets here, he can go elsewhere."

"Well, you can tell him that. I won't."

"I'll tell him," the man said, filling the cup. "Have the bastard step over here if he has anything to say to anyone."

The fat man looked at the serving girl, a lascivious smile on his thick features as his eyes moved up and down her, and he patted her buttocks. "Let's us go up the stairs, Moll."

"Fuck off, goat breath," she replied, moving her hips away from him irritably as she counted the coins on the counter. "I can do without the pox, as well as the foul smell of you. Here, put my threepence change in my box there, Tom." She pushed the coins toward him, picked up the cup, and started to turn away from the counter. Her eyes passed across Santee, and she stopped, smiling brightly. She looked at his cup, then at the man behind the counter, and pushed the cup toward him. "And freshen this cup a drop, why don't you, Tom?"

The man behind the counter nodded, picking up the coins and Santee's cup. The girl moved away from the counter, fluttering her lashes as she smiled up at Santee. Santee looked at her with a flushed grin, speechless and frantically wishing he knew what to say. The fat man glared at him, then looked at the girl sullenly. "Mayhap you have in mind taking him up, then?"

"Better him than you, sod. He has more look of a man and a far better smell about him."

"He has the look of a scavey pup to me," the fat man

growled, turning back to the counter. "A man can't have a sip anymore without having pups underfoot."

Santee stiffened, anger swelling in him. The girl stopped again, her eyes moving between Santee and the fat man. Santee glowered at the man. "If there's something bothering you, why don't you move it aside?"

"We'll have no trouble here," the man behind the counter said, putting the dripping cup in front of Santee. "I don't run a rowdy house."

"He'd be no bleeding trouble," the fat man chuckled sourly. "I'd box his ears and send him home to his dam."

"Then fetch your ladder and be at it," Santee said quietly. "I'd hang your scalp on my belt if someone hadn't been there before me, but I'll settle for skinning your arse and selling the hide for a skunk's pelt."

"Hear him!" the girl whooped with laughter, as the fat man whirled toward Santee angrily. "You'll not run over him with your slimy tongue, sod!"

"I said I'll have no trouble!" the man behind the counter shouted. "And you get that geneva over to that table and stop enticing it on, Moll!"

The fat man trembled with rage, glaring at Santee. The girl moved away, her white teeth shining as she smiled at Santee. The man behind the counter glanced at the two men moving back toward his stool. The fat man slowly turned back to the counter, his features working. Santee grinned at the girl, then reached for his cup.

A crushing blow exploded on the side of Santee's head, the room spun around him, and the floor came up and slammed into him. His mind reeled numbly, and there was motion, noise, and confusion all around him. He blinked and shook his head to clear his vision, and he saw the fat man standing over him, his heavy features twisted with savage triumph as he lifted his foot. Santee rolled. The fat man's foot slammed down onto the sawdust and borings. Santee, climbing to his feet, saw the fist at the last instant, filling his vision. The knuckles ground into his left eyebrow, and brilliant flashes of light burst all around him as penetrating pain lanced through his eyebrow. The floor came up and slammed into him again.

Searing pain enveloped his side and his breath was forced from his lungs as the fat man's heavy shoe thudded

into his ribs. The girl's shrill squealing blended with hoarse
shouts and laughter around him. Awareness that he was
being whipped was a sickening torment, and it brought
fiery rage. Then motion was effortless. The man's foot was
drawn back for another kick. Santee sprang up, slamming
his right fist into his attacker's crotch as he rose. The man
howled with pain as his face twisted, and he began dou-
bling over, holding his groin. Santee punched the man's
face with a short left to lift it, then brought his right fist
around, leaning forward and putting his weight behind it.
Blood flew, and the fat man's features were flaccid and
loose as his nose and lips disappeared under the gushing
blood and he staggered backward, arms windmilling.

Santee's vision was blurred, and he was completely blind
on the left side, blood streaming from his eyebrow and filling his eye. He shook his head to clear it and jerked away
from the men closing in around him. The fat man stumbled
back against the counter, sagging toward the floor. Santee
rushed at him, pounding with both fists. The man's head
jerked from side to side, cuts opening on his forehead and
cheeks, saliva and blood flying from his loose lips.

Men closed in around Santee again, laughing and shouting, and pinioned his arms as they pulled him back. The fat
man was collapsing to the floor. The man behind the
counter was bellowing angrily, and the girl was laughing in
delighted approval. Then the men around Santee scattered
as someone shouted in alarm.

"Knife! He has a bloody knife!"

The blade of the knife in the fat man's right hand shone
dully in the dim light as he pushed himself to his feet, panting hoarsely. He wiped the blood out of his eyes with his
sleeve, and there was a deathly silence in the room as he
came toward Santee in a crouch, moving the blade from
side to side. Santee shook his head again to clear it and
tried to wipe the blood from his left eye as he poised himself to dodge the blade. The fat man closed in, then slashed.
Santee leaped to one side, knocked the man's right arm
down, and slammed his right fist into the man's forehead.
The man staggered, then recovered and slashed at Santee's
arm. The keen blade of the knife trimmed pieces off the
long fringe hanging from Santee's arm. Santee knocked the
man's right arm down again and hit him in the mouth with

a right. The fat man staggered, then reeled, his right arm
drooping. Santee leaned forward and put his weight behind
his right fist as he hit the fat man on the chin. The man's
head snapped back, lolling on his neck, and his right arm
fell to his side as he stumbled backward.

Santee followed him, hitting with his right, his left, and
his right again. The fat man fell against the counter, and
Santee stood over him, pounding with his fists. Victory was
a heady, triumphant joy seething through his veins. And it
stirred a driving, churning need for total victory, a dark
impulse to crush and destroy. He threw his last reserves of
strength into his arms, flailing with his fists. But the blows
seemed weak and ineffectual, doing no more than had already been done. The knife had fallen from the man's limp
hand. Santee snatched it up, gripped the man's thin hair as
he slumped toward the floor, and jerked the man against
the counter as he lifted the knife. Memories stirred in his
mind, echoes of wolves baying in savage victory at the moment of the kill and the shrieks of war parties around their
campfires, and the whoop burst from his throat of its own
volition as he poised the knife to plunge it into the man.

"*Santee!*"

The commanding, imperative bellow cut through the
shouts of alarm around him. Santee froze, looking at the
door. Raines stood in the doorway, glaring at him. There
was an instant of utter silence, then a babble of sound
again. Raines pushed through the people, shoving them
aside, and reached for the knife. Santee's fingers were
frozen on the handle. Raines gripped his wrist, twisted the
knife out of his hand, and threw it down. He shouldered
Santee back, grasped the fat man's shirt, and held him up
as he looked at him. The fat man mumbled weakly through
his battered lips, pawing feebly with his hands. Raines
grunted as he released him and dropped him to the floor.

"No lasting harm done there, it appears. Let's have a
look at you, Santee. Aye, you're a bloody mess, aren't
you?"

"That sod there started it!" the girl shouted, pushing
through the men. "The lad was only having his cup of beer,
and that bastard—"

"You keep your mouth out of it!" Raines barked at her.
"I'd be bloody loath to take the likes of you as witness to a

magistrate, and you may be bloody assured of that!" He glanced around. "Is that you, John Hughes?"

"Aye, it's me, Isaac."

"You saw what happened, did you?"

"We all saw. They scuffled, the lad got the best of the fat bugger, and the shitstick pulled a knife. It wasn't the—"

"You'll remember that if a question arises, then, will you?"

"Aye, I'll be a witness for the lad, if need be. We all will, won't we?"

There were murmurs of assent, and Raines nodded, taking Santee's arm. "Well and good, and you might take a look at him and see that he's alive, if somewhat the worse for wear. I don't expect trouble of this, but I like to be prepared. Come along, Santee."

Santee's knees were suddenly weak and rubbery, and Raines gripped his arm more firmly, moving toward the door with him. The light outside was blinding, even though his vision was still blurred and he couldn't see with his left eye. People passing by did doubletakes at him, looking startled. The taste of blood was strong in his mouth, and it was thick in the back of his throat as it trickled from his nose. He spat out a mouthful of blood and wiped at his nose and eye with his sleeve. Raines took both of his arms and guided him along as he weaved through the traffic on the street, wagons and riders slowing as men looked down at Santee.

The three children's heads were in a row along the edge of the side of the wagon, their eyes and mouths open. Martha's expression of horror became mixed with indignant satisfaction. "No harm in him having a sip when he does a man's work and has a man's money in his pocket you said, didn't you? Well, it didn't take him long to find what he'll get instead of a sip in some—" She broke off as Raines looked at her stolidly, then she cleared her throat and stirred on the seat. "Do you want me to help him?"

"He's not hurt. Can you climb up there, Santee?"

Santee nodded, grasping the edge of the sideboard on the wagon, climbing the wheel spokes and pulling himself up. As Raines gripped his belt and lifted him, Santee slid over the edge of the sideboard and fell into the wagon. The children moved away, staring at him. Raines climbed onto the

seat beside Martha, released the brake, and clucked to the
team as he snapped the traces, and the wagon began jolting
along the street.

Raines and Martha looked straight ahead in silence. The
three children sat in a row behind the seat and gaped at
Santee. He slowly dragged himself around to a reclining
position against the sideboard, keeping his head down so
people on the street couldn't see him. The wagon rumbled
along the streets, turning at intersections and jarring more
heavily as the streets became more pitted, and the sounds
of traffic around the wagon gradually diminished.

His head throbbed, seething with pain that was centered
on the left side around the eyebrow, and his ribs ached
where he had been kicked. His knuckles were raw, his
hands sore and swollen, and his left eyebrow was a burning
mass of open flesh, still seeping blood. A numb lethargy
gripped him, and he felt weak and lifeless.

The wagon stopped. Raines handed the traces to Martha
and climbed down from the seat. "Unharness the team and
turn them into the pasture, and leave the wagon by the
pasture. I'll unload it when I get there. Come along, Santee."

Santee lifted himself and crawled over the edge of the
sideboard. Raines helped him down and steadied him on
his feet. Martha clucked to the team and snapped the
traces. The wagon moved away, and Santee and Raines
walked slowly along the path toward the Bledsoe cabin.

"You had no call to speak to that girl the way you did.
She was kind to me."

"If you'd offered her two and sixpence, she would have
been kinder yet," Raines said acidly. "She's no worse than
those who spend their time searching for her sort, but that's
saying nothing. I'm no parson, but I've no time for any of
that bloody lot."

Bledsoe was working on the door of the corn crib. The
dog began barking as Santee and Raines passed the tilled
area along the side of the stock pens. Bledsoe put down his
hammer and walked to the corner of the stock pens, looking at Santee with alarm. "What the bloody hell's this?
What did you come afoul of, Santee?"

Raines folded his arms and looked at Santee. "Tell him."

Santee cleared his throat and spat blood, then touched his left eyebrow cautiously. "I got into a fight."

"Did you now? I would have never bloody known it. How many of them were there?"

"One."

"One? One, did you say? One regiment, was it? Did you get your arse leathered, then?"

"The man was well set up," Raines said. "I would have had my hands full with him, but Santee leathered him. But that's not the end of it. Tell him the rest, Santee."

"It was in a tavern."

"A tavern, was it? Aye, well, you'll learn that trouble meets you more than halfway in a bloody tavern."

"That's not the end, yet," Raines said. "Tell him, Santee."

"He pulled a knife on me."

Bledsoe nodded and started to say something, then he stiffened with apprehension. "Did you cut him?"

"No."

Bledsoe relaxed and nodded with relief. "Well, then there's no harm done if you—"

"He was about to," Raines said. "If I'd got there a blink of an eye later, he would have had him gutted out like a slaughtered hog. He was waving that knife over that man and howling like a Shawnee taking a scalp, and it made my blood run cold, I'll tell you. Now Caleb, I'm not one to put my mouth into another man's affairs, but you're my friend. And this lad is my friend as well, and I like him. But it's no secret as to why he started going with us when he was no more than a boy. As much as I like him, I know he has a bloody mean streak in him. And it's coming to the point where it'll get him on a gibbet if something isn't done about it."

Bledsoe sighed despondently, looking away and stroking his beard. "Santee, why did you do it?"

"He started it, I didn't."

"That has nothing to do with it," Raines snapped impatiently. "He started a fight with you, you leathered his arse, and that's all well and good. What I'm talking about is the way you were going to cut his heart out."

"Why did you do that, Santee?" Bledsoe asked again.

Santee looked away, pondering. He spat out a mouthful of blood and shook his head. "I don't remember it."

"You call me a liar, and you'll think the one you just fought was a babe in arms," Raines said.

"I didn't say you were lying," Santee said resentfully. "I said I didn't remember it. And when my eye gets to where I can see with it, we'll have a go anytime you wish."

"Here, now!" Bledsoe barked angrily. "How's this to talk to the one who's helped you?"

"Leave him be," Raines chuckled, putting his hand on Santee's shoulder. "He's feisty, and there's nothing wrong with that. It's his mean streak that concerns me, and only because I like him."

"Santee!" Hannah shrieked at the side of the cabin. She dropped an armload of washing and ran toward them. "Santee, what happened?"

"He got into a fight, Hannah," Bledsoe said. "There's no cause for alarm."

She stopped, her expression becoming wary, then she walked toward them, looking from Raines to Bledsoe. "Did he hurt anyone?"

"Nothing was done that won't heal," Raines said, turning away. "I've work waiting at my cabin, Caleb."

"Aye, I'll see you again, Isaac," Bledsoe said. "And we're much obliged to you."

Raines nodded, walking rapidly along the path toward the road. Nina came around the cabin and trotted heavily toward Santee, looking at him in consternation. Hannah's eyes narrowed suspiciously. "There's more to it than that. What is it?"

Bledsoe drew in a deep breath and exhaled with a heavy sigh, lifting his hands and dropping them in a helpless gesture. "Santee was about to do the sod with a knife, and Isaac stopped him."

Hannah's face flushed with anger as she glared at Santee, then her features became drawn and gray. Her lips trembled and her eyes filled with tears as she slowly shook her head. "You've a bloody streak in you, Santee," she whimpered in anguish. "You'll come to no bloody good end, and I know it as well as I know I'm standing here."

"Now, Hannah," Bledsoe said in a placating tone, reaching for her. "There's no need for—"

"Leave me be!" she shrieked, jerking away from him. She began sobbing as she moved toward the cabin. "Why couldn't he be like Jubal . . . never a thought of any trouble. . . ."

Nina trotted past Hannah and Bledsoe and reached up to look at Santee's eye. He pulled away from her, looking at Hannah resentfully. "Perhaps I should just take myself on back to the hunting grounds so I won't be any bother, then."

"Good bloody riddance!" Hannah shouted, wheeling around. "Take yourself back among the wild bloody Indians, where you'll be with your own kind!"

"None of this, now," Bledsoe said to her, frowning darkly. "You don't know what you're saying, Hannah."

"I know what I'm saying," Hannah wailed, her voice muffled as she buried her face in her hands and shook with sobs of despair. "When he was only a tyke, I had a constable here because he'd cut a boy with a bloody knife. He was put on the whipping post in town as a common rowdy, and then he . . . all the other things. I've laid awake at night worrying about him, because I know he'll come to no good end."

Her voice faded into gasping sobs. Bledsoe put his arms around her and led her toward the cabin, murmuring to her. Nina pulled at Santee's shoulder, and he turned and sat down against a post at the corner of the stock pen. Nina leaned over him and looked at his eyebrow closely, glanced over him for other injuries, then straightened up and walked toward the cabin.

She returned with a basin of water and a rag to wash the blood off his face, and a pot of salve for his eyebrow. The salve was soothing, but her attitude was far more soothing. She was solicitous and comforting, with no hint of censure, not even caring what he had done or what had happened. Her love was total, unmixed with any other consideration. Resentment over the attitude taken by Raines. Bledsoe, and particularly Hannah churned within Santee, and tears of wounded anger burned in his eyes. Nina was a refuge from the world, and it was tempting to put his arms around her and bury his head against her bosom to seek the healing she had always given him as a child. And she seemed to perceive his need. When she was finished, she put the things aside and knelt in front of him, her hands on his shoulders and a smile on her brown face. But he wasn't a child. He patted her shoulder as he got to his feet and walked away.

Santee sat against a tree near the creek. The afternoon dragged by. Bledsoe hammered on the corn crib and moved around the barn. The cow began lowing, and someone went and milked her. The sun set, thunder muttered in the distance, and the breeze promised rain. Jubal's horse clopped along the path. The smoke from the chimney thickened, rolling down toward the creek.

Darkness fell, and the rumble of thunder became more distinct. Santee got up and walked up to the cabin. The shutters were open and the windows were squares of yellow light, but there was no sound of conversation inside. Santee opened the door and went in. Bledsoe was on his stool by the fireplace, smoking his pipe and whittling. Hannah was on her stool, breaking up beans to cook for the next day. Nina was on her stool, sewing. Jubal was at the table, reading a book by the light of a taper. He looked up.

"Your appearance bears out the story of the brawl in a tavern, and more."

"Mind your own flaming affairs, you."

"I am. It's of little help to me in the conduct of my affairs to be known as the brother of a common rowdy."

Santee turned, went back outside, and sat on the bench outside the door. Nina came out with a plate of food, patted his cheek with a gentle touch of her fingers, and went back inside. Santee ate, got a drink of water from the rain barrel, and went back inside. Nina took the plate and spoon, and he went to his room.

The thunder moved closer. The sounds of activity and movement in the cabin died away. It began raining softly. Santee listened to the patter on the shingles overhead, staring up into the darkness. After a time, he dozed off. The first sound of movement in the cabin wakened him. It was still raining. Bledsoe coughed and wheezed as he dressed. There were other movements in the cabin, then the rattle of pans and skillets and the smell of food cooking. Voices murmured. Jubal left, Hannah telling him to be careful to keep his feet dry. Santee got up and dressed.

Bledsoe was on his stool by the fireplace, smoking his

pipe, and he nodded silently. Hannah was washing dishes at the washstand. She looked over her shoulder at Santee, her eyes red and her features pale and rigid, then she turned away coldly. Nina smiled, filling a plate with food for him. He sat at the table and ate part of it, then got up from the table.

"Will you help me shoe my horses?" he asked his father.

Bledsoe glanced toward the fire, puffing on his pipe and stroking his beard. The water in the basin on the washstand stopped splashing as Hannah looked at him. Nina stopped halfway across the room to the washstand, holding Santee's plate and spoon. Bledsoe sighed heavily as he stood up and put his pipe on the mantel, and he nodded as he walked toward the door. Hannah began washing the dishes again. Nina's features twisted, and she began silently weeping. Santee followed Bledsoe out.

The soft rain continued pattering down. Bledsoe started a fire in the forge and put in pieces of iron to heat, and Santee brought in his horses from the pasture and tethered them outside the toolroom. They removed the old shoes and trimmed the hooves flat, then forged, shaped, and tempered new shoes for each horse. When the shoes were on, Bledsoe got one of his horses and went to town to get bullet lead and fresh gunpowder, and Santee sharpened his fighting knife and tomahawk to a razor edge, then took out his packsaddles and began putting them on his horses.

Santee got a flitch of bacon from the smokehouse, filled bags with dried corn, peas, and beans, filled smaller bags with salt, peppers, and sage, and collected his other supplies and equipment. When Bledsoe returned from town, Santee was loading the bags of supplies on a horse. Bledsoe put the powder and lead in a bag and helped him. Then the horse was loaded, and he was ready to leave.

"Just watch yourself until you get well past the border settlements, son. After you're past them, you should be all right."

"Aye."

"And you'll be better off south of the Holston and in the deep mountains, away from buffalo country. Buffalo draw a lot of Indians, and you should find good deer hunting in the mountains."

"Aye."

"You might run into some forest fires, because lightning starts a lot of them in the deep forest in summer. The only thing you can do is circle around to the upwind side of them."

"Aye."

"And you might ought to . . . well, I could talk all bloody day. And waste my breath while I'm doing it, because you're as good a long hunter as ever wore moccasins. You'll know what to do when the time comes. Let me step into the cabin a minute before you leave, son."

"Aye, all right, Pa."

Bledsoe turned and walked toward the cabin, limping on his right foot, his white hair and buckskins soaked with rain, his shoulders slumped. Santee assembled the horses into a train, tying halter ropes to packsaddles, and the halter rope on the horse loaded with supplies to the back of his saddle. Bledsoe came back around the cabin, his face pale and resigned, with only Nina following him. Nina put her arms around Santee, sobbing, and he bent over her and kissed her.

"I'll see you in a few months, Nina."

"Be careful, Santee. Be careful."

"Aye, I will." He kissed her again and patted her, then held out his hand to Bledsoe. "I'll see you in a few months, Pa."

Bledsoe nodded, his lips thin and tight, and squeezed Santee's hand with a firm grip. "Be careful, son."

"I will."

Santee mounted his horse and lifted the reins, and the horse began plodding toward the corner of the stock pens. The other horses began moving along behind as the halter ropes tightened, their hooves splashing in the mud and shallow puddles on the ground. The train of horses moved along the side of the stock pens at a slow walk, then passed the tilled area. The furrows Santee had plowed the day before were becoming blurred by the rain. Bledsoe's horses in the pasture lifted their heads, cocked their ears, and flared their nostrils as Santee rode along the side of the pasture. The milk cow and oxen lay under a tree and chewed their cud, looking at the train of horses in aloof indifference. Santee was almost at the end of the path when he heard her.

"Santee! Santee! Santee!"

Tears were blended with the rain on her wrinkled face, and she gasped for breath as she ran heavily. The rain had plastered wisps of her gray hair to the sides of her face and soaked the shoulders of her homespun dress. Bledsoe and Nina were running far behind her on the path, trying to catch up. Santee got down from his horse and trotted back to her, and she threw herself into his arms, her fingers digging into his back as she squeezed him and sobbed against his chest.

"Be careful, Santee. Be careful."

"I will, Ma. I'll be careful."

"I love you, Santee."

"I love you, Ma."

# Chapter Eight

The sound was like that of a quail, but it wasn't a quail's call. Santee froze, listening, becoming acutely aware of every whisper of sound over the soft murmur of the breeze in the foliage. A twig popped a hundred feet behind him. A throaty whistle like that of a bobwhite rang through the trees again. The first one had been off to his left, the second one to his right. There was someone behind him. They were trying to surround him.

His first step was in a full, headlong run up the slope ahead. A war whoop rang out behind him, a chilling shriek that battered at his ears. An arrow whispered past him and slammed into a tree trunk ahead. Other whoops rang out, to the sides and behind him. A rifle popped, and the ball whined off a tree. Leaves churned as feet raced toward him.

He ran. The certainty of dire peril was clamor in his mind, and he channeled all the strength and energy he possessed into his legs, racing up the steep slope. The whoops continued to ring out behind him. His thighs and calves began cramping, then the pain became excruciating. His breath began coming in ragged gasps. He ran on.

A large outcropping of rock appeared through the trees ahead, a shelving plateau on the side of the mountain. As he burst from the trees and underbrush and darted across the open rocks the side of the mountain came into full view above. There was more deep forest, then another plateau of rock. The whoops of the Indians were far behind him, but not far enough. He had to reach the rocks before the Indians. Trees closed in around him again. The thick bed of decaying leaves was slippery underfoot, and underbrush snatched at him. The slope rose steeply and his steps became labored. He summoned reserves of energy, running on.

The whoops stopped as the Indians put all their energy into the chase. The pain in his legs passed beyond pain, and they became numb. He breathed in hoarse gasps. The slope leveled off for a few yards, and he lunged across it. Pinpoints of light seemed to dance in front of his eyes and he felt lightheaded, the trees swimming around him. He ran on. After an eternity, glimpses of gray rock were visible through the trees ahead. He struggled the last few steps, staggered out of the trees and onto the rocks, then began climbing.

From the top of the rock the plateau below was in full view across the treetops. The straight-line distance was just on the edge of maximum rifle range. He checked the priming in the pan on his rifle, closed the lid, then took long, deep breaths as he watched the rocks below. There was no disturbance in the forest to indicate where the Indians might be. The thought that the Indians might have crossed the rocks while he was in the trees was a gnawing worry.

They came into sight. There were five of them, Cherokees, three with rifles and two with bows and arrows. He stretched out comfortably, shouldered the rifle, and took aim on one carrying a rifle. His breathing was still rapid, and his hands trembled. The bead swam back and forth across the Indian. Santee steeled himself, drawing in a deep breath, and the bead steadied. The wind was from the right, not much more than a slight breeze, but it would carry the ball well off the point of aim at maximum range. The shot would take ample elevation. He put the bead above and to one side of the Indian's left shoulder, and slowly released his breath as he squeezed his right hand together, pulling the trigger.

The hammer slapped forward. Santee continued tracking the Indian with the bead as the pan flashed. The sharp crack rang out across the trees, and smoke boiled from the muzzle of the rifle. Santee leaned to one side, looking around the smoke. The Indian was down, sprawled on the rocks, and the others were leaping for cover. Santee pushed himself to his feet, slid off the rock, and began trotting on up the mountain.

Losing one of their number would slow them down and make them more cautious. But they would follow. He pondered about where they might have picked up his trail. It was possible that they had simply crossed his trail shortly before, and started tracking. But it was also possible that they had happened across his horses and followed him from there. His supplies and hides might be scattered and spoiled, and more might be waiting for him where his horses were hidden. He pushed the nagging thought out of his mind.

He came out on another plateau of rock, staggering and gasping for breath, and looked around. The mountain extended on up above him, the top far away. Off to the left a fire had swept up the mountain and into a shallow cuplike valley on the mountain side. Wind or rain had stopped the fire, because the foliage was still thick on the upper edge and the sides of the valley, but the heat had been intense and growth had been cindered. He looked at it for a long moment, thinking, then he trotted on along the plateau of rocks and angled off the side, running down the mountain toward the burn.

The breeze carried the lingering odor of smoke and burned wood up through the trees on the side of the mountain. He caught his breath as he ran down the mountain, taking long, bounding strides and weaving through the trees. A deer burst out of cover ahead of him and raced away, and a pair of turkeys exploded from a patch of underbrush. He came to the edge of the valley and stopped, then ran on downhill and across the burn. Several rains had fallen since the burn, but the ashes were so thick that they hadn't soaked into the ground or washed away. Virtually all growth in the valley had been consumed by the fire, with only a few short stumps and partially burned logs remaining, and the ashes stirred up around him as he ran through them.

His trail through the ashes was clearly visible across the valley. It passed several partially burned logs, rocks, and shallow dips. It could be interpreted as the trail of panic-stricken quarry with no thought but to wildly flee, or as the trail of more cunning quarry that had doubled back to hide under a burned-out log or in a dip to wait until danger had passed. He waited, listening and watching the edge of the trees at the top of the valley. His breathing returned to normal, and the cramping pains in his legs turned into the ache of sore muscles driven to the limits of tolerance. Time dragged by, minutes turning into an hour. He sat motionless on the limb in the tree, waiting and watching.

The sound of a bobwhite quail that wasn't made by a quail rang out sharply, hanging in the air. It came from one side at the upper edge of the valley, the same side he was on. A more distant whistle rang out, coming from the upper edge on the opposite side of the valley. The foliage stirred, and two Indians stepped into the open, crouching furtively as they eased forward. They had split up, two coming down the sides of the valley and two coming down the center, covering all the possible routes he might have taken to evade them, and they would converge on his trail at the bottom of the valley and continue tracking. In a single sweep they were eliminating all the possibilities except one. They had overlooked the possibility that it was a trap.

But it would be a trap of his own making if the Indian on his side of the valley got past the tree he was in. The foliage in the tree was thick, and it was possible that the Indian would slip by, out of his line of vision. Then the Indian would spot the trail he had made and would immediately know where he was. Santee slowly pulled his feet up and stood on the limb against the trunk of the tree, checking the priming in his rifle. The foliage in the tree had been scorched thin, and the two Indians crossing the burn were clearly visible. They spread apart and moved out onto the slopes of the small valley, walking slowly along and looking at stumps, burned logs, and depressions. The one nearest him was going to pass within easy rifle shot. The quail whistles continued to ring out occasionally, the Indians coming down the sides of the valley calling to each other to keep track of each other.

A soft, fleecy cloud in the rich blue sky overhead floated past, casting a shadow over the burned valley. A crow cried in the distance, a squirrel chattered a few yards away, the whirring of cicadas rose and fell in monotonous rhythms, and the breeze stirred the leaves. The presence of death seemed incongruous in the bright daylight, more in keeping with dark nights split with flashes of lightning and rolling peals of thunder than with the drowsy atmosphere of the forest dozing through another of its centuries of long, hot summer afternoons. Santee wondered if he had taken the right course of action, or whether it would have been better to flee. But attack was the best defense. And more importantly he had been attacked, the odds weren't insurmountable, and he had to respond. And he had to win.

A quail whistle rang out twenty yards from the tree, then there was silence. Santee stood motionless, his eyes searching and his ears sampling every breath of sound. The two crossing the burn were absolutely silent, moving like ghosts. The one nearest him was well within easy rifle shot. A rustle came to his ears over the whisper of the breeze, then a cracking sound, a moccasin pressing down on a twig and lifting again before the twig broke. Then there was a movement on the ground below. Santee glanced quickly at the Indian in the open, then looked down, taking three rifle balls from his pouch and putting them in his mouth, lifting his powder horn in his left hand and loosening the stopper with his thumb and forefinger. The Indian below came into sight, crouched low with his rifle across his chest, moving around a clump of brush below the tree. It was point-blank range. Santee held his powder horn and rested the rifle across his left forearm as he shouldered it, and he looked down the barrel at the left side of the Indian's chest as he tightened his right hand.

The rifle boomed, and the heavy thrashing in the leaves as the Indian went down blended with the rippling echoes of the shot rolling through the trees. Santee dumped powder into the barrel, spat the three rifle balls into it and rapped the butt against the limb, then lifted the rifle and dumped powder into the flash pan as he looked for the nearest Indian in the burn. The Indian was dimly visible through holes in the foliage as he ran for cover. An arrow slammed into the tree trunk by Santee's head. Santee pushed the stopper back into the powder horn and dropped it, shouldered the rifle, elevating the barrel to keep the rifle balls in the powder as he snapped the pan closed and pulled the hammer back. He sighted down the barrel at the Indian through the foliage, tracking him, and jerked the trigger back. Smoke blossomed from the overcharged pan, then a huge cloud of smoke boiled from the muzzle of the rifle. He lowered the rifle as he leaped to a limb below. The limb began breaking under the heavy shock of his weight, and he leaped for a lower limb and caught the end of another to break his fall. The limbs cracked, and leaves and twigs rained down around him as he hit the ground, looking toward the valley. An arrow thudded into the ground near his feet, and the Indian on the other side of the valley was notching another arrow. The Indian nearby was down, two large spots of red on his back. A puff of smoke came from the edge of the trees, then the thudding report of the rifle carried across the valley. Another arrow hissed past. Santee turned and ran.

The whoops behind were different from before, shrill shrieks to vent frustrated rage instead of exultant baying on the trail. Santee continued running down the mountain for a time to put distance between him and the Indians, then he slowed. There were only two left, and they would be slower and more wary, cautiously examining every potential ambush. But they would follow.

The slope led down to a fold in the mountain, a valley with a creek running through it. Santee stopped by the creek, cleaned out the touchhole by the flash pan in his rifle and reloaded the rifle, then drank his fill from the creek and crossed it. An ancient, massive oak was a hundred yards up the rise on the other side of the creek, and Santee scratched the bark on the tree in a couple of places to make it look as though he might have climbed the tree and be hiding in it, then he walked backward to the creek, placing his feet where he had stepped before. When he was in the water again, he waded up the creek. The dry bed of a wet-weather rivulet joined the creek a few hundred yards along it, and he walked by it for a hundred feet, stepping on large stones to hide his tracks, then he climbed the bank, leaving a clear trail. He walked to another tree, marked the bark, backed to the dry bed, and walked down to the creek.

A large oak overhung the creek farther along, clinging to the bank with part of its roots underwashed by spring floods, and a thick branch of the tree hung low over the water. Santee jumped up and caught the branch, broke a twig so the fresh break was in clear sight from the creek, then dropped back into the water. The creek became more shallow and narrow as he waded farther up, and the high clay banks became lower and rocky in spots. He waded past a tall, slender hickory, then past a large oak. Then he stopped and looked back.

There were rocks around the hickory that could be used as a path, but there was clay and soft mast around the oak, which made it impossible to reach the oak without leaving a glaring trail. He waded back to the hickory, climbed out onto the rocks around it, and began climbing the tree, careful not to break any limbs. The tree was over sixty feet high, slender and pliant, and it began bending under his weight as he climbed toward the top. He swung his weight under it, bending it toward the oak, and continued climbing. The foliage at the top of the hickory dipped into that of the oak as it bent farther over. Santee climbed a few more feet, swinging his weight so the hickory would sway over a thick limb jutting out from the oak, and he dropped onto the limb. The hickory whipped back upright. Santee crawled along the limb to the trunk, then settled himself comfortably.

Time dragged by, one hour, then two. The damp air around the creek became cooler as the sun inclined toward the west. The tension and exertion had almost exhausted Santee, the steady murmur of the creek was soporific, and he struggled to stay alert. Then a jay shrieked raucously back along the creek, disturbed on its nest or while feeding, and Santee stiffened, no longer struggling to stay alert. The bird hadn't cried out when he passed, so either the bird hadn't been there or something was moving on the banks instead of along the center of the creek. He slowly pulled his feet under him, then stood on the limb and leaned back against the tree trunk, his eyes darting around.

The jay cried out a few more times, its sound moving along the creek at about the slow pace of an Indian watching for an ambush and searching for tracks. Then the jay was silent. At a flicker of motion on the other side of the creek Santee turned his eyes toward it, watching through holes in the foliage. The Indian came into sight, creeping along the creek bank. Santee turned his eyes back and looked down, searching the bank below him. A limb of brush at one side of the opening below him was bent back at an unnatural angle. A bow with a feather on its end was holding the limb back. The Indian stepped into view, and the brush moved soundlessly back into place. The Indian glanced around, then walked across the opening toward the oak, looking in the soft clay and mast for footprints.

Santee slowly lifted his rifle, his eyes moving between the Indian below him and the one across the creek. The one below approached the trunk of the tree. The one across the creek was in clear view through an opening in the foliage. Santee settled the butt of the rifle against his shoulder, sighting down the barrel at the Indian across the creek, then he glanced down again. The Indian below was almost directly under him. Santee put the bead in the center of the back of the Indian across the creek, between his shoulder blades, and he tightened his right hand.

The rifle boomed. Santee turned, gathered himself, and leaped. The Indian was looking up with a stunned expression under the paint on his face, lifting his bow. His breath burst from his lungs with a hoarse grunt as Santee hit him, striking at his head with the butt of the rifle, and he jerked his head out of the way of the blow as he went down. The arrow skittered away as he dropped his bow. Santee dropped his rifle, rolling and leaping to his feet. The Indian was already on his feet, snatching at his tomahawk and knife. Santee jerked out his fighting knife with his right hand and his tomahawk with his left. The Indian sprang forward in a feint, waving his weapons and shrieking. Santee's war whoop exploded from his throat without conscious effort as he leaped forward, brandishing his weapons. The Indian's expression of savage ferocity became mixed with startled, wary cautiousness as he turned the feint into a sideward shuffle. They circled, glaring at each other and searching for an opening.

The Indian was several years older than Santee, with a lean, wiry build, a wily, seasoned fighter with scars of combat on his naked arms and shoulders. And he moved his weapons with blinding speed. But Santee was larger and his weapons were better, his tomahawk heavier than the Indian's and his long fighting knife almost a sword compared to the Indian's. They watched each other's eyes to anticipate moves, and Santee could easily see the Indian's naked arms on the edges of his vision. But the long, flowing fringes on his sleeves confused the Indian and he had to move his eyes to watch Santee's arms.

The tomahawks clanged and the knives rattled. The Indian's whoop rang out, and Santee's echoed through the trees. They circled again, then closed. The tomahawks clattered, then locked. They pushed and pulled, slashing and stabbing. Burning pain enveloped Santee's right forehead and cheek. The Indian's arm dropped with the force of the slash, and Santee stabbed. The wide, heavy, razor-sharp blade went deep into the Indian's stomach. The Indian began collapsing. He snapped forward as Santee jerked the knife out. Folds of entrails protruded and blood gushed from the wide gash in his stomach as he dropped his weapons and clutched his stomach. He fell, and his body began snapping in hard, driving convulsions, forcing deep grunts from his chest.

Raw terror gripped Santee. He was blind on the right side. The right side of his forehead and his right cheek were a mass of seething agony, and he could feel raw flesh with the tips of his fingers as blood poured down his face. The deep cut was halfway down his forehead to his eyebrow, then across his cheekbone. His hands trembled violently as he felt it gingerly, and he couldn't tell whether or not his eye had been cut open. He turned his head to the right, cautiously trying to wipe the blood from his eye with the tips of his fingers. Thick, heavy drops spattered on the ground. He still couldn't tell if his eye had been cut. He staggered to the creek.

The water turned crimson as he bent over it, splashing it into his eye. He held his head sideward, dipping up handfuls and washing out his eye, then he blinked and carefully felt the eyelid. It didn't feel like it had been cut. He held it open. Vision on the right side was a blur. He dipped up more water, washing the blood from the surface of his right eye, then it cleared. He collapsed in relief, panting and trembling, then gathered his strength and began crawling through the low undergrowth along the edge of the creek, holding his head to keep the blood out of his eye as he searched for cobwebs.

The fragile wisps of cobwebs shredded in his trembling fingers as he blindly tried to stick them on the open wound. The blood continued streaming from the cuts, leaving a wide trail behind him as he crawled through the brush. Then the drops began thickening as clots began forming, and the bits of cobweb he got into place seemed to help staunch the flow of blood. It became a trickle, then it oozed slowly enough that he could keep it out of his eye when he held his head upright. But he was so weak it was difficult to hold it upright. Nausea seized him, and he retched dryly. Then he lay on his side in the underbrush, his strength near its end.

After resting for a few minutes he pushed himself wearily to his feet and stumbled back to the tree. He gathered up his knife and tomahawk, picked up his rifle and leaned against the tree as he reloaded it, then pushed himself away from the tree and turned to walk back along the creek. Then he stopped. He turned and walked to the Indian, taking out his skinning knife. He ran the point of the knife around the top of the Indian's head, jerked the scalp off, and stumbled across the creek to scalp the other one. The rifle on the ground was a new one of French manufacture, and a good one. He scalped the Indian, gathered up the powder horn, shot pouch, and rifle, and walked back along the creek.

Throbbing pain enveloped the side of his head, nausea churned in his stomach, and his legs were unsteady. Each step seemed to require a gigantic effort, and the extra rifle was a heavy, burdensome weight. The blood continued oozing into his eye for a time, then finally stopped. He had to rest frequently, slumped on a rock or against a tree, and each time it was a greater effort to go on. It was almost dark when he reached the burn. One of the Indians had been armed with a bow and arrows, and the other with a new rifle of French manufacture. He scalped them, took the ammunition, and staggered on up the slope until he found a deadfall.

A numb, pain-wracked daze approaching sleep settled over him, interrupted occasionally by the sound of predators fighting over the bodies down the slope. At daybreak his right eye was swollen closed, and he could see with it only when he pushed the swollen eyebrow out of the way and held the lid open. The grinding pain in his head made it difficult for him to focus his other eye and concentrate on his surroundings. Every muscle in his body was sore and cramped, but the rest had restored his strength to a degree. He walked cautiously along and frequently stopped to listen to the forest around him.

Foxes and other small animals had fed on the body of the first Indian he had killed, and birds were clustered around it. The rifle was another new one of French manufacture. He scalped the Indian, pushed the scalp under his belt with the other ones, and continued down the mountain.

The Indians had been traveling to the north, had crossed his trail, and started following him. A bundle of belongings they had been carrying was tied in a tree where they had left it. It contained blankets, bags of corn, jerky, and pemmican, two bottles of rum, and an extra tomahawk. He took a drink of the rum, put the powder horns and shot bags he had collected into the bundle, tied the rifles to it, and slung it over his back and walked along his trail, eating a handful of the corn and jerky.

Finding the bundle in the tree made it seem unlikely that there had been a sixth one who had gone along his back trail to find his horses, but he still cautiously approached the valley where his horses were hobbled. He crept down into the valley, pausing frequently to listen and look around. The trees opened out into a wide, grassy glade with a rivulet running through it, and he crawled to the edge of the trees and lay in the shadows for several minutes, looking around the valley. Everything appeared normal.

He circled around the valley to his cache of supplies and hides. They were untouched. The jerky the Indians had been carrying had a sour taste, and he opened his own supplies, ate another piece of jerky and a handful of corn, and drank several sips of the rum. The rum made the pain in his head diminish and restored his energy, and the sinking nausea in his stomach disappeared. He gathered pieces of white oak bark to build a smokeless fire, took out his camp kettle and put on beans, peas, and jerky to boil into a stew, then he went down to the rivulet and cut several thin limbs from willows. He brought them back to the fire, peeled them and tied them into hoops with bits of vine, then took out his awl and strips of rawhide to lace the scalps to the hoops where they would dry and tan.

# Chapter Nine

The thick odor of woodsmoke from a forest fire blanketed other scents, but a hint of a smell of horses seemed to be underlying the smoke. And the horses had their ears cocked and their nostrils flared, looking up the valley. Santee dismounted, tied the reins to a sapling, and began walking slowly up the valley.

A distinct smell of horses now hung in the air. The trees opened into a clearing ahead, and he walked to the edge of the trees, stood in the shadows, and studied the valley. There were broken openings in the trees and a small creek ran down the center of the valley. It was possible that he had happened upon an Indian camp, but unlikely. The hunting in the area was poor, and they usually camped on lower ground rather than high in the mountains. The only reason they would remain in such a valley would be if nightfall found them there, and it was now afternoon.

But approaching the camp of another hunter could be as dangerous as stumbling over Indians, unless peaceful intentions were clearly announced at the same time as one's presence was made known. Santee moved back into the trees and slowly worked his way forward. There was a click of a horseshoe against a rock in an opening ahead, then a sound of a horse stamping its foot to drive flies away. The only time an Indian had a shod horse was when it had been recently stolen, so it was almost certain that it was a hunter's camp ahead. Santee moved around to the downwind side of the horses, then crawled to the edge of the opening. There were four horses, with packsaddle marks on their backs.

Santee moved on around the uphill side of the opening where the horses were hobbled, and he froze, looking at the ground. There was a heavy trail in the weeds and brush where something had been dragged along the ground. He took a few more steps forward, looking at the trail where grass and weeds had been pressed down and uprooted, and the leaves and earth had been furrowed. The trail led directly to a briar patch up the hill from where the horses were hobbled. It looked as though the hunter had dragged all his packsaddles and other equipment along the ground. Santee turned his rifle over, holding the barrel in both hands and lifted the butt high into the air, and he walked up the trail toward the briar patch.

"Hello the camp!"

There was a scuffling sound in the briar patch, then a man's voice replied, sounding thin and weak. "Who's there?"

"My name's Collier!"

"Step on up where I can see you."

Santee walked on up the trail and through the opening into the briar patch, still holding his rifle butt over his head. A tall, heavily bearded man in buckskins was lying against a packsaddle with his left leg bundled in a blanket, aiming a rifle at the opening. His face was pale and drawn above his thick mat of beard and moustache. His hair was a long, tangled mass around his shoulders and his buckskins were worn and tattered. The barrel of the rifle weaved from side to side as he strained to hold it up, and there was a strong stench of feces, urine, and putrefied flesh hanging in the air in the briar patch. The man dropped the rifle and slumped weakly back against the packsaddle.

"Lord God, I thought I'd never live to see another white man," he panted in a relieved tone. "Come on in, come on in."

Santee lowered his rifle, walking toward the man. "Have you been taken with something?"

"No, my bloody horse fell with me and broke this leg . . . what did you say your name is?"

"Collier. Santee Collier. My pa is Caleb Bledsoe."

"My name's Harnett, Simon Harnett. Aye, I know of you. You and your pa hunt with Isaac Raines, don't you? I've met Isaac a time or two. Where are they?"

"In Wilmington. I'm out by myself."

"By yourself? Bloody hell, you're hardly old enough to

be out at all, much less by . . ." His voice faded, and his eyes moved between the scabs on Santee's forehead and cheek and the scalps hanging on his belt. "But it appears that you can take care of yourself better than most men. Met some Indians, did you?"

"Aye. How long's your leg been hurt?"

"Over a week now, and I've had the devil's own chore seeing to my things and dragging my saddles about. It took me a whole day to make camp here, and I thought I'd just stop here after that. How many Indians did you meet?"

"Five. Your leg's that bad, is it?"

"That, and more," Harnett grunted, sitting up unsteadily and wincing as he pulled at the blanket. "Here, have a look for yourself."

The odor of feces and urine was stronger as he moved and stirred the blanket, and the sweet, cloying odor of decayed flesh was thick in the air. The left leg of his buckskin breeches was slit open, and his left moccasin was off. His foot was puffy and an unhealthy bluish color. His leg was grotesquely swollen, a mottled gray and black, and the skin had broken open and was oozing pus in spots. Streaks ran up his thigh from his knee. Santee kept his features neutral. "It's bad enough," he said, turning away and walking toward the opening in the briars. "I'll fetch up my horses and hobble them, and I'll see what I have to eat."

"I'd be obliged, because I'm bloody starved, Santee."

"I'll be back in a bit, then."

Santee walked back along the trail, then angled down the valley toward his horses. The smell of Harnett's horses and their manure was strong, and the problem would be compounded when his horses were with them. It was a very dangerous situation.

He led his horses up the valley and hobbled them, carried his packs up to the briar patch, and opened his supplies. Harnett began eating the jerky and corn ravenously, gulping it down, and Santee chewed a mouthful as he sat against a packsaddle and looked at Harnett's packs. They were heavily loaded with thick stacks of beaver and otter pelts.

"Are you still out from last winter?"

Harnett nodded. He tried to swallow, choked, and took a drink of water, then swallowed and took another bite. "I've been out for onto a year now. And I've had a bloody time of it, I'll tell you. I ran out of salt two months or more ago, I'm down to my last dozen charges of powder and ball, and I haven't tasted tobacco for so long that I've forgotten what it's like. And now this has happened to my leg. But I made myself a bloody good catch."

"I can see that."

"You've a goodly lot of deerskins there, it appears. And a bloody good catch hanging on your belt. When did you run into them?"

"About three weeks ago down to the south of here. I was coming up this way to swing over across Blue Ridge to the Yadkin and go on home. It won't be many weeks until my pa and Isaac get ready to leave for the winter, and I wouldn't want to miss them or have to track them down."

"Aye, well, I'd say they would wait on you. You must be a good man on the hunt, from what I can tell. I can't name three or four men who could go up against five Indians and win, much less any other lad of your age." He looked at the extra rifles tied on a bundle of deerskins on one of Santee's packsaddles. "And three of them had rifles, did they?"

Santee nodded, digging in his supplies, and he took out a bottle of rum and handed it to Harnett. "Here, have a drink of this. How long has your leg been as bad as it is?"

Harnett took a drink of rum, swallowed and coughed, then took another drink and handed the bottle back. "For a few days now. How did you go about killing them?"

"We had a running battle, with me doing most of the running. Do you still have feeling in your leg?"

Harnett shook his head, taking another bite of jerky. "No, not for a few days now. How did you keep the rest of them from jumping you while you were reloading after shooting one of them?"

"My rifle will reach out a good piece to bite, so I just shot and reloaded as I ran. I'm no chemist, Simon, but I believe that leg wants seeing to. It appears to me that it might take you with it unless you have it off. I've never carved on anything except something to eat, but I'm the only one here and I'll have a slice at it, if you wish."

Harnett looked away, chewing, then swallowed. He pondered for a long moment, then sighed as he looked back at

Santee. "Well, I'm obliged for the offer, Santee, and I'll think about it."

Santee nodded, searching in a supply bag and taking out a handful of cord. "I don't have any more peas or beans, and they would probably taste good to you. But I can go set a rabbit snare or two, and that would be better on your stomach than more jerky."

"Aye, it could be."

"I'll be back when I've caught a couple, then."

"Aye, very well, Santee."

Santee picked up his rifle, walked out of the briar patch, and went toward the upper end of the valley. There were numerous rabbit runs in the openings in the trees, narrow paths in the deep grass. He picked out several spots where the paths ran between rocks, trees, thick brush, and other natural obstacles, made nooses with the cord and hung them over the runs, then walked up toward the top of the hill.

The sun was going down, and the breeze had died. The odor of the horses was very strong in the still air. He sat down under a tree at the top of the hill and looked down at the valley, anxiety gnawing at him. It was tempting fate to remain in the valley. But Harnett was too ill to move and he needed help. He would have to stay.

An hour before sunset a thrashing noise came from where he had set one of the snares. A few minutes later he heard another distant thrashing sound. He walked back down the hill. There were rabbits in three of the snares, and he took up the rest of the snares and went back to the briar patch. Harnett's eyes were closed, and he was breathing with a deep, regular rhythm. Santee moved around quietly, cleaning and skinning the rabbits and building up the fire. The shadows were growing longer, and the fire cast a thin, wavering light in the briar patch as it blazed up. Santee hung two of the rabbits in a bush, salted the other one, and put it on an iron skewer, then suspended it over the fire between two stones as the fire burned down to hot coals. The rabbit began roasting, and he took out handfuls of corn and spread it on the stones by the fire to parch.

Darkness fell. The embers in the fire glowed red then yellow as a breath of a breeze stirred. Santee rolled the skewer to turn the rabbit over, then sat back and glanced at Harnett as he moved.

"That smells good, Santee."

"It's a young, fat one, so it should taste good. Would you like a sip of rum?"

"Aye, I'll have a sip if you have some."

Santee took the bottle out of the bag and handed it to him. The bottle gurgled as he drank. He panted softly, took another drink, and handed the bottle back. Santee sat back on his heels and put the bottle in the bag.

"An Indian could probably smell my horses ten miles away now, as long as they've been here," Harnett said.

"No, there's a forest fire a few miles away, and the smell of the smoke from it is heavy."

"Still, it's more than a bit dangerous to loiter about here any longer."

"It's not all that different from anywhere else, and it doesn't worry me. We're off the trails here, and it's safe enough."

"A man's scalp would be safer in a fresh stopping place, though. We could think about it tomorrow."

Santee tested the rabbit with the point of his knife, then slid it off the skewer and onto a stone to cut it in two. "We can think about it, but I see no reason to be in any great hurry to move."

Harnett made a doubtful sound in his throat. Santee cut the rabbit in two down the backbone and stirred the corn and turned it over. The coals began burning out, and Santee handed Harnett half the rabbit and the corn, feeling for his hand in the darkness. They began eating.

"You say you were on your way home? What way are you taking?"

"By Fort Dobbs, then down to the Cape Fear River."

"Would stopping by the Catawba be far out of your way?"

"No, it wouldn't be far out of my way."

"If something happened to me that I couldn't make it home, would you take my furs to my woman?"

"Nothing's going to keep you from taking them yourself."

"I'm just talking about if something did. It wouldn't be hard to find the place. You can pick up the Catawba Trace

south of the Yadkin, and follow it on down to Pollock's
Landing. Not more than five miles past Pollock's Landing
a slough crosses the road, and there's a wagon road by the
slough. Take the wagon road up to where the slough turns
into a creek, and you're there. There's a half-built barn that
I never did get finished off. But I did build her a bloody
good cabin, with twice as many rooms as she could ever
need."

"A woman likes a good cabin."

"She likes a man at home, too, and I let her down on
that. All the bloody time off hunting and trapping, and I
should have stopped at home more. Her name's Ellen, and
I was lucky to get her. She's a redhead, as pretty as you'll
find, and not much older than you. I should have studied
her more, but it's done now and it's futile to worry about
what's past. I have twelve guineas in my pocket, and you
can take that, my rifle, and one of my horses if you'll take
the pelts and the other horses to her."

"If it came to it, she'd have it all. But it won't come to
it."

"Aye, I just wanted to be sure she'd be all right if it did.
The pelts would be ready money, and she'd have no trouble in finding another man, God knows. She's as pretty as a
man could find."

Santee took another bite of the rabbit and chewed. His
appetite had left him. He put the rest of the corn back into
the bag, tossed the remainder of the rabbit away, and took
out his blanket. He put his fighting knife and tomahawk on
the ground beside him, put his rifle by them, and wrapped
his blanket around him. Harnett finished eating in silence.
Santee looked up at the stairs, listening to the sounds
around him and waiting for sleep.

"Santee, if you were running and shooting all the time,
how did one of those Indians get close enough to give you
that slice on the face?"

"It just happened."

Harnett chuckled softly. "Aye, and I believe I haven't
heard a tenth part of the story. It could be that you had as
hard a bloody battle as a man ever fought, and you don't
wish to boast. Killing five Indians is no easy thing, far
more than I'd ever want to take on myself. You know, I've

always preferred to be on my own in the wilderness, but I wouldn't mind having you along."

"We can think about it when you have that pin back under you."

"That we can, Santee, that we can. Sleep well."

"Aye, and you."

Santee looked up at the stars again. Harnett moved slightly, settling himself, then began breathing deeply. Santee closed his eyes. The horses stirred, and Santee opened his eyes, listening. Minutes passed, and there were no more movements among the horses. Santee closed his eyes again, and slowly drifted off to sleep.

When Harnett groaned softly, Santee opened his eyes and looked up at the stars. It was shortly before daylight. Harnett murmured and whispered softly, talking in his sleep. Santee sat up, folded his blanket and put it aside, put his knife and tomahawk back in his belt, picked up his rifle as he climbed to his feet, and walked out of the briar patch. The forest was still in its predawn hush, the air was motionless, and the smell of the horses was thick in the air. The light of the stars was bright, and the path down to the horses was clearly visible. Santee walked down to the horses, checked their hobbles, walked up the hill and gathered an armload of wood, and went back to the briar patch.

The stench from Harnett was almost overpowering in the still air in the briar patch. Then a breeze began stirring, sweeping some of the stench away. The birds began trying their voices as daylight broke, and their chirping and singing swelled in volume as they flew about, beginning a new day. The fire burned down to a bed of coals, and Santee put both of the rabbits on the skewer over the coals, put handfuls of corn on a rock to parch, then took Harnett's leather-covered water bottle down to the stream to refill it. Harnett was awake when he returned.

"How are you feeling, then?"

"I must still be alive, because I've shit myself again. But it's not hurt all that bad for the past day or two unless I move it."

"I could pull you down to the creek and give you a swill, if you wish."

"Oh, I've lain in it until I'm used to it now, Santee. But it's not very bloody pleasant for you, I daresay."

"It's no bother to me, Simon."

Santee put the water bottle by Harnett and sat down by the fire, testing the rabbits with the point of his knife. He took them off the skewer, put one aside and split the other one, and gave Harnett half of the rabbit and corn. Harnett's movements were weaker and more faltering than the day before, but his attitude seemed strangely cheerful and bright. Santee ate, put his blanket away, and looked through his supplies.

"How are the horses, Santee?"

"They're all right. You did a good job of hobbling your horses, broke leg or no."

"Well, I had to scoot about, but I've hobbled horses so many times I could do it in my bloody sleep." He put the last grains of his corn in his mouth and leaned back against the packsaddle, chewing them. "I've been thinking about things, Santee, and I've decided that it's no good to tarry about here any longer. Another day or two with all the horses we have here, and this valley will draw any Indian who passes within ten miles. So what I'd like you to do is pack everything onto all the horses, go on a piece and find another good place to camp, then return for me."

Santee shook his head. "We'll wait here a bit longer and see how your leg does. And we haven't talked about whether or not you want me to take a cut at it."

"Aye, well, I've thought about that, and I've decided it would be futile. And I've also decided on what I asked you to do. It's what I want you to do, Santee."

Santee looked away for a long moment, thinking, then he silently nodded and rose to his feet. He picked up his bridles, walked over to where Harnett's bridles were scattered on the ground and gathered them up, then walked out of the briar patch and down toward the horses.

They were silent as Santee moved back and forth between the briar patch and the horses, carrying Harnett's packs and packsaddles down, then his own. Santee could feel Harnett's eyes on him, and he avoided Harnett with his eyes. He finished carrying all the furs and hides down, then returned for his supplies. As he knelt to tie up the bags and rope them to the packsaddle a leather purse was on the ground by the bags, where Harnett had tossed it.

"That's the twelve guineas I mentioned to you, and there's odd shillings in there as well. I'd like you to keep it for me so we don't forget it."

Santee nodded, put the purse in one of his supply bags, and tied them up. He started to lift the bags onto the packsaddle and hesitated. "Perhaps you'd like me to leave the rum with you while I'm gone. In event I'm gone overnight. It gets cold without a fire."

"No, but thank you all the same, Santee."

"I could put this other rabbit here where you can reach it, then, in event you want a bite."

"Aye, do that. Those were tasty rabbits, Santee, and I might feel like another bite."

Santee put the rabbit where Harnett could reach it, tied his supply bags to the packsaddle, and picked it up and carried it down the hill. He put the packsaddle on a horse, fastened the girth, then walked back up to the briar thicket and stood at the opening.

"Well, be careful, Santee. And I'm obliged."

Santee tried to speak and couldn't. A thick, choking feeling filled the back of his throat. He nodded, turned away and walked back down to the horses, and waited. A moment later there was a sharp crack of a rifle in the briar thicket, and the horses tossed their heads. Santee took the spade out of Harnett's belongings and walked back up to the thicket. The rabbit was pulled apart, and Harnett had eaten a few bites of it. Santee put his rifle down and began digging a hole.

# Chapter Ten

A few settlers had moved west of the Blue Ridge, spreading out along creek lines and into the rich, fertile bottoms. Many isolated farmsteads among them had been attacked, burned out, and the crop fields destroyed. But others had clung tenaciously to the land they had cleared, and farmsteads clustered near small community blockhouses and forts were still occupied.

The scabs on his forehead and cheek came off as he was crossing the Blue Ridge. The tender skin under the scabs was sensitive to the direct rays of the hot late summer sun, burning and peeling for a time, then it toughened.

East of the Blue Ridge, signs of Indian attacks were scattered. In areas where there were expansive stretches of virgin forest the attacks had been more frequent, but in the more settled areas they had been rare. Some farmsteads had been burned out and abandoned, but others were being rebuilt, the fields freshly plowed and late crops planted. Nearer the Yadkin, signs of attacks were relatively rare, and a couple of new settlements had sprung up. People talked about the heavy Indian raids in Virginia along the Shenandoah, and some of the people were those who had moved south from the Shenandoah. They talked sadly about relatives massacred and tortured to death, and they spoke bitterly about the impotence of the militia.

Harnett's directions had been accurate. Santee passed through the settlement of Pollock's Landing and continued along the trace. It crossed a slough at the lower end of a long valley a short distance from the settlement, becoming a muddy trail of heavy logs that had been laid to support wagons across the boggy ground, with numerous deep holes where wagons had mired and had been dug out. A wagon road led off to the right, up the valley, and Santee turned onto it.

The slough became a gurgling creek, and the late afternoon sun shone down on the thick, lush growth in the fertile valley. The smell of woodsmoke hung in the air, the scent of a cheerful hearth rather than of mountain ridges enveloped in licking flames on dark, sultry nights. An ax rang against wood, a dog barked, and a cow lowed at a farmstead buried in the thick trees off to the side of the road, then the trees opened into gentle contours of rolling meadows as he continued along the road. Furry cedars covered the bulging slope at the head of the valley, and their fresh sweet scent blended with the musky, gravid odors of the rich soil.

The cabin was large, as Harnett had said, with chimneys on each end. The log framework of the unfinished barn stood by the old barn, a small structure of half a dozen stalls, with a fodder loft and a toolroom behind it. The stock pens were large, looking almost empty and vacant with only two milk cows and a span of oxen in them. The corn crib was large, but the harvest from the crop of tall corn looked like it would overfill it. The vegetables were in neat, straight rows, the cabbages huge, and beans, peas, and the tops of the root plants luxuriously large and abundant. A strip of new ground had been turned at the side of the tilled area, and the rich soil gleamed in the sunlight.

Two small children were playing by the woodpile in front of the cabin. A rangy dog trotted from behind the cabin and barked. Chickens scratching and pecking in the dust at the corner of the cabin scattered as a woman came around it. She leaned a hoe against the cabin and walked along the front of it as Santee approached, snapping her fingers at the dog, looking at Santee curiously, and smoothing her apron and touching wisps of hair into place in an automatic effort to make herself presentable to receive a visitor. She was small and young, about twenty, and she was a very capable-looking woman, with lines of independence and self-assurance in her face. And she was very pretty, with red hair and a round, freckled face. Her homespun dress fit neatly, her sleeves were rolled up to her elbows, and her bare feet were dusty from hoeing in the vegetables. The two small girls were fair, more like her than Harnett. Santee reined up.

"Are you Mistress Harnett?"

She glanced along the line of horses, recognizing some of them. The freckles stood out on her cheeks as her face blanched, her lips tightened to a thin white line, and her green eyes were wide with despairing knowledge of what he had come to tell her. She nodded tautly. Santee cleared his throat uncomfortably and looked away, not knowing how to tell her.

"Is Simon dead, then?"

"Aye."

Her shoulders slumped, and she looked down at the ground. "I knew it had to come," she murmured softly, her lips trembling. She swallowed dryly, shaking her head. "I knew there would be a time when he wouldn't be coming home, because . . ." Her voice faded into a sob as her features twisted and her eyes filled with tears, and she turned and stumbled blindly into the cabin, weeping wildly.

The children sidled toward the door, looking at Santee with frightened expressions, and darted inside. The dog sat down by the door, looking up at Santee and panting. Santee sighed heavily, dismounting from his horse. He unloaded Harnett's horses, piled the packsaddles and loads on them in front of the cabin, then led the horses around to the stock pens. The horses were thin and weary from their long trek, but they scampered about and rolled on the ground in the pen as Santee released them. He carried corn from the corn crib and fed them, and went back around to the front of the cabin.

The sun was setting, and the light from the fireplace played on the panes of glass in the windows in the front room of the cabin. The woman had stopped weeping, and Santee could hear her snapping testily at the children as she rattled plates. Santee took Harnett's purse out of his supplies, gathered up Harnett's rifle, powder horn, and shot bag, and went inside. The children were sitting quietly at the long deal table, and the woman was kneeling by the hearth. He put the rifle against the doorjamb and hung the powder horn and shot bag on a peg inside the door, then crossed the room to the table and put the purse on it.

"There's some money he said he wanted you to have—

twelve guineas and odd shillings. And his furs are out here."

She glanced at him over her shoulder and looked back at a skillet on the hearth. "Sit and eat."

Santee hesitated unsurely. Her sorrow had apparently changed to a grim, hard resentment. "I'd rather my horses had their fill . . ."

"Go feed them, then," she said impatiently, carrying a plate to the table. "There's ample corn."

Her resentment didn't seem to be necessarily directed at him, but her manner was less than hospitable. She looked tempery, and it was clear that those who knew her didn't want to call attention to themselves or provoke her. The two girls at the table were quiet and meek. The dog had been following Santee around and had been standing in the doorway. He abruptly disappeared at the note of irritation in the woman's voice. Santee nodded, turning toward the door.

"And stop by the trough long enough to throw some water on yourself before you come back in. A layer or two less dirt won't hurt you. Stop! What's that you have there?"

Santee's anger was stirred by her imperious tone and manner, and he frowned at her as she glared and pointed suspiciously at the scalps on his belt. "Scalps."

"Get those fucking things out of my cabin!" she shouted, her face twisted with revulsion. "Scurvy, bloody savage, you are! Call yourself a flaming human being, do you? Call the bloody Indians savage, do you? You're no better yourself, you bleeding bloodthirsty swine! You get those out of here, and you leave them outside when you come back in!"

Santee recoiled from the explosion, then boiling anger swelled within him. He glared back at her, then shook his head as he turned and walked toward the door. "No, I've no need to listen to this to get food for myself or for my horses. I've ample, and I'd do without first. I'll be on my way."

"You'll bloody do as you're told!" she barked. "You go wash yourself and leave those outside when you return!"

"I'll bloody do as I wish!" he snapped, turning back at the door. "I'm sorry you lost your man, and you've my sympathy for your grief, as short-lived as it was. But I've no patience for a common scold, and I'll not be around one. And if you're so bloody loose with your tongue with everyone who passes, you need your ears boxed to teach you better, is what you need."

Her eyes widened and her face blanched as she became tense with rage. The children ducked down out of sight behind the table. Ellen walked slowly toward Santee, her bare feet soundless on the floor. "When you've killed all the Indians who roam the forests, then you return here to box my ears for me, sod," she said in a soft, steely tone. "And on your way back here, you might reflect on the fact that the main part of the chore you've taken upon yourself lies ahead of you. The man who can box my ears will never be born." She stopped inches from him, her eyes sparkling as they bored into his, then she drew in a deep breath and turned back toward the fireplace. "Now we'll have an end to this where it stands. You go feed your horses, wash, and leave those outside when you return."

"No. As I said, I'll be on my way. I'll not stay where I've been called what I have here, and I'm too accustomed to doing as I please to be told what to do by someone I meet along the way."

She stopped and looked back at him, her lips pursed. "You'll stop and eat," she said quietly. "No one comes here and leaves empty, and you'll eat what's been prepared for you. And as far as being called goes, you called me a common scold, and I'll let that pass. And there's been few times when I've listened to someone give me a name like that and let it pass, you may be bloody assured. So far as being told what to do goes, I don't think it's too much to ask that you come to my table with clean hands and a clean face. Nor do I think it's too much to ask that you come in without the grisly bloody trophies from the bodies of poor, benighted heathens you've slaughtered."

Her tone and manner were a tentative peace offering. The food smelled good, and he was hungry. He looked at her, considering it, then nodded and went out the door. The dog had taken refuge behind the woodpile, and he came out and trotted to Santee, looking apprehensively at the doorway. Santee unloaded his horses, took the scalps off his belt and put them in one of his supply bags, then led his horses around to the stock pen. He put them in the pen and put out more corn, stopped at the watering trough and washed his hands and face, and walked back around the cabin, pulling his hair back and retying the thong at the back of it.

Daylight was fading, and the front room of the cabin was lighted by the yellow light from the fireplace. The children sat motionless, their plates in front of them. Ellen sat at the end of the table, her arms folded as she waited. There was a full plate, spoon, and cup at the other end of the table. Santee sat down, reaching for the spoon, then put it back down and bowed his head as the woman began praying. Her voice was a soft murmur as she prayed quietly for a moment, then they began eating.

They ate silently, the only sound the rattle of the spoons against the plates, and Santee devoured his. The food was delicious. The lean slices of pork had been fried until they were crisp on the outside, and tender and succulent on the inside. The corn was creamed and had subtle tastes of molasses, mustard, and other things in it, the green beans had been cooked with bits of pork, the potatoes were parboiled and fried with onions, and there was sweet nutty-tasting gritted bread made with corn still in the milk.

Ellen looked at him and his plate in satisfaction as he cleaned it off, and she put her spoon down and rose. "You can eat, can't you?" she said in a pleased tone, stepping along the side of the table to take his plate. "I like to see a man with an appetite. What's your name?"

"Santee Collier."

"Santee? There's an odd name, but I must say it goes with someone who roams the forests. My name's Ellen, if you didn't know." She took his plate and started to turn away, then she looked at him again as she stepped back so the full light of the fireplace was on him. "Bloody hell, you're but a lad!"

"I'm onto seventeen," he said defensively.

She smiled and nodded, sucking her teeth and swallowing. "Aye, I can see you are, now that some of the rust has been scraped off and your hair is out of your face. And with those great blue eyes, you're as comely as most girls, but for that huge gash down your face."

Her manner was almost friendly as she looked down at him, holding his plate and moving her tongue around her teeth. She looked very pretty with a pleasant expression on her face and the firelight catching highlights in her red hair. There was a sudden tension to the silence as they looked at each other. Ellen's smile faded, then she flushed hotly. She turned and carried his plate to the fireplace, and she rattled lids on pans with unnecessary force as she refilled his plate. There was a subtle difference in the atmosphere that Santee could detect but couldn't classify. She brought his plate back to the table, took his cup and refilled it with buttermilk, and went back to her place at the table, her footsteps quick and silent and her eyes avoiding him.

"How did you get that scar?"

"While I was hunting."

"I didn't think it was while you were praying, and a knife did that, or I'll miss my guess. Did a deer come at you with a knife, then?"

Her tone approached being light again, and he smiled and shook his head. "No."

"Do I have to guess, then? Was it an Indian?"

"Aye."

She nodded and sighed, looking down at her plate and taking a bite. "And you don't wish to talk about it."

"There's little to talk about."

She looked at him again, taking a drink of buttermilk. "I daresay most would find enough in it to talk about for days at a time. Where are you from?"

"Wilmington."

"What does your ma have to say about your wandering off into the forests by yourself?"

"It's nothing to do with her. I went with my pa and another man for three years, and I went by myself this summer."

Ellen looked at him, then nodded and looked back down at her plate. They ate in silence for several minutes, then one of the children murmured. Ellen looked at them and nodded. "Go ahead then."

The children got off the bench and took their plates, cups, and spoons to the washstand, then carried in wood from the pile by the chopping block and piled it by the hearth. Ellen pushed her plate away and put her elbows on the table, sipping her buttermilk and looking at the children as they went back and forth across the room. They finished stacking the wood, and one of them murmured something again. She nodded. "Go ahead. And say your prayers. I'll be in presently to tuck you in."

They went into another room. Santee finished eating what was on his plate and sat back with a sigh, patting his stomach. Ellen put her cup down and started to get up, and he lifted his hand and shook his head. "I've had my fill. It's as good as I've ever tasted and I'd like to eat all night, but I've nowhere left to put it."

She smiled slightly, nodding, then her smile faded as she looked down at the table, moving her cup around on it. "Was he killed by an Indian, then?"

"No, his horse fell on him and hurt him, and it was too late to do anything when I found him. But he didn't suffer at the end, and he was at rest in his mind. He talked about you, and he said that he wished he had studied you more and spent more time at home."

"He's decently buried, then?"

"Aye."

She sighed heavily, rubbing her face with her hands. "It's well that he should say that he should have spent more time at home, because we've been married onto five years, and he's scarcely spent more than as many months here. And it's well that you should say that my grief was short-lived, because it's as though I've lost what I never had."

"I said that in anger, and I beg pardon. It's not up to me to call you down. And I know you're sorry he's gone, because I can see it."

Her eyes became misty, and she nodded, rubbing them with her knuckles. "Aye, I'm sorry," she sighed. "It could be that another would be more sorry. It could be that one who hadn't done the plowing, planting, hoeing, harvesting, tending the stock, making the clothes, repairing the roof, cutting the wood, and all else I've done would be more sorry, because my labor and my loneliness have turned me hard. But I am sorry, Santee, I am." She got up and crossed the room to the washstand, took a rag and a pot of soap from under it, and brought them back and put them on the table. "You can spend the night. And you can wash yourself before you lie on my sheets."

She seemed a mercurial woman of rapidly changing moods, and her reflective sadness of a moment before had changed to aloof, reserved detachment. Santee nodded, rising and picking up the soap and rag, and Ellen began gathering up the dishes. He went outside and around to the stock pens, and he stood on a rock by the trough to strip, douse himself with water, and lather with the soap. The night air was cool, and the powerful homemade woodash soap tingled on his skin. He rinsed and dried, put his buckskins back on, and went back around the cabin. Ellen was feeding the dog at the front door, and she pointed to a doorway opening off the main room as she walked back toward the fireplace.

"In there."

He nodded as he took the soap and rag to the washstand, and he stepped back to the door and picked up his rifle. "I'll lie down, then. Sleep well."

She silently nodded, her back to him as she knelt in front of the fireplace and scooped up ashes with a wooden shovel to bank the fire. He went into the room and closed the door. The shutter was closed, and it was dark. He felt his way to the bed, put his rifle against the wall by the bed and his fighting knife and tomahawk on the floor by it, then undressed and got into bed. The cornshucks in the mattress rustled, and the sheets and blanket were rough, smelling strongly of soap. He stretched out and relaxed.

The large meal and the fatigue from the long day made him drowsy, but the unfamiliar surroundings and slight noises from the main room pulled at his consciousness, keeping him awake. Ellen rattled a pan lid and moved one of the table benches or something heavy on the floor, then she went outside, speaking to the dog. The front door closed a few minutes later, the bolt on it clattered closed, and the bolts on the shutters on the front windows closed. Then there was silence.

Then the door to his room squeaked. Her feet whispered against the floor as she crossed to the bed, and her dress made a soft sound as she took it off. The blanket moved, and the cornshucks rustled. She settled herself, drawing in a deep breath and releasing it in a sigh, then she was silent.

Admonishing voices spoke in his mind. He remembered a pale, drawn face with a cheerful smile on it as he had been leaving, the pain-wracked voice, the leather purse on the ground by his supply bags. But his hand reached out to her as though of its own accord. The voices and memories were overpowered by a swelling surge of urgent responses as her hand lifted, taking his and pulling it to her breast. He moved toward her.

Her lips were damp and hot against his, and the tips of her fingernails moved down to his neck and shoulders. The scent of her hair filled his nostrils, and the feel of her body against his made a fiery, throbbing need explode within him. She made a sound of protest in her throat as he pushed on top of her, surging violently. The sound of protest changed into a gasp and her fingernails dug into his back, on the verge of penetrating his skin. He stopped moving, seething with a frenzy of desire. She pulled his hands to her breasts and wrapped her arms around his neck, and her breath was warm against his face as she bit at his lips. Then she moved her hand down his body, and there was a swift, plunging rush.

He dozed, then woke when she moved in her sleep. She made a drowsy, interrogative sound as he put his arms around her, pulling her to him, then she murmured in acquiescence as she held him. Her fingers moved over his shoulders and arms, and her hands grasped him as her yawn turned into an urgent sound. It was slow and leisurely, gradually building up to violent frenzy and a wrenching end, and she panted breathlessly and held him to her as he went back to sleep.

The rustle of the mattress woke him. She slid out of bed, crossed the room, and the bolt on the shutter rattled. Bright moonlight flooded in as she opened the shutter. She pushed her hair back, folded her arms, and stood looking out the window. The moonlight gleamed softly on her skin and made highlights in her long hair. He lay and looked at her, then he got out of bed, crossed the room, and put his arms around her. She sighed, leaning against him and putting an arm around his waist.

"I'm a bloody slut, I am. The day I hear my man's gone, and I can't wait to lie with some wild boy who roams the bloody forests killing Indians and carrying their scalps around. But a pretty boy, as well. Those great blue eyes will bring you many a smile if you can keep from having any more of your face cut off."

"Come on and lie down again."

"I won't say no, slut that I am, because I need a man here for more than to cook for and talk to. But you're to leave in the morning, do you understand? If I'm to find myself a good husband, I can't have people talking about what a baggage I am. So you're to leave tomorrow, do you understand?"

"Aye, come on."

It was daylight when he woke again. She was gone, and his clothes were gone. A pair of boots and a pile of neatly folded homespun clothes were on the floor in place of his clothes, and he got up and put them on. The clothes and boots were a poor fit, made to different proportions, but they weren't uncomfortable. He went into the front room, and Ellen was moving around the fireplace, preparing breakfast. Her face was bright and flushed, her eyes twinkled, and a smile played around her lips as she looked at him.

"Get that smirk off your face if you don't want it slapped, sod. I took those filthy animal skins you use for clothes and put them to soak in the creek, because they were making my cabin smell like an offal pit. You can leave as soon as they're washed and dried."

"Well, I'll work on the barn while I'm waiting, then."

"You will not! Every bugger for five miles about would be able to see you up on those beams, and I've my reputation to consider. You can yoke the harness and plow the rest of that new ground I've been cutting in up there. Or do you know how to do anything but kill poor bloody savages and tear their hair from their heads?"

"I can plow, but I'll need someone to lead the oxen."

"Not those oxen, you won't. You keep the plow in the ground, and those oxen will do the rest. And you'll want a good breakfast to keep your strength up. For plowing, sod!"

She bit her lip to keep her flushed smile from spreading as she carried a plate to the table and slammed it down in front of him. He grinned widely as he began eating. The children came out of their room, and Ellen kissed them and patted them affectionately as she pushed them to the table.

After eating Santee went out and took the oxen out of the pen, yoked them and hooked them to the plow, and led them around the tilled area. The plot of new ground was marked off by a single furrow, about a quarter of it had been plowed, and Santee began plowing the rest. The oxen were exceptionally well broken, trudging back and forth in meticulously straight lines. The feel of the unfamiliar clothes and the boots was bothersome, but there was a satisfying feel to the plow digging deep into the rich, moist soil, and the earth parted into neat, straight furrows as he followed the oxen back and forth, holding the plow in the ground.

At noon Ellen came out of the house with a plate of food and a water bottle. Santee unhooked the oxen and led them into the deep grass to rest and graze, and walked back to the tilled area. Ellen was looking at the corn, and he took his food and the water bottle into the shade of the corn rows to sit on the ground and eat. She sat by him, and they conversed desultorily while he ate and drank. Then he put the plate and water bottle aside and put his arms around her, pulling her to him.

"Not here, sod! I might be a slut, but I'm no flaming whore to lie about in a cornfield and . . . oh, bloody hell. Come on, then. And be quick about it. As soon as those animal skins you call clothes are dry, I want your arse on your horse. . . . I'm waiting, Santee. And you don't have to be so quick that my oxen don't have a moment to rest. . . ."

Afterward she was flushed and scolding, pulling her dress down and straightening it as she gathered up the plate and water bottle. He dodged a slap as he kissed her, then he walked toward the oxen. Ellen walked back toward the cabin, biting her lip to keep her smile from becoming wide as she glanced at him over her shoulder. The oxen looked at Santee in patient resignation as he approached, and they trudged along behind him as he led them back to the plow.

At sunset half of the plot Ellen had marked off was finished. He drove the oxen back to the pen, fed them, and put the yoke, chains, and plow away. The children were playing in front of the door, and they smiled up at him. The dog was lying near them, and he wagged his tail. Santee went inside, and Ellen was sitting on a stool in front of the fireplace, sewing on his buckskins.

"You're as fond of baubles and kickshaws on your clothes as a girl, aren't you, Santee? Some of these beads were coming loose, so I thought I'd repair them and put on a few more I have here."

"That's kind of you, and I'm obliged, Ellen."

"Aye, well, I'll be obliged if you'll use some of that soap when you go to swill tonight. There was as much in the pot when you brought it back in last night as when you took it out, and you needn't be concerned that you'll use up all my soap. I keep plenty of it on hand, and I can make more anytime I need it. And you can spend the night, but you're to leave tomorrow, do you understand?"

"Aye."

She put his buckskins aside and began preparing dinner. Santee went out and washed his face and hands in the trough, and the children were at the table when he came back in. Ellen put the food on the table, prayed quietly, and they ate. The children carried in wood and went to bed, and Santee finished his second helping, took the soap and a rag, and went to bathe at the trough. Ellen looked over her shoulder with a flushed smile when he came back in. He went to his room, and she came in a few minutes later.

The boots and homespuns were by the bed the following morning, and he put them on. The day was a repetition of the previous one. Ellen constantly referred to his imminent departure, he plowed another quarter of the new ground, and he spent the night again. The boots and homespuns were by the bed the following morning, and he put them on again. Ellen had finished sewing on his buckskins and had hung them in a corner, and she was more subdued and thoughtful during the day. Santee pondered the situation as he plowed the remainder of the new ground, and he decided that he wanted to stay and marry Ellen. When she lay in his arms that night, he brought the subject up to her, and she flatly rejected the idea.

"Santee, Santee, you are but a lad, aren't you? That would be folly of the worst sort, Santee."

"But you act as though you're fond of me, and as for my part, I want to stay and be a proper husband to you and a—"

"I'm more than fond of you, Santee, and that's why I've been a fool and cruel to both of us by allowing you to tarry. For my sake and the sake of my children I have to have a settled man here. And now I'll have to see to it without delay, because you might have me with child the way you've been going at me. And me at you."

"But I'm settled enough to be a proper—"

"Santee, you're a lad. A lovely, wild, and beautiful lad. Come autumn, wild ducks will settle on the slough down there. Lovely things they are, and I couldn't kill one of them even if I were starving. Do you think I could coop one of them to put with my chickens? No sooner would I take you as a husband, Santee. Now we'll have an end to this, and I won't say another word on it."

Her voice was a soft whisper, almost breaking with tears as she finished. He pulled her closer to him, and she turned, put her arm around him, and burrowed her face against his chest. Her breathing was ragged, and her tears were damp against his chest. He looked into the darkness, trying to think of a more convincing argument, unable to contemplate leaving but unable to think of any way to make her let him stay.

She woke him getting out of bed. He lay with his eyes closed, listening to her dressing, going into the front room, and moving around. Then he heard her come in and take the boots and homespuns, and put his buckskins in their place. The buckskins were fresh and clean, and the rows of beads were bright. He put on his belt, put his fighting knife and tomahawk in the back of his belt, and picked up his rifle as he turned toward the door.

Ellen's eyes were red, and her face was drawn and pale. Santee went out, led his horses around from the pen, and began loading them. Ellen brought out a bag of food and put it on his supplies. Santee tied the bag to the horn of his saddle, finished loading the horses, and went back inside. Breakfast was on the table, and the children were glancing timidly around as they ate. Santee ate a few bites, then got up and went to the door. Ellen followed him, her face trembling and her tears starting to spill over. Santee kissed her, and she turned and ran into a back room, sobbing. He got on his horse and turned it toward the road, and the train of horses plodded along behind.

# Chapter Eleven

Indian summer was hanging over the border country when Santee, Bledsoe, and Raines passed through it. For those in the east it was a pleasant interlude of late-season fair weather without the heat of summer, a time to enjoy before winter set in. For the border settlers it was a time of terror, a dreaded period when the Indians would have their crops gathered and larders stocked for the winter, and could raid in full force, unhampered by winter weather. A few burned cabins were still smoldering when they passed them, and a few families of settlers were fleeing to the east with the possessions they could load on their backs and their remaining animals. Santee, Bledsoe, and Raines passed through the edge of the settled area without meeting Indians, and when they returned in the spring, the signs of raids that had been made during the winter were widespread all along the border.

Santee rested his horses and fed them heavily while he helped Bledsoe plow and put in the crops, then he left again. He made it through the border country safely, spent the summer months north of the Holston without meeting Indians, then recrossed the border settlements safely. On the way back he considered going by the Catawba and through Pollock's Landing, then dismissed the idea. It was a certainty that Ellen had remarried the previous year.

Jubal was uncharacteristically warm and friendly when Santee returned, and they had several conversations. He had finished his apprenticeship the year before and had been working for Porter for wages, and he wanted to enter the business with Porter as a full partner. The capital was available, money that had been in their mother's possession when Bledsoe had rescued her, and Jubal wanted to use the entire amount to buy the partnership in Porter's firm. Bled-

soe had made passing reference to the money in a number
of conversations with Santee, and it was a matter that
didn't particularly interest Santee. Each year's pelts and
hides had brought in more money than was spent during
the year, and the difference had become substantial since
Santee had started hunting during the summer. Santee had
all the horses he could safely take into Indian territory, he
had the best weapons that could be bought, he had what he
considered a large amount of money buried in an earthenware pot near the barn, and he didn't know what he would
do with any more money. He willingly agreed to turn over
to Jubal the entire amount that had been in their mother's
possession.

The winter was unusually cold and severe, Bledsoe developed a hacking cough that lasted until spring, and his
foot and other aches and pains bothered him all winter.
For years he had made comments about his age and had
talked about each trek being the last, but for the first time
he began to sound as though he meant it. But the warm
summer weather on the estuary made the memory of his
aches and pains of the winter fade, and he was ready to
leave again when Santee returned from his summer hunt.

The border country continued to shrink to the east as
the conflict between the British and French intensified and
the Indians armed by the French drove deeper into the settlements on their raids. Encouraging news came from the
north, where the regulars and large units of militia were
battling the French and their Indian allies. General Am-
herst took the French fort at Louisbourg, and General
Forbes led an army to victory over the French at the forks
of the Ohio, capturing Fort Duquesne and renaming it Fort
Pitt. But the outcome of clashes between huge armies to
the north was of little interest to border settlers clustered in
groups of a dozen families for defense against raiding parties of a dozen to twenty Indians, and the battle for the
frontier was being lost. When Santee, Bledsoe, and Raines
crossed the border, Bledsoe pointed out areas where he had
once hunted that had become deserted again. But the areas
were spotted with burned and abandoned cabins, denuded
of game, and a gauntlet of danger from moving war parties.

The Assembly began a more active recruitment campaign for the militia, raising more companies to send to the

north and to the border, and Raines was offered a lieutenancy. He took the commission, talked to Santee about joining, and brought his commanding officer to talk to Santee. Santee flatly rejected the offer. He had seen the militia on their drill grounds in Wilmington and at Fort Dobbs, and he wanted no part of what he had seen.

The winter camp was drab without Raines and his jovial, boisterous humor. Bledsoe developed a bad cough again, and his right foot became so painful during the trip back that they had to camp for a week for him to recuperate. When they arrived in Wilmington, they found that changes had taken place during the winter. Porter had died, and Jubal had taken over the firm. He'd had new warehouses and offices built on the outskirts of Wilmington, and he was expanding the business to include a trading post and pens for dealing in livestock. Jubal had also moved out of the cabin.

There were indications that Porter's widow and other heirs had taken exception to how they had been dealt with by Jubal. The matter was under litigation in the courts, but it was mentioned only in hints around Santee and was of no interest to him. What did interest him was the daughter of a man working for Jubal. Andrew Martin, a mild-mannered, learned, and congenial but somewhat reserved man, had recently arrived from England. He had been a schoolmaster in England, which was borne out by his manner and disposition, and he had started working for Jubal when he was unable to find employment in Wilmington as a schoolmaster. And his daughter was a strikingly beautiful girl of eighteen named Alcey.

But while Martin was friendly and forthright enough in his own way, interested in the wilderness, in where Santee had been, and in what he had seen, Alcey was withdrawn, her wide blue eyes darting away every time Santee looked at her. There was no valid reason for Santee to spend any time at Jubal's firm once the furs and hides were delivered, but he stopped in at every opportunity because Alcey also worked there, casting accounts. And he continued to stop in, even after Jubal's cold and acid hints that he was in the way and interfering with business became more blunt.

Her voice was soft and muted, like her demeanor, and the rich, ringing tones of her English accent were like a tiny bell. Her hair was a light brown, with streaks of paler shades that caught any ray of sunlight and glinted with shimmering sparkles, and it fell down over her shoulders in thick tresses. Her features were delicate, dominated by her large, blue eyes. She wore dresses like those he had glimpsed on women in carriages about the town, frilly and bright garments that hugged her slender shoulders and arms, and she always wore a scarf or shawl of some sort to conceal the outline of her bosom under the bodice of her dress, an engaging modesty that made her bosom a matter of intense interest. A light and alluring scent always hung about her, and she was the essence of femininity as she sat at her desk with her lips pursed and her quill in her small, graceful hand or walked about with some piece of paper in her hand, no ripple of her skirt betraying the slightest hint of her hips swinging, and only her feet appearing to move as the hem of her dress swept along the floor. She was fascinating.

Before the interim between the time he returned from the winter trip and left on his summer hunt had been interminable, but somehow it flew by. His horses were rested, the crops were planted, and there was no reason to delay. He left. And he frequently thought about Alcey.

And his thoughts ranged to wider aspects of the situation. Alcey was a highly educated woman. In Santee's conversation with Martin he had made a couple of wry comments about her knowledge of some things exceeding his. Insofar as it was possible to tell anything about what Jubal was thinking he seemed interested in her in his cold, detached way. Jubal knew many of the large landowners, government officials, and similar people, and it was likely that he would one day be as wealthy as anyone in Wilmington. Alcey wasn't the kind of woman seen barefoot by a cabin boiling clothes. She properly belonged with someone who could provide for her in a way that was consistent with her background. And she probably thought the same. What he had interpreted as demure shyness had probably been polite repugnance.

His beard had been thickening during the past years, and he had usually more or less scraped it off when in Wilmington as a gesture of sorts toward making a presentable appearance while in town. On his return trip from the sum-

mer hunt he stopped over in his last camp outside
Wilmington to clean up and make himself as presentable as
possible. He soaked his buckskins in the creek where he
camped, carefully shaved with his skinning knife and
chopped off his hair to a neat length in back, then repaired
the beading on his buckskins and washed the mud off the
horse he was riding.

During the spring work had still been going on around
the complex of buildings and pens where Jubal had his
business, and the construction had been completed during
the summer. It was a wide area off the side of the road and
surrounded by a high fence, with the warehouse, trading
post, and offices in the center, the stock pens on one side,
and a row of houses where Jubal and some employees lived
on the other side. When Santee rode into the yard, Jubal
was on the loading dock castigating a clerk about something, and he greeted Santee with his usual remote indifference, glanced over the load of hides, then invited Santee in
for the obligatory drink of rum.

Alcey was at her desk, her lips pursed with concentration and the end of her long quill moving as she wrote in a
thick ledger. She was even more beautiful than he remembered. Her long thick lashes lifted as they came in, and she
looked up as Santee greeted her. She nodded and murmured a reply, her features neutral. Her cold eyes seemed
to hesitate on the scar on his face and the scalps hanging
on his belt. Santee had the drink with Jubal, got his bill of
credit for goods in the trading post, and left, his feeling of
anticipation over arrival having turned into a somber and
depressing disappointment.

At the cabin the next day Bledsoe mentioned that Alcey's father had been ill several times, and that Jubal had
hinted that he and Alcey might get married. Santee didn't
return to Jubal's firm until it was time to get his supplies
for the autumn trip, then he only went into the trading post
to exchange his credit bill for goods and cash. When Santee
and Bledsoe returned in the spring, Alcey's father had died
and she and Jubal were married.

During his summer hunt Santee ranged to the north
across the Holston, crossing the Clinch River and the rugged Clinch Mountains, looking for Cumberland Gap. Bledsoe had been ill again the winter before, and it appeared

certain that he would give up hunting and trapping in the near future. Santee toyed with the idea of going into *Kentake* on his first trip by himself. He didn't find Cumberland Gap, but he did find abundant evidence of the recent presence of large numbers of Indians. As he approached the Holston on his return trip, he detected the presence of other horses. He cautiously investigated and found the camp of another hunter, a man named John Schilling. Schilling was traveling in the same general direction as Santee, intending to turn south and across the French Broad River at the point where Santee would turn east to cross the Nolichucky, and they traveled together for two days. Schilling had found Cumberland Gap and turned back because of the numbers of Indians in the vicinity, and he gave Santee specific directions for finding it. During their conversations he also mentioned that the summer Indian raids into North Carolina had been very heavy, and the Indians had penetrated deep into the Catawba.

The evidence of the raids was on every side as Santee crossed deserted border country where farms and small settlements had once been thick and well established. He moved rapidly and cautiously, traveling along wooded creek lines and avoiding open areas where timber had been cleared and crop fields had once been. And as he moved deeper into North Carolina, he thought more often about Ellen and about what Schilling had said about raids along the Catawba. When he reached the Yadkin, he turned south toward the Catawba.

The destruction had been heavy, and few isolated farmsteads were occupied. Pollock's Landing had grown larger with people moving into it from outlying areas for protection, and as Santee rode through, men called out to ask if he had seen any Indians. The roadway across the slough had deteriorated, most of the logs had sunk into the mud, and there were few wagon tracks. Santee turned up the wagon road, restraining himself from whipping his horses into a run, and reined up when the farmstead came into sight. The cabin and outbuildings were piles of ashes and rubble. The new ground he had broken for Ellen years before had been planted in corn during the spring, and it was trampled down.

He rode back toward Pollock's Landing. The nearest occupied farmstead was less than a mile from the settlement, a short distance off the road. The crops were still standing, smoke was coming from the chimney in the cabin, and a man was chopping wood in front of the cabin. Santee turned onto the narrow road leading to the cabin. Dogs ran out from the cabin and barked, and the man called them back as he shaded his eyes with his hand and looked at Santee. A woman came to the door of the cabin, a swarm of children behind her.

Santee reined up in front of the cabin. "My name's Santee Collier, and I wonder if you could tell me anything about the people who lived up at the head of the creek above the slough down there."

"Santee Collier?" the man said, walking forward with a wide smile. "Aye, I've heard of you. Step down and make yourself at home. I'm Jacob Holt, and this is my wife Mary."

Santee dismounted, shook hands with the man, and nodded to the woman. "I'm pleased to meet you."

"We're pleased to meet you, and there's God's truth. I like the look of what's hanging on your belt there and all, by God. Aye, I've heard of you and what you've done, but I had in mind that you'd be a good bit older than you look. At the head of the creek, you say? That'll be the Elders. A big bunch of Indians came through in the first part of July and got them and several more. All of them were killed except a couple of their little ones they hid in the springhouse, and we have one of them here. Were they friends of yours, then?"

"I believe I knew them. Would that be the same woman who was known as Ellen Harnett?"

The man shook his head blankly and looked at his wife, and she nodded. "The same. You remember her first husband, Jacob. He was Simon Harnett, the hunter."

"Oh, aye, I remember now," Holt said. "That's been a few years ago, hasn't it? And I see now why you're asking. You must have known Simon."

"Aye, I knew him. And you say the man and woman both were killed?"

Holt nodded, sighing morosely. "The only ones who got away were two of their little ones. The Johnsons over in Pollock's Landing took one, and we took the other one in.

Not that we needed another mouth to feed, because I have nine here now and only four of them properly mine. But I could spend the rest of the day naming off people who've been killed around here, and I couldn't face myself if I turned a homeless child away."

"It's easy for you to talk," his wife chuckled good-naturedly. "Who does the cooking around here? But if I'm going to be up to my knees in anything, I'll have it little ones if I have my rathers. And the little Elder boy is no trouble. He's as pretty as a girl, too." She turned and beckoned to a child. "Come here, boy. He's a pretty thing, but it's a puzzle to me as to where he got his coloring. His mother had hair like a flame, her first husband had brown eyes and hair, and her second husband had . . ."

Her voice faded and her smile died on her lips as she pulled the boy to the door, looking from him to Santee. The boy was much like any settler's child seen along the way, about three, and a tall, sturdy child. Barefoot, in shapeless homespun trousers to the middle of the shin, the wide waist caught up with a thong for a belt, and a blousy homespun shirt with wide sleeves down to the middle of his forearms, sturdy garments that had been patched, sewn, and passed down through several children. His hair was a thick mop of coarse, black hair, and his eyes were deep blue. At first glance Santee for some reason thought the boy vaguely resembled Jubal. Then he realized that the boy's features were a miniature of his own.

The woman's face was crimson with embarrassment. Holt looked from the boy to Santee a couple of times, a frown of disapproval forming on his face, then he cleared his throat gruffly and looked away. "Well, I expect you might want to water your horses and have a bite to eat. . . ."

"I'm obliged, but I'd rather not tarry." Santee looked at the boy thoughtfully, then at Holt. "I could take the boy with me, if it's all the same to you."

The woman opened her mouth to object, then closed her lips without speaking. Holt's frown darkened as he looked from Santee to the boy again, and he shook his head. "I don't go with passing little ones from hand to hand like they were a cat or a dog. But I've heard of you, and it's plain to see that . . . anyway, what will your woman have to say about it? I'd never send a little one to where he'd be mistreated, and I couldn't blame a woman for not taking up with—"

"I don't have one, but my ma would be glad to see to him."

Holt looked at Santee narrowly, shaking his head again. "A man should have a woman," he said emphatically. "I'm not one to mind another's affairs, because it takes me all of my while to see to my own. But I do believe a man should be properly married, be he farmer or whatever. And that comes from the Bible." He looked at his wife. "What do you think about it, Mary?"

She pursed her lips, looking down at the boy and pondering, then shrugged. "It's for you to say, Jacob. The boy's no trouble and we have ample to eat, but we do have nine. That's a passel to see to when there's trouble and we go into Pollock's Landing to stay with the others. I'm fond of the boy and I wouldn't be glad to see him go, but there's a right and wrong in this somewhere. It's up to you to find it."

Holt nodded absently, stroking the stubble on his chin. "Would he be seen to properly?"

"That, and more. My ma's a good woman."

Holt nodded again and looked at his wife. "I believe it's right that the boy should go with him, Mary. I can't deny the evidence of my own two eyes."

"Aye, very well, Jacob," she said, taking the boy's shoulder and turning back into the cabin. "I'll get his few things together, and I'll put up a packet of victuals for them to take along."

"Aye, do that." Holt looked back at Santee. "I do think it's a good thing for a man to be properly married, and I think it's . . . well, when do you think we might see some militia up this way, then?"

Santee shrugged and shook his head. "I wouldn't look for it soon. Most of what they have out this way is west of here, and from what they're doing out there, I don't believe they would be of any assistance if they were here."

"They'd be of more assistance than what we have now, because we've bloody nothing."

"How is it that you're still here, then?"

"Because I won't leave, that's how. I've fought swining

tax collectors, sodding cheats of land surveyors, and every other sort of slimy bugger you can name for this land. This land has my sweat on it and I have my life in it, and I'll fight every other sod who attempts to drive me away, including flaming Indians."

"Then that's what you have, and it's a lot more than nothing."

Holt looked at him with a puzzled frown, then he smiled slightly in understanding. "Aye, I suppose it is. But I'd welcome some militia to go along with it."

"They're recruiting more right along, and they might start building forts at all the larger settlements. When their tax revenues start falling, they'll do something."

"You have it there," Holt laughed grimly. "You're right there, no bloody fear. When the sods in Wilmington start hurting in the purse, they'll do something to cure it." He turned to the door as the woman came out with the boy. "Well, here we are. Now you be a good lad, do you understand?"

The boy was clutching a bundle tied up in a blanket, and he looked up at Holt and Santee, his toes moving nervously in the dust and his eyes wide with fright and lack of comprehension. He nodded uncertainly. The woman had a bulging homespun bag of food, spots of grease seeping through the thin, worn material, and she bent over the boy and kissed and patted him, then handed the bag to Santee.

"Here's a bite for you and the boy to eat along the way."

"I'm much obliged." He tied the bag onto the canvas bags of supplies on the second horse and lifted the boy onto the canvas bags. "I'm obliged for everything."

"Come back and see us when you're by here," Holt said, extending his hand. "Let us know how the boy's doing, and see if you can't have a few more of those hanging on your belt."

Santee nodded, shaking hands with him, and he nodded to the woman as he turned to his horse. "I'll stop in if I'm by. And the boy will be seen to properly."

"Aye, I've no fear there," Holt replied. "We know all about you here, and I only wish we had fifty more like you living in these parts. Travel safely."

"Aye, and you hold onto your land here."

"I will. We'll be here when you come back by."

Santee mounted his horse and turned toward the road, smiling as the man and woman waved. While the pack train followed his horse, the woman and some of the children waved to the boy. He rocked from side to side on the bags of supplies as he looked back at them with a frightened, forlorn expression on his small face, his fingers digging into the bundle he was clutching to himself. The horses plodded along to the main road, and Santee turned onto it. The children were playing around the front of the cabin. The man was chopping wood again. The woman was standing in the doorway of the cabin with her arms folded. The boy watched her until the farmstead disappeared from sight behind a low rise in the road.

Santee reined the horses off the road, turning to the east. The boy was still holding the bundle to him instead of resting it on the bags of supplies, and Santee stopped, dismounted, and stepped back to the second horse, reaching for the bundle.

"We'll tie this on, and you won't have to bother holding it."

The boy released the bundle reluctantly, looking down at Santee apprehensively. Santee loosened a rope, tied the bundle onto the bags by the bag of food, and started to step back to his horse. Then he turned and looked at the boy again.

"You're old enough to talk properly, aren't you?"

The boy nodded nervously.

"What's your name, then?"

He opened his mouth and tried to speak, then swallowed convulsively and replied in a whisper, "Simon Elder."

"Aye, that's a good name. Well, it's Simon Collier now, and that's what you're to say when people ask you. Do you understand?"

The boy nodded unsurely. Santee smiled and patted his leg, then stepped back to his horse.

"When are we going back?"

Santee hesitated, then mounted his horse and looked back at the boy. "Back there, do you mean? We're not, but you'll like it where you're going. There are two good women to see to you, a snug cabin, and ample good food. You'll be happy there."

It took Simon a couple of seconds to realize that he

wouldn't be returning to the cabin he had known. Then he looked at Santee with an appalled expression, tears filling his eyes as his lips and chin trembled. Santee wondered if the boy was going to start crying, and he frowned. The boy's face stiffened with fright as Santee frowned, and he pressed his lips together tightly and breathed rapidly, controlling the sobs that were about to begin. Santee turned back to the front, nudging his horse. The horses began moving again, plodding up a slow rise where large trees had been cleared, making the cover sparse and thin. Santee checked the priming in his rifle and glanced around at the boy again. The boy was looking off to one side with an expression of hopeless despair, tears trickling down his cheeks.

Near dark Santee stopped and made a cold camp in a thick belt of forest. Simon had little appetite, eating only a mouthful of the cornbread and pork the woman had put in the bag. He watched Santee roll up in his blanket, and he untied the blanket around his belongings and wrapped it around himself. He began trembling and shivering with cold, and presently he began weeping softly. Santee listened to him, wondering what to do. Then he sat up, unwrapped his blanket and pulled Simon to him, and wrapped his blanket around both of them as he lay back down. Simon stopped shivering and crying, and he was tense as he lay against Santee. He gradually relaxed, nestled closer, and went to sleep. The boy slept restlessly and dreamed constantly, twitching, jerking, murmuring, and occasionally crying out in his sleep. Santee's sleep was only an intermittent doze with the boy beside him, but it didn't irritate him.

Santee rose just before dawn, caught the horses and loaded them, and opened the bag of food again. Simon shivered in the chill of the misty half-light as he awkwardly tried to tie his bundle, his face sleepy and his hair a tousled mop. Santee tied the bundle for him and gave him a piece of bread and pork.

"Where do I swill?"

"You don't. We'll have a wash-up in a few days, before we get there."

From his expression that was a bright spot in the upheaval he had suffered, and he ate with better appetite than he had the night before. When they began riding along again, he looked around with more interest in his surroundings. The sun rose, and the boy slumped and dozed on the horse occasionally, swaying with the packsaddle. Near the middle of the day Santee stopped in a clump of trees near a burned farmstead, and after eating he went to search for corn for the horses in the remains of the outbuildings. Simon raced after him, not wanting to be left alone. Hulled walnuts had been spread out in a corner of the barnyard to dry, and Simon began trying to crack them between stones as Santee dug in the ruins of the corn crib. Santee found a large basket among the corn and gave it to the boy so he could gather up the nuts, and he took him to the trampled tilled area so he could pull himself some turnips to gnaw as they rode along.

When they stopped and made camp again, Santee looked through the boy's belongings. There was another pair of trousers and another shirt in the bundle, both patched and sewn homespun that was soft and bleached from many washings, a wooden top that the boy said the Elder man had whittled for him, a knotted length of cord to go with the top, a broken knife, a handful of bright stones that the boy had collected, and other small treasures meaningful and valuable only to him. What appeared at first to be a couple of cheap, faded bracelets were wrapped in a scrap of homespun, and Santee recognized what they were after examining them for several minutes. They were threaded beads that Ellen had taken from his buckskins when she had washed and repaired them.

As they traveled farther east, the evidence of raids gradually diminished, then disappeared. And as the days passed, Simon's despondency faded and he began to find satisfaction in the respite from the chores and the daily routine he'd always known. He enjoyed having a fire and cooking over it, and he scuttled around and gathered wood when they stopped to camp at night, then hovered around the fire and turned potatoes in the coals as they baked. When he became more accustomed to Santee, his timid silence turned into streams of questions as they sat by the fire at night and cracked walnuts.

"What happened to your face there?"

"I got cut and it grew back this way."

"What do people call you?"

"Santee Collier. But you call me Pa."

"You're not my pa."

"I am now."

"Have you been in many fights?"

"A time or two."

"With Indians?"

"Once or twice."

"Did you whip them?"

"Now and then."

"Who's going to be my ma?"

"My ma."

"How can you be my pa when we have the same ma?"

"Just because. Here, eat this walnut. And this one too. And here's a tasty apple."

It rained for several days, and Simon huddled in his blanket and shivered as the horses plodded along through the downpour, then the weather cleared again as they traveled along the Cape Fear River. When they approached Wilmington, Simon was grimy, his face dirty and sooty from campfire smoke, his thick hair tangled and full of twigs, leaves, and clumps of mud, and his clothes wrinkled, torn, and stained with mud and food. They camped by a creek, and Simon had an attitude of grim resignation as he scrubbed in the creek and got his clean clothes out of his bundle of belongings. Santee picked the debris out of the boy's hair and trimmed it with his knife, shaved and cleaned himself up, and they went on into Wilmington.

Jubal's business complex had a settled, established, prosperous appearance. The stock pens were crowded with animals; the wagon yard behind the warehouse was parked full of wagons and drays. A dray was being unloaded at the warehouse dock, and horses and wagons were thick in front of the trading post as people went in and out. Santee turned into the yard by the warehouse, reining his horse around toward the end of the dock. The clerk overseeing the laborers loading the dray walked along the dock as Santee dismounted and tied his horse, glancing curiously at Simon and smiling and nodding to Santee.

"Good day, Mr. Collier, and it's a pleasure to see you again. It appears you have a good lot there, as usual."

"It'll do," Santee replied, lifting Simon off the horse. He climbed onto the dock. "Is Jubal within?"

The clerk nodded again. "He's in the trading post, I believe, if you'd like to step in. I'll have your hides unloaded
and weighed in as soon as the men are through there.
That's a healthy-looking little one, isn't he?"

"Aye, his name's Simon and he can travel with the best,
come rain or shine. I'll be inside when you get the tally
taken, then."

The clerk glanced over at Simon once more and walked
back toward the dray. Santee strolled along the dock toward the front of the building, Simon following him. As he
passed the office door, he glanced in. Then he stopped. Alcey was at her desk, and she had looked up.

"Good day, Alcey," he said.

She started to reply politely, then she looked at Simon as
he caught up with Santee. Her eyes opened wide in surprise, and she glanced back and forth between Santee and
Simon with a puzzled expression. Then a smile began forming. It spread, becoming brilliant, and she put down her
quill as she rose and moved around her desk toward the
door, her eyes fixed on Simon. Santee nudged Simon, pushing him into the office.

"What a lovely child! Such an absolutely lovely child!"
Her dress rustled as she knelt in front of Simon, pushing
his hair back, and she pulled him closer and kissed him.
She smiled up at Santee and started to ask a question. Then
she blinked, her smile became embarrassed, and she
flushed hotly as she took Simon's hands and held them.
"Such a lovely child."

"Pay your respects, Simon," Santee said. "This is Mistress Collier."

"Pleased to meet you, ma'am," Simon whispered, trying
to edge away from Alcey.

"And I'm delighted to meet you, Master Simon," Alcey
murmured affectionately, pushing at his hair. "Would you
like a boiled sweet, Master Simon? Of course you would,
wouldn't you?" She took his hand firmly. "Come along,
then, and we'll find you one. Jubal is just within, Santee,
and I'll tell him you're here."

"I'm obliged, Alcey."

Simon glanced over his shoulder at Santee apprehensively, then looked up at Alcey as she led him toward a
door at the side of the office. Jubal walked through the

doorway, glancing from Alcey to Santee, then he did a doubletake at Simon and stopped, staring down at him.

"What's this, then?"

"This is Master Simon, Jubal," Alcey said. "Isn't he lovely?"

Jubal looked from the boy to Santee again, an expression of disgust forming on his face, and he lifted his eyebrows and shrugged in dismissal as he went into the room. "So you've returned, Santee? Did you bring any hides with you, or were you too occupied on other matters to hunt?"

"Aye, I brought a few."

"Step on in, then, and we'll have a sip." He turned and looked at Alcey as she began leading Simon toward the doorway again. "What are you about, may I ask?"

She stopped, her smile fading. "I'm taking Simon to get him a boiled sweet."

"Are you now?" Jubal said acidly. "You have nothing better to do? I would I had such ample leisure."

Fear of him flickered on her features for an instant, then her face became totally expressionless. "I have work to do to no ends," she said quietly. "But better? No, I have nothing better to do." She turned and walked through the doorway, pulling Simon along behind her.

"I'll pay you for the sweets, Jubal," Santee said, annoyed at Jubal's attitude toward the boy. "I wouldn't want you to be out anything on my account."

Jubal glanced at him absently, his pale cheeks flushed with anger, and he looked back at the doorway. "Churchmouse before the wedding, and defiant wench afterward," he murmured grimly. "I'll bloody see that right, no fear."

Santee frowned thoughtfully, leaning on his rifle. Except under the most unusual circumstances interference in the relationship between a married couple was strictly proscribed by custom. But Jubal could be cruel. His anger was extreme in comparison with Alcey's mild comment. And fear of him had been plain on her face. They hadn't been married long and Santee hadn't been around them at all to have an idea of how smoothly their marriage was going, but he didn't like the hint that had just been revealed. "I wouldn't want any bother between you and Alcey over the boy, either."

Jubal turned and glared at him. "What goes between me and my wife is none of your bloody concern."

"Aye, you're right there. Unless it came to the point that you were mistreating her or abusing her over naught. Then I'd make it my concern."

Jubal stiffened and his nostrils flared, and he started to reply angrily. Then he hesitated, shrugged, and turned toward the doorway at the rear of the office. "Did you get enough hides to make the trip worth the effort?"

"I'll live," Santee replied, following him. "Even with you twisting me out of half the value."

Jubal glanced over his shoulder at Santee with a sour expression as they walked into his office. "You're free to go to Wilson's anytime you wish. I'm leaning more heavily toward shipping, produce, and livestock as it is, because we're not taking in sufficient hides and pelts for the bother. Most of the Indian traders have either remained in or haven't been heard of."

"I'm not surprised, because all of the friendly Indians are either with the militia or in the north fighting with the armies. The only pelts other Indians are interested in come off the heads of whites. And as far as my going to Wilson's is concerned, I'd as soon go there as you would have me go, but it would bother Ma and Pa. How are they, by the way?"

Jubal grunted and shrugged as he took cups and a bottle off a shelf. "I've only seen them once since you have. They came to the trading post for some goods, and I talked to them for a few minutes." He poured rum into the cups and handed one to Santee. "Here's your health."

Santee nodded and took a sip, then leaned his rifle against the wall and sat down on a chair. "You haven't had Alcey over to see them?"

"I have business affairs to occupy my time and attention," Jubal said impatiently, sitting down at his desk and taking a drink from his cup. "In talking to some of the upriver settlers in the trading post, I've found that a shovel I sell to a dealer here for two and sixpence goes for a guinea there, and a lot of barrel staves that costs me a guinea fetches two and sixpence there."

Santee chuckled, taking another sip from his cup. "Have

you just found out that you're not the only bloody twister in the world?"

Jubal looked at Santee in irritation, then sat back in his chair and looked out the window by his desk. "I'm considering putting a post up by Cross Creek and using drays to supply it from here. Do you think there would be any difficulty with Indians?"

"At Cross Creek? No, they've not been coming that far east. But there are no less than four trading posts around Cross Creek now."

"Aye, but I'd take in produce instead of demanding money and have the produce transported back here. I could charge little more than what I do here for goods and get the produce at a bargain, and make a profit on both ends by shipping the produce out of here. I have it that a lot of the produce from upriver is being carted to Charleston because of the prices the traders up there are charging, and I believe I could take a lot of that away from the merchants in Charleston."

Santee shrugged and shook his head. "I know nothing about business affairs, and care less."

"I'm not asking you about business affairs, I'm asking you about Indians. You say there wouldn't be any trouble with them at Cross Creek?"

"No. If they start raiding that far east, the Assembly will have every man in the Colony in the militia."

Jubal nodded and grunted, taking a drink from his cup and looking out the window again. The clerk from the dock came in quietly, smiling nervously, and put a piece of paper on Jubal's desk and left. Jubal sat forward and looked at the paper, picked up a quill, dipped the tip, and jotted figures on the paper. "It comes to eighty-six guineas, ten shillings, and sixpence. Do you want the money or a bill?"

"I'll take a bill and trade it for my goods and the difference in money when I get ready to leave again."

Jubal took a piece of paper from a stack on the desk and wrote on it rapidly. "From what Father said when I talked to him a few weeks back, he might not be going this winter."

"Aye, I've been looking for that, and it's just as well. He's getting old, and he has enough money saved up to last them."

Jubal shrugged indifferently, signing the paper, then pushed it toward Santee and sat back, picking up his cup again. "You'll probably get more pelts going by yourself, because he is that old that I fail to see how he even manages in the wilderness. And you'd undoubtedly get many more pelts if you'd devote your energies to trapping instead of such larrikin ventures as that boy evidences."

Santee nodded agreeably, draining his cup as he stood. He picked up his rifle, put the cup on the desk, and took the piece of paper. "Aye, well, I'll stop such as that when you give the Widow Porter and her children their just dues."

"They've had their just dues!" Jubal snapped. "And I'll ask you to mind your own bloody affairs!"

Santee nodded again, turning toward the door. "Let's both of us do that, then."

Jubal made an angry sound in his throat, pulling some papers on his desk toward him, and began shuffling through them as Santee walked out. Alcey was standing on the porch outside the front office, smiling down at Simon and talking with him. Simon was rolling a large boiled sweet around in his mouth and holding another in a twist of paper in his hand as he grinned up at her. Alcey turned to Santee as he came out onto the porch.

"Santee, I'm truly tempted to steal him from you. You will bring him again, won't you?"

"It appears I'll have trouble keeping him away now. Aye, I'll bring him back, and you'll be seeing him at the cabin, no doubt."

Her smile faltered and her eyes dropped, and she nodded uncertainly. She bent over Simon and kissed him, then moved toward the door. "Do bring him back soon."

"Aye, I will. Come along, Simon."

Alcey stood in the doorway and smiled and waved to Simon as he followed Santee along the porch. Simon looked back at her, grinning and waving. As Santee turned the corner, Simon caught up with him, and he smiled down at the boy and ruffled his hair. Simon sucked the boiled sweet noisily and rolled it around in his mouth. Santee hopped down from the dock, lifted Simon onto the supply bags on the second horse, then mounted his horse and turned it away from the dock. The horses plodded across the yard to the road, their steps more lively in anticipation of the end of the journey as Santee turned them onto the road. The sunlight was bright, and the interior of the office where Alcey worked was dim and distant from the road, but it looked as if Jubal was standing by her desk. A wagon rattling noisily along the road ahead of the horses drowned any sound that might be coming from the office. But from the way Jubal was standing, he seemed to be berating her. Santee frowned, looking at the doorway until the interior of the office was out of his line of vision.

Bledsoe was working on a gate at the front of the stock pens. He shaded his eyes and looked as the dog began barking, then he cupped his hands around his mouth and shouted toward the cabin as he walked along the front of the stock pens, limping heavily. The dog came racing along the path, barking madly and leaping into the air. Bledsoe stopped at the corner of the stock pens and shifted his weight onto his left leg, waving. Santee smiled and waved. Bledsoe looked closer, shading his eyes with his hand again and craning his neck to one side to look at the boy, his mouth opening in surprise.

Nina and Hannah came around the side of the cabin. They slowed, looking at the boy, then Nina rushed around Hannah and hurried toward the path. Santee dismounted by the stock pens, and Nina ran up to him, looking from him to Simon with speechless surprise and mounting joy. She hugged Santee perfunctorily, then rushed to the second horse and pulled Simon down with a squeal of delight as he made a sound of alarm. Hannah stopped in front of Santee, looking blankly from him to Simon as Nina held the boy to her and kissed him, tears running down her cheeks, then Hannah stepped to Nina and took the boy from her. A wide, elated smile covered her face as she pushed his hair back, kissed him and held him to her.

"Nina, isn't he the prettiest little thing? He's the prettiest little thing I've ever seen, and he's the pure image of . . ." Her voice faded, her smile fading into a suspicious frown. "Now what is this, Santee? Who is this boy, and where's his ma?"

"His name's Simon, and she was killed in an Indian raid."

"Aye, but . . ." She pushed Simon's hair back, then closed her mouth with a snap and glared at Santee as she hoisted Simon in her arms. "Nina, let's get this poor mite inside and give him a good wash and a good feed. He looks like he hasn't had a bite to eat this week nor a wash this past year." She looked up at Santee narrowly as she carried the boy past him, Nina walking beside her and patting the boy. Then she glared at Bledsoe. "I've a good idea I know what's been afoot here, and it's up to you to put it right! You're the man of the house!"

Bledsoe nodded vaguely, stroking his beard and looking at the two women as they carried the boy toward the cabin. "Well, who is that boy, Santee? And who was his ma?"

"His name's Simon, and his ma was a woman named Ellen Harnett."

"Harnett? Harnett, you say? I've heard that name."

"Her husband was Simon Harnett."

"Oh, aye, I know of him. Someone said he's dead, as I remember. His wife, you say? Well, that's not right, is it?"

"No, it's not right, Pa."

"Aye, enough said, then. It's good to see you back, son. Let's get your horses into the pen and give them some corn. Did you get a good load of hides?"

"Just under three hundredweight."

"That's good enough, I'd say. Well, this foot has been a misery to me all summer, Santee, and I might just lie in this winter."

"Aye, I thought you might, Pa."

"It's time, because I'm old beyond counting. I'm older than Alvah Raines was, and he passed on this summer. Did you know that? Aye, he did and all. Well, where do you think you'll go this winter, Santee?"

"I have in mind going to *Kenta-ke*."

"*Kenta-ke?* Well, you'll have to be mightily careful, Santee."

"Aye, I'll be careful, Pa."

# Part Three

# ALCEY

Part Three

# Chapter Twelve

Alcey concentrated on the bill of lading and the ledger, keeping the wall of detachment firmly in place around herself and allowing the scathing tirade to impinge on her consciousness only to the extent necessary to be aware of pauses. The next listing on the bill was two bales of bolted drugget, one gray and one brown, twelve bolts of twenty yards each in each bale. She made the entry in the ledger, carefully forming the letters and numbers in the pattern that had been drilled into her in childhood. His voice paused.

"I understand, Jubal."

"Understand? You understand, do you? You understand flaming naught, and there's God's bloody truth. But I warrant you'll come to understand, no bloody fear. You'll understand that I won't be . . ."

The curving sweep down from the shoulder of a character 2 was too wide, just a fraction beyond the allowable margin of tolerance that the countless hours of concentrated practice under the watchful eye of her father had instilled in her. It could have been an unconscious tremble of her hand from his voice penetrating to a sensitive level without her being aware of it. Or the point of the quill could be shredding on one side. She wiped the point on the lip of the inkwell, then rolled it in her fingers, looking at it. One side of the point was slightly burred. It was a good quill and she had written only a couple of lines after sharpening it, so she had been pressing too hard. His angry voice had been penetrating her control. She picked up the knife from its slot, scraped the burr off the side of the point, and replaced the knife and dipped the point in the inkwell again. His voice paused.

"Very well, Jubal."

"Very well, you say? You'd have it pass with that, would you? Aye, I'm bloody sure you flaming would and all. But you'll find that you'll either have a sodding mind to your saucy tongue or you'll suffer the bloody consequences. I'll not listen to flaming scavey such as I had from you, and I'll not . . ."

The lines flowed smoothly as she moved the quill with controlled motions of her wrist, concentrating on the pressure on the paper. The motions of her wrist were automatic, requiring no conscious volition, the letters of the ill-formed, ungainly scrawl on the bill of lading keying responses that produced the motions, with hesitations only when she translated the spelling to that which had been taught her by her father. Only her wrist moved, her fingers remaining absolutely motionless in obedience to dictums deeply embedded in her mind, prohibitions that were the ghostly memory of her father's quietly reproving voice in distant childhood, when her fingers had been tiny and had tried to move the quill to ease the aching of her wrist when weary from practice. His voice paused again.

"I shan't alter my behavior, Jubal."

"Shan't alter my behavior," he sneered, mimicking her accent. "Parading your learning again, are you? If you were so bloody intelligent, you would have kept your flaming tongue still, woman. But you'll rue the day when you talk back to me again, and you may be bloody assured of that. Furthermore I'll not have you make a fool of me the way you did with that whelp Santee dragged in here. Save your affection for an heir of mine, if indeed there be affection in that cold gizzard. I'll not have my own wife shame me before the bloody world by making such a do about some get of a wandering ruffian and some backwoods strumpet, and I'll not have . . ."

But his sense of shame didn't extend to others. On the edge of her vision she saw one of the overseers, Price Hugh, come in. Hugh hesitated, then started to back out. Jubal snapped his fingers and motioned him in, still glaring down at Alcey and continuing the vituperative, profane berating. Hugh folded his arms and stood inside the door, moving his feet uncomfortably. The next entry on the bill of lading was four casks of coarse salt, four hundredweight each cask. She dipped the point of the quill and began making the entry in the ledger. His voice paused again.

"Very well, Jubal."

"It'll be very well before it's over, you may be bloody assured. You might have your long nose in that ledger and ignoring me now, but we'll have another word on this later. And I'll have your attention then, I'll wager." He turned and looked at Hugh. "Is the drover finally up and about, then?"

"Aye, he's out at the pens, Mr. Collier."

"Has he been at the rum today?"

"Aye, he's had a cup or two to cure his head. Or more, from the look of him."

"Perhaps he's ready to talk a fair price, then," Jubal said, walking toward the door. "How much did the tavern girl cost me?"

"Five shillings."

"That's little enough if it's put him in a set of mind to reduce the price by a shilling or two per head. Let's go talk to him, then, and see what return I'll have from five shillings for the serving wench and ten for rum. Are they all healthy?"

"Aye, they want feeding up after being driven that far, but I'd say that they are as healthy as one might reasonably expect, considering . . ."

Their voices faded as they walked along the porch, Hugh's deferential manner reflecting dislike for the method of doing business and resentment over being required to serve as a panderer. A more intense dislike had been in his voice and attitude some months before, when a drover had brought in a herd of swine dying of some disease, and Jubal had bought them for a low price and quickly sold them to a processor of foodstuffs, making an enormous profit on the transaction.

Hugh was about fifty, heavyset and gray-headed, always in well-washed and patched homespuns and heavy, clumping boots. A good man, the honest accent of his native Wales thick in his voice, a recent immigrant aware of his limited knowledge of the dangers of the border settlements, and a farmer who had been driven into Wilmington from some outlying area because of fear for the safety of his wife and two children. And a helpless man, an honest worker at a time when workers were flooding in from the outlying areas, other colonies, and from ships docking in the port, a man forced to work for poor wages and do things he considered dishonest and immoral in order to support his family.

A man rendered helpless by circumstances. A man of a type Jubal always sought to work for him. A man such as her father had been.

Even in England circumstances had conspired against her father. Considered by some as unsuitable as a schoolmaster because of his libertarian attitudes and because of the religious convictions of his second wife, a Quaker, he had earned enough for bare necessities by filling small posts in schools for the children of working people, by tutoring children whose parents were tolerant of academic political eccentricities, and by doing some translating for publishers. The frail, delicate wife had died, eagerly relinquishing her infirm grip on life with composed satisfaction and in avid anticipation that the scorn and abuse heaped upon her in life had accrued a bountiful reward after death. But the association with her religion had lingered, the reputation from the attitudes had remained. The teaching posts had become smaller, the tutorial opportunities fewer, and the stipends from translating assignments rarer.

A bequest from a relative had enabled them to emigrate, but the libertarian attitudes had been more unwelcome in Wilmington than in England. And not surprisingly his forthright abhorrence of slavery as an institution had been a barrier to being engaged as a tutor by wealthy landowners who were also slave owners. Then, just as the indebtedness for the cramped, filthy lodgings had been mounting to the point that the landlord was threatening legal action, he had found employment for both of them with Jubal.

And before the debts were fully discharged, he succumbed to a winter illness, the fate of many immigrants. Then she had been helpless. In her wrenching sorrow and confusion, with the firmament turned to shifting quicksand under her, Jubal's prosaic and matter-of-fact offer of marriage had been the only refuge, her only escape from appearing before a magistrate to declare herself indigent and to be bound out as a governess, maid, or tutor to discharge the indebtedness left by her father. And even in retrospect there had been no other choice, even if she had avoided bondage by submitting herself to a kind of slavery.

The point of the quill left a tiny blob of ink at the bottom of a character, and she wiped it on the lip of the inkwell and lifted it, examining it. It was fraying. She picked up the knife, made a diagonal slice through the quill above the point and cut it off, and began shaping another point, shaving tiny slivers from each side and making a smooth, symmetrical curve on each side. Heavy footfalls approached the doorway from along the hall to the trading post, and a man came in. On the edge of her vision, she saw it was Beasley, the overseer for the warehouse, a man of another type Jubal sought to work for him. Men who were servile toward him, and who had no morals or scruples. Beasley crossed the room to her desk and put a sheaf of papers on it.

"There's the warehouse inventory, Mistress Collier."

His voice had a note of sarcasm. He and some of the other men were frequently slyly disrespectful, staring at her and making coarse comments they knew she would overhear. It had developed slowly as they analyzed the situation and concluded that they had nothing to fear from Jubal through her. But they weren't completely sure of themselves, because it never happened when Jubal was present. At the same time it had steadily become more forthright when Jubal wasn't present.

"Thank you."

He remained by her desk. It was one of his ways of being impudent, and he would walk away as though he had just put the inventory down if Jubal came in. It also happened when she came upon him somewhere in the building. He would stare at her, waiting for her to look at him, then he would smile or laugh sarcastically and go on about what he had been doing. Other men did the same. When it had dawned on her that they considered her meeting their gaze as a victory of some kind, and that they considered it a contest of wills, she had stopped looking. It was a contest they couldn't win, because it was an arena in which she had the strength of steel. It was in the arena of control, and she simply ignored them, blotting them out of her awareness. And she easily ignored many things far more bothersome than their presence and their stares.

"I trust you'll be able to read it, pitiful scribble that it is. But you see, my clerk and the rest of us don't have your ladyship's pretty hand with a quill."

The quill had been hardened with heat just a fraction more than when preparing raw feathers, but it wasn't brittle. She scraped away a couple of rough spots, slit the point with a deft push of the knife, then put the knife down and dipped the point in the inkwell, glancing at the bill of lading. The next listing was twenty ingots of bullet lead, one hundredweight each. She wiped the point on the lip of the inkwell, then began writing the entry in the ledger. Beasley made an angry sound as he turned and walked back toward the doorway. It was a distant, vague impression on her consciousness.

It was easier to hold the quill motionless because of a slight stickiness on her fingers, a residue from handling the boiled sweets she had given the child. It had been unwise to be demonstrative, because a moment's reflection would have warned her of Jubal's displeasure. But she had been caught unaware, and a sudden flood of warmth had swelled up within her, something that had never happened before that she could remember, and it had taken control. The boy was angelic, a small cherub with huge blue eyes, smooth, pretty features, and pitifully rude little garments and bare feet. And he was a tiny copy of Santee.

A strange and different name for a man, and a strange and different man. When she had first seen him, she had expected him to be a brawling, boisterous lout from the comments Jubal and others had made in her presence. But he was a quiet man, talking less than most, and he had always been remote and withdrawn around her, despite the indications of boyish, puckish humor that sometimes glinted in his eyes. There was also a feeling of restraint about him, as though he always held himself in check, always poised to move suddenly and moving about as silent as a shadow despite his enormous size. And he looked as though he might have a violent temper. Significantly Jubal was cautious with him. With his foster parents and others Jubal varied from being indifferent to being casually insulting, but with Santee he was more wary, as he was with powerful businessmen and Crown officials. He would venture slyly cutting remarks, but he was judicious, never going too far. And from subtle undercurrents that suggested what Santee might be like when angered, it seemed wise to not go too far.

Santee was also extremely handsome. He had seemed to find her father interesting and had talked to him frequently. Her father had teasingly suggested that Santee might be interested in her, but there had been no outward indications of it. It had seemed unlikely, because it was obvious that they were too different. And beyond the fact that he was a handsome man, some of Santee's characteristics were repellent. He was a man of the deep, distant forests, wild and dangerous. She had been aghast when Jubal mentioned that the hairy balls dangling on thongs from Santee's belt were Indian scalps. The boy was visible proof of an uncontrolled and rakish side to his nature. He had met some desirable, willing woman somewhere who had reveled in his lusty, brawny strength, and the boy had been the result.

The thought made her cheeks burn, and the point of the quill trembled on the paper. She pushed the thought firmly out of her mind, dipping the point of the quill and wiping it. The inkwell lid was on its side and several inches from its place by the inkwell, where it had rolled when Jubal had brushed it with his sleeve while leaning over the desk and berating her. She put it back in its place and began writing again, sighing softly. Jubal had been furious with her, enraged by her comment about her work, as well as by her show of affection for the boy. The comment was a mistake that would continue to cost her for a long time to come. But the comment had slipped out, protectiveness toward the child and indignation over Jubal's arbitrary treatment of the child giving rise to a surge of temper that overcame her fear of him.

Her father and her stepmother had admonished her about temper in her childhood until she had learned to exercise almost absolute control over it. Her father had been a retiring, self-effacing man, far less inclined than most to assert himself, and it appeared that any temper she had inherited had come from her mother. She had only dim, distant memories of her mother, a redheaded woman from a family of redheaded people named Cosgrave, and her father had rarely mentioned her. But she remembered her mother's brother well, a volatile man named Malatish Cosgrave, who had a flaming red beard and shock of hair. He had been constantly embroiled in one difficulty or another until he had emigrated to one of the colonies with his long-suffering wife and unruly mob of redheaded children. And her father had often used that family's difficulties as an example when admonishing her about her temper.

The last entry on the bill of lading was ten casks of tea, one hundredweight per cask. She filled out the line in the ledger, put the quill in its slot by the inkwell and blew on the ink to dry it as she glanced at the doorway. The long shadows of late afternoon were stretching across the porch. It was near time to go to the house and too late to make a reasonable beginning on the inventory, which would take at least two or three days of searching through stacks of bills of lading and sales statements to reconcile it with the inventory ledger. She closed the ledger, carried it into Jubal's office and put it on the shelf, then crossed the outer office and stepped out onto the porch, looking toward the stock pens.

Her daily schedule was unvarying, but mentioning to Jubal when she was leaving the office was a symbol of asking permission that gave him a feeling of satisfaction. In view of his mood, it was a time for attention to the details and nuances that gratified him, but he wasn't in sight. He didn't like her wandering around among the men, and it always aggravated him when dinner was late. She turned and walked toward the other end of the porch. A couple of men were standing outside the door of the trading post, with two or three children around them, and Alcey dropped her eyes as the men looked at her. A man and woman in home-spuns were coming up the steps to cross the porch to the trading post, and they hesitated on the top step, looking at Alcey and waiting for her to pass ahead of them. Alcey plucked at her skirt in a motion of a curtsy and smiled. The woman stuttered a greeting, a flushed, confused smile on her face. A small boy was standing on the steps at the end of the porch and noisily chewing a piece of toffee, and Alcey smiled at him and patted his head as she walked down the steps.

The houses were in a row at the side of the complex, with the board fence around the perimeter, across a dusty expanse that was dotted with large rocks, holes, and splintered remains of stumps, and scored with wagon tracks. The house Jubal had had built for himself at the end of the row was much larger than the others, with two chimneys and a porch in front, but it was plain, blocky, and functional, its weathered, unpainted wood fading in with the other houses, the board fence, and the jumble of dwellings and other buildings at the edge of town.

It was hot and stuffy in the house, and Alcey left the doors open and raised the windows. A breath of the humid, sultry breeze moved through the house, heavy with the stench of the stock pens and the smell of the tide flats on the estuary, and thick with the pall of woodsmoke. The heat in the kitchen was intense from the smoldering fire in the fireplace, and she opened the window in the kitchen as she put on her apron and rolled up her sleeves. The joint on the spit was almost done, the bread in the pan on the hob was baked, and the beans on the edge of the fire were cooked through. She poured more water into the beans, built the fire up, and took potatoes out of a bin, peeled them, and put them on to boil.

The heat in the kitchen became torrid as the fire blazed up, and it felt almost cool on the back porch. She dipped water from a rain barrel into a tub, took Jubal's shirt and her petticoats from the tub where they had been soaking in Castile soap, rinsed them and wrung them, and began hanging them over the porch rail to dry. On the edge of her vision, she saw a movement at the rear of the adjacent house. It was Meghan, Price Hugh's wife, coming out the back door of her house to throw scraps to the chickens cooped behind her house. She smiled and waved to Alcey, and walked a few steps toward her.

"I would have done those few things through for you if I'd known they were there, love."

"It's very little to do, and it gives me a breath out of the kitchen. How are you today?"

"I can scarcely breathe in this heat, but my megrims are leaving me be, so I'm thankful. It must be torture for you over there at your writing table on days such as this."

"I'm accustomed to it, and I don't find it too difficult."

"Aye, and you're a tiny thing compared to my great size, so the heat won't plague you as much. Still, it's little wonder that you're small, what with all the running back and forth you do. But we all bear our burdens in the hope of a better tomorrow, don't we?"

Alcey smiled and nodded as she spread the last petticoat over the porch rail and turned toward the door, wiping her hands on her apron, and Meghan waved as she walked back toward her door. She was a short, stout woman in her forties, with a round, red, honest face, and she was always friendly and motherly. When her children collected apples, peaches, or other fruit from somewhere, she always left a share on the back porch and frequently offered to help with the housework, dropping hints that working in both the office and the house was too much. But she was also a little diffident and unsure of herself, because they weren't close. From the first days of their marriage Jubal had discouraged her from forming friendships with the employees' wives, so she was no more than acquainted with any of them.

Or with anyone else, because Jubal was close to no one. She had met the wives of several of Jubal's business associates at church, but Jubal had declined invitations to visit and forbade her to invite anyone. He frequently went to see other businessmen or government officials at night, sometimes going to their homes and at other times meeting them at taverns, but there were no social relationships as a married couple. The wedding had been a civil ceremony, taking only a few minutes in the office of a justice of the peace. His foster father and Santee had been gone, so his foster mother and the Indian woman Nina had been witnesses. They had come to the house after the wedding, embarrassed and uncomfortable because of Jubal's cool indifference, and pitiful in their attempts to regard the wedding as a momentous, joyous occasion. On several occasions Jubal's foster father had extended invitations to visit when he had been at the trading post, but Jubal had always pleaded the pressure of his business affairs. His foster parents and Nina were simple, honest people, good people, and after Alcey heard the story of Jubal's and Santee's birth, it seemed that the ones who reared them were much in the position of chickens that had hatched ducks. Neither Jubal nor Santee were like them, or like each other beyond a similarity of features and the color of their hair and eyes. But it appeared that Santee was affectionate toward his foster parents and Nina.

Her father hadn't been a socially inclined man, and the isolation from others wasn't unendurable. She had worked hard all her life, so the work didn't bother her. As a child she had been assigned long hours of studies and exercises, as well as household chores. When her father's second wife died, she had housekept, transcribed work for her father, and made odd shillings by taking in work from a seamstress. But she'd had a few friends along the street in Cheltenham. And her father had been voluble in his praise about what she did. Other women had harder lives, poor food, numerous children, and endless toil in tiny cabins. But it was difficult to remember that, at times. Things seemed very drab and hopeless. She had to maintain constant control over herself.

The joint and potatoes were done, and darkness was falling. She put the meat on a plate on the hearth to keep warm, poured the potatoes into a bowl and salted and buttered them, then lit a Betty lamp and carried it into the parlor and put it on the table. The sound of a couple of wagons rumbling along the road blended with the laughter and conversation of several men somewhere in the wagonyard and the sounds of the animals in the stock pens. The breeze coming in the front door and windows had freshened, and it was cooler, bringing the salt scent of the sea with it. A lantern someone was carrying along the road was a speck of yellow light bobbing along in the darkness.

Jubal came in. His cold glance was a silent reminder of his anger. Alcey put the food on the table, and he ate in silence as she washed the cooking utensils. When he left he took his frock coat with him, indicating he was going to someone's house or to a tavern instead of back to his office. Alcey ate, put the leftover food in the food safe, and washed the pewter plates, cups, and spoons. The clothes over the rail on the back porch had dried enough to iron, and she built up the fire in the fireplace, put the flatirons on the fender and folded a blanket on the table in the kitchen, and ironed the clothes, picking up the flatirons with the handle and replacing them on the fender as they cooled.

The seams on one of the petticoats were coming loose, and she took it into the parlor and sat by the lamp on the table to mend it. The petticoat was also becoming worn, as were many of her clothes. They were made of good, durable cambrics, calicoes, calamancoes, and linens, but they were getting old. And it was a subject she hesitated to bring up to Jubal, even though there were many bolts of cloth in the warehouse, because he was penurious in most things. The house was sparsely furnished, and the scattered pieces were a motley assortment of things from unclaimed shipping consignments he had picked up by one means or another. The wall around the fireplace in the parlor was different from the other walls, because it had been finished off later. Jubal had intended to have a cast-iron, five-plate Dutch stove installed, but had changed his mind because of the cost. He kept close check on the amounts of foodstuffs she took from the trading post, as he did with the employees.

The latest copy of the *Gazette*, the local news sheet, was on the table, and she glanced through it. It contained an account of an Indian raid on a small settlement to the west, minutiae of affairs conducted by the Assembly, a notice of recruitment for the militia, notices of arrivals and departures from the port, advertisements for a land company being formed, rewards for runaway slaves and bound servants, and various items for sale or barter. There was also a stack of month-old news sheets from England, but she had read most of them, and most of the news in them was about the war in Europe.

She put the clothes away, banked the fire, and went into the bedroom and changed into her nightgown. She walked back through the house and out onto the back porch, and listened in the darkness for several minutes to make sure no one was around. Sounds of conversation, arguments, laughter, and children at play came from the other houses, and there was no movement around her house. She undressed, dipped water from a rain barrel and bathed with a scrap of Castile soap, then dried herself, put her nightgown back on, and went back through the house to the bedroom.

It was quieter, with no traffic on the road and the animals in the stock pens settled for the night. The soft murmur of crickets and other insects around the house was restful and relaxing. Then Jubal came in.

His footsteps were loud in the darkness, the heavy footsteps of when he'd had a lot of rum, but not the unsteady footsteps of when he'd had too much. He went out to the privy, came back in and closed the doors, then entered the bedroom. Alcey looked up at the ceiling in the darkness, gradually becoming more and more tense as she listened to him undress. He got into bed, coughed and cleared his throat, and pulled the cover up. Alcey bit her lip, rigidly tense. He shifted in the bed, turning over and moving toward her. Alcey summoned her self-control, forcing herself to relax and not recoil as he began pulling up her nightgown.

His breath smelled strongly of rum, and he was sweaty. He didn't bathe often, and he frequently had boils on his chest and back. The coarse, day-old growth of bristles on his face scratched. It hurt, because he was always impatient and hurried. But it took only a moment, then he was motionless and panting on top of her. He moved off her, slid over to his side of the bed again, then relaxed, sighing heavily.

He began breathing with a deep, heavy rhythm, then began snoring. Alcey was alone in the darkness, and she could relax her control. The tears began welling in her eyes, and she wept quietly.

# Chapter Thirteen

Immigration had offered escape. There had been an expectation of a fresh start in a bright, new place where old difficulties and problems would be left behind. There had been a promise of a new life. Broadsides and pamphlets had given glowing descriptions of the healthful climate and the bountiful opportunities for all trades and professions. News sheets were filled with details of new ventures and investments being undertaken, and of fortunes reaped from past undertakings. People with relatives who had emigrated had talked about letters they had received describing vast tracts of land being sold for pence per acre, of soil so fertile that a few seeds broadcast by hand produced bountiful harvests. There were stories of those who had sold themselves into bondage for the price of their passage, then worked off their indebtedness and became landowners within a few years. There had been stories of transported felons who had worked out their periods of servitude and become respected, wealthy citizens. It had seemed assured that a schoolmaster and his daughter could find themselves a comfortable niche.

Reality had fallen short of the promise. The voyage had been a tortuous ordeal to endure. They were packed into crowded, unsanitary quarters, with poor, scanty food, and the constant heaving motion of the ship. People had become ill, and several had died. The ship had battled through terrifying storms, with the screams of the panic-stricken blending with the grinding of timbers being twisted and battered by the howling winds and towering waves. Life had been a nightmare.

The arrival had been disappointing. A long, suspenseful wait had followed the sighting of land, while some difficult passage was being negotiated, then she had eagerly crowded onto deck with the others for a first glimpse. The ship was moving through a narrow, muddy stretch of water with a dead dog floating nearby. She had seen only a shore-line littered with debris and refuse piles, with log huts scattered among the scraggly trees above the waterline. Then the docks and part of the town had come into sight. The town seemed very shabby, with an atmosphere of the temporary pressed into service beyond its useful life. The piers seemed hardly more extensive than the wharfs for small pleasure boats on the Severn, but far more spindly, rickety, and battered, thin poles and sagging boards tilting to one side or the other.

An officer from the naval and customs office examined papers and impatiently snapped questions as they stood on the pier, dazed, numb, clutching the things they'd had in the cabins, and still swaying with the motion of the ship. The smells were different, and there was a different quality to the air, a different feel. Bystanders watched in amused, patronizing curiosity. Everyone had talked with strangely blurred accents. Vendors moved among the new arrivals and shouted their wares: fruit, food, drink, furs, snakebite remedies, weapons for fighting Indians, and amulets and medicines to ward off the illnesses to which newcomers were prone. Others had harangued, offering to be guides, offering houses for sale, and offering transportation to the best lodgings and eating establishments. They walked into the town, and she had kept wondering when they were going to reach it. Everyone wanted money for something, and everything was expensive. The lodgings had been tiny, dirty, and expensive, and her father carried their trunks to the lodgings one at a time to save the expense of hiring a cart. The food was strange and unappetizing. On the second day both she and her father had fallen ill, with high fevers and severe stomach cramps.

And she wished they had never left Cheltenham. In Cheltenham the cottages and shops along her haunts had been bright and cheerful, each familiar from earliest memories, with its individual visage comprised of leaded windows and black beams against white plaster, and the thick walls matched and joined with precision to form solid lines on each side of the cobblestone streets, straight with the street when it was straight, and curving with it when it curved.

Time had rested lightly, a tilting lean in one building being compensated for by its neighbor's; stone stoops grooved by the footsteps of generations leading past thick oak doors shaped to fit the outline of jambs, sill, and transom prepared to endure eternity; and a workman repairing a slate roof repaired by his grandfather did his work carefully so his grandson wouldn't be ashamed of him.

Window boxes and tiny back gardens had been brilliant splashes of color from flowers growing in profusion, but a controlled profusion in which each flower was tended and assigned its spot in the pattern. Ancient oaks overlooked the graves of four generations of Martins in the sleepy churchyard by the blocky, ivy-covered stone church where the Martins had always worshiped. Paths led out from the common to meadows above Cheltenham, crossing a stile at every fence and a footlog at every rivulet, and from the meadows the distant white specks of sheep had been visible on the Cotswolds, grazing on pastures where sheep had grazed when the tax levied on wool had been paid to Rome. The patina of centuries had been comfortable. Mossy stones covered any bank in danger of sliding down, a neat growth of hedge covered any angular, jutting edge of a wall, and any unruly growth had been clipped back to meld into the harmonious whole.

In Wilmington a wild mélange of structures had been erected from boards hurriedly ripped from trees, with little thought beyond the needs of the immediate moment. Some streets had been paved, masses of stone sinking into soil yet to settle and stabilize, and others were beds of mud when it rained and dust when it was dry. The luxury of ample space turned into a drawback when openings between buildings became dumping grounds for refuse, and in the frenzy of seizing the fleeting crest of opportunity, a warehouse receiving goods one week might be partitioned into lodgings for the next. Businesses were located on the basis of where there were openings to build or vacant buildings to occupy, and goods for sale varied with what was available and the whims of the owner more than the character of the business, so that it might be necessary to pass taverns along any approach to a shop to buy a ribbon or thread to repair a gown, and cheeses for sale might be displayed on the shelf above the ribbons and thread. A more consistent pattern emerged near the center of town, where the streets were even and the buildings more durable, but even the brick buildings had a raw self-conscious atmosphere of newness, in settings that had the awkward appearance of more haste than forethought.

The people were also different, few of them fitting into known categories, many of totally new categories, and most partaking of a bewildering mixture of characteristics from several categories. Tradesmen and plantation owners wore better wigs, rode in larger carriages, and lived in more luxurious homes than the governor, and a woman screaming invectives at the driver of a dray for splashing mud on her gown might be a goodwife of the town rather than a harlot. A sword was worn more often as a weapon than as an accoutrement of a gentleman, and the purse in the leather breeches of an artisan might be heavier than that in the waistcoat of a Crown official. And with the collapse of forms order also fell into disarray. Official pronouncements were often received with derisive jeers, and unpopular officials venturing abroad in the town were often greeted with bits of offal flung from side streets. The atmosphere and deportment in the Assembly occasionally resembled those of a tavern more than of the chambers of a legislative body, and a magistrate sitting in judgment frequently found his intelligence, motives, and the regularity of his birth called into question by the accused.

The change from Cheltenham to Wilmington had been catastrophic. But while life had followed patterns and order, it had never been easy for her. And past generations had suffered calamity and shock. Husbands and fathers had been impressed to man ships, leaving their families penniless, and when they had lived to return, they had found their wives and children hungry, ragged, and destitute, but alive. Fate had inflicted other blows on past generations, demonstrating that life is not necessarily stable, not necessarily just. And she had suffered adversity herself, the handicap of the death of her mother at an early age, and the toll exacted from her because of her father's political convictions and the religion of his second wife. And when life had turned into a seething maelstrom around her, failed hopes bringing bitter disappointment, an unyielding bedrock of endurance had asserted itself. On her second day in Wilmington she had struggled up from the pallet she used for a bed, fighting the nausea, agonizing stomach pains and fever of her illness, and she had set about making the dingy, cramped lodgings into as much of a home as she could.

The further disappointment of her marriage when she had only begun to adjust to her surroundings also failed to uncover despair. From vague hints she had gathered, the marriage between her father and mother had been less than ideal, the marriage between her father and stepmother had been an arrangement rather than a love match, and many other marriages were similar. As there was no returning to Cheltenham from Wilmington her married state became an immutable fact. To live in Wilmington she had to accept Wilmington. Similarly she accepted her marriage, her physical disgust for Jubal, his cold and cruel nature, her fear and mistrust of him, her absolute dependence upon him and his authority over her, and she worked within those boundaries to make of her life whatever she could.

With her strong, healthy constitution, she required little sleep and rest, and she always woke well before daylight and well before Jubal. His abuse of the day before had generated resentment that gnawed at the back of her mind as she woke, and she immediately pushed it out of her thoughts. Dwelling on it might make her prone to saying something she shouldn't again, and it would take him long enough to get over her anger from the day before. Jubal had turned toward her and was snoring heavily, and his breath was sour and still heavily laden with rum. Alcey pushed the cover aside and got out of bed.

Summer mornings were pleasant, usually cool and fresh, and sometimes almost chilly when an offshore breeze was strong and it was raining. The early morning was quiet, only the sounds of the insects and the occasional call of a night bird, and fireflies speckled the darkness beyond the windows. The fireplace filled the kitchen with a cheerful light, and the food cooking smelled appetizing. As day began breaking, the birds began calling and the animals in the stock pens stirred. Then Jubal arose.

His face was pale and he looked drawn and ill from the rum the night before. He washed and shaved at the washstand, ate his breakfast, and left without speaking. Alcey ate, washed the dishes and utensils and put them away, started rice and peas soaking in pans of water to cook later in the day, then began cleaning the house. The dust from the road, the wagonyard, and the open space between the houses and the main building always carried into the house when the ground was dry, and it was thick on the furniture and floors. The heavy timbers of the floors were rough and porous, with cracks that had opened as they seasoned, and they couldn't be kept as clean as those made of timbers that had been expertly finished and joined, polished by the footsteps of generations. When she finished cleaning, she gathered up dirty clothes and put them in a tub of soapy water to soak, then got ready to go to the office.

Hugh was in Jubal's office, going over some papers with him, and he looked up and greeted her cheerfully when she went in for the inventory ledger and the current stacks of bills of lading and sales statements. Jubal glanced up, then impatiently called Hugh's attention back to what they were discussing. Alcey stacked the bundles of bills and statements on the ledger, carried the ledger out to her desk, and began on the inventory.

The first few items on the inventory were in agreement with the ledger, then there were minor variances that she reconciled by leafing through the statements and bills, adjusting the amounts shown in the ledger by computing amounts received and sold. Then there was one she couldn't reconcile. The inventory showed four cases of five-pound ax heads, and the inventory ledger showed five. There had been two cases on the previous inventory. Bills and statements reflected that six more cases had been received and three had been sold, so there should have been five. She went back again to recheck it, and arrived at the same answer as before. She glanced over her shoulder at the doorway to Jubal's office, pondered for a moment, then went on to the next item on the inventory.

Jubal's voice became louder as he and Hugh came through the doorway into the outer office. ". . . tell him no more than six guineas per head, and see what he says. I doubt that he'll get more than seven anywhere in Wilmington, the way the market is at the moment."

"Aye, I believe you're right, Mr. Collier, and he might

take it, to be shot of all of them at one place. What shall I do about those beeves I put off to one side, then?"

"Call Wesley the butcher to have a look at them, and do it before they get down and can't get back up. If he'll pay five guineas each, then let him have them."

"Aye, I'll send someone to talk to him now, then," Hugh said, walking toward the door. "And I'll take care of that other, and let you know what he'll take."

Alcey looked at Jubal as he nodded to Hugh and started back toward his office. "There's an error somewhere in the stock or in the inventory on ax heads, Jubal. The inventory I have from Mr. Beasley shows four cases, and the inventory ledger shows five."

"What's this?" he said irritably.

"On five-pound ax heads the inventory shows a case less than should be on hand." She picked up the first stack of bills and began thumbing through them. "The last inventory showed two cases, here two more were received, and here another—"

"I've no time to muck through that," he snapped impatiently, turning toward the door at the side of the office. "I'll have a word with Beasley about it."

Jubal's footsteps faded along the hallway to the warehouse, and a moment later they returned, followed by Beasley's heavy tread. They came into the office.

"What's this about me stealing a case of ax heads?" Beasley laughed in a patronizing, somewhat nervous and overly hearty tone.

"I said nothing about anyone having stolen anything, Mr. Beasley," Alcey replied quietly, looking down at the ledger and annotating it. "I said there is a discrepancy between the inventory and inventory ledger on five-pound—"

"Well, bloody show it him!" Jubal barked. "We haven't all day to deal with this!"

Alcey jumped involuntarily from his loud tone, and she stiffened her hand to keep it from trembling as she put her quill in the slot by the inkwell. She sanded the wet ink on the open page, then turned the pages to where the ax heads were listed. "You see here, there were two cases on hand at the time of the last inventory." She picked up the first stack of bills and thumbed rapidly through them. "Here two more were received, another one here, and one here." She put the stack aside and picked up another one, leafing through it. "And here two more were received. Here are the sales statements, and they show one case was sold here, one here, and another in that lot there."

Beasley shuffled his feet and scratched his beard, looking at the stack of papers. "Does that make five, then?"

"Two plus six minus three is five," Jubal said. "So where are they? We just looked at them back there, and there were bloody four."

Beasley cleared his throat and shook his head, looking away. "I know naught about ledgers and such. All I know is . . ." He hesitated, thinking, and looked at Jubal. "Stop a minute. Didn't you tell Johnson to take a case of ax heads a week or two ago?"

Jubal frowned with thought, then nodded. "Aye, I did and all. That's it, then, isn't it?"

"By God, I should hope so," Beasley laughed in a relieved tone. "I was worried there for a moment, and that's no lie."

Alcey glanced at the stacks of papers and looked up at Jubal. "I don't have a receipt from the trading post."

Jubal shrugged, turning away. "Receipt or not, there's where it is. And it's naught to make such a fuss of, so mark the ledger and have done with it. A case of ax heads is a case of ax heads, and we don't need a receipt as long as we know where it is."

"Well, a case of ax heads in the warehouse becomes twelve ax heads in the trading post, and . . ." Her voice faded as he glared at her, color flooding into his face, and she turned and reached for her quill.

"Have done with it, I said!" Jubal shouted angrily, stalking toward her. "I said to mark the flaming ledger and be done with it. Now do as I bloody said!"

On the edge of her vision Alcey could see Beasley grinning widely, looking from Jubal to her. She pressed her lips together tightly. "Very well, Jubal."

"No, it's fucking not!" he stormed, snatching the quill from her hand, and he crushed it and threw it down. "It's not bloody——" He leaned closer, shouting at the top of his voice as he mocked her accent. "——very well! I'd be in a bleeding sad condition indeed if I needed some sauce to tell me how to conduct my flaming affairs! I have no need for advice from the likes of you, and I'll not—"

He broke off suddenly. Alcey was looking down at the ledger, struggling to block the awareness of his raging voice thundering in her ears. The doorway had darkened. She lifted her eyes. It was Santee.

Santee's features were neutral, the slightly withdrawn expression his features always assumed in repose. His darkly tanned face didn't look different from any other time, but at the same time it was entirely different. It looked as though it were carved from stone. The deep scar on his forehead and cheek was a lighter color against his tanned skin, and a muscle was moving in the side of his face.

A ghost of a wide smile of anticipation and greeting remained on Simon's small face, and his eyes were wide and round as he stood behind Santee, peering around his leg at Jubal with a frightened expression. Jubal straightened up and turned toward the door, clearing his throat with an embarrassed rasp. He made a subvocal sound as though he were going to say something, but he remained silent. Santee stepped into the room, his moccasins soundless on the floor, and the long fringes on his buckskin breeches and tunic swaying and rippling. He looked at Beasley.

"Leave."

His deep voice was quiet, almost soft, but somehow the impact of the single word was greater than Jubal's shouting had been. Beasley's face paled, and he glanced from Santee to Jubal, opening his mouth to object. Then he swallowed noisily, and walked rapidly to the door. Jubal cleared his throat again, and his attempt at a bantering tone was hollow and false as he spoke.

"What's this, then, Santee? Are you taking it upon yourself to come to my place and order my people about?"

Santee ignored him, taking out a buckskin purse as he stopped by Alcey's desk. The musky scent of his buckskins and the fresh scent of the sun and open fields eddied around him. The boy stood behind him, still looking apprehensively at Jubal. Jubal made an uncomfortable sound in his throat. Santee took two pennies out of the purse and put them on the desk.

"I'd be obliged if you'd take the boy to the trading post and get him a tuppence of sweets, Alcey."

Alcey rose and picked up the coins. The boy stepped from behind Santee, grinning up at her. Alcey felt the tension fading from her, a smile spreading on her face as she walked toward the door with him. They went through the doorway and along the hall toward the trading post, and she heard Jubal's voice rise in an aggravation. Santee's deep voice was a soft, penetrating rumble, cutting him off.

"Well, what have you been doing, Master Simon?"

"Getting my hair cut, getting swilled, getting shot of nitties, and getting fitted for new breeches and shirt that my grandma and Nina are sewing. My pa took me fishing this morning, and I caught a goodly lot. But he caught the biggest one."

His thin, cheerful voice chattered on as she led him into the trading post and through the crowded aisles to the counter. At the jars of sweets she gave him a piece of maple toffee, then she took the top off the jar of boiled sweets and began wrapping them in squares of greased paper stacked by the jars. Simon chewed the end of the toffee, still rattling on about what he had been doing. Alcey smiled and nodded absently, pondering about what had happened.

Wishful hope battled with dark, fearful apprehension in her mind. Help had materialized unexpectedly. It was obvious that Santee was angry over Jubal's treatment of her, and obviously that was what they were discussing. But there was a large and enormously important question as to whether Santee's involving himself would actually help her or make things much worse. Her father wouldn't have allowed Jubal to publicly humiliate and abuse her, and most fathers and brothers would similarly come to the assistance of female members of their family, but Jubal was legally within his rights, because what he had been doing would be defined by law as discipline, not mistreatment. Santee was putting himself in the position of a brother to her, and it was likely that Jubal was cautious enough of him that the public humiliation would stop. But Jubal would be furious and might wreak his anger on her in private. On the other hand Jubal might be afraid that she would tell Santee if he did. The situation had several ramifications, but it was deeply comforting to know that there was at least someone willing to help, when she had thought she was all alone, with only herself to depend upon.

She stayed in the trading post for several minutes talking with Simon, then led him back across the trading post and slowly along the hallway, listening. There was no sound of voices in the office, and she approached the door and looked in. Jubal was shuffling papers in his office, and Santee was standing on the porch outside the office, leaning against the railing and looking along the road. Alcey bent over Simon and kissed him, pressing the two pennies into his hand.

"Don't drop your sweets, Simon, and don't eat too many on the way home and give yourself a bad stomach. And here's tuppence for you as well, but don't show your father until you're well away."

His eyes were large as he looked at the two pennies and clutched them, grinning widely with delight. Alcey kissed him again and took his hand and led him across the office toward the doorway. She looked at Jubal from the corner of her eye as he came into her line of vision, but his face was averted and she couldn't see his expression. Santee turned away from the rain and stepped across the porch to the door.

"Aye, there's a nice lot and all, isn't it? Did you thank Mistress Collier? You did? Come along, then. Good day, Alcey."

His smile was courteous, and there was nothing in his expression or eyes that indicated the outcome of the conversation between him and Jubal. And she didn't know whether to consider that promising or ominous. She forced a smile and nodded. "Good day, Santee."

Santee walked toward the corner of the porch, where his horse was tethered, and Simon looked back and grinned as he followed. Alcey smiled and waved to Simon, then turned away from the door and walked back to her desk. She picked up the broken quill from the floor, dropped it into the wicker refuse basket by her desk, then sat down and took another quill from the recess in the side of her desk.

The sound of Santee's horse moving away from the building came through the window, and the hoofbeats faded into other noises outside. She trimmed the end of the quill into a point, her tension and nervousness mounting as she waited breathlessly to see what Jubal was going to do or say. Papers rustled in his office, and there was an occasional sound of movement, his chair squeaking or his foot moving on the floor. Alcey put the knife down, looked at the inventory for where she had left off, and began working on it again.

Jubal's chair scraped on the floor. Alcey's hand jerked convulsively, and she lifted the point of the quill just in time to keep from dragging it on the paper and leaving a blob of ink. His footsteps moved away from his desk and through the doorway into the front office. Alcey swallowed dryly, dipping the point of the quill and wiping it on the lip of the inkwell, then she concentrated on the entry she had been making in the ledger. Her hand trembled violently. She stiffened her hand. He passed her desk, looking at a piece of paper, walked out onto the porch, and turned toward the loading dock. Alcey drew in a deep breath, released it in a soundless sigh of relief, and began writing again.

When the sun began to approach its zenith, Alcey went back to the house. The peas and rice were beginning to soften, and she built up the fire, put them on to cook, then went out onto the porch and stirred the clothes she had left soaking in soapy water. She came back in, took out the leftover beans and bread from the day before and heated them, and began cutting up strips of salt pork to fry. Her nervousness began mounting again as she wondered if Jubal had been waiting for privacy to vent his anger.

Jubal came in while she was still cooking. Before having to wait for his meal had always brought at least an acid remark or two, but he only glared at her silently, sat down at the table, and took some papers from his coat pocket and looked through them as he waited. She put the food on the table, and he silently ate and left. The tension had taken away her appetite, but she choked down a few bites. She cleaned up and used the leftover meat from the day before to make a stew to cook during the afternoon. Then the food she had eaten made her feel nauseated.

Drays from the port were unloading at the warehouse dock when she returned to the office. Beasley and a driver argued over a bill of lading in loud, profane voices, the laborers from the warehouse and workmen from the port cursed hoarsely as they strained with bales and crates, heavy hogsheads rumbled across the dock as they were rolled into the warehouse, and Jubal's voice was audible through the uproar as he talked to someone on the dock. Alcey began working on the inventory again. The noise on the dock diminished, a whip cracked and the driver shouted, and the wheels on the dray squeaked as it moved away from the dock. Another dray moved up to the dock, and the noise began again.

There was a movement in the doorway, and Alcey glanced up. It was Hannah, Alcey put her quill down and rose, smiling with pleasure. "Mrs. Bledsoe! How good it is to see you again!"

Hannah's wrinkled face was wreathed in a smile as she walked in. Her gray hair was pulled back in a bun so tightly that the skin on her forehead looked taut, she was in a shapeless, faded, spotlessly clean homespun dress with an openwork shawl around her shoulders. "Aye, it's good to see you again and all, love. Are you keeping well?"

"Very well indeed, thank you. Here, have a seat here, if you would. Would you care for some refreshment? I believe there's some small beer in the trading post."

"No, but I'm obliged, love. And I'll just stand, if it's all the same. I was down this way with Caleb, and I thought I'd stop in and see you while Caleb's having a word with Jubal."

"I'm delighted you did. How is Nina?"

"Oh, she's well, and she sends her best. And I'll tell her you were asking after her." Hannah cleared her throat, her smile becoming tentative. "Caleb's having a word with Jubal about dinner on Sunday."

Alcey blinked, puzzled. "Dinner on Sunday?"

"Aye, well, Santee mentioned that he'd spoken with Jubal, and that they had agreed we were all past times getting to know each other better, seeing as how we're family and right close to each other. And Santee allowed that you and Jubal might be over to dinner on Sunday."

"How lovely!" Alcey gasped with delight. "Jubal hasn't mentioned it to me because he's quite busy today, but I'm pleased beyond measure."

Hannah's smile became wide again, and she nodded.

"Aye, then I'm happy you're pleased, love. You know how these men are—they go at everything like a hog in a corn crib and never think to ask a woman her mind, and a right pickle they make of things at times."

Alcey looked at her, puzzling over what she had said, and shook her head. "But did you contemplate that I might think anything else? Mercy, I couldn't be more pleased."

Hannah nodded again, her smile softening. "I wasn't sure what to think, love. We're plain folk, and I know that you have much to do with your time, mayhap things that give you more pleasure than having to do with us lot. But now I see that—"

"But how could you think so poorly of me? Of course I've nothing to do that would give me more pleasure than to—"

"No, no, I didn't think poorly of you, love," Hannah chuckled, patting Alcey's arm. "I didn't think poorly of you at all. All I'm saying is that when I'm in a woods I've never been through before, I watch where I put my feet. And it's rare that the likes of us have to do with people of proper quality such as yourself, you know. So when Caleb had asked Jubal to bring you to the cabin and Jubal has allowed his business was pressing him, we've let it go at that. But Jubal lets his business weigh on his mind overmuch and we all know that, so I'll own fault for not setting it aright and getting to know you better by just coming here and taking you away, if by no other means. And I'll do my best to repair my end of it from now, so let's leave it at that."

"And so shall I," Alcey replied, smiling warmly and putting an arm around Hannah's shoulders. She squeezed her fondly and kissed her cheek. "Moreover I'll be looking forward to Sunday as I have nothing before."

"As I will, love," Hannah said, holding her and patting her. She sighed and moved away, turning toward the door. "Well, I'll get back out before Caleb starts looking for me and . . ." She hesitated and turned back, her smile fading. "No, there's one thing yet I've overlooked saying. It's much on my mind that you're a gentle girl with no proper family here of your own. If you've ever a mind to visit someone, it would please me no ends to have you visit me." Her eyes looked straight into Alcey's, her wrinkled features unsmiling. "And stay as long as you've a mind to."

The old woman's voice was firm, and her face was stern, in rigid lines of an offended sense of right and wrong. Santee had talked to her. Gratitude swelled within Alcey, and a choking feeling formed in her throat. She smiled and nodded, kissing Hannah again. "You're very kind. And I'm very grateful."

"Aye, well, it's something that needed to be said, and it's been said," Hannah replied, patting Alcey again, and she turned back toward the door. "Well, I'll get back on out and see if Caleb's finished talking with Jubal, and then I'll see what the boy Simon's into now. It takes me and Nina both to keep track of him, and we need two extra arms apiece when it comes time to scrub him."

"Isn't he a lovely child, though," Alcey sighed, following Hannah to the door. "He's so pretty, and such a friendly child."

"Aye, he's a sweet nipper, for all the trouble he is." Hannah chuckled wryly, shaking her head. "That rascal Santee. I'd have at him with a fence rail over that business if I could stand on a ladder and lift a fence rail at the same time. That scamp has been into one thing or another all his life. Raising that pair of boys has put the gray hairs in this head and moved me to the edge of my grave, no fear." She stopped in the doorway, looking into the distance with a musing expression and shaking her head again. "I thought that Santee was going to be the death of me, what with his high spirits and hot temper, you know. But he's got a handful of himself so that he's not one part in ten as mean as he used to be, even though it's still a good idea to stay out of his road when he's got his wind up. Jubal was never a bit rowdy or trouble of that sort, but he . . ." Her voice faded, then she blinked and smiled brightly at Alcey as she stepped out onto the porch. "I'll be on my way, then. And I'll see you again on Sunday, love."

"I'll be looking forward to it. Thank you so much, Mrs. Bledsoe. Thank you for everything."

"You're more than welcome, love. Good day."

"Good day, Mrs. Bledsoe."

Alcey walked back to her desk and sat down, feeling weak with relief. The situation had turned out far better than her wildest hopes. The possibility of help from Santee had turned into direct and effective help from the entire family. Jubal's foster parents had always been somewhat diffident toward him, but they wouldn't permit what they considered mistreatment of a wife. Santee had talked to them, and their response had been immediate. They were drawing her into the family, making her one of them. And for the first time since she had come to Wilmington, life had a cheerful glow about it. Tears of happiness welled up in her eyes, and she blinked them away as she reached for her quill.

Jubal's footsteps came along the porch, hard and heavy. Alcey glanced up as he came in the door. His face was flushed and his lips were a tight, thin line. He stamped across the office and into his office. The rum bottle rattled against the cups as he snatched it from the shelf, and rum gurgled into a cup. He slammed the bottle back on the shelf and sat down heavily in his chair, gulping a drink of the rum. He sighed heavily and made a sound of disgust in his throat, taking another drink. A moment passed, then his chair scraped against the floor as he pushed it back. He slammed the cup back on the shelf and stamped out of his office. He passed without glancing at her, going out the door toward the dock.

The sounds of the drays unloading continued, then they stopped and the last dray squeaked and rattled away. Jubal came back in and went into his office. He poured himself another drink of rum, sat down at his desk, and papers rustled as he shuffled through them. Alcey continued working on the inventory, turning the pages in the ledger and leafing through the bills and statements. Beasley's footsteps came along the hall. He came into the office, crossed it to Alcey's desk, and put a stack of papers on her desk.

"Here are the bills from the loads we got today, Mistress Collier."

His tone was slyly sarcastic, and he remained standing by her desk. The sweaty, unwashed stench of his body swirled around her, and she knew he was looking down at her with a sneer, waiting to see if she would notice him. She pursed her lips, thinking, then looked up at him from the corners of her eyes.

"Beasley, I shall not tolerate further impudence from you," she said in a clear, ringing voice. "Kindly take yourself out of here, and do not return until you learn how to conduct yourself in a fitting manner."

Beasley's mouth dropped open in consternation, and he backed away from her desk, looking from her to the door of Jubal's office as Jubal's chair scraped on the floor and his footsteps came to the door.

"What's this?" Jubal barked irritably.

"It's naught, Mr. Collier," Beasley stammered in confusion. "I fear that Mistress Collier might have misunderstood, and I meant no impudence and meant to conduct myself—"

"Well, see that you bloody do!"

"Aye, I shall, Mr. Collier," Beasley said, nodding rapidly and walking toward the door. "I certainly shall, Mr. Collier. Aye, I shall . . ."

He went through the doorway and along the hall, still nodding and stammering. Alcey dipped the point of her quill and wiped it on the lip of the inkwell, looking back down at the ledger. Jubal stepped back to his desk, then came out of his office and crossed the outer office toward the door to the hallway, carrying a piece of paper. He stopped in the doorway and turned, looking at Alcey.

"And you don't go getting on any bloody high horse, you! If you try that with me, you'll find what it gets you soon enough."

His tone lacked the firm note of confidence of before. He was angry, but it was resentful rather than furious. There had been a subtle shift in their relationship. His authority was no longer absolute. Alcey lifted her quill and rolled it in her fingers, looking at the point. He had made sarcastic remarks and mocked her accent from time to time. indicating that her accent irritated him. She replied in her most pear-shaped tones.

"Indeed I shan't, Jubal."

He grunted, turning away. "You'll bloody see that you don't, if you're wise."

"While we are discussing matters pertaining to me, I might mention that I shall require a few bits of fabric from the trading post to make another odd garment or two. And perhaps something to wear while I'm at work here, to protect my sleeves and bodices from the dust of the road that collects."

"How much is all that going to take?"

She picked up the knife and scraped at a burr on the side of the point on the quill, then put the knife down and turned her head slightly, pursing her lips. "I will look through the fabrics, select a few bits, and let you know."

The paper he was holding rustled as his hand tightened on it, his face flushed, and he glared at her. Then he wheeled, went through the doorway, and stamped heavily along the hall. Alcey looked at the point on the quill again, then glanced out the doorway and across the porch. A wagon was moving along the road, dust boiling up from its wheels, and a fine haze of dust was drifting into the office. The breeze had died away, and the heat of the afternoon was approaching, humid and stifling. But it seemed a very bright and cheerful day. She dipped the point of the quill and looked down at the ledger with a satisfied smile as she began writing again.

# Chapter Fourteen

Dust hung over the road as carriages, chaises, wagons, and groups on horseback moved along it. There was a distinctive atmosphere of Sunday afternoon, a relaxed feeling of anticipation of enjoyment and entertainment. Souls cleansed by prayer and sermon, and consciences stilled by substantial offerings in the poor box, people were seeking respite between the toil and pressures of the week past and those of the week to come.

In Cheltenham oldsters had gathered on the benches under the oaks on the common to reminisce, while the edge of the common had served as a promenade for the nubile to display their beauty and new Watteau gowns, and for the handsome to display their wit, strength, and agility. In Wilmington all who could streamed out of the town toward the beach. Young couples chattered, laughed, and called to friends in other carriages, mothers snapped at their children and smacked small hands trying to pry into baskets of food, fathers sat in detached isolation from the uproar of their offspring around them and guided their wagons around rough spots in the road. Young men raced their high-spirited horses along the edge of the road, and the wealthy and powerful exhibited the trappings of their station. Families who lived in tiny, rude cabins along the road sat on rough benches in front of their cabins and munched watermelon and cantaloupe, gazing at the parade passing a few yards away.

Jubal turned off onto a narrow road, jerking the traces and making the horse toss its head. The narrow road was hardly more than a path along the side of a pasture enclosed by a rail fence, but it was less rutted than the main road and the chaise rocked with a gentle swaying motion as the horse trotted along. Alcey brushed at the dust on her

dress, looking ahead. There was a pigsty in the corner of
the pasture, a thin scattering of trees between the pasture
and a large tilled area, then stock pens, outbuildings, and
the cabin. Santee and Simon were behind the cabin, tossing
horseshoes at a stake in the ground. Simon was in conspic-
uously new homespun trousers and shirt, a band of linen
was around his neck in the form of a cravat, the dirt on his
face looked fresh, and he was barefoot. Santee looked enormous beside the small boy, his buckskins a rich tan with
bright lines of beading, and his white teeth gleamed against
the darkness of his tanned face as he said something laughingly to the boy and ruffled his hair. A dog ran toward the
chaise, barking excitedly, and Santee called it back. Jubal
snapped the reins to make the horse run the last few steps so
he could pull up sharply.

"Good-day. That's a fine-looking horse, Jubal."

"Aye, I had him off a man who brought him from Virginia, but don't get your eye on him. You don't have anything that'll trade for him."

"I'm sure I don't, but I think I'll stay with my Chickasaws all the same." He took Alcey's arm, handing her
down from the chaise. "How are you today, Alcey?"

"I'm very well, Santee, thank you. How are you?"

"Very well, thank you. Simon, show your aunt around to
the door. I'll give you a hand with the harness, Jubal, if
you'd like to turn your horse into the pen for a bite of corn
and a rest."

"No, we're not stopping for the night, you know. I'll just
take him out of the shafts and tie him over there."

Alcey bent over Simon and kissed him as he grinned up
at her, and she took his hand as they walked toward the
cabin. "How are you, Master Simon? You look very handsome in your cravat."

He grimaced and pulled at the band of linen around his
neck. "Grandma put it on me, and it's choking me to
death. We've apple pie to eat after dinner."

"Indeed? That sounds delicious. What have you been
doing, then?"

"I went to church this morning with Grandma and Nina,
and Grandma pinched me when I went to sleep. And then
I got leathered for eating a dish of berries that Grandma
had put by for something or other. . . ."

Alcey smiled down at him as he rattled on, and she glanced around as they walked along the side of the cabin. The bare ground by the cabin had been broomed, patterns of lines showing in the dirt, the chickens had been chased away, and the wood pile was meticulously neat. The gleam of the estuary was visible through the trees on the slope between the cabin and the edge of the tide flat, and a fresh, cool breeze was blowing in from the Cape.

"Aye, I thought I heard someone," Hannah chuckled as she came out of the cabin. She put her arms around Alcey and patted her, then pulled her toward the cabin and pointed her finger at Simon. "Come on in, love. And you stay away from this door, you scamp. I've not forgotten what you did, and you're liable to get another hiding yet." She smiled wryly at Alcey, shaking her head. "I had a bowl of dewberries all sugared and ready to put in a pie, and that scamp got into them and ate every last one. It would have made me so bad in my stomach that I would have been in bed for a week, but it didn't even make him belch. I don't know what I'm going to do with that boy. Come on in, love. Nina, Alcey's here."

Nina turned away from the fireplace as they entered, a beaming smile on her smooth, brown face, and she walked toward Alcey. "How are you, Alcey?"

Alcey put her arms around Nina and kissed her damp cheek. "Very well, thank you, Nina. How are you?"

"Hot, hot," Nina laughed, plucking at her heavy, home-spun dress. "You look nice and pretty."

"Thank you, but I fear I'm in disrepair after the road. I do believe everyone in Wilmington is abroad today, and the dust was choking."

"Aye, it does get dusty," Hannah said. "We get it all the way down here to the cabin on some Sundays, when the wind is right. Here, you sit down on this bench by the door, love, where you can get a breath of air."

"Oh, no, I'm sure there's something I can do to help, and I'd much rather do that than—"

"No, it's about all done, love. I'm just waiting for Caleb to bring up a fresh crock of buttermilk from the spring-house so I can mix up a batch of . . . oh, here he is now. They're here, Caleb."

His baggy homespuns were fresh and clean, his shirt was

buttoned to the throat, his heavy shoes were glistening with blacking, and he looked somewhat hot and uncomfortable in a shapeless tweed coat. He stepped carefully over the threshold with a large earthenware jar, favoring his right foot, and his eyes twinkled above his thick, white beard and moustache as he smiled at Alcey and nodded to her. "Aye, I heard them. How are you, Alcey?"

"I'm very well, thank you. How are you, Mr. Bledsoe?"

"Well, I might live until supper if I can find somewhere to put this crock down."

"Here, put it right here," Hannah said, taking another earthenware jar off a stand in the corner. "You know where it goes as well as I do."

"I know that every time I find out where things go, you change them back to front," he grunted, lifting the jar and sliding it onto the stand. "Hand me down that rum and some cups, and me and the boys will have a sip while we're waiting."

"Aye, all right, but don't sip so much that you can't find the door to get back in. You know how rum sets to your head lately."

"It set to it a lot worse when I was twenty, so hand me the bottle and don't worry about my head and me finding the door. I've found my way across miles of wilderness. Santee's better at it than I ever thought of being, so between us we ought to be able to find the door. Just hand me the bottle."

Their banter was cheerful, laughing, affectionate. Hannah pushed at his shoulder fondly as she handed him the bottle and cups, and he winked at Alcey as he walked toward the door with them. The interior of the cabin was unpretentious, with primitive, homemade tables, benches, and stools that were smooth and shiny with age and use, but the atmosphere in it was precious.

Hannah took Alcey's arm and led her to a bench just inside the door. "Now you just sit down there, love, and we can all talk while Nina and I are finishing up here. And let me prop this door a little wider so you can get a breath of air."

"If you wish," Alcey said as she sat down on the bench. "But I do feel helpless, just sitting while others are working."

"It's past times you had a rest, love, because I know you work harder than most." She crossed the room to a table and began stirring the contents in a mixing bowl. "Have you settled to where you like it here, now? I know it must be hard on you, with it being so different from England."

"Oh, it's quite different from Cheltenham, of course, but I've accustomed myself to it and I've come to like it very much."

"It's Chatham you're from, then? Aye, I don't recall that it was mentioned when we've talked before."

"Cheltenham," Alcey said slowly.

"Cheltenham, is it? Give me no mind, love, because I'm so accustomed to hearing the lot I usually have around me that I can't understand proper English. Are you plagued still with the sickness that new people get?"

"No, I was ill for only a short time after I arrived, and I haven't been again. I'm blessed with good health."

"Aye, I can see that, love. And you want to protect it, because it's a precious gift. They say that carrying a bag of asafetida around the neck will help, but I daresay that's as many things one hears . . ."

The three men and Simon passed across Alcey's line of vision as Hannah continued talking, and Alcey glanced at them. They sat down on a rough bench under an oak a few yards in front of the cabin, and the old man handed cups to Santee and Jubal and poured rum into them. Their voices were a distant murmur as they talked. Jubal talked mostly to the old man, his features in the vaguely dissatisfied lines that was his neutral expression, and he sat the way he usually did, his legs tightly crossed and his shoulders bowed, looking drawn into himself. By contrast Santee was relaxed on the bench, his feet out in front of him, taking the room needed to accommodate his large, powerful frame. The way he sat showed a disregard for social niceties, too much of a sprawl for those schooled in parlor manners, but it also had the freedom, lack of restraint, and animal grace of the way he walked. Simon had brought him a leather ball stuffed with flax, and he was repairing a seam on it as he smiled at the boy and talked to him.

Hannah and Nina finished the cooking and put the food on the table, and Hannah went to the window and called the men and boy in. The old man and Hannah sat on stools

at the head and foot of the table, and Alcey sat with Jubal
on a bench at one side, across from Santee, Simon, and
Nina. Some of the pewter plates and spoons looked new, as
though they had been bought for the occasion. The old
man murmured a brief prayer, then there was a flurry of
motion, dishes being passed, laughter and conversation,
and Hannah smacking at Simon's hand as he snatched at
things. Fine china, linen serviettes and tablecloth, and silver utensils would have clashed with the atmosphere in the
cabin, and the lack of it failed to detract from the meal.
The food was abundant and delicious: a white, flaky fish
steamed and soaking in hot butter; a pork joint roasted on
the spit until it was tender and its crust of molasses, cloves,
and pepper was crisp; sweet potatoes glazed with maple
sugar; potatoes fried with onions; a wide variety of vegetables well seasoned and spiced; cornbread; and cups of buttermilk.

The differences between Jubal and the rest of the family
were highlighted in the conversation around the table. Jubal remarked on the propensity that King George III was
showing over his predecessor for personal rule and control
of the government ministry, a subject of intense interest to
many. Hannah was only politely interested, Santee was totally disinterested, Nina didn't know what Jubal was talking about, and the old man seemed confused about who
was king. The conversation moved on to the growing resistance of some of the settlers in the Piedmont and areas
farther west to tax collectors, surveyors, and other government officials, and there was a direct clash of opinion. Jubal characterized those who were resisting as an unruly
mob in opposition to the lawful force of government. The
old man disagreed, of the opinion that the government officials were arbitrary and unfair in many instances, and he
observed that he would move elsewhere if he were in the
position of some settlers. Santee commented that if he were
in that situation, he would pay his tax through the barrel of
his rifle. Jubal became indignant, and Hannah broke up the
conversation as it started to turn into an argument by going
to the hearth and bringing back a large apple pie for des-
sert.

After the meal, the men and boy went back outside, and
Alcey rolled up her sleeves and insisted on helping clean

up. Hannah limited the cleaning up to putting leftover food away and stacking the dishes, and they took one of the benches from the side of the table to carry it out to the shade of the tree where the men were sitting. Simon was slumped in the crook of Santee's arm, comfortably full and dozing, and Santee stirred him, rose from the bench, and stepped to the cabin to take the bench from Alcey, Hannah, and Nina as they came out the door with it. It wasn't a show of strength, and Hannah and Nina seemed to expect it of him, but it was impossible not to notice the way he carried the heavy bench without apparent effort, the only indication of strain a tightening of the shoulders of his tunic. He put the bench down facing the one under the tree, pressed the legs into the soft ground so it wouldn't rock, and sat down, smiling at Simon and pulling him closer again.

The breeze had freshened, birds chattered in the trees, chickens clucked lazily in the brush down the hill, and the whirring of cicadas was a rising and falling drone. The shade under the tree was deep, and there was a feeling of privacy. The sounds from the other cabins were muffled by the screen of trees, and the rattle of tackle and shouts of sailors on a ship moving up the estuary were distant and thin.

"This is very pleasant here, isn't it?" Alcey commented. "It has the aspect of a private garden."

Hannah nodded, fanning the collar of her dress and wiping sweat from her brow with her sleeve. "Aye, Nina and I sit here often of an afternoon, don't we, Nina? The breeze is nice after the heat of the cabin."

"And all the trees about make it restful. I've always enjoyed greenery about me."

"Shall I plant you some trees about the house, then?" Jubal commented sourly. "You'll have a wait for that."

"There's nothing wrong with having a tree to sit under," Hannah said firmly. "And one should have leisure to collect one's wits now and again."

"And I have more need of room to park and move my wagons about than I have for trees," Jubal replied, shrugging, then looked at Santee. "I fail to understand why you want to go to this place you're talking about. You've been catching all your horses will carry where you've been going."

"I'll load them with nothing but beaver and otter," Santee replied.

Jubal snorted in disbelief and shook his head. "Then we'll see you again come Saint Geoffrey's."

Santee shrugged nonchalantly. "If I can't get the beaver and otter, then I'll take deerskins."

"You may get all the beaver and otter you want, and then some," the old man said drowsily, yawning. "But you'll see all the Indians than it'll take to satisfy you, and on that I've no doubt."

"Are you onto *Kenta-ke* again, Santee?" Hannah sighed. "Son, my heart stands in my mouth all the time you're gone to the places you've been going. Why can't you be satisfied with going there?"

"The catch of the furs and hides is far from the end of it, Hannah," the old man chuckled. "The going is half of it, and more. You know that."

"Well, I know that," Hannah replied morosely. "With a husband whose feet couldn't rest until he was far past the age when they should have been warming on the hearth of a winter, and a son who's far and gone worse than you ever thought of being, well I know that."

"Where are you talking about?" Alcey asked.

"*Kenta-ke*," Santee replied. "It's south of the Ohio, and far to the west of the mountains west of here. A few traders and hunters have been there, but not many and not much is known about it. It's said that the trapping and hunting there are far better than anywhere else."

"What is it like in the wilderness?"

Santee looked away with a musing expression, then smiled slightly and shook his head. "It's hard to tell someone about it."

"I've talked with aplenty who had no difficulty telling about it," Jubal said. "Mountains, rivers, trees beyond counting, and a bloody Indian behind every tree waiting to scalp the first white man who comes along. We're past times dealing with that lot so the settlers can grow their crops, tend their animals, and conduct their commerce in peace."

"We'd be well on the way to dealing with them if we

dealt with our own," Santee said quietly. "About three years ago a group of Cherokee who had been fighting with Colonel Washington against the French and their Indians were on their way back to their village, and they were waylaid in Virginia by some white men. It's not hard to understand why most of the Cherokee are against us after that, and any settler who is attacked by the Cherokee can thank those in Virginia as much as the French."

"That's strange talk, considering what I've seen hanging on your belt," Jubal laughed dryly. "And they were probably mistaken for hostile Indians, with all the trouble that's been going on."

"I'll fight when I'm attacked, and I'll leave those alone who leave me alone," Santee replied. "And they weren't mistaken for hostile Indians. They were killed to get the thirty guinea bounty that's paid in Virginia for Indian scalps. There are many Indians who won't live in peace with anyone, white or Indian, and there are a lot of whites who are the same. If we can ever get shot of that lot, Indian and white, then we'll be well off. And if we can ever have an end to the trouble between England and France, then we'll be far better off than we are now."

"All this talk of killing," Hannah sighed. "This is the Lord's day, we're all together to enjoy each other's company, we've had a good meal, and we've the promise of many more. Let's dwell on what we have to be thankful for, not killing."

"I agree," Jubal said. "But I have so much work undone that I can scarcely think of anything else. That was a most enjoyable meal and this has been a pleasant respite, but we'll have to leave directly."

"Stop awhile, Jubal," Hannah said plaintively. "We've hardly had a chance to talk to Alcey, we've not seen you for a long time, and there's a watermelon cooling in the springhouse for later."

"Aye, stop awhile," the old man said, shaking off some of his drowsiness as he looked at Jubal. "This is the first time you've brought Alcey to see your ma and Nina, and they want to visit. And to that end it'll be good that we'll all be seeing each other every Sunday from now on."

Jubal frowned and moved irritably on the bench. "I don't trap in season or grow crops by the sign of the moon, you know. My work continues at all times, regardless of the season or weather."

The old man's grizzled eyebrows drew together. "Aye, well, leave then, if you must," he said flatly. "I'll see that Alcey gets home safely and before dark."

There was an instant of stiff, strained silence. Jubal flushed, and Santee looked away, smothering a smile. Hannah cleared her throat to say something, the old man glanced at her, and she remained silent. The old man looked back at Jubal, frowning. Jubal shrugged, his face flushed and his lips tight with aggravation. "I didn't say we were leaving now."

The old man's frown disappeared, and he nodded amiably as he yawned and looked away. "That's right, stop awhile, Jubal."

"Aye, we don't see enough of you, Jubal," Hannah said placatingly. "Since you moved out, we've seen hardly anything of you. I know it plagues you to be doing nothing, but you should rest now and again for the good of your body." She looked at Alcey, smiling brightly. "That's the way both of these boys have been all their life—always doing something. That Santee has never been able to bear having a hill in front of him that he hasn't climbed, and Jubal has never been able to leave a bit of work undone."

"It's their Dutchman's blood," the old man murmured, then chuckled. "Not a mark like me. I could stop until grass grows up around me as long as I didn't get hungry or something didn't step on me."

"Caleb!" Hannah laughed scoffingly. "You know that's not so even as you say it, because there's never been a lazy bone in your body. But you're right that it's the boys' blood that makes them how they are."

The old man nodded and yawned, stroking his beard. Silence fell, a silence with a hint of stiffness from Jubal's annoyance as he looked down at the ground with a discomfited frown. Santee looked down at Simon and tickled him, and Simon whimpered sleepily, pushing at Santee's hand. Nina clicked her tongue and shook her head at Santee as she rose, and she gathered up the boy with an effort and sat back down, cuddling him on her lap. Simon nestled against her, settling himself comfortably, and Nina hummed tunelessly as she rocked back and forth with him. Alcey looked at Simon, then at Nina, and they exchanged a smile. Alcey became conscious that the old man's eyes were on her, studying her thoughtfully.

"Were you a schoolmistress in England, then, Alcey?" he said musingly.

"No, sir. I was some years short of the age most head-mistresses require for their staff, and . . . well, I wasn't quite old enough."

"Whatever are you thinking of, Caleb?" Hannah chuckled. "She's but a girl now, so she could hardly have been a schoolmistress in England, could she?"

He smiled at Alcey. "But you know enough to be one, don't you?"

"Well . . . that would depend on the school and the requirements of the position. I could deal with grammar school and some forms in a girl's day school, but my qualifications in foreign languages aren't up to the requirements for instruction in the advanced forms of a girl's day school."

He nodded slowly, stroking his beard. "Do you opine that Collier is a Dutchman's name?"

Alcey hesitated. Jubal had impatiently brushed aside her questions about his and Santee's birth, but there had been mention several times that their mother had been Dutch among the sketchy details she'd heard. And she'd had strong doubts about it. They didn't look typically Dutch, and Collier obviously wasn't a Dutch name. But there had also been mention of possessions of their mother's with the name on it, which was reasonable, or they would have been named Bledsoe. And the confusion over nationality could be a matter of terms. During her time in the Colony she had found that English colonists with poor or no education, which included most of them, ordinarily referred to Germans as Dutch because of a misunderstanding over the German word *Deutsch*, and it wasn't unknown for English colonists to refer to foreigners in general as Dutch. She'd heard that Jubal's and Santee's mother had died within hours of being rescued, so if the woman had been unconscious and had been wearing clothing that looked foreign to the Bledsoes, they could be referring to her as Dutch in either a general or a specific sense. Alcey felt uncomfortable because of the suddenness of the question. She still wasn't completely at ease with the family, and she wanted to make a good impression. Hannah seemed perturbed, squirming on the bench and making subvocal sounds in her throat. It was clearly a time for tact.

"As the name of a person from Holland, do you mean, sir?"

The old man nodded again, still stroking his beard. "Aye."

Alcey hesitated again, thinking rapidly, then nodded. "I wouldn't consider it at all remarkable. The name would be originally English, I believe, but that could be readily explained. A large number of Royalists fled to Holland in 1649 or thereabouts, great numbers of Separatists went to Holland some years before that, and there have been other instances when English took up residence in Holland for one reason or another. I have no direct knowledge on the matter, but I wouldn't be at all surprised if there were any number of people in Holland, good Dutchmen all, who have English names from English forebears."

"Now there's an intelligent girl," Hannah said in a pleased voice, patting Alcey's shoulder. "Mercy, how quickly all that came from behind those pretty eyes. And she knows the times, the names of those who went, and all, doesn't she?"

"Aye, she does and all," the old man agreed, smiling at Alcey.

Hannah chuckled and patted Alcey's shoulder again. "If I had the burden of the hundredth part of what she knows, I'd have brain fever, and there's God's truth."

"If more than the hundredth part of what she knows was of benefit to man or beast, I'd be well off," Jubal said sourly, glancing at Alcey and looking away.

Silence fell, his tone chilling the congenial atmosphere. Alcey controlled the aggravation that sprang to quick life within her, keeping her pleasant half-smile in place. "My father took the view that education serves its own purpose. Accordingly many of my studies were on matters of no direct and immediate utility."

"Which was utter nonsense," Jubal snorted scornfully.

"Aye, you may be right," the old man said quietly, looking at Jubal and frowning slightly again. "You may be." He turned his head and looked at Alcey, his frown

disappearing and his eyes smiling. "But again you may be
wrong. It may be a matter that could be judged in different
ways, depending on who's doing the judging. If I understand Alcey rightly, that is. She has a precious way of
speaking that's a pleasure to hear, but now and again I'm
left floundering as to what she meant. But if I understood
rightly, I've done the same thing. From time to time I've
ventured a good way with no other purpose than going,
and never a thought of a hide or pelt at the end of the trip.
That might have been nonsense, but it suited me. And the
moccasins and horses I was wearing out belonged to me. If
what she knows satisfies her as well as my ventures satisfied me, then who's to call it wrong? And I'm well pleased
to have someone in the family as learned as she is."

"Aye, we all are," Hannah said. "Alcey, I've had in
mind getting some roses and making an arbor just down
the hill there. That would be nice, wouldn't it?"

"Indeed it would. And the smell of roses always makes a
place to sit more pleasant and refreshing."

"Aye, I like flowers. Last year I scraped out some flower
beds up by the cabin there to plant a few, but the chickens
couldn't wait until I was back in the cabin to dig up the
seeds and eat them, then they made dust wallows in the
beds."

Alcey laughed at the wry note of humor in Hannah's
voice. Silence fell again, Jubal's displeasure and impatience
to be gone serving as a damper on the mood of the gathering. Simon was snoring on Nina's lap, sprawled across her
as she strained to hold him up, and Hannah sat forward
and looked at him.

"Nina, that boy's going to break your arms, trying to
hold him up that way. Put him on the ground, and let him
. . . no, give him here. I need to go in and make sure the
fire's banked properly, and I'll take him in and put him on
the bed."

The old man looked at Hannah as she rose and bent
over Nina, gathering Simon into her arms. "Bring out that
Bible that belonged to the boys' mother and let Alcey have
a look at it, Hannah."

Hannah frowned, shaking Simon impatiently as he
squirmed sleepily and almost fell from her arms. She
looked at the old man, hesitated, then cleared her throat. "I

don't know as I could put my hand on it without searching, Caleb. Let's just—"

"It's right in the top of the trunk in the corner of the bedroom. I saw it there when I was working on the latch on that trunk a month or two ago."

Hannah started to say something and hesitated again, then turned toward the cabin. "I'll have a look for it, then."

The old man nodded, stroking his beard and looking away. Nina rubbed her arms and smiled wryly at Alcey. Jubal sighed heavily and moved his feet. The sun was starting to incline to the west, and the surface of the water in the estuary was catching its rays and reflecting them through the trees with a brilliant gleam.

"We made out her name to be Sheila," said the old man. He was looking at Alcey musingly, studying her face.

She nodded. "Yes, sir. That was what I understood."

"I've always thought it would be good for one of the boys to name a daughter after her when they had one."

"Yes, sir. That would seem to be very appropriate."

Jubal moved his feet again. Santee sat motionless, totally relaxed, at the same time gathered and poised, immediately ready to move. The light coming through the trees from the estuary gradually became brighter, and dappled bright spots swam on the ground and in the foliage from the reflections off dancing waves. Hannah's footsteps returned from the cabin, and Alcey turned and smiled at her as she sat down on the bench.

"Well, here it is, love. And a pretty thing it is and all, just like that poor girl was . . ."

She was nervous and trying to conceal it. Alcey glanced at her again, puzzled, and looked down at the Bible as she put it on her lap. It was a beautiful book, richly bound in expensive leather. It was in elaborate German Gothic type, each letter bristling with curling serifs. Primary letters in paragraphs were enlarged into the left margins, and chapter headings were illuminated in patterns, designs, and figurines picked out in bright colors and gold foil.

An icy chill raced through her as the full implications registered. Collier was no more a German name than it was Dutch. She turned to the front of the Bible. It took a second glance to decipher the writing in ink, because it had been blurred by water and was in the German script alpha-

bet. The slanting, angular lines were in a distinctly femi-
nine hand, the spidery calligraphy forming a pleasing pattern.

The blinding glare of the reflection coming through the
trees was in her eyes, blotting out the others around her,
and there was a hushed quiet as she looked numbly at the
line of writing, her mind reeling. Names were pillars of
existence, one of the primary reference points through
which the place among others and in the world at large was
established. It was staggering that something as basic as a
name could be wrong, a matter of a mistake. It turned accepted patterns of life into chaotic disorder.

But in a way, it wasn't totally dissimilar to the chaos of
her life after arriving in Wilmington. And painfully and
gradually new patterns had evolved, amid the agony of fitting into them. The Alcey Martin who had gazed at the
gravestones in the churchyard in Cheltenham in the belief
that she would contribute some small ripple to the
centuries-old flow and ebb of Cheltenham then join the
names in the churchyard had been sloughed off. A different
person had evolved. And she was still changing. Before
when she had worked on the inventories and other things,
she had painfully and with difficulty worked around irre-
concilable matters and told Jubal about them when the opportunity presented itself. Toward the end of the last inventory she had been pouncing on discrepancies and tracking
Beasley down in the warehouse to get an explanation. Before she had avoided the men who stared at her insolently.
Now they avoided her.

So it was possible that names were among the other
things that had assumed roles of less importance. And perhaps it wasn't completely inappropriate for the name to be
selected by chance or error when the severance with the
background and forebears had been as dramatic and complete as it had been with Jubal and Santee. But however
the name had been chosen, and regardless of what name it
was, it had acquired a veracity and life of its own through
use, because it had come to represent people. And under
the circumstances an injudicious display of erudition
would be dangerous. Education in a larger sense was the
wisdom required to know when to use learning. And this
wasn't the time to use it.

But the truth of the matter had to be preserved. And it did seem pathetic and somehow wrong that the one who had relinquished life in giving life hadn't been known by her real name in death. But the years had passed, and she was known again, if only by one. To the degree that the memory of the names of the dead among the living conferred immortality, Frieda Kohler lived once again. And the kernel of truth would remain in the Bible.

Alcey composed her features into a polite half-smile as she looked up from the Bible, and she closed it and gave it back to Hannah to get it out of her hands before she replied. "It is a lovely Bible, isn't it? And you were quite correct. Her name was Sheila Collier, and she was Dutch."

# Chapter Fifteen

They came to her house the following Sunday, and disaster seemed to hover threateningly over everything she did. The fire died down too low during church, and the rack of lamb had barely started to cook through when she got home. Then she built up the fire too high and had to take the lamb off to keep it from burning. A wind had blown the house full of dust, the mint sauce wouldn't thicken, and the flour had been wet and was full of lumps. Nina came an hour before the others and turned calamity into success. Everyone ate heartily, and Jubal was in an expansive mood and approached being gracious because of some turn of events in his business affairs. Santee wasn't there, having gone to Kinston to look at some horses, and the group was incomplete, the gloss taken from a bright day.

Santee bought enormous quantities of supplies before he left for the distant hunting and trapping grounds he had talked about, and it was a week after he was gone that Alcey was sure she was pregnant. And for some reason that escaped analysis and identification, she was glad that he didn't know. Jubal changed toward her, becoming solicitous about her health, if still distant and withdrawn in attitude.

A late summer storm came, black rolling clouds covering the skies and drenching rain pouring down, and the old man came and woke them late at night to warn Jubal that the storm was becoming severe. As a dramatic illustration of Jubal's change toward Alcey, his first thought was of her rather than the business. He helped her gather some of her things, harnessed the horse to the chaise and took her to the safety of the Bledsoe cabin, and left to assemble men to drive the livestock to safety and secure the trading post and warehouse. The storm raged for three days, with shingles ripping from the cabin and tree limbs and other flying debris thudding into the walls, and the roof began leaking heavily when the shingles were completely stripped off the heavy timbers of the ceiling. Alcey spent most of the three days huddled with Simon over a slate in the dim half-light, working with him on his spelling and ciphering to pass the time and keep her mind off the storm.

Jubal sent a boy from the warehouse with the chaise for her, and the signs of the savagery of the storm were all along the route to the other side of town. Trees were down across the road, small cabins along the road had been demolished, many buildings in the town had been destroyed or heavily damaged, the docks had been destroyed, and dead animals, pieces of buildings, and parts of shredded trees were scattered everywhere. One side of the warehouse had been damaged, part of the livestock pens was destroyed, one of the employee houses had been damaged beyond use, and the shingles on all the houses, the trading post, and the warehouse had been stripped away, allowing the rain to pour in.

Days of frenzied activity followed the storm, one of the worst in years. All routine business was suspended and Jubal didn't need Alcey at the office, so she cleaned the house, carried out bedding and clothing to dry in the sun, and did what she could about water damage to the furniture. Jubal drove himself relentlessly, missing half of his meals, working until late at night and rising before Alcey every morning, and he was ill, with a hoarse cough, a high fever, and bouts of vomiting. His attitude of satisfaction in spite of his illness and in the face of what appeared to be a severe setback was inexplicable until Alcey found out that the storm had produced windfall profits and an unprecedented opportunity for him to expand the business. An immediate shortage of food had developed in the town and surrounding area, and perishable foodstuffs that had been water damaged were being sold off at substantial profits before they had a chance to spoil. Most of the livestock had been saved, and each animal was bringing an enormous price. A ship loaded with durable goods had run aground in the estuary and was in danger of breaking up from tidal action, and Jubal had bought the ship and was having it unloaded and refloated. A man who owned a lumber mill had been killed in the storm, his widow wanted a quick settlement of her affairs so she could take her children and go to her parents in Virginia, and Jubal had bought the mill and was having it expanded for the anticipated demand for lumber when Wilmington began rebuilding.

Repairing and rebuilding on the houses and the main building started, the stock pens were repaired, and Jubal bought more land at the side of the stock pens to expand them. The warehouse and trading post were expanded at the same time they were repaired, and Jubal hired a boy to work in the office and more men to work in the trading post and warehouse. The overseer of the trading post, a man named Johnson, had difficulty controlling the activity in the trading post after it was expanded, and Jubal fired him and hired a man named Harris. Alcey had a period of relative rest while the rebuilding and repairing was going on, cooking, taking care of the house, visiting frequently at the Bledsoe cabin, and making herself new clothes as her waist expanded. Then Jubal began to suspect pilferage in the trading post as things settled down to a routine, and he had Alcey inventory random stocks at irregular intervals. The inventories established that some pilferage was taking place, and Jubal fired Harris and hired a man named Swann. Jubal agonized over a decision about the damaged ship for a time as it lay at anchor in the river, then sold it to an entrepreneur who sold subscriptions to local investors to refit it and buy a cargo for a voyage. As part of the transaction Jubal sold a large amount of lumber to the man for cargo on the ship. The ship foundered on the Frying Pan Shoals at the mouth of the Cape as it was leaving, the naval and customs office recovered much of the cargo, and Jubal bought the lumber back and resold it as cargo on another ship.

A comprehensive warehouse inventory was needed. Inventories were too complex for the boy in the office to do accurately, and Alcey went back to work in the office, making up a new ledger and documenting warehouse stocks on hand. The leaves fell and the wind took on the chill of winter, and Alcey resumed a routine much as she'd had months before, taking care of the housework during early and late hours and in the middle of the day, and spending most of the day in the office. After the weeks of confusion there was a satisfying feeling of order and normality, and she enjoyed the work. When the task of preparing the new ledger and documenting the inventory began approaching an end, she suggested to Jubal that she do a complete inventory of the trading post. He was as sensitive and cautious as ever about any hint of her encroaching on his control over his business affairs, and her suggestion was received in silence. Then a couple of days later he told her to inventory the trading post when she finished with the warehouse.

Swann was a small, thin man with a nervous, harried disposition, and he met her at the door the morning she began the inventory, bowing, washing his hands in the air, grinning anxiously, and offering to help. Alcey tactfully explained that the inventory was to document stocks rather than check on the operation of the trading post, but he either didn't understand or didn't believe her, because he followed her around as she and the boy helping her started the inventory, peering worriedly over her shoulder. After a short time of the slow, dull repetition of the boy counting the items and Alcey checking his count and annotating the amount, Swann's anxiety faded and he wandered away.

The business in the trading post had diminished with the onset of cold weather, fewer people from outlying farms coming in, the people in the town staying closer to home, and all of them having less money to spend. Activity in the trading post was a low murmur of movement and conversation that barely impinged on Alcey's consciousness as she moved slowly along the shelves in the rear of the room. She was uncomfortable, because the cold draft in front of the shelves cut through her heavy wool dress and thick shawl, her fingers were so stiff and numb with the chill that it was difficult to write, and she had to watch the boy closely, because he had trouble counting any amount larger than the number of his fingers. The sound of horses outside and of heavy boots coming in registered remotely on her awareness, and the scuffle of boots and the men's voices faded into the other sounds in the room. Then as she and the boy moved to another shelf, she glimpsed a tall man with red hair and a red beard walking toward her and looking at her with a smile.

"Alcey?"

She turned and looked at him. He was in a uniform, a tall, heavyset man with a bushy, bright-red beard and hair. There was something vaguely familiar about the beard and hair, as well as his features, but she didn't recognize him. "I fear you have the advantage of me, sir."

"I'm Anthony, Alcey. Anthony Cosgrave."

"Anthony!" she gasped in surprise. "Why, my goodness . . . mercy, little wonder I didn't recognize you, Anthony! How you've shot up there!"

"Aye, and you're hardly the bit of a girl you were when I saw you last," he chuckled, his eyes politely avoiding her swollen stomach. "But I recognized you straightaway when I saw you back here. Of course you're not hidden behind such as this lot of hair I have in front of me here."

Alcey laughed and clicked her tongue. "I'd be a sight if I were, wouldn't I? My goodness, it's a pleasure to see you again, Anthony. How are Uncle Malatish, Aunt Julia, and the rest of the family?"

His smile faded and he sighed heavily as he shook his head. "We've had our losses, Alcey. Pa died about five years ago and Ma came to live with me and my family, and she died two years ago this winter. Simon, his wife, and all his children were killed in an Indian raid on his farm in the Shenandoah two years ago last summer, and Thomas was in Colonel Washington's forces at Duquesne and was killed there. John is well. He and his wife have three, and they're living in Richmond. Ellen married a man from North Carolina. They lived up on the Catawba River and he was some kind of hunter or something, he got killed and she remarried, then she and her second husband were both killed by Indians. Beatrice is doing well. She and her man have a tobacco plantation on the James, and they have four little ones. Ma and Pa had one more and named her Rachel. She's still a tyke, and she's staying with me and mine. My wife and I have two sons, and I allow the name of Cosgrave will go on, but we've had our losses."

"You have indeed, Anthony," Alcey said, shaking her head sadly. "My father was taken ill and passed on not a twelvemonth after we arrived."

"I'm truly sorry for you, Alcey. That was a great loss to people at large, and I know how close you and your pa were."

"Yes, it was a grievous time for me, and I'm sure your losses have been a trial for you. You have my condolences for such comfort as they may be, Anthony. But I was fortunate enough to marry a well-situated man of a good family, so I have much to be thankful . . ." She glimpsed Jubal approaching them along an aisle between barrels and stacks of goods, a questioning frown on his face. "Oh, here he is now. Jubal, this gentleman is my cousin, Anthony Cosgrave. Anthony, this is my husband, Jubal Collier."

"Major Cosgrave of the Virginia Militia at your service, sir."

Jubal's attitude thawed appreciably as he heard the title, and he smiled thinly as they shook hands. "I am at your service, sir, and it's a pleasure to meet you. Alcey's cousin, are you? Then you'll stop for dinner with us, won't you?"

"Nothing would give me more pleasure, Mr. Collier, but I am overdue on affairs of some importance. I'm on my way to Fort Dobbs to talk with Captain Raines, then I must be back to Virginia with all haste. Perhaps you'd be so good as to allow me to defer the invitation."

"Indeed I will, Major Cosgrave. You'll have a ready welcome at any time."

A man in buckskin breeches, tall boots, and a uniform greatcoat and tricorn approached, looking at Cosgrave respectfully, and he touched the peak of his tricorn as Cosgrave turned to him. "We got everything, and the men are all ready, sir."

"Aye, go ahead, then, and I'll be right out." He looked at Jubal and extended his hand again as the man turned and walked away. "Well, I must be on my way, and it was a pleasure meeting you, sir."

"It was for me as well," Jubal replied as they shook hands. "I wish you well, and I'll look forward to talking with you at greater length when we meet again."

"As I do, sir."

"I'll see you to the door, Anthony," Alcey said as Jubal nodded and walked back along the aisle. "And do try to make time to tarry awhile when you're here again."

"I'll do my best, Alcey. And you have my sincere congratulations on your marriage. Your husband seems congenial and is well situated indeed."

Alcey nodded as they walked toward the door. "Yes, I'm

more fortunate than most. When you see Captain Raines please convey our wishes that he fares well, and tell him that Martha and the children are well. He is a friend of the family, particularly my father-in-law, and my brother-in-law, Santee."

"Santee?" Cosgrave said, looking down at her in surprise. "Why, of course—I didn't connect the name in my mind. Santee Collier is your brother-in-law, isn't he?"

"Yes, he is. You've heard of him, then?"

"Who hasn't?" Cosgrave chuckled. "I've heard enough that I'd give this good right arm to have him in my regiment. Aye, one hears a lot about Santee Collier, some of it hardly to be credited as the truth. About a month ago I heard a man talking about Santee in a tavern, and he swore that Santee had come up against a band of twenty-five Indians when he was no more than fourteen or so, and that he killed all of them."

Alcey laughed and shook her head. "Santee talks very little about what he's done, but I'd say the story missed the mark by at least a year or two and some twenty Indians."

Cosgrave laughed heartily and nodded. "Spinners of tales in taverns rarely let the truth interfere with a good story, do they?" He chuckled and shook his head, stepping forward and opening the door. "Where is Santee now?"

"He left during the autumn for a place he calls *Kentake.*"

"Aye, I've heard of that place," Cosgrave said, following her out and closing the door. "Someone said Daniel Boone from over on the Yadkin has been there. There's another man I'd give an arm to have in my regiment."

Alcey chuckled as she shivered in the wind sweeping along the porch, and she pulled her shawl up over her head and held it under her chin. "My word, Anthony, you'll run out of arms before you have a proper platoon, never mind a regiment." She looked up at him, her smile softening. "Do take care, dear Anthony."

He took off his tricorn, bent over her, and patted her shoulder as he kissed her cheek. "And you beware of this weather in your delicate condition, love. A slip and fall could be dangerous."

"I shall. Do give my best wishes to your good wife, give your children and my cousin Rachel kisses for me, and tell the rest of the family when you see them next that they are in my thoughts."

"I will indeed. Good-bye, love."

"Good-bye, Anthony. Travel safely."

Cosgrave turned and trotted down the steps, where the mounted men were waiting. There were ten of them, wearing mixed assortments of buckskins and homespun, some with uniform greatcoats and tricorns, others with fur caps and plain coats. One of them handed Cosgrave his horse's reins, Cosgrave stepped lightly into the saddle, and he lifted his tricorn as his horse sprang forward. Alcey waved, and a couple of the other men waved, The horses galloped along the road, and Alcey stepped to the edge of the porch and looked along the road, holding her shawl tightly and waving as the wind tugged at her clothes.

He had been about fifteen the last time she saw him. His clothing had been torn, dirty, and rumpled, blood had been trickling from his nose, and he had been arguing fiercely and tearfully with the wooden-faced constable dragging him along the street to his home to talk to his father. He and his brothers and sisters had been rowdies in Cheltenham, willful, disrespectful, and ill-tempered, always in a fight with someone and always breaking or stealing something.

But he had turned out to be a fine man, and she had immediately felt a deep fondness for him. Tall, handsome, and affable, and with an air of command about him, he didn't seem the same person as the boy of fifteen she remembered. She felt intensely proud that he was her cousin. Tears from something more than the stinging wind stood in her eyes as she waved until the horses were out of sight, then she turned and went back into the trading post, touching a corner of her shawl to her eyes.

The wind increased when she went to the house to prepare lunch, and a fine, cold rain fell during the afternoon, whipped along in stinging sheets by the wind. It turned colder, the wind moderated, and the rain continued for several days. Alcey's legs and back began aching from the constant standing as she worked on the inventory, and she had the boy get a stool for her and carry it from place to place as they moved around the trading post. Jubal was torn between wanting the inventory done and concern for

the welfare of the baby, and he put another boy with her to
help her. When she finished the inventory of the trading
post, he had her stay in the house.

On Christmas they went to the Bledsoe cabin after
church. In the corner was a tiny tree decorated with col-
ored scraps of cloth, balls of flax, and tiny wooden figures
and a wooden star the old man had whittled, and the cabin
was bright and cheerful. Hannah and Nina had cooked a
large meal, and after eating they sat around the roaring
fire. It was a pleasant day, but one with a bittersweet feel
of melancholy as Alcey stared into the fire and felt the
baby stirring in her stomach, fragmentary memories of
other Christmases racing through her mind. And it was too
soon ended, turning into a cold ride back through the frigid
darkness to an empty and cheerless house.

The practice of having Sunday meals alternately at the
Bledsoe cabin and Alcey's house continued. On a Sunday
shortly after the New Year Nina brought her belongings
when the meal was at Alcey's house and moved in to stay.
Jubal was darkly and silently disapproving for a few days,
which Nina ignored with bland disregard, then he became
resigned to the situation. Alcey was delighted. She was restless and bored with having nothing to do, heavily burdened
by her pregnancy, and Nina's warm and smiling companionship was invaluable.

The winter hung on, drab cold days of leaden skies and
frigid winds following one after another. The baby's movements became so frequent and violent that uninterrupted
sleep was impossible for Alcey, and for the first time during
her pregnancy she had periods of nausea. Then a warm
breeze moved in from the south, and the ground began
drying out. When Alcey and Nina took their walks around
the houses and stock pens, they saw tiny shoots of grass
pushing up through the ground. The sun became warmer,
the days longer, and buds were visible on the trees during
the drives to the Bledsoe cabin.

The first pains came during the darkness of early morning, and within seconds Jubal was gone and Nina was
there. Then Meghan Hugh was there, and a few minutes
later Hannah and Widow Fanning were there. The alternating waves of agony and periods of apprehensive and suspenseful waiting for the next pains became a rhythm as

Nina and Hannah sat by the bed and murmured encouragingly, and Widow Fanning and Meghan moved quietly around the room and muttered. It dragged on, pain and effort draining her energy, and time seemed to collapse into the rhythm, becoming one with it. Widow Fanning probed and felt, nodded confidently, and lifted Alcey's head to give her sips of soup and a bitter, nauseating draught. The pace of the rhythm increased, the periods of release becoming shorter, and the pains became more wrenching and demanding. Nina and Hannah patted Alcey and coaxed her to greater efforts, and Widow Fanning leaned over her and rasped commands in her dry, husky voice. Alcey's strength faded as she became numb, wracked with the surges of excruciating pain, and exhaustion approached. Then the pains began to gather an impetus of their own, carrying her along against her will and finding new reserves of energy to tap. At the limits of endurance, when she was beginning to shrink within herself, it was over and they were rushing around in the bedroom as the baby wailed in a thin wavering cry.

Impresssions were vague and indistinct through the haze of exhaustion. Hannah and Nina moved Alcey around on the bed and pulled at her, talking in happy murmurs, and the meaning of their words gradually penetrated. It was a boy. They chuckled as the baby pulled at her breast, and she turned her head with an effort and looked at it. It was tiny and red, a small, wrinkled face buried in an envelope of covers. Widow Fanning made loud, knowledgeable pronouncements in the next room, and men's footsteps shuffled in. The old man bent over the bed and chortled as he looked. As Jubal leaned over the bed it was the first time Alcey had seen him smile happily.

During a conversation some months before Jubal had told her that the child would be named Jude if it was a boy. Alcey didn't like the name, but she hadn't argued because Jubal had given her the choice of naming the child Sheila if it was a girl, a name the Bledsoes suggested and one that Jubal didn't like.

Jude was a small, weak baby, and during the first days Alcey's fiercely protective love gave rise to a sickening fear that he would waste away. But he gradually gained strength until he was slobbering greedily at her breasts and wailing angrily when he was hungry. Nina remained and Hannah was at the house every day, and they said the baby was identical to Jubal when he had been born. And within a few days the baby was gaining weight, the fine down on top of the baby's head was growing into black hair, and his eyes were a deep blue.

Widow Fanning came back every day for several days, and Meghan visited often. There were long conversations between them and Nina and Hannah over the efficacy of various teas for babies, sassafras, walink, watermelon seed, rattleroot, white oak bark, and others, and they brewed up various potions and gave the baby sips. Widow Fanning was satisfied with the baby's progress, and her visits diminished and stopped. Meghan's visits became social, and Hannah's diminished to three or four a week. Nina remained at the house, helping Alcey with the housework and the baby.

Shortly after the christening the activity in the business began to build toward its summer peak. Jubal was having the lumber mill expanded and was spending a lot of time at it, and a large influx of goods was pouring into the warehouse. The boy in the office was having difficulty in keeping up with the bills of lading and other things, and the inventory ledger on the warehouse was so inaccurate it was useless. On several occasions Jubal brought up the subject of Alcey's returning to the office, but the necessity to nurse the baby frequently presented too much of an obstacle. Then the wife of a man who worked in the warehouse had a stillborn baby, and Jubal made arrangements to hire her as a wet nurse.

Both Nina and Hannah were silently disapproving, and Alcey had strong reservations. It was contrary to all her instincts, and she had a deep-seated need to hold and fondle the baby. She didn't trust another woman to care for the baby properly, and the situation had the feel of giving up her child. But Jubal's concern for Alcey had been transferred to the baby when it was born, his next concern was the business, and he wanted Alcey in the office. The woman's name was Alice Lambert, a young, strong woman, and the stillborn baby had been her first child. Her grief immediately turned into affection for Jude, and she was patient, loving, and careful with him. Nina stayed on at the house for a few more days to help Alice, then she moved back to the Bledsoe household.

Alice became a part of the household, sleeping on a pallet by the baby's crib in the second bedroom, with her belongings in a box in the corner. Her husband was more than satisfied because of the additional wages he collected through her, and she seemed happy. She was a simple and uneducated but amiable and industrious woman, and she gradually took over all the cooking and other housework. Hannah and Nina were still silently disapproving, but they liked Alice and she fit smoothly into the group at the Sunday gatherings. Jubal never held the baby or played with him, but he had an intense interest in him, frequently talking to Alice about him and watching her with him at night. His only interest in Alcey was that directly related to the office. She waited for him to begin taking her again at night, and she continued waiting. Weeks turned into months, and she felt a sense of relief over his lack of interest in her, combined with a vague foreboding.

Early summer brought the welcome news of the Treaty of Paris, ending the war between Britain and France, and acknowledging British control over territories in the Americas previously claimed by France. But the news sheets also reported Indian uprisings against the British forts in the north, including Detroit, Pitt, Sandusky, and Presque Isle, and reports of Indian attacks on isolated settlers continued to come in. Jubal began the final preparations for an expansion he had planned for some time, that of placing a trading post up the Cape Fear River at Cross Creek. Wagons were loaded and parked in the yard, and Jubal selected men from the warehouse and trading post to work in the new trading post. The convoy of wagons left, and Jubal returned a month later, exhausted and ill. A trickle of wagonloads of produce began to come back along the road from the new trading post almost immediately, then a few livestock began arriving every few days. The amounts increased rapidly, and rafts of logs for the lumber mill began coming down the river from the trading post.

Santee was mentioned less frequently as the months of the summer wore on, and the fact that he hadn't returned became a constant undercurrent in the conversation during and after Sunday meals. Hannah had periods of effusive, demonstrative affection for Simon, thinking of Santee. Nina would sit in musing silence and look at Simon, and occasionally tears would fill her eyes. Alcey thought about the stories she'd heard of hunters who hadn't returned or been heard of again, and of the dangers of the wilderness. Several weeks passed during which there was no mention of Santee in conversation, then autumn came, the weather turned cool, and leaves began falling. And there was a reversal to the grim silence about Santee. The old man began talking about him again, telling long, rambling stories about their trips together into the wilderness. Hannah and Nina began discussing what they would do when Santee returned the following summer.

Winter brought a minor business reversal. Jubal had invested money in a land company organized to survey and parcel land somewhere in the west, and the company collapsed upon news of the Royal Proclamation restricting settlement to the east of the headwaters of rivers flowing into the Atlantic. Jubal was also dissatisfied with the profits from the trading post at Cross Creek, and he made a trip to the trading post just before Christmas. Christmas at the Bledsoe cabin was heavily melancholy under the veneer of artificially bright conversation about Santee. Jubal returned from Cross Creek shortly after Christmas, weak and feverish with a severe chest infection, and he sent men up to replace those he had fired.

Alice's husband was killed in a fight in a tavern during late winter, and Jubal took charge of her affairs, selling her tiny cabin and few sticks of furniture, and moving the rest of her belongings into her room at the house. Several men who worked in the warehouse, trading post, and stock pens began trying to make her acquaintance, talking to her when she went to the trading post for foodstuffs for the house or when she was taking Jude out for fresh air. Jubal fired one of them, and the rest left Alice alone.

When the activity of business began reviving after the winter slump, Jubal had Alcey keep a close check on the goods sent to the trading post at Cross Creek and the value of the return. She started separate ledgers, listing the livestock and the board feet of raw lumber that came in first, then the hogsheads of pitch and tar, kegs of butter, and bales of hides, and she listed the goods that were loaded into the wagons returning to Cross Creek. The season advanced, and raw flax, wool, and indigo began to come in, then the first of the tobacco and preserved hams and flitches of bacon. Jubal pored over the ledgers from time to time, satisfied, and began making plans to establish another trading post.

The optimism about Santee in the conversation at the Bledsoe cabin took on a note of desperation as the weeks passed, and Alcey worried about him often, sitting at her desk and staring blankly at a ledger or bill in front of her. Then the heat of late summer came, bringing worries over Jude that took precedence over everything else. He had thrush and hives, and Alcey stayed at home to help Alice with him as he worsened. Jubal brought a surgeon from town, Hannah brought Widow Fanning, and Widow Fanning threw out everything the surgeon had left and gave Alcey solutions to soak him in and draughts for him to drink. He gradually became better, the angry red welts disappearing and the white patches in his mouth fading.

Then he developed a high fever and began having bouts of vomiting. The illness came on with ominous suddenness, and Alcey sent Alice for Widow Fanning. By the time she arrived, Jude's tiny body was burning with fever, he seemed to be having difficulty breathing, and Widow Fanning's anxious expression as she examined him struck terror into Alcey's heart. Widow Fanning wrapped him in cool, damp cloths and began giving him sips of an infusion of Jesuit's bark. There was no improvement for hours, his breathing still labored and his stomach rejecting the infusions all during the long sultry hours of a stifling late summer afternoon. Then near dark his fever subsided. Hannah and Nina stayed through the night, taking turns changing the cloths and giving him sips of the infusion, and by morning he was eating small spoonfuls of pap and nursing on Alice's breasts again. He was still weak and feverish, vomiting part of the time, but Widow Fanning came back during the morning and nodded in satisfaction when she looked at him.

He was completely recovered the following morning, eating his pap hungrily as Alice clucked and giggled happily over him, and Alcey felt as though a heavy weight had been lifted from her shoulders as she got ready and went to

the office. The sun seemed brighter, the sounds of the birds
sounded more cheerful, and the faces of the people standing on the porch in front of the trading post looked more
amiable and congenial. The boy was slouched at his desk
when she went into the office, oblivious to the dust and
grime that had settled on everything during the days she
had stayed at home, and his sleepy grin of greeting changed
to a guilty expression as she glanced around in disapproval.
He got up from his desk, took the straw broom from the
corner, and began sweeping. Alcey took a rag from the
recess in the side of her desk and started to dust the desk
and stool, then put it back when the cloud of dust from the
broom the boy was wielding became thick in the room. She
sneezed, then walked back toward the door, lifting her
hands and dropping them in a gesture of resignation.

She walked out onto the porch, stifling another sneeze.
A large dray of lumber drawn by two yoke of oxen was
rumbling along the road, a load from Jubal's mill enroute
to the docks. She looked at it as she stepped across the
porch to get away from the clouds of dust billowing from
the office doorway, and she glanced idly along the road.
Then she stiffened.

His buckskins were the pale color of skins that had been
tediously kneaded inch by inch until they were soft, pliable,
and almost white, with long fringes of a contrasting buff,
and even at a distance of a hundred yards, the elaborate
patterns of beading were clearly visible, brilliant splashes of
color. He was bareheaded instead of wearing the fur cap he
sometimes had on when arriving, his thick, black hair tied
back in a clout, and his black hair and darkly tanned skin
made his buckskins look even lighter. His buckskins had
always shown a taste for decoration, but he had never before gone to so much trouble and such lengths in decoration, and the effect was eye-catching. Such bright colors as
the beading against the pale buckskin would have looked ostentatious and gaudy on other men. The long, flowing
fringes hanging down from his sleeves, shoulders, and the
seams of his breeches would have looked showy on others.
But on him, the colorful, fanciful dress looked magnificent.
And he looked magnificent, large, powerful, and masculine
on his horse.

A feeling of panic shot through her. During the days of

Jude's illness, she had given little thought to her appearance. It had been days since she had washed her hair, and she had put it up hurriedly to come to the office, her mind still occupied with thankfulness over Jude's recovery. Her dress was one of her worst, dull and faded from washings, not flounced properly because she was wearing only one petticoat, and wrinkled from being indifferently ironed. She felt pale, wan, and drawn. A sudden impulse to run to the house and do something about her appearance seized her. But he had already seen her. He shifted his rifle and lifted an arm and waved, the fringes hanging down from his sleeve rippling. Alcey waved, restraining the impulse to flap her arm frantically, and she walked toward the end of the porch, feeling her hair and tucking in loose ends, and tugging at her dress.

The road was crowded, his other horses were more or less hidden behind him, but from glimpses of them they looked heavily laden, and there appeared to be more of them than he had left with. Alcey stood at the end of the porch and glanced down at the drape of her skirt as she straightened her shoulders, resting her hands lightly and gracefully on the railing. Then she gripped the railing.

Santee hadn't devoted all the time and labor it had taken to make his buckskins so magnificent. It had been done for him. The girl's buckskin smock and moccasins with knee-length leggings were the same pale color as those Santee wore, perhaps even more richly decorated with beading, with a short buff fringe around the hem of the smock. She was small and slight, and looked very young at a distance. And very beautiful. Her hair was in thick braids that hung down her back, and she had a wide beaded band around her forehead. A heavy, bulky blunderbuss cradled in her arms looked out of place. The sagging sling of buckskin draped across her shoulder and hanging partly behind her back was the cradle Indians used to carry babies about.

The crushing despair was devastating in its suddenness, a yawning, hollow pit opening around her. And it was also totally inexplicable. Anger, resentment, disappointment, and agonized hurt struggled to assert themselves. Tears of anguish rose to her eyes. An imperative urge to flee seized her, clamoring in every recess of her mind. She struggled to compose herself, summoning all the protective defenses and

control that she had, and at the same time her mind reeled
as she struggled to understand the welter of confused emo-
tions gripping her. Santee was turning toward the yard by
the warehouse dock, waving again, and the girl was looking
at Alcey. Alcey waved, then walked toward the dock, fighting to get her features under control.

The girl was bewitching, breathtakingly beautiful. She
was part Indian, with an olive tone to her smooth skin,
delicate features, and large dark eyes. Hardly more than a
child, about sixteen or seventeen, with a daintily thin build,
slender arms and shoulders, and gracefully long and slender legs that were somewhat immodestly outlined by her
smock. There was a charming quality of girlishness in the
lines of her small face and candid stare, but at the same
time there was a torrid, voluptuous beauty about her, hints
of a fiery, wild, and uncontrolled nature smoldering in her
massive eyes, and the potential of a savage temper in the
lines of her lips and chin. She looked fiercely proud and
independent. And suddenly the huge blunderbuss she was
carrying didn't look out of place in her thin arms.

Santee hopped lightly onto the dock, smiling widely, and
he put his arm around Alcey and pulled her to him, bending down and kissing her cheek affectionately. "Alcey, it's
good to see you again, and there's no need to ask you how
you are."

She flushed with confusion, pulling away from him.
"Yes, it's so good to see you again, Santee, and . . .
mercy, what a surprise this is, and we were all so worried."

"Worried?" he laughed, turning back to the edge of the
dock. "There was nothing to worry about. Here, let me
give you a hand, Aimee." The girl had already put her
blunderbuss on the edge of the dock and leaped down as
easily as Santee had, holding the baby's sling with one
hand, and a flash of a smooth thigh showed as her smock
crept up. Santee took her arm, turning back to Alcey. "This
is my wife Aimee. Aimee, this is Alcey I've told you
about."

What he had told her had apparently led her to expect
friendship, because her smile was wide, totally open and
guileless. Her teeth emphasized the girlish naïveté of her
frank smile as they gleamed white against the dusky color
of her lips and her small, beautiful face, but her eyes had

limitless depths in them. The baby in the sling had started crying, and she rocked it with an absent movement of her shoulder as she stepped toward Alcey. "*Enchanté. Excusez-moi*, no much English, me."

Her voice was soft and melodic with a husky quality and a hint of a lisp mixed with the heavy French accent. Alcey felt large, dowdy, and clumsy as she put her hand on Aimee's shoulder and kissed her cheek. "I'm so pleased to meet you, Aimee, and I know we shall be fast friends."

"Aye, she doesn't speak much English, Alcey," Santee said. "She can understand about anything, though, if you talk slow, and . . . but you speak French, don't you?"

"Not up to the requirements for conversation, I fear, because my training in French was in reading and writing. But I'll speak slowly, and I'm sure we'll understand each other, won't we, Aimee?"

"*Oui, très bien*," Aimee said cheerfully. "No talk too bleeding fast, I understand."

Alcey blinked, keeping her smile in place. "Yes, well . . . well, what a healthy-sounding baby. May I see the baby? Mercy, Santee, this is all so sudden."

Aimee pulled the sling around in front of her, spreading the top open. "Name Genesee."

It was a large, chubby baby, and it stopped crying as it looked up at them. Thick black hair covered its head, and its eyes were deep blue. The sling was padded with mossy vegetation, the baby was swaddled in soft fur, and looked as if it was coated with some kind of grease or oil. "Her name is Genesee? Well, she's a very lovely little—"

"*Non, non, garçon*. Boy. Boy baby."

"Oh, I do beg your pardon, how stupid of me. Of course, he's quite large, much too large to be a . . . and that's a lovely name for a boy. Yes, Genesee is a lovely name."

"It's where Aimee's ma was from," Santee said. "Her ma was a Delaware, from the Genesee, and her pa was a French trader."

"Yes, I see. . . ." A couple of men came out of the warehouse, and she beckoned to them. "Come and unload these furs, if you would, please. And ask a couple more of the men to step out and help you." She looked back at Santee. "Oh, Jubal and I have a child, by the way, and it's also a boy. We named him Jude."

"I'm very pleased for you. Is Jubal within?"

"No, he's at the lumber mill. Goodness, Santee, along with everything else, it appears you have an enormous amount of furs."

He nodded as he glanced at the men climbing down from the dock and unloading the horses, and he stepped to the edge of the dock, hopped down, and began untying the load on one of the horses. "Aye, I didn't get to *Kentake*, but I found plenty of beaver and otter."

"Yes, I see you did. Well . . ." She looked at Aimee, smiling at her and taking her arm. "Santee, I'll just take Aimee over to my house so we can sit and have a nice long chat. There are simply thousands of things I want to ask her."

Santee hesitated and looked at her as he pulled a bundle of pelts off the packsaddle on the horse, then he tossed the bundle onto the dock. "Aye, well, I'd like to get on home without delay."

Alcey flushed with confusion and clicked her tongue in disgust with herself. "Of course, how stupid of me. I really don't know what I'm thinking about or saying, because everyone has been frantic with worry about you and you mustn't delay. Jubal and I will come over this evening."

"Aye, it'll be good for us to all get together and have a talk. I'll just leave the furs for now and pick up my tally later."

"Yes, very well."

A gnawing headache was beginning to throb in Alcey's temples, and mortification over the gauche, nonsensical comments she had made seethed within her. The odor of the pelts forming a large pile on the dock was nauseating. Her face ached from keeping her smile in place. Aimee tucked the top of the sling closed and pushed it around behind her back, leaned toward Alcey and kissed her cheek, then moved toward the edge of the dock.

"*Au revoir, ma copain.* I am seeing you *ce soir?*"

"Good-bye, dear Aimee. Yes, my husband and I will be over this evening."

Aimee knelt and put her hand on the edge of the dock, steadying the sling with her other hand, hopped down from the dock, and picked up her blunderbuss and walked toward her horse, smiling up at Alcey. Alcey smiled and nodded, her mouth dry and her hands hot and damp as she clenched them together behind her back. Santee lifted Aimee onto her horse, mounted his own, and they smiled and waved.

The men began untying the bundles of pelts on the docks and sorting through them, counting them, and the nauseating odor from the pelts became intense. Alcey walked along the dock to the porch, waving at Santee and Aimee again as the horses turned onto the road, and went back into the office.

The headache became blinding, and she couldn't concentrate on anything she read. Her hand trembled violently and she couldn't write legibly. She went to the house, looked in on Jude, talked to Alice about lunch, then wandered through the house distractedly, thinking about what she had to do. She decided to wash her hair, and the soap got in her eyes and brought stinging tears. She ironed a fresh dress, and the toe of the iron caught a seam and tore it. Her headache, her trembling fingers, and her tears made it difficult to thread the needle to repair the seam. She ate a few mouthfuls of lunch, then became nauseated and went outside and vomited.

# Chapter Sixteen

Jubal shook out his shirt with an impatient jerk and began putting it on. "This is a bleeding bother," he grumbled. "In the future I'd be grateful if you'd ask my leave before you commit my time for me."

Alcey straightened the collar on her dress, then turned from side to side and looked in the mirror as she tugged on the waist of her dress to settle the bodice to a firm fit. "He's your brother. And he brought you an enormous lot of furs on which you'll make a handsome profit, rather than taking your oft-repeated invitation to deal with Wilson."

"It's still a bleeding bother. And all for some Indian wench."

"Half Indian, and his wife and your sister-in-law, not some wench. And a lovely young woman and all."

"Half or all is the same, as far as I'm concerned. But I should have known that he'd never find himself a proper wife, knowing him."

Alcey picked up the comb and tucked a wisp of hair into place, then looked out the window absently, thinking. She slowly nodded. "Yes, it took me aback at first. Indeed I might say I was quite shocked. But it was the lack of warning that startled me. I was quite upset. I've always thought of Santee as not the sort of man to even be married, to which poor Simon is unfortunate proof, lovely lad that he is. And coupled with that I found little to recommend his choice at first thought, although it's not my choice to make and Aimee is a lovely young woman. But having married her he'll not be gone for time without end, because it's clear at first sight that Aimee is as much at home in the wilderness as a sweet little deer." She looked back at the mirror and turned her head from side to side, touching loose hairs into place with the comb. "If he'd married a good girl hereabout, he would at least be home once a year, and give your poor mother and father some peace of mind. And Nina as well of course. They deserve that much."

Jubal finished buttoning his shirt and stuffed the tail of it into his breeches, looking at her. "Upset, were you?"

"Indeed I was. I was quite out of my wits for a moment, to the extent that I was on beam's ends presenting myself well to Aimee."

"You'd do well to concern yourself more with your affairs and less with Santee's."

Alcey put the comb on the table and turned, looking at him coldly. "My affairs are sufficiently well ordered to my likes. And I did say that Santee's choice of a wife is not my choice to make. On the other hand it's long been clear that I regard your family with far greater affection than you. And through this affection I find concern for their welfare."

He pulled on the waistband of his breeches and reached for his cravat on the bed as he looked at her stonily. "I'll ask you to have a mind to your tone when you address me. And I'm the one who's to say when your affairs are well ordered and when they're not, not you. As far as your affection goes you've a child and heir of mine to shower whatever affection you might possess upon. To my way of thinking your affection for Santee surpasses proper limits."

Alcey stiffened, her eyes widened with indignation, and she flushed. "What a swining, bloody, scurvy thing to say!"

Jubal frowned darkly, glaring at her. "I said to have a mind to your tone, woman!" he barked. "I'll listen to no bloody talk such as that from you!"

"You won't, will you?" Alcey raged, seething anger suddenly exploding to life within her. "Then you'll have a mind to your own bleeding tongue, you flaming get!"

His mouth dropped open and he took a step backward, looking at her in outraged disbelief. Then his face turned crimson, and he trembled with fury. "I'll not hear this from you, woman! Now you address me in a proper tone and words!"

"I'm to address you properly, am I? While you concoct fabrications which could come only from an evil mind such as yours, and then reproach me with them? I'll bloody address you as I'm addressed, is what I'll flaming do!"

He was speechless for a moment, his face twisted with wrath as he trembled violently, then he lifted his fist and shook it at her. "I'm warning you, woman! I'm your husband, and I'll take you in hand!"

"My husband!" she sneered scornfully. "You're not even a bloody man! No, nor a human being!" She leaned toward him, shouting at the top of her voice. "You're naught but a bleeding ledger with a pair of spindly shanks under it!"

His face blanched, becoming drawn and haggard as he looked at her in helpless rage. He opened his mouth and closed it, then snatched up his coat from the bed and stamped toward the door. "By God, I'll not have to do with you until you have yourself under control, or I'll not be responsible for my own actions!"

"Bugger off, then! I'm sick of the bleeding sight of you!"

The door slammed behind him with a boom. His heavy footsteps thumped through the house, then the front door slammed closed. Alcey turned back to the table and leaned on it, trembling. Her anger diminished, leaving behind a clean, wholesome feeling, a cheerfully bright sense of satisfaction. Apprehension over what she had done and over Jubal's anger stirred, and she mentally shrugged it off. Cursing and shouting at him had been a long stride but was in the same direction their relationship had been moving for months. There was a nagging shame over cursing, but her self-condemnation wasn't as severe as it would have once been. She turned away from the table and walked to the window. Jubal was stamping toward the wagon yard to get the chaise. She went back to the table and picked up her comb, again touched a couple of wisps of hair into place, then picked up her reticule and put the comb in it as she walked toward the door.

Alice was humped on a settle in the parlor, the baby on her lap and her eyes wide with fright over the argument. She smiled timidly at Alcey.

"Has he had his pap, Alice?"

"Aye, he has, ma'am."

"Come along, then."

They went outside and waited in front of the house. It apppeared the sound of the argument had carried a considerable distance. Loiterers in front of the trading post were collected at the corner of the porch, looking toward the house. Four men working on a dray in the wagon yard glanced furtively at the women. There were surreptitious movements in the front windows all along the row of houses as women peeked out, and a cluster of employees' children was at the corner of the third house, peering around it. The chaise came toward the rear of the wagon-yard, Jubal snapping the traces and the horse trotting smartly. Jubal pulled up the horse and stopped the chaise by Alcey and Alice, his eyes straight ahead and his face in rigid lines of boiling anger. Alcey took the baby from Alice as she climbed in, then handed her the baby and climbed in. Jubal snapped the traces and turned the horse toward the road. Alcey hummed softly, pulling the cover closer around Jude. Jubal darted an enraged glance at her, snapping the traces harder. Alcey braced herself against the motion of the chaise as it picked up speed, looking around cheerfully and humming louder.

The dog ran around the Bledsoe cabin and barked as the chaise swayed and bounced along the road toward the rear of the cabin, and he yapped with excitement as he recognized Alcey.

They were sitting on benches under the large tree in front of the cabin, looking expectantly toward the corner. Aimee sat between Hannah and Nina as they clucked over the baby. A smile spread over Aimee's face. Alcey still felt strong reservations, a repugnance for the situation and a shrinking unwillingness to probe her feelings on the matter too deeply, but it was impossible to have reservations about Aimee as a person. Her smile pathetically begged for acceptance, and as they looked at each other, Alcey felt a genuine and warm fondness for the slender, beautiful woman, coupled with understanding and sympathy for one in strange and unfamiliar surroundings without adequate defenses, a turmoil she had experienced herself. Aimee's smile became brilliant as she sprang up and rushed to Alcey.

"*C'est épatant* you are here! You are so long coming."

"I came as quickly as possible, dear Aimee," Alcey laughed, as they embraced and kissed. "And here is my little Jude. A bit less sturdy than your Genesee, I daresay, but he'll be walking within the month the way he's been tumbling about."

Aimee gasped with admiration as she took Jude from Alice and began cooing over him. He squirmed strongly in her arms and wailed angrily, trying to get back to Alice. Jubal came around the corner of the cabin, his face in sullen lines of satisfaction. He glanced at Aimee sharply and started to walk on toward the others, and Alcey turned Aimee toward him.

"Jubal, this is our sister-in-law. Aimee, this is my husband."

Jubal looked at Alcey with a searing glance, then forced a thin smile and bowed shortly as Aimee murmured and nodded. "Delighted, I'm sure," he said, and walked on toward the benches. "Well, Santee, from the furs you left at the warehouse, it appears your trip was worth the effort. And I brought along your tally—here it is."

"Aye, very well. Yes, I didn't get to *Kenta-ke* as I had planned, but it was a goodly catch of furs."

For an instant Aimee's face was much less like a girl's as her eyes lingered on Jubal, dislike and mistrust plain in them, then she smiled again as she looked at Alcey, kissing Jude again and handing him back to Alice. Jubal sat down with Santee and the old man, talking about the trip with them, and Hannah and Nina made room on the other bench for the younger women. The antagonism between Alcey and Jubal was still intense enough for the others to detect, but the conversation was cheerful and animated. Hannah, Nina, and the old man were exhilarated with relief over Santee's safe return. They were extending themselves to make Aimee welcome, and were delighted with Genesee. Alcey tried her limited conversational French with Aimee, but her standard French was incomprehensible, and Aimee's French was a dialect that Alcey couldn't understand except for scattered words and phrases. But Aimee's English was adequate for conversation, even if somewhat garbled, heavily accented, mixed with a jumble of French, and spiced liberally with profanity.

Aimee was as inclined as Santee to reticence and understatement about herself, but from what she said and from snatches of the conversation between the men that Alcey overheard, she found out a number of essential facts about

Aimee. She had been an only child. Her father had raised her much like a boy, and she didn't carry the huge blunderbuss around for the purpose of handing it to Santee when he needed it. Santee laughingly remarked on the lethal effect with which Aimee used the blunderbuss, and on her deadly skill with a knife and tomahawk. She also knew a lot about hunting, trapping, and caring for skins and pelts.

And Alcey pieced together how Aimee and Santee had met. Somewhere far beyond the mountains to the west Aimee, her mother, and her father had been traveling eastward from some gigantic river the Indians called the Mississippi, and they had been set upon by a band of Indians. Santee had been in the vicinity and heard the gunfire. He had joined the fight, surprising the attacking Indians and driving them away. Aimee's father had been seriously wounded in the fight and died a few days later, and her mother had died during the winter.

The story was very romantic, a rescue from death in the depths of the remote wilderness. And it was a very fitting way for them to have met. A conventional meeting and courtship would have been totally inappropriate. Walks on the common among meaningful glances from others, businesslike meetings between parents, posting of banns, and exchanging of vows in the staid atmosphere of a church ceremony would have been entirely too dull and prosaic. The stalwart Santee could only have met the wildly and torridly beautiful Aimee in the terror and clamor of battle, could only have won her by charging into battle to rescue her from death. And they seemed so compatible. They both had an expansive freedom about them, the demeanor of those who tread boundless spaces and do as they wish. Aimee's lithe and slender body was the perfect counterpoint for Santee's brawny strength. The hints of potential for savagery lurking in the lines of Aimee's sweet, beautiful face complemented the suggestion of attractiveness under the dark tan and scars on Santee's strong, somewhat intimidating features.

It was a pleasant, enjoyable evening. The gathering was congenial, the conversation lively and interesting. And Alcey found Aimee even more delightful as the evening wore on, their friendship rapidly becoming close as they chatted.

But Alcey developed a headache and became nauseated and her regret wasn't unmixed with relief when it grew late and time to return home.

Santee and Aimee remained only two days, and a soft, misty rain was falling the morning they lined up their horses to load their supplies. Aimee stood on the porch and talked with Alcey as Santee and clerks from the trading post tied the bags of supplies on the packsaddles, her demeanor melancholy with leavetaking and parting from a newly found friend, but with joyful anticipation of the trip and satisfaction in leaving the town. Alcey felt a comparable but different conflict over seeing them leave. When the supplies were loaded, Santee kissed Alcey and said goodbye, and Alcey and Aimee embraced and kissed. They rode away, with Aimee relaxed comfortably on her horse, oilskin wrapped around the lock on her blunderbuss, heavily greased buckskin draped over the sling holding Genesee, and the rain unnoticed as it trickled down her face. Alcey walked along the porch to the corner as the horses plodded along the road, waving as Aimee looked back. They continued waving until the horses faded into the misty rain, but Alcey had long since been blinded by her tears.

The acrimonious argument between Alcey and Jubal wasn't mentioned in open conversation, but it was a constant undercurrent in the atmosphere in the house. And it was a landmark in their relationship. Jubal became even more distant and withdrawn toward her. He did or said nothing to deliberately provoke her temper, and their conversation was limited to brief exchanges concerning business affairs.

The business affairs were expanding rapidly, and Jubal hired another boy to work in the office and help with the growing amount of correspondence with factors in England, the other colonies, the West Indies, and other ports in the Caribbean. The volume of trade at the post at Cross Creek was beginning to rival that of the main post, and Jubal proceeded with plans to establish another post on the Yadkin, as well as one at Kinston to intercept part of the increasing volume of tobacco that was being shipped out by factors in New Bern at the mouth of the Neuse. The Indian attacks on settlers on the frontier had decreased; a lively trade was carried on with people buying livestock, wagons, and supplies to take to the interior and settle; and the news sheets had reports of a large increase of expanding settlements on the fontiers of all the colonies.

The news sheets also had reports on the deliberations in Parliament concerning the colonies. The national debt in England had doubled as a result of the war with France, plans were being considered to permanently station several thousand regulars in the colonies to protect them, and various proposals were being studied to establish taxes in the colonies to retire a part of the national debt and to contribute a portion to the support of soldiers stationed in the colonies. And some of the proposals were drawing fire in the colonies.

An issue of the *Gazette* contained the text of a speech by Benjamin Franklin before the House of Commons in which he made a distinction between external taxation, a duty established on commodities, and internal taxation, a proposed stamp duty on legal documents, transfers of property, and publications. His viewpoint was that an external tax became a part of the price of an article and the purchaser was at liberty to buy or not buy the article, but an internal tax on wills, bills of lading, news sheets, leases and property titles, and similar items, was an involuntary tax that Parliament was prohibited from levying on the colonies by English common law, because the colonies weren't represented in Parliament. This viewpoint was supported by William Pitt, who had been replaced as prime minister by King George III, as well as by others in Parliament. Most of the editors of colonial news sheets also supported that viewpoint as strongly as they could without risking having their presses closed down.

Alcey was also adamantly opposed to taxation without representation. Her father's libertarian views were a cornerstone of her education, and he had viewed common law as the bulwark of defense of the individual against unwarranted intrusion by government. In reading the news sheets and pondering the matter Alcey could see that it was only fair and reasonable for the colonies to assume costs for supporting soldiers stationed in defense of the colonies and to pay the costs for military operations against the French that had been undertaken in behalf of the colonies. But not in violation of common law. For the first time she began to regard the interests and purposes of the colonies as a matter apart from the interests and purposes of the British Empire as a whole. She discovered that a fundamental shift in attitude had occurred, and she regarded herself as a colonist first and as British second.

Jubal was less concerned with the niceties of common law than with business, and he was adamantly opposed to any kind of taxation, internal or external, because it would increase costs and diminish the potential for profit. He was also less concerned with the possibility of future problems than he was with immediate problems at hand. The drift of more people into the Piedmont and across the Blue Ridge had decreased the number of unemployed laborers in Wilmington at a time when he needed more. He needed men to man the proposed trading posts at Kinston and on the Yadkin, and he was hiring more men to raft lumber down from Cross Creek and drive wagons between Wilmington and Cross Creek. The decrease in men available for hire had also resulted in an overall increase in wages being paid to laborers, which compounded costs and problems.

When the men were finally hired and the preparations were being made to establish the new trading posts, Jubal began suffering from periods of vomiting and diarrhea. Occasionally he was so ill that he had to spend a day or two in bed, which was extremely unusual, because he had always managed to find the energy to go about his business affairs. He was too ill to go with either convoy when the wagons and men were ready to leave, and he gave the men in charge detailed instructions and sent them on. The bouts of vomiting and diarrhea diminished as autumn approached, but he contracted a skin disease on his head, and sores broke out on his scalp, and his hair came out. He had his hair cut off and started wearing a peruke, keeping the raw spots on his scalp covered with a rancid-smelling ointment.

The trading post at Kinston was in operation in time to garner autumn tobacco harvests from smaller farmers, and wagons loaded with hogsheads of tobacco trundled in to reload with trade goods to take back. The return from the trading post on the Yadkin was only a trickle, then the winter slump in business set in, and Jubal sat in his office and fumed over the bills from the Yadkin post. When the weather became cold, the lesions on Jubal's head healed into shiny scars and he stopped using the ointment, but his hair grew only in spots, and he continued wearing a peruke.

The debate over taxation continued to be reported in the news sheets, and concrete actions began to take form and were announced as initial steps in a new colonial policy during late winter and spring. A currency act was being promulgated, requiring all colonies to retire paper money they had issued and to cease issuing paper money. Jubal was forewarned of the act by a factor in London, and he disposed of the bulk of North Carolina currency he had on hand before the value began falling. But he was disgusted with the situation as a whole and foresaw a reduction in the overall level of trade within the colony because of the shortage of English specie that had always plagued the colonies.

News of the next action being taken came during late spring, and it had more far-reaching implications. A sugar act was being passed, increasing the duty on various kinds of sugar and establishing a duty on coffee, indigo, and other things. The *Gazette* simply reported the matter, because the act in itself was of no great consequence in North Carolina. But the news sheets from Massachusetts, Rhode Island, and other predominantly commercial colonies had long editorial tirades condemning the act. And Jubal was infuriated by it. The duties were a minor irritant, but in conjunction with their enactment actions were being taken to eliminate illegal trade with the foreign West Indies by reorganizing and enlarging the customs service and by stationing more ships of the Royal Navy in American waters. This was much more than a minor irritant, because Jubal and other merchants had been trading with factors in French ports in the West Indies, in violation of the Navigation Acts.

The penalties and fines for illegal trade were also increased, and Jubal took no chances when the risks outweighed the potential for profit. By the time the Sugar Act was in force, he had severed association with the factors in the French ports in the West Indies and had broadened his contacts with factors in London and in the other colonies. As the summer wore on, the loss of the profits from trading with the French was more than recovered in the overall volume of business. The increase in the number of settlers in the west was reflected in the massive influx of commodities arriving at the warehouse, and in the constant bustle of wagons loading goods to replenish the stocks in the trading posts. The income from the trading post on the Yadkin was still well below what Jubal expected, but he was ill again during the summer and unable to make a trip to the post, so he was limited to venting his displeasure in vitriolic letters to the manager of the post.

A small, thin child, Jude had been slow in learning to walk, but he was precociously rapid in learning to talk. He showed indications of picking up Alice's accent and ungrammatical speech when he began forming sentences, and Alcey tried to spend as much time as possible with him after the summer was past, playing with him, talking with him, and coaxing him into forming sentences and pronouncing words properly. But she was limited in the amount of time she could spend with him, because there was no real slump in activity in the office, even after cold weather set in. Jubal was having the warehouse expanded again to build up large stocks of goods for the coming summer, and he hired another boy to work in the office. At the same time the overall level of business had increased to a continuing flow that was maintained during the winter, goods were arriving at the port and shipments were being dispatched, and all the trading posts kept up a moderately high turnover of goods.

The developments connected with the proposal for an internal stamp tax in the colonies continued to be reported in the news sheets. The prime minister had asked the colonies for suggestions for alternative means of raising revenue, and the texts of replies from colonial assemblies that were printed in the news sheets consisted of vigorous protests against any taxation. There was a report that colonial agents, headed by Benjamin Franklin, were working with Parliament and the prime minister in an attempt to reach an accommodation on the matter. The *Gazette* also had several articles on William Tryon, who was to arrive the next spring or summer to become the next royal governor.

The chest congestion and other illnesses that frequently bothered Jubal during winter didn't materialize, and in late winter he began making preparations to visit the trading post on the Yadkin before the spring surge in business activity. The volume of business had multiplied several times over what it had been during his last absence, and even in winter it was at a level that required daily decisions from someone in overall charge. But Jubal was intensely jealous of his prerogatives as the owner of the business. He was secretive about many things he did, and he was reluctant to relinquish any authority to anyone else. He gave detailed instructions to the men in charge of the lumber mill, warehouse, trading post, and stockyards, and he gave Alcey detailed instructions on activities in progress in the office. He left in early February on a wagon transporting goods to the Yadkin.

It was a clear, frosty morning when he left, but clouds began moving in and covering the sky during the afternoon. By the next morning a fine, misty rain was falling, and the cold was damp and penetrating. The fire in the fireplace in the office looked bright and cheerful, but the drafts sweeping in around the door and through cracks in the walls and floor made the office frigid a few feet from the fireplace. The three boys sat humped over their desks in their greatcoats, sniffling and wiping their red noses on their sleeves as their quills scratched busily. Alcey sat at the desk with her heavy wool shawl pulled up around her ears, fingerless wool gloves on her hands and her fingers numb with cold, painfully deciphering price quotations from a factor in London and comparing them with another quotation. Occasionally one of the boys asked her how to spell a word, or brought her something to decipher and lingered in front of the fireplace on his way back to his desk.

At midday one of the boys went to the trading post for a beaker of beer for them to have with their bread and cheese, and another went for more wood for the fire. Alcey went to the house for lunch, spent a few minutes in the warmth of the kitchen with Jude, then put her coat and shawl back on and walked back through the rain toward the office. There was no relaxation in the atmosphere due to Jubal's absence, because everyone knew he would check on what had been done when he returned. Wagons were moving in and out of the wagonyard, their heavy wheels splashing through puddles and sinking into the mud, and the patient oxen drawing them were dark with rain. Stock was being moved around in the pens to make room for a herd that had arrived, and a low bustle of activity in the trading post was audible as she climbed the steps at the end of the porch. She walked along the porch to the office, then hesitated outside the door to give the three boys a moment longer in front of the fire, and she pulled her shawl closer and looked absently along the road.

Traders had been going out among the Indians again, and at first glance she thought it was an Indian trader. But the line of dark shapes of horses through the swirling mists of rain was short, far fewer horses than most traders had. And the figure on the first horse was very familiar. She ran to the corner of the porch and strained her eyes to make out details through the rain, the cold forgotten as she leaned over the rail and rain spattered against her face.

But it was much too early for him to be coming in. The mountains to the west were still in the grips of hard winter, and the Bledsoes and Nina weren't expecting him for months, because he had planned a two-year trip into *Kenta-ke*. There were only five horses. Santee was the only rider. Alcey turned and ran toward the dock.

His buckskins were ragged and torn, a buffalo hide was pulled around his shoulders to serve as a greatcoat, he was unshaven and haggard-looking, and his hair was loose and around his shoulders and the sides of his face, plastered down by the rain. He clutched his rifle and a large bundle of buckskin to him with his right arm, and he dismounted slowly, favoring his left shoulder and limping heavily on his right leg. Under the buffalo hide a wide gash gaped in the left shoulder of his buckskins, surrounded by a dark stain. The right thigh of his breeches had a long cut in it, and a crude, bloody bandage showed through the rent.

Alcey stood frozen, stunned with shock. Santee put his rifle and the bundle of buckskin on the edge of the dock and began painfully pulling himself up onto the dock. The buckskin stirred, then fell open, and Genesee climbed to his feet, holding the buckskin around him as he shivered. His hair was a tangled mat, he had dark bruises and cuts on him. He was wearing a buckskin shift that came halfway down his small legs, one foot was bare and the other had a small moccasin on it, and he fumbled with the buckskin wrapping as he tried to pull it around him, his small frame shivering and his teeth chattering with cold. His tiny face was a mask of shrinking fear. Alcey darted to him and snatched him up, pulling the buckskin and the end of her shawl around him. He squeaked something in French in fright, struggling with her, then he lay still and looked up at her apprehensively through the hair hanging down over his eyes.

Santee climbed to his feet on the dock. Alcey looked from him to the horses. Aimee's blunderbuss was tied to the bundles of pelts on one of the horses. Santee was thin, drawn, and slumped with exhaustion. His face was lined with physical and mental pain, and his eyes were dull with grief. Alcey held Genesee tightly as she began weeping.

"Oh, God, Santee . . . God . . ."

"I'd like to get shot of the furs and get my supplies. I'm going to take the boy to Ma and be on my way."

His voice was flat and lifeless, a heavy monotone. Alcey wiped her eyes and tried to control her tears as she turned away. "Get someone from the warehouse to take the furs. I'll send someone from the trading post."

He turned toward the warehouse door. Alcey walked rapidly along the dock toward the trading post. Genesee was a sagging weight in her arms, much heavier than Jude, and he was still shivering with cold and looking up at her with numb, fearful apprehension in his large blue eyes. Alcey went into the trading post, and people in the crowded, cluttered aisles stepped out of her way, looking curiously at her and the boy. Swann and two of the clerks were behind the counter at the rear, dealing with a cluster of people gathered in front of the counter. Alcey pushed through the people.

"Santee is at the dock, and he wants his supplies without delay. Take someone with you and find out what he wants, then collect it and take it to him. Get his tally, and if he is due money, take it from your cash box and I'll give you a receipt from the office for it."

Swann looked at her, frowning with concern, then nodded, motioned to one of the clerks, and hurried toward the door. The people around Alcey moved aside as she turned away from the counter, and they looked at the boy and murmured curiously among themselves. Alcey carried

Genesee around behind the counter, lifted the top off a barrel of ship's biscuit and took one out. Genesee snatched it from her hand and began devouring it ravenously, like a small, starved animal. Alcey walked on along behind the counter to the cheese, shaved off a piece and gave it to him. He stuffed part of it into his mouth with the biscuit he was chewing, and choked and gagged as he tried to swallow. Alcey crossed the trading post to the keg of small beer, filled a cup, and went to a back corner and leaned into the corner, holding Genesee and forcing his hands down with the cup to make him take sips of the beer and wash the cheese and biscuit down. He stopped choking as he gulped the beer, and he hungrily crammed more biscuit and cheese into his mouth.

Swann and two of the clerks bustled back and forth along the aisles and shelves, filling canvas bags and carrying them out. Genesee finished the biscuit and cheese, and Alcey put the cup on a shelf and held him to her, rocking back and forth with him. The buckskin had a damp, moldy odor, and the boy had a sour, unwashed smell, covered with grime over his cuts and bruises. The fear and suspicion was gone from his small face and blue eyes, and he murmured something in French and looked puzzled when she whispered to him soothingly, rocking him back and forth. His eyelids became heavy, and he nestled closer to her. Swann walked up to Alcey, clearing his throat diffidently.

"Ah . . . we took everything out, Mistress Collier. From Mr. Beasley's count of the furs he had another thirty-six guineas and odd shillings due, and I took it out of the cash box, as you said."

"Thank you. I'll send you a receipt for it presently."

Swann nodded and walked back toward the counter. Genesee had dozed off, and he stirred and muttered in French as Alcey pulled the buckskin tightly around him and walked back to the door. A man held the door open for Alcey, and Genesee moved and whimpered in her arms as she carried him along the porch in the frigid wind. Santee, Beasley, and another man from the warehouse were tying the bags of supplies on the packsaddles on two of the horses. The horses were thin and weary, and their heads drooped. Santee limped heavily and dragged his right leg as he moved around.

They finished loading the horses, and Beasley and the other man began taking the bundles of pelts into the warehouse. Santee picked up his rifle, dragged himself onto his horse, and moved the horse closer to the edge of the dock. Alcey stood on the edge of the dock, leaned over, and carefully handed Genesee to him. Santee took the boy, then looked at her dully. She looked back at him, wanting to say something but not knowing what to say. Santee shook the reins, and the horse turned away from the dock. The other horses followed as their halter ropes tightened, and they plodded across the yard in the rain, toward the road. Alcey walked back along the dock to the porch, weeping.

# Chapter Seventeen

The arrival of a new governor was a momentous occasion, but the event was almost crowded out of even the local news sheets by the passage of the Stamp Act, which was to take effect on the first day of November. And while other actions by Parliament had been of intense interest only to political and business leaders, the Stamp Act dominated everyone's conversation. When Alcey went to the Bledsoe cabin, Hannah and Nina sighed with fond exasperation over Simon's and Genesee's mischievous tricks, and they talked about the Stamp Act. In the trading post farmers, artisans, laborers, and their wives talked about the Stamp Act rather than the weather, crops, work, and children. Jubal went to the reception for Governor Tryon and was in an expansive and unusually talkative mood when he returned, the result of ample good port and brushing elbows with the wealthy and powerful. He talked about the Stamp Act, but his attitude about it was markedly less critical than before, apparently a result of Governor Tryon's persuasive personality.

The reaction was more widespread and vehement than Alcey had expected, and instead of dying away as most things did after a time, it continued to grow. It was reported that the speaker of the Assembly informed Governor Tryon that North Carolina would resist the Stamp Act to the death. An organization called the Sons of Liberty was formed. A congress of delegates from all colonies was called in New York City to consider the Stamp Act and other legislation passed by Parliament relating to the colonies. Governor Tryon refused to call the Assembly into session in time for North Carolina to choose delegates for the congress, for which he was roundly criticized in the news sheets and reprimanded by the Assembly when he did call it into session.

Editorials and pronouncements of colonial political leaders about the Stamp Act and similar matters continued to fill the news sheets during the summer, and numerous pamphlets denouncing the Act were published and circulated. News sheets from other colonies reported a few scattered public demonstrations, then more frequent demonstrations. Men and women talking in the trading post began sounding angrier. On an afternoon during late summer, Alcey saw a large body of men leaving town along the road, shouting and singing, and one of the boys in the office told her there had been a demonstration in front of the courthouse. Jubal informed all the employees through the foremen and overseers that lawful and orderly conduct was a condition of employment in his business, which enraged Alcey.

Another demonstration took place in Wilmington on the first Saturday in October. The Sunday meal was at the Bledsoe cabin the following day, and Alcey asked about Simon when she didn't see him. Hannah told her that Simon and one of the Raines boys had been at the demonstration in town the previous day, pelting the courthouse with stones from their slings, and both of them had been thrashed and locked in their rooms for the weekend.

On the third Saturday in October Alcey saw a large number of men streaming along the road into town during the afternoon, and several hundred had passed by the time she left the office and went to the house. A roar of chanting and singing carried out from the town, rising and ebbing as the crowd moved through the streets. When she went to bed, she saw a glow of a large bonfire somewhere in the town, and Jubal muttered under his breath when he came to bed. A short time later the sounds of shouting and singing became louder, and the gleam of torches shone through the windows. Individual voices became audible in the crowd as over a hundred men came along the road, beating on doors and rousing people from cabins and houses. The noise became an uproar as men were summoned out of lodgings on the other side of the fence around the complex, then men with torches began streaming into the open space between the houses and the trading post and warehouse building.

A couple of men beat on the door and shouted for the man of the house to come out, and others beat on the doors of the employees' houses. Jude began screaming with fright in the other room, and Jubal snarled curses as he jerked on part of his clothes. Alcey put a shawl around her shoulders and went into the other room, where Alice was calming Jude. He began screaming again as Alcey took him, trying to get back to Alice, so she handed him back and went into the front room to look out the window as Jubal left. The crowd was noisy, boisterous, and good-natured, many of the men drunk and capering about as they waved their torches, but there was also a mood of demanding insistence about them, an indication that they could become ugly. Jubal laughed and talked with them, his shirt loose and hanging out of his breeches, his shins bare, and his bald head shining in the light of the torches. Someone gave him a bottle and demanded that he drink to liberty, property, and no stamp duty, and he did. The employees had been roused from their houses, and wild cheering broke out when Jubal sent Swann for bottles of rum from the trading post. The crowd milled around and gravitated toward the trading post as Swann trotted toward it. The gleam of the torchlight faded in the front room, with dark shadows dancing over the side of the building as the men moved about and waved the torches. Alcey went back to bed. Jubal returned an hour later and got back into bed, cursing furiously.

Another demonstration took place on Halloween, the night before the Stamp Act was to take effect. The next day a tense, steely quiet hung over the town. Many activities were at a standstill. Everyone knew about the Act, but no official notice or copy had been received from England, and no stamps had arrived. No clearance papers for ships could be issued without stamps, and the port was paralyzed, ships unable to enter or leave. Courts were closed for the lack of stamps to authenticate legal documents, and no news sheets, books, or pamphlets could be distributed. And Jubal was in a towering rage. He had cargo in ships waiting to leave the port, as well as goods in ships unable to clear into the port and discharge cargoes. He had also been in the process of purchasing a strip of land to enlarge the lumber mill, as well as other transactions requiring stamps.

There was little diminishment in the work in the office, and the activity in the trading post and around the stockyard and wagonyard even increased slightly. After a few days the *Gazette* began circulating again, with a skull and crossbones in the spot reserved for the official stamp. On a morning in the middle of November Alcey heard a disturbance in the town, and one of the boys in the office told her about it when he returned from an errand. The official stamp distributor for North Carolina had arrived the night before to present his credentials to Governor Tryon, and during early morning some three hundred of the Sons of Liberty had marched to his lodgings behind a flag and drums and had escorted him to the courthouse. There he had written and signed a resignation from his post, and the Sons of Liberty had delivered the credentials and the resignation to the governor and went about their business.

Jubal was one of the fifty political and business leaders who received invitations to dine at the governor's mansion in the middle of November. He had little to say about the affair the following day, but he called in all the foremen and overseers and reiterated that lawful and orderly conduct was a condition of employment with him. During the afternoon four other Wilmington shippers and one from New Bern came to talk to Jubal, and Alcey caught snatches of what they were discussing in Jubal's office. The men, members of the Sons of Liberty, were proposing an agreement between all shippers and merchants to cease importing goods from England and force the recision of the Stamp Act through economic pressure. The discussion was cordial, and Jubal was affable and courteous with them, pouring rum and talking with them in a friendly tone. And he was also totally noncommittal.

At the end of November the sloop of war HMS *Diligence* entered the harbor with supplies of stamps and stamped documents, accompanied by the HMS *Viper*. With no official stamp distributor to accept the stamps and documents the warships idled at anchor among the trading ships waiting to be cleared into or out of port, watched by curious onlookers and Sons of Liberty on the docks. A boat attempted to take supplies of fresh victuals to *Diligence* and *Viper*, and the Sons of Liberty seized it and dumped the supplies overboard. The next Sunday Alcey was at the Bledsoe cabin, and Simon was again locked in his room. He and the Raines boys had been pelting the warships with pebbles from their slings, an irate coxswain from one of the ships had thrashed them, a member of the Sons of Liberty had thrashed them, and they had been thrashed again and locked in their rooms when they got home.

During the second week in December three of the five men who had come to discuss a nonimportation agreement returned. The tones were less cordial and considerably louder, and Alcey had no difficulty in overhearing one of the men naming off all the merchants and shippers who had signed the agreement. And she had no difficulty in overhearing Jubal's refusal to sign. That night there was a commotion outside the house, and through the bedroom window Alcey could see the trading post and warehouse silhouetted by flames leaping up on the opposite side of the building. Jubal jerked on his clothes and ran out as employees rushed from their houses, and Alcey dressed, put on her coat and shawl, and went out. The livestock moved restlessly about in the pens, and the flames leaping high into the air gleamed on the puddles of water and mud as Alcey walked around the end of the wagonyard. Five barrels of pitch had been placed in a row in the yard by the warehouse dock, well away from all structures that might be damaged, and were burning brightly. Jubal and the other men were scooping up mud to extinguish the burning pitch.

Jubal didn't return to the house and was still gone when Alcey arose the next morning. She heard him in his office when she arrived at the office. During the middle of the morning the three men returned with the nonimportation agreement. There was no discussion, and Jubal signed it. The men left, and Jubal called Alcey in and told her to cancel all orders of goods from factors in London. He was pale and drawn with rage, and Alcey kept her features neutral and her eyes downcast to conceal her glee.

Jubal became even more morose and remote, so preoccupied that he paid hardly any attention to Jude. He had always spent long hours in his office, and he began spending most of his time there returning after dinner each night. There were some matters he had always been secretive about, dealing with the correspondence himself and keeping it locked in his desk. Alcey had glimpsed addresses on incoming and outgoing correspondence a few times, to investment brokers and several shippers in London and the colonies, but there had never been any incoming bills of lading or outgoing shipment invoices. Jubal began poring through his private files frequently, covering them and looking up with a frown when Alcey came into his office. He was frequently closeted with Beasley for hours at a time, talking in quiet murmurs. On Christmas Day he was too busy to go to the Bledsoe cabin. Alcey had a man from the stockyards harness the horse and hitch him to the chaise, and she took Alice and Jude. It was an enjoyable day, and Simon wasn't in trouble for once, even though his black eye, swollen lip, and scraped knuckles evidenced something less than completely orderly behavior.

In early January the merchantmen *Dobbs* and *Patience* out of Philadelphia entered the harbor, and they were seized by the captain of HMS *Viper* because their clearance papers from Philadelphia weren't stamped. The governor queried the attorney general of the colony for a legal opinion on whether the seizures were legal and if legal proceedings in a vice-admiralty court should be initiated, and men began gathering from the outlying areas and assembling in Wilmington to await the decision. The attorney general ruled that the seizures were legal, and proceedings should be instituted in Nova Scotia rather than in North Carolina so an unbiased judgment could be reached.

The Sons of Liberty, numbering some one thousand armed men, assembled and marched on the docks and the governor's residence. The governor's residence was surrounded, the papers of the seized vessels were taken, and a delegation of the Sons of Liberty boarded *Viper* and demanded the release of the seized vessels. The captain of *Viper* capitulated. The Sons of Liberty gathered all the Crown officials except the governor, and the officials took an oath not to use stamps or stamped documents in the execution of their offices. *Diligence* and *Viper* sailed out of port, the stamps and stamped documents still on board.

Alcey glowed with pride over what had happened, and she reflected that it was an incident that would have been very gratifying to her father. Rights guaranteed by common

law had been protected, and it had been in the face of the
threat of drastic retaliation. None of the Sons of Liberty
had made any attempt to conceal their identity, and many
were prominent citizens personally known to the governor
and other Crown officials.

The incident had been unique. There had been protests
and demonstrations in other colonies, and Chief Justice
Hutchinson's house had been burned in Boston. Other scattered and minor incidents took place, but the most direct
action taken by the other colonies had been petitions to the
king and appeals to Parliament. But in North Carolina action had been taken with force of arms. For the first time
in history armed colonists had faced British authorities.
And they had achieved their objectives.

The news sheets reported that the official activities
halted in November were functioning again, but the flow of
work in the office was ebbing. It was near the time of year
when there would normally be heavy correspondence, and
the stockpiling of goods for the summer would be in progress. But the Stamp Act was still law and the nonimportation agreement was still binding. Ships were entering and
leaving the harbor, but those coming from England anchored in the estuary and remained unloaded. A story circulated about a merchant in New Bern who was tarred, feath-
ered, and carried through town on a rail for violating a
nonimportation agreement.

When the work in the office had diminished substantially
Jubal fired one of the three boys, and the other two became
more industrious, worried about their jobs. Jubal continued
working late at night and most weekends, and his quiet
conferences with Beasley continued. Then Beasley disappeared. Alcey suddenly realized it had been several days
since she had seen him, but when she asked Jubal about
him, he acidly told her to mind her own affairs.

Several nights later she was awakened by activity around
the warehouse. Jubal had gone back to his office after dinner and hadn't returned. And it was very late at night. Alcey got out of bed, walked quietly through the house to the
front room, and listened at the door. Wagons were moving
around on the other side of the warehouse, by the dock. It
wasn't unusual for wagons to come in from one of the trading posts late at night, but Jubal didn't meet them and they

always waited in the wagonyard until the next morning to be unloaded. It sounded like wagons being unloaded, even though there was no gleam of lanterns from the other side of the warehouse. Heavy crates, bales, and hogsheads thumped and scraped across the dock, and there was an occasional clatter of harness chains and squeaking of wagon wheels and timbers. The rough boards of the floor were cold under Alcey's bare feet, and the icy draft cut through her nightgown as she held the door open a crack and listened for a time, then went back to bed. An hour or more later Jubal quietly entered the house.

He was still asleep when Alcey got out of bed. Alice was in the kitchen, bright and cheerful as she bustled around preparing breakfast, and Alcey helped her and got ready to go to the office. Eight large drays that hadn't been in the wagonyard the day before were parked in a row near the rear, their wheels and sideboards covered with mud. When she entered the office one of the boys said that Jubal had gone to the lumber mill and would be there most of the day. Alcey looked through the bills of lading waiting to be posted in the warehouse inventory ledger, and there was only one waiting from the day before, a small shipment of earthenware, rifle flints, and other miscellaneous items from Baltimore. She pondered for a moment, then went through the doorway at the side of the office and along the hall to the warehouse.

Heavy articles were being moved around at the opposite end of the long, dim room, and voices and laughter were coming from the tiny office by the dock door. Alcey pulled her shawl closer and walked along the center aisle, glancing at the narrow aisles that opened off on each side between the bales, crates, and hogsheads. Fresh gouges in the floor timbers led into one of the aisles and clumps of wet mud were smeared on the floor at the end where fabrics were stored and large bales were stacked up on each side, segregated by type. The heavy canvas coverings on one stack were damp and muddy, and she read the lettering on the bales of calico consigned from a shipper in London to a merchant in Charleston.

Quick, heavy footsteps came up behind her as she walked back toward the office. "Were you looking for something, Mistress Collier?"

It was Beasley, his tone worried and suspicious. She shook her head, walking on along the center aisle. "I don't require any assistance, thank you."

He hesitated for a long moment, then slowly walked back toward the small office at the side of the warehouse. Alcey went into her office and sat down at her desk, aimlessly shuffling through papers on her desk and staring at them blankly. The condition of the drays were proof that the goods hadn't come in at the port, as was the consignee, because ships from London weren't being unloaded at the port. But the goods hadn't come from Charleston by dray, because Beasley hadn't been gone long enough to get to Charleston and back over muddy winter roads, and it would have been much cheaper and easier to ship them on a coastal vessel. The goods had been acquired directly from a vessel out of London, possibly one that had been unable to discharge its cargo at Charleston because of a nonimportation agreement among the merchants there. Jubal had probably contacted associates in ports up and down the coast to find ships with goods on board that were in short supply in the warehouse, a rendezvous had been arranged with the captain of a ship, and the ship had put in at a nearby cove along the coast and lightered the goods ashore to the drays.

Burning anger swelled within her. Other men had risked all in fighting the Stamp Act. They had jeopardized their lives and property, and they had chanced arrest and prosecution for everything from riotous and unlawful assembly to armed insurrection. But Jubal couldn't even forego a minimum amount of short-term profits. And it would only be short-term at most, because the nonimportation agreements were working. The news sheets from London were already reporting restiveness among merchants, and it would shortly be alarm. When the powerful merchant interests in London became alarmed, Parliament would react. But every ship that managed to discharge its cargo would prolong the process. More than that, every ship that managed to discharge cargo eased the fear of economic reprisal in general, decreasing its effectiveness as a weapon. Most of all a fist lifted in defiance could not be permitted to tremble. And that collective fist was partly hers. Some London merchant would laugh sarcastically in satisfaction when the ship returned with the cargo sold. And that laugh would be directed partly at her.

Then her anger turned into a drab, hopeless resentment. There was nothing she could do about it. Jubal would be furious and tell her to mind her own affairs if she mentioned it to him, and moreover, it would do no good to mention it to him. And it would be impossible for her to tell anyone else about it. Beyond the fact that it would be irrational because it would have an impact upon her and Jude, she was prohibited from telling anyone else because of loyalty. Jubal was her husband. She didn't love him, but she had to be loyal. As a basic tenet of her upbringing she had to be either loyal to him or a traitor to herself.

She sighed heavily, stacking the papers in a pile and pulling her shawl closer. The damp chill had a feel of coming change in it, of life stirring in growing things and of warmer days ahead, but the buoyant uplift in spirits the promise of spring usually sparked in her was missing. She took her fingerless wool gloves from the recess in the side of her desk and pulled them on, then took her quill out of the slot, cut the point off, and shaped another. She put the knife down, took the top off her inkwell, and pulled the stack of papers closer.

Jubal's footsteps came along the porch. Alcey glanced at the boy who had told her that Jubal would be at the lumber mill most of the day, and he shrugged slightly and looked back down at his desk, writing busily. The footsteps approached the door, and Alcey looked down at the papers in front of her. Jubal came in, closed the door, and walked slowly toward his office. Alcey glanced up. His face was in stern lines of contained anger, and he indicated his office with his chin as he looked at her. She suddenly realized why he had returned from the lumber mill. Beasley had either gone there or sent word that she had been in the warehouse and looking at the goods that had been unloaded the night before. Apprehension began within her, and she controlled it as she put the top back on her inkwell, put the quill in the slot, and rose.

He closed the door as she stepped into the office, then turned and glared at her. "What were you doing loitering about in the warehouse?"

Alcey lifted her chin and looked back at him, staring

into his eyes. "I heard the wagons being unloaded last night and I saw no bills to be entered in the ledger, so I went to see what had been unloaded."

"And your only concern was the accuracy of the ledger?" he sneered.

"No. I was also passing curious as to why wagons were being unloaded in the night."

His face flushed and his eyes narrowed as he started to shout something. Then he stopped himself, looked at her with a musing frown for a moment, and turned away. He crossed the room, took off his hat and put it on his desk, and straightened his peruke as he took the rum bottle and a cup from the shelf. He splashed rum into the cup, replaced the bottle on the shelf, and walked to the window and looked out, sipping the rum.

"Jubal, it's foregone that the Stamp Act will be abolished. It's only a matter of time, and it's contrary to reason to risk—"

"Hold your tongue!" he snapped over his shoulder. "I've no need for your bloody views on the intentions of Parliament, the state of the world, or whether or not it's bloody raining." He took another drink of rum, then turned away from the window and walked back toward his desk. "Go to the house. I'll discuss this with you there."

"Now, do you mean? I was seeing to that—"

"Yes, I mean now! Forget the bloody work, not that you'll have a chore doing that, considering the extent to which it occupies your mind!"

Alcey stiffened and glared back at him, suppressing the scathing retort that rose to her lips, and she turned to the door and went out. The two boys glanced up, then quickly looked back at their work. Alcey took off her gloves, put them in the recess in the side of her desk, and pulled her shawl up over her head as she crossed to the office door and went out.

Alice stepped to the kitchen doorway and looked at Alcey with a puzzled smile as she came in the front door. "Back so soon? Are you well, Mistress Collier?"

"Yes, thank you. My husband wishes to talk with me about something, and he asked me to come here to discuss it."

"It's naught I've done, is it?"

"Oh, no, it doesn't concern you, Alice."

"Aye, well, I never know when I've . . . Come on and sit by the fire, then, Mistress, and I'll make you a nice cup of tea. I've just put little Jude to bed for his morning nap, and I was doing this bit of cleaning up here. A nice cup of tea goes down good on a morning such as this."

Alcey hung up her coat and shawl, went into the kitchen, and sat down on a stool by the hearth, warming her hands and feet. Alice continued chattering as she bustled about and filled the teapot from the kettle, her manner communicating a cautiously guarded, uninvolved sympathy in event Alcey was having some difficulty with Jubal. She gave Alcey a cup of tea and put the pot on the hearth in front of her, then put on a shawl and went out onto the back porch to do washing. Alcey sipped the tea and looked into the fire, pondering. Jubal's anger had lacked the explosive heat that had always characterized his temper. It had been cold and hard, more intense. And somehow more threatening because of the musing, thoughtful element in it.

Alice came back in, shivering and warming her hands at the fire, then went into the front room and began cleaning. The minutes dragged slowly by. Jubal's tone had suggested that he would be coming to the house immediately. The delay seemed auspicious, indicating that the matter wasn't of paramount concern to him and of sufficient importance to put everything else aside. But in another way the delay seemed ominous. Alice finished in the front room and went into the bedrooms.

Jubal's footsteps crossed the porch, and the front door rattled as he came in. His pace was slower and more deliberate than usual. Alice came out of the bedrooms and made a nervous sound of greeting.

"Take the boy to Hugh's house."

"Ah . . . well, he's just taking his nap, and he—"

"Then wake him up!"

Alice scuttled into the bedroom. Jude whimpered querulously, and Alice murmured soothingly. Her footsteps came out of the bedroom, crossed the front room, and went out. Jubal came into the kitchen. He took a bottle of rum from a shelf, poured some into a cup, then walked to the fireplace and stood on the other side of the hearth.

"Have you thought that you'd like to return to England?"

The anger was gone from his voice, and it was almost conversational in tone. She looked up at him, puzzled. "Return to England? What do you mean?"

"I mean I'm finished with you, and I'd as soon make the ending of this sorry affair as easy and simple as possible."

It took an instant for his full meaning to register, then she sat up on the stool as indignant anger flooded through her. "Finished with me?" she snapped. "Do you think I'm a pot to be cast aside when it's broken or an ox to be sent to slaughter at will? Regardless of your views and of how I've been treated, I'm a human being. And I have rights under the law."

He took a drink from the cup and looked into the fire, shrugging. "I know more about your rights than you do, I daresay, such as they are. Now answer my question—do you wish to return to England?"

Her anger began fading as dark apprehension formed. She shook her head and swallowed dryly. "No, I'll stop here. And I see you've been contemplating this for some time."

He nodded nonchalantly. "I'm not caught unawares when I can avoid it, which you'd know if you'd ever taken the trouble to study me. I made it my business to find out how to get out of a marriage before I got into one."

"I'm not totally ignorant on the subject, even though I lack your scheming cast of mind, and it might not be as simple as you expect. There was a time when you rode roughshod over me, but that time is well past."

"Aye, mouse before the wedding and scold afterward," he sneered. "Well, that was part of your undoing. That, and the foolishness your father instilled in your mind. But now I'll tell you a few things you mightn't have thought of. It's not that long gone that everyone in these houses here heard you screaming like a fishwife at me, and they'll testify to that. I've also men who'll testify to how your meddling has interfered with my business, and men who'll testify . . ." His voice faded and he shrugged again, taking a drink from his cup. "I've ample testimony to support a bill of divorcement, and it's a matter of placing it before the Assembly, which is easily done. I know enough members of the Assembly that it'll pass without even a hearing. But as I said, I wish to make it as easy and simple as possible. To that end I'll arrange passage to England for you, and I'll settle an amount on you that will see you comfortably set up."

Fear gripped her as she looked up at him and studied his face. He meant it. It wasn't a threat to ensure her silence over what she had seen in the warehouse or to keep her from prying further. He had made a decision to divorce her. And he could, because he had acquaintances among the various Crown officials as well as in the Assembly. It was a staggering, devastating blow. She had expected a confrontation and a reprimand from him, a warning to contain her curiosity. Instead everything was falling to pieces around her. What had been a solid foundation for life, if less than happy and comfortable, had turned into a quaking morass under her. She felt numb, and tears burned in her eyes. She blinked them back, swallowing to keep her voice from trembling.

"Jubal, I can well believe that you could fail to consider loyalty as a matter to be reckoned with, because it's foreign to your nature. But I could never tell another of what I saw or that you've been—"

"That's only part of it," he interrupted impatiently. "And not the largest part, by far. You think you've the station in life of a man. You have a head full of foolishness, and I can't trust you. And I won't have someone around me that I can't trust. Furthermore I've determined my course and I won't be turned aside from it, so it's wasted talk to discuss it."

Alcey blinked and swallowed again. "I wasn't attempting to. I was about to observe that your decision might be costly to you, because you'll pay a pretty penny to replace me as a clerk. But you have your reasons, and perhaps they're more important to you than the cost. I would also observe that while I've become outspoken, and possibly to excess on one occasion, saintly Job himself might pluck out his beard in wrath were he to have concourse with you to the extent that I have. But that aside I'll not beg to stay where I'm not wanted, and I'll find my own road if I'm to go. I'll take my son and leave, and I'll put you to no—"

"You will not take him!" he snarled, emphasizing each word. "You will go alone, and you'll return to England where you—"

"I shall take him!" she hissed in fury, glaring up at him. "I am his mother, and I shall take him wherever I go!"

Jubal put the cup on the mantel and looked down at her, his face in hard, rigid lines. "Now hear me out," he said quietly, pointing his finger at her. "And listen to every word I say. I wish to make this simple and easy, but the choice in that is yours. My son does not regard you as his mother, and that you well know. If you were to try to take him away from Alice, he would bring the house down about your ears, and that you well know. He stays with me. I will book your passage to England and ship your belongings for you, and I will settle a goodly amount on you. But if you contest this with me, you'll find yourself in a worse condition than you were when I married you. If need be I can see you penniless in the street, dragged there and out of this house by the bailiffs. I can do this, because I have witnesses who will testify to your loose and profane tongue. I also have witnesses who will testify to your meddling in my business." He leaned toward her, his eyes narrowing. "And I also have witnesses who will testify that you've been a common whore behind my back. Now you bloody think on that, woman!"

A heated denial rose to her lips as she looked up at him in shock, then she closed her mouth. He had said he had witnesses. And among the men who worked for him he undoubtedly had. She looked at the fire, her eyes filling with tears and a sob catching in her throat. "If there be a God in heaven, you will suffer for this," she murmured, her voice trembling. "If there be a God in heaven, you will rue this day."

# Chapter Eighteen

She shrank from the dangers and privation of a sea voyage, and returning to England to no family and no fixed situation was as forbidding as the voyage. And even through her confusion and turmoil she realized that she could go back in space but not in time, and that it would be a mistake even to attempt to return at all.

The Cosgrave family was a source of assistance. But they were weeks away in terms of the time it would take to get a letter to them and get a response, while her predicament required immediate action and she had no money to travel. There was also pride that made her reluctant to beg their assistance. Other than the Cosgraves her only refuge was the Bledsoe cabin.

The tension in the cabin was nerve-wracking. Hannah and Nina were affectionate and loving, they wanted to make her welcome, and they were appalled by what Jubal had done. But their love for Jubal went far into the past. The old man had always been more impatient with Jubal, and his actions were direct and effective. Jubal was enraged over her refusal to go to England and had forbidden her to take any of her belongings out of the house, and the old man hitched the oxen to the wagon and went for them. While he was there, he demanded and got from Jubal an amount equivalent to clerk's wages for the length of time Alcey had been married to him, an amount in excess of eighty guineas.

The logical course of action seemed to be to find employment as a governess or tutor. Alcey picked out eight families from those she had read about in the *Gazette*, those who had children of various ages and might not have a governess or tutor, and she wrote letters to them, detailing her qualifications. Hannah and Nina sighed admiringly over Alcey's handwriting and the neat packets the letters made, and they talked enthusiastically about how many requests for interviews she might get. The old man and Simon rowed across the estuary to deliver six of the letters to plantations on the west shore, and they delivered the other two to residences in the center of town. The cheerful talk continued for a couple of days after the letters had been delivered, then it gradually disappeared under an embarrassed veneer of talk on other subjects as the days passed and no replies were received.

Total dependence on the charity of others was galling and humiliating, but any hint of moving elsewhere made Hannah and Nina distraught, fearful that something they had said had been misconstrued, or that they hadn't been hospitable enough. But the old man had perceptiveness and a degree of sensitivity that surprised Alcey. He owned a wide swath of land that extended from the road to the estuary tide flat, and without mentioning the subject, he began building a small cabin and outbuildings in the corner of the pasture near the road.

Isaac Raines had come home to work on his cabin and plant his crops, and he brought two of his sons and helped. Other men who lived nearby came to help for varying amounts of time. Still others brought stones for the hearth and step, boards for the door and shutters, and seasoned wood for shingles. A man whose wife had died some time before came and asked Alcey to marry him, and she stuttered a negative, taken aback by the bald question. The man ruefully chuckled and said that he hadn't thought she would, and he cheerfully helped on the cabin for a couple of days. It was finished within a few days, with a rail fence around it and its outbuildings to separate it from the pasture. When it was completed, the old man and Simon went to Jubal's house and returned with a table, stools, a large mirror, a wooden tub, rain barrels, and other things. Simon told Alcey about it, laughing gleefully as he described Jubal's raging fury while the old man had stolidly carried things out of the house and loaded them into the wagon.

The story of what had happened to Alcey spread through the nearby cabins, but the people showed less open curiosity about details than Alcey had expected. Alcey candidly declined to discuss the subject, and it wasn't brought up again. All the people were sympathetic, the assistance of some of the men seeming more generous than if her situation had been different, and the women even more supportive. Martha Raines brought a spinning wheel, another woman brought a churn, another brought a nesting chicken with six eggs, and others brought small pieces of homespun and small articles needing repair. On the second day Alcey was in the cabin, a bailiff brought her an approved bill of divorcement that had been passed by the Assembly.

Alcey felt an aching sorrow over the separation from Jude, a constant gnawing melancholy where there had once been fulfillment. But she realized the loss was less wrenching than it could have been under other circumstances, because she had been gradually losing him from the time Alice had come into the house. From that point he had become less than the primary motivating force in her life. And she had become virtually nonexistent to him. But as at least a partial compensation for the loss of Jude, she had a sense of utter freedom. The depressing, hateful cloud of Jubal's presence was gone and would never have to be suffered again. She had companionship, because she saw Hannah and Nina all the time and there were visits from Martha Raines and other women who lived nearby. But she also had moments to herself. She had an intensely satisfying feeling of ownership toward the cabin, a feeling she had never before known. A sense of accomplishment came from finding a crack between two logs and mixing a handful of mud to chink it. It was gratifying to simply sit in front of the cheerful fire at night and look at the firelight playing on the walls and her things placed neatly about the cabin.

She also felt independent for the first time in her life, in control of herself and her situation. The old man told her in his blunt and straightforward but kindly way that she could share in the milk from the cows in exchange for tutoring Simon for an hour each day, and that she could help with the gardening and share in the crops. The eighty guineas was virtually untouched, and it became certain that it would last indefinitely when word got out that she was expert in reading and writing. Some of the people in the surrounding cabins were illiterate, and others could read and write after a fashion but preferred to seek skilled help when it was available and inexpensive. Writing a letter or deciphering a letter and writing a reply was a service that cost ninepence or a shilling in town, but Alcey set no established charge and they brought what they could, a piece of gammon, a basket of vegetables, a chicken, a jar of honey or molasses, or a bag of corn. One man who wanted seven letters written brought a thin, spindly pig with a long snout and an ear-splitting squeal. They were grateful that she would take what they offered, and Alcey was grateful that she could help them. Whenever she sat at the table and waited while a quiet, unassuming couple in homespuns discussed in soft tones what to say next in their letter, Alcey felt that her education had found fulfillment.

The ground became dry enough to plow, and Nina gave Alcey a sun bonnet and an old homespun dress she had cut down for her. The old man plowed and harrowed, and Alcey, Hannah, Nina, and Simon carried compost to fertilize lettuce and onion beds. The work was grueling, and Alcey could hardly get out of bed on the second day. Then the soreness disappeared, and the others had difficulty in keeping pace with her. She stopped wearing a petticoat under the homespun dress and cut off a pair of pantaloons above the knees for comfort, then she began going barefoot because of the difficulty in walking in the soft soil in shoes. There was a two-day respite to wait for the right phase of the moon, then they began the planting. A soft, warm rain began falling before they finished. The feel of the rain soaking through her dress to her skin, the soft feel of the freshly turned earth under her bare feet, and the moist odor of the soil struck a responsive chord within Alcey.

After the planting Simon began coming to Alcey's cabin each morning for his hour of lessons. He was a strapping nine-year-old with features strikingly like Santee's, of a size that indicated he would be as large as Santee, and a quick temper and aggressively independent personality that made him difficult for Hannah and Nina to control at times. But he was less sure of himself with Alcey, and she wasn't a doting grandmother. Her education had been based solidly on discipline, there was a thick birch switch prominently on the table with the slate and chalk the first morning he came, and she had no difficulty in controlling him. Genesee was Simon's small shadow, able to climb, run, and swim much better than boys twice his age, and Alcey enjoyed talking and playing with him while Simon was busy with the slate. Genesee was quieter than Simon but possibly more mischievous, impossible to keep fully clothed, frequently catching snakes to put in the cabin to scare Hannah and Nina, and playing other tricks. He was supple and slender, his features much like Santee's, his hair coarse, thick, and black and his eyes a dark blue like Santee's. But there was a faint olive tone to his skin and a softness to his features reminiscent of Aimee.

Simon and Genesee fished along the creek and at the mouth of the creek almost daily, and Alcey went with them and learned how. The old man caught a large flounder in the estuary, and by watching Hannah and Nina she learned how to salt and smoke fish to preserve it. Hannah and Nina also showed her how to make soap with woodash lye and pork fat, and how to card, spin, and weave wool and flax.

Simon was learning to fire a rifle, but it was a slow process. Powder and lead were too expensive for aimless shooting, and Simon had to wait until the old man had time to take him hunting for small game, so the powder and lead could be used to kill meat for the table. Alcey had happened across the formula for gunpowder in one of the books her father had left her, and she talked to the old man about it. He was doubtful, because others had tried it and come up with a very poor grade of gunpowder at best. Niter for curing meat and brimstone for fumigating cabins was readily available in town, both of them were inexpensive, and Alcey sent Simon for a small amount of each and made a charcoal furnace in the ground by her cabin. Smoke trickled from the air hole in the top of the furnace for a day, turf covering the billets of hickory remained hot for another three days, and the two boys waited impatiently. Simon was bemused that books could be used in practical applications as well as in mental torture, and Genesee was interested in anything that interested Simon. When the furnace cooled, Alcey made scales from string, a stick, and two small gourds. She dug out the charcoal and used a large wooden spoon and bowl for a mortar and pestle to mix the ingredients. The boys hovered around breathlessly as she carried the bowl outside, and the results were more spectacular than she had anticipated when she touched the tip of a firebrand to the pile of powder, the swirling ball of flame singed the front of her hair and took off Simon's and Genesee's eyebrows, and the huge cloud of smoke obscured the end of the pasture as it billowed across it. But it was unquestionably gunpowder, and of commercial quality. The old man had difficulty believing it at first, then he was amazed and delighted when Alcey mixed another batch and he fired a charge with his rifle.

While fishing at the mouth of the creek with Simon and Genesee one day, Alcey found an injured dog. It had apparently washed down the estuary and was more dead than alive, feebly trying to crawl out onto the bank as the tide came in. They pulled the dog onto the bank, and Alcey washed off the mud with creek water and examined it. A large male dog, with wide, strong shoulders and a thick, heavy neck, it looked like some sort of hound, with long ears and large spots of black and brown. But its ears were frayed, and it had deep wounds along with numerous scars from previous encounters. They made a stretcher of poles and sticks and carried it to her cabin.

Simon went for the old man, who brought a pot of turpentine and shook his head over the dog as he daubed the wounds. He said it was a Black and Tan hound, probably a fighting dog that had been wounded beyond recovery in the dog fights or bear baiting in the pits at the head of the estuary. He didn't believe the dog would live. Alcey made broth and poured trickles of it into the dog's mouth as it struggled to swallow, eyes glazed with pain.

When it began to appear that the dog would live, the old man shook his head for a different reason. He was a large, powerful fighting dog, a dangerous animal. But the dog didn't seem to be aggressive or vicious as he regained his strength and began moving painfully about. He didn't like to be petted and would move away from Simon and Genesee with a warning glare if they approached him. But it made no attempt to attack people who came to the cabin to get Alcey's help with letters. Alcey thought about what to call the dog as he became more active and started gaining weight, and she decided to name him Dock.

Alcey's life took on a quality of deep, serene satisfaction far surpassing that of any other period in her life. The days were full, but she had ample time for privacy and contemplation. It was pleasant to stand in the doorway and look out at the rain, to feel the wind against her face and the earth under her bare feet, and to awaken to the sound of her rooster crowing in the tree by the cabin. The colors of sunrise and sunset were richer. She felt vibrantly alive, browned by the sun and pared to minimum weight by physical labor. Food tasted better, and her sleep was sound. Each day began with buoyant, cheerful expectations and ended with measurable results achieved. Fatigue came from aching muscles rather than frayed nerves. She could shrug off an all-day stint of bending over the hoe with a night's sleep, and none of the others could keep pace with her. The hogs rooted out of the sty one afternoon when they were all working in the crops, and they ran to herd them and drive them back into the pen. Simon was chagrined because Alcey effortlessly outran him along the path, her skirt gathered up around her knees and her bare feet slapping the hard-packed earth.

When the children weren't around, Hannah or Nina occasionally mentioned Aimee's death in a sad murmur, and a few times one or the other of them referred to the day Santee had left Genesee at the cabin and rode away without dismounting from his horse. They frequently discussed Santee in hushed, worried tones, but the old man was confident about Santee's well-being. There was some speculation as to whether he would be in during the summer, and the old man was firmly of the opinion that he wouldn't. As the days of the summer slowly passed and the summer heat began moderating, it became evident that the old man was right.

Alcey dug a root cellar under her cabin during spare moments and made bins for the cellar from pieces of boards and shingles that had been left over from building the cabin. The crops began maturing, and they started gathering them. The pace was moderate at first, picking beans and peas and drying them in the sun, then it became more rapid as the mornings turned chilly, collecting cucumbers and cabbages before the frost touched them. The cornstalks began turning, the long leaves becoming dry and rustling in the wind, and they collected the squashes, pumpkins, and corn. Then they dug potatoes and pulled onions, turnips, and carrots. The root cellar Alcey had dug was filled, and her cabin smelled of the bunches of onions hanging from the beams and the bags of corn, peas, and beans.

The old man killed three of the hogs on a cold, windy morning, and it took all day to butcher them. They hung the carcasses on a trestle to clean them and let them cool, then sorted out the entrails and cleaned them. The wind whipped the roaring fire under the large, black kettle in which the lard was rendering, and they took turns standing in the warmth of the fire to stir the kettle and dip out the lard into wooden kegs. They took the carcasses down and put them on a puncheon table to cut up, smearing the hams, shoulders, and bacon flitches with niter and hanging them in the smokehouse to cure, and salting the rest. It was a long, hard day in the cold, but Alcey felt contented as she sat in front of her fireplace after a dinner of rich, lean pork ribs, with Dock lying by the hearth and contentedly gnawing a bone.

There was less to do after the weather turned cold and rainy, and Alcey kept Simon and Genesee at her cabin for half the day or longer, working with Simon on his lessons and reading to them. Simon was progressing, and at times his curiosity in a story stimulated him to concentrate harder on his reading, but it was obvious that his interests and the main thrust of his talents lay in directions other than his studies. He and the old man frequently went hunting rabbits in the scrubby, sandy fields on the other side of the road, and the old man began asking Alcey to go with them. When she went, the old man would occasionally give her a rifle to shoot, and he wanted her to reload it each time a shot was taken. The rifle was heavy and cumbersome, difficult for her to hold steady enough to aim it accurately, and the snap of the hammer as it slapped down made her jerk the rifle off the target at first. She became accustomed to the noise of the hammer and her accuracy improved to an extent, particularly when shooting from a rest, and she became almost as adept as the old man at reloading.

Near Christmas she went into town with the old man to do some shopping, and it was unpleasantly crowded, noisy, and odorous after the months of being away from it. She went to a fabric shop for the needles, ribbons, and other things she needed, then she went to a sundries shop and picked out Christmas presents for the boys, a pocketknife for Simon and a top and string for Genesee. As she left the shop and walked back toward where the old man had parked the wagon, she came face to face with Jubal. He looked ill, his face drawn and haggard and his shoulders bowed in his heavy greatcoat. And he looked smaller. His eyes widened as he saw her, and he stopped. Alcey stared at him coldly. His eyes dropped, and he averted his face and walked on. The gray, gloomy day was brighter and Alcey felt unusually cheerful as she went back to the wagon and waited for the old man.

Stock thefts were common along the road during late winter, and Alcey was awakened one night by Dock scrambling out of the hole he had dug under the bedroom lean-to at the rear of the cabin. He rarely barked, usually expressing suspicion or dissatisfaction by baring his teeth and growling, but now he burst into deep, ringing baying as he leaped the fence around the cabin and raced toward the other corner of the pasture. The baying changed into a ferocious snarl, a man bellowed in pain, and the loud crack of a rifle echoed across the pasture. Alcey leaped out of bed, snatched her coat from a peg as she ran through the cabin, and raced outside.

Another rifle cracked, and a momentary flash of bright yellow cut through the darkness on the other side of the pasture. Two men cursed and shouted in pain and alarm as Dock fought them, snarling viciously. The oxen lumbered about in the darkness of the pasture, and a horse whinnied and stamped in fright. Alcey hesitated, then pulled her coat around her and ran toward the fence, her bare feet splashing through the cold mud and water. She climbed over the fence and ran across the pasture, shouting at Dock and urging him on. The horse squealed in pain, his hooves scrabbling on the road, and raced away along the road toward town. The sounds of the fight between Dock and the two men began moving along the road toward town. The bobbing light of a lantern came along the path from the Bledsoe cabin as Alcey approached the corner of the pasture, and Alcey called Dock back. The old man ran up with his rifle and the lantern, puffing breathlessly, and looked around. One of the rails at the corner of the fence had been taken down, and torn pieces of homespun splotched with blood were scattered on the ground by the fence. Dock came back along the road, limping from a heavy blow on one shoulder, a shallow furrow across his back where a rifle ball had grazed him, and his mouth full of bits of homespun and blood. The old man chortled gleefully as he went for turpentine to put on the furrow on Dock's back, and he stopped in the smokehouse to bring Dock a large pork bone covered with thick chunks of meat.

Before the cold rain and winds of winter had been only a discomfort to be endured, but a wall of detachment had disappeared and Alcey felt in closer harmony with what went on around her. There was a kind of empathy, and she detected a change when the wind lost the edge of its driving force and the cold became less biting as a prelude to the arrival of spring. Then the chickens and other animals moved about more, and there was a burgeoning feel and smell in the earth.

Hannah had been bothered with a painful stiffness and swelling in her joints during the winter, and the old man's right foot troubled him. When the weather warmed, the old man limped less, but Hannah improved only to a degree. Her legs and back were stiff and her fingers were swollen and clumsy when Alcey sat with her and Nina in front of their cabin on warm afternoons and helped sort out the seeds for planting. She remained at the cabin and prepared meals for the others when the plowing and planting began, and Alcey threw herself into the work to make up for Hannah's absence. Hannah wavered on becoming bedridden for a time after the planting, and Alcey went with the old man on one of his trips into town and brought back a pot of aromatic liniment salve. The weather became much warmer and Hannah used the salve and potions Nina made and slowly improved.

A leak had developed in the corner of the roof on Alcey's cabin during the winter, one which would ordinarily be ignored because it let in only a tiny trickle of water, but having anything wrong with her cabin bothered Alcey. The old man was working at the forge in the toolroom when she went for the pole ladder hanging on the side of it, and he told her that repairing a roof was men's work. Alcey laughed and shrugged it off, taking down the ladder, and she dragged it along the path to her cabin.

The wind had pushed one of the shingles sideward, its edge was warped and had slid up over the edge of the adjacent shingle, and it had swiveled on the wooden peg holding it to the rafter, opening a crack through which the rain had leaked. Alcey turned the shingle back straight, climbed down and found a thick stick, then climbed up and wedged a piece of the stick between the warped shingle and the adjacent one to keep it from turning again. She started to climb back down, then hesitated and looked around. The trees had yet to develop their full summer foliage, and she could see some of the cabins on adjacent properties through the trees. The grass in the pasture was becoming thick and the oxen and cows were grazing contentedly, a haze of green covered the tilled area in straight rows, and the gleam of the bright sunshine on the estuary was visible through the trees on the slope in front of the Bledsoe cabin. The air was fresh and damp, and rich with the smells of growing things. She glanced along the road, then she looked intently.

A string of horses was moving along the road at a trot. Alcey shaded her eyes with her hand, looking at the rider on the first horse. Even from a distance it was unmistakably Santee.

# Chapter Nineteen

Alcey climbed rapidly back down the ladder, then hesitated at the bottom. A frenzied urge for activity clamored within her, an imperative need to do something. But she didn't know what to do, and she felt confused and nervous. She pulled the ladder away from the side of the cabin, lowered it to the ground, and began dragging it back toward the toolroom.

As she pulled the ladder along the path by the tilled area, Simon came around the side of the cabin with a bucket of slops for the hogs. "Simon, your pa's coming! Go tell your grandma and Nina!"

He stopped, his mouth and eyes opening wide. He put the bucket down and ran back around the cabin. Alcey dragged the ladder around the corner of the stock pens and past the corn crib to the toolroom at the rear of the barn, and she looked in the doorway. "Mr. Bledsoe, Santee's coming. He's coming along the road from town."

"Santee?" he shouted excitedly, his hammer poised as he held a hot piece of metal on the anvil with a pair of tongs. He tossed the piece of metal into a bucket of water and dropped the hammer and tongs, trotting toward the door. "Santee's coming? Well, I'll be . . ."

He ran out of the toolroom and around the barn, limping heavily. His voice joined those of Hannah and Nina as they exclaimed with delight, seeing Santee turning onto the path. Simon and Genesee whooped and shrieked, their voices fading as they ran along the path. Alcey lifted one end of the ladder to a peg on the side of the toolroom, then walked along it and lifted the other end to a peg. An irrational urge to flee and hide gripped her. Her hands trembled violently, her knees quivered, her mouth felt dry, and her stomach churned with nausea. She walked around the corner of the toolroom toward the others.

The horses trotted swiftly along the path. Simon sat on the horse in front of Santee, and Santee held Genesee on his thigh as he laughed and talked with the two boys. He was cleanshaven, his hair was pulled back neatly and tied, and his buckskins were clean. Some of the lines in his face were more pronounced and he looked older, more settled and mature, but there was nothing of the agony of grief that had been on his features the last time she had seen him. He pulled up his horse at the corner of the stock pens and dismounted, and Hannah and Nina rushed to him, hugging and kissing him tearfully. The old man limped forward, and he wrung Santee's hand and joyfully pounded his back and shoulder.

Then Santee looked at her. She was in a shapeless homespun dress, the sleeves short to free her arms, and the hem well above her ankles so she wouldn't stumble and fall. Her hair was pulled back and tied with a string, her arms and face were brown from the sun, and her feet were bare and dusty. But his eyes looked past all that. The seething agitation within her abruptly faded as she saw the look in his eyes. She suddenly realized the previous summer and winter had been a period of waiting to see how he would look at her. And perhaps years before that had been a period of stasis, of waiting to wait. In retrospect it seemed that, in a way, life itself had been a twisting path that had gradually led her to this minute and this meeting. His teeth were very white against his bronzed face as he smiled slightly, his dark blue eyes on hers. He was very tall. And very handsome. Alcey felt her smile spreading out of control and a flush forming on her cheeks under her tan. She walked forward and held out her hand.

"I'm pleased to see you again, Santee."

"And I'm pleased to see you, Alcey."

He held her hand, smiling down at her. The others were absolutely silent, looking between them. Alcey felt herself turning crimson, and she pulled back and folded her hands in front of her. The old man cleared his throat self-consciously.

"Well, you see, there was this falling out between Jubal

and Alcey, Santee, and Alcey came here to stay with us. That's her cabin out by the road. . . ."

Santee nodded. "I heard about it."

"Of course he heard about it," Hannah said. "He's been by Jubal's factory to get shot of his furs, hasn't he? How is that boy, Santee? Mercy, it's been so long since we've—"

"I went to Wilson's."

There was another moment of silence. Simon pulled at Santee's arm. "I'm shooting a rifle pretty good now, Pa. Maybe we can go hunting while you're here."

Santee smiled, ruffling Simon's hair. "Maybe we can, son."

The old man cleared his throat briskly and rubbed his hands together. "Well, what are we all standing here for? Let's get these horses penned and find a sip of rum, Santee. Have we got something good cooking for supper, Hannah?"

"I'll cut a piece of ham and put it on to roast. That's some really good ham we put up last year, Santee." She smiled at him, starting to turn toward the cabin, then looked at Alcey. "You're coming in, aren't you, love?"

"I have some milk souring and about ready to churn, and a couple of other things to do."

"Well, you come on and have supper with us when you're finished. It'll be nice, all of us sitting around the table."

Alcey smiled and nodded, turning away. On the edge of her vision she could see Santee looking at her as the old man said something to him and Simon pulled at his arm. She walked along the path toward her cabin, and she could hear them unsaddling the horses. And she could feel Santee's eyes on her. A lighthearted, joyous elation suffused her, and she felt like running and skipping along the path.

It seemed both ostentatious and unnecessary to do too much about her appearance. When she finished the things she had to do, she pulled the tub into the cabin and bathed, combed her hair back and tied it, and picked out a calico dress. All of her clothes were slightly large because of the weight she'd lost, and all of her shoes were tight because her feet had spread from going barefoot. She put a sash around the waist of the dress to pull it in and slipped on a pair of moccasins that Nina had given her at Christmas, emptied the tub and hung it outside the cabin, and walked along the path to the Bledsoe cabin. The sun was sinking into the west, and the fleecy clouds scattered across the sky glowed with a soft flush of gold and pink.

It was a cheerful, noisy meal. Hannah and Nina were still in a flush of joyful excitement over Santee's arrival, and the old man was expansive and talkative from the rum he'd had. He was astounded over the catch Santee had made. Santee had found the hunting and trapping grounds he'd been searching for, and he described it as a virtual paradise, thick forests of huge trees, prairies filled with herds of buffalo, rivers teeming with fish, and enormous quantities of deer, elk, turkey, beaver, otter, and other game.

When they finished eating, Alcey helped Hannah and Nina wash the dishes, and they sat back down at the table and joined the conversation again. An hour after dark the old man's eyelids became heavy, and he started nodding. He looked at Santee and Alcey with a blank, drowsy expression as Santee told her more about *Kenta-ke*, and his eyes slowly closed and his chin dropped to his chest. He sat up straight, opening his eyes wide, scratching his head, and smothering a yawn as Santee looked at him and chuckled.

"Are you about ready to roost, Pa?"

"Oh, no, I'm all right, son. Maybe we ought to have another little sip."

"You do, and you'll fall over and go to sleep on the floor," Hannah chuckled. "You'd do better with a cup of tea. Maybe we could all use one. Do you fancy a cup, Alcey?"

"I believe I'll decline, because it's past time I was going," Alcey said, rising. "Thank you very much for the delicious supper."

"Mercy, you did half of it yourself, love. Are you sure you won't stop for a cup of tea?"

"Thank you, no. I believe I'll get on home."

"I'll walk you there," Santee said, rising.

Hannah looked at him quickly, her expression indicating she wasn't sure whether or not it violated her sense of propriety, then she smiled and nodded. Alcey glanced around and said good night, walking toward the door, and the others murmured and nodded as Santee followed her out.

The moon was full, shining brightly on the path when they were out of the shadow of the cabin. His hand was large and warm on her arm, a gentle touch, and there was a feel of restrained and controlled strength, strength more than sufficient to keep her from falling if she stumbled. They were silent as they walked along the path. Santee's footsteps made no sound, and there was only a whisper of a rustle from the long fringes on his buckskins. Alcey controlled her breathing, but she had no control over her heartbeat, and it pounded with a force she felt had to be audible to him. He stopped at the gate halfway along the pasture, dropped the rails for her, then replaced them and took her arm again as they crossed the pasture toward her cabin. There was a movement in the darkness by her cabin, and Dock growled deeply.

"You be quiet, Dock," Alcey called. "Don't try to pet him, Santee. He doesn't even like me to pet him but now and again."

"Aye, Pa told me about him. He said he had his doubts about him at first, but he lost them when that pair tried to make off with some of the stock during the winter."

"He's a good watchdog, and he fears nothing. And it's little wonder that he has little use for people, poor beggar. When I found him, he was on death's doorstep from being pitted against other dogs or a bear or whatever. I wish I could do the same to those who did it to him."

Dock approached the fence around Alcey's cabin and sniffed noisily at Santee as he slid the rails in the gate aside for her. "He looks a handsome dog."

"He is, but for his scars. He's a hound, and it appears he had lovely long ears before they were cut and chewed from fighting."

"Aye, he's a Black and Tan, isn't he?" Santee said, following her through the gate. "A good Black and Tan will fetch as much as a good horse."

Alcey stopped and looked at Santee uncertainly. He finished replacing the rails, then folded his arms and looked at Dock, making no movement to leave. She motioned toward the bench in front of the cabin. "Would you care to sit down?"

"Aye, I will, thank you," he said promptly, taking her arm again and walking toward the bench. "I was in Cross

Creek when I heard what had happened between you and Jubal. It's always seemed that Jubal had ten people's share of intelligence in making money and less than his own share in other things, but until I heard that, I'd never known he was such a bloody fool."

Alcey shrugged as she sat down on the bench, smoothing her skirt. "I think it was more on the order of rectifying what was a mistake to begin with, Santee."

"It could be," he replied as he sat down. "Whatever it was, it's in the past and best left there." He folded his arms and leaned back against the cabin, relaxing. "Well, I had good fortune on my return trip. I was in two minds on whether to come in this summer, and I thought I might trade my furs at the post on Stony Creek and go back to *Kenta-ke*. But I couldn't get a tenth of their value from that thief of a trader at Stony Creek, so then I came on in to Cross Creek, still of two minds on whether or not to do my trading and go on back. Then I heard what had happened between you and Jubal, and I almost killed my horses getting on in. And I had my rifle freshly primed all the time as well, in event I arrived just in time to intercept you on the way to a church with some man."

There was a light, playful overtone of humor in his voice, but it was only an overtone, with a strong undercurrent of earnest meaning. Alcey swallowed to control her voice and chuckled softly. "Extravagant talk isn't like you, Santee."

His teeth shone in the dim light as he smiled down at her, and he looked away. "No, but it's God's truth that if the service had been started, it would have stopped until I had a word with you. And if I live to be a hundred, I'll never understand this slow lot hereabout. They could fall over an anvil made of gold, and they'd walk away swearing and rubbing their knee. Pa said no one's even been calling on you."

Alcey looked up at him, lifting her eyebrows archly. "You asked your father about me? That was a cheek."

"I wanted to know without delay," he chuckled. "And Pa was ready to tell me, I might add. He thinks a lot of you, and Jubal lost mightily in his eyes over what he did to you. In any event I didn't mean to go behind your back and ask about you, and I would have . . ."

His voice faded as he turned his head and looked across the pasture. Dock was lying a few feet away, and he lifted his head and looked across the pasture. Simon jumped down from the fence by the path and ran across the moonlit pasture toward the cabin.

"Ma'am?"

"What is it, Simon?"

"Grandma can't find her needle with a big eye to do a bit of sewing she has. She'd like the loan of yours, and for Pa to bring it with him when he comes back."

"You can take it back, son," Santee said.

"Aye, all right, Pa."

Alcey rose and went into the cabin, stirred the ashes in the fireplace, and pulled splinters from a piece of wood and tossed them on the hot coals. They blazed up, and she put a couple of pieces of wood on the fire and opened her sewing box. Santee walked quietly into the cabin and sat on the settle at the side of the hearth, tossing another stick onto the fire. Simon followed him in. Alcey took out her packet of needles, trying to keep her fingers from trembling, and separated a needle with a large eye. She put the packet back in the sewing box, and pulled a splinter from a piece of firewood. Simon pointed to the table.

"There's the stick Mistress Alcey clouts me with when I don't pay attention to my lessons."

"That is a switch, Simon, not a stick," Alcey said, pushing the needle into the splinter. "And I've only tapped you in warning."

"That's a sight less than you'll have from me if you give her any trouble," Santee chuckled. "It's good of her to bother with you."

"Well, she hasn't really leathered me."

"I will if you lose my needle," Alcey said, smiling at him. "Here, hold this bit of wood in your hand like this, and you won't drop it."

Simon cupped the splinter in his palm and went back out the door. Alcey walked to the settle and sat down. Santee picked up another stick and tossed it onto the fire. "A fire makes a place cheerful."

"Yes, and the nights still have a touch of chill. Was it cold where you were this past winter?"

He laughed wryly and nodded. "Colder than cold. And it

snowed a lot as well. But it's the richest land I've ever seen, so the cold and snow are easy enough to bear." He was silent for a moment, looking into the fire and musing, then he glanced at her, picked up the poker, and jabbed at the burning wood with it. "I didn't mean to rush at you a bit ago, Alcey, and if I didn't properly consider your feelings, then I'm sorry."

Alcey smoothed her skirt, looking down at it, and shook her head quickly as she cleared her throat nervously. "No, you didn't . . . that is, I didn't think . . . I'm not upset, Santee."

Santee looked at her, then put the poker down and sat back on the settle, looking into the fire again. The wood popped as it burned brightly, making a pool of light in front of the fireplace, and the silence between them was tense. Santee looked at her again. "Well, I don't want to rush you, Alcey, but I want to make myself plain to you. I love you, and I'd like you to marry me."

Alcey looked down at her hands on her lap, her lips pressed tightly together, and she lifted a hand and pushed at her hair as she cleared her throat softly. "Santee, my situation isn't such that . . . well, there are others to consider. Your mother and father took me in because I had no other recourse after Jubal divorced me, but Jubal is their son. I flatter myself that I have their affection and they certainly have my love, but it isn't a simple matter. And what you suggest would be even more difficult for them. It would set them totally at odds with Jubal."

"How could they be more at odds with him? He never sets foot across their threshold."

"You are talking about Jubal's feelings for them. I am talking about theirs for him, which is another thing again."

"Then would it satisfy this if you were elsewhere? There are a number of farmsteads for sale at Cross Creek. That's far enough away to be removed from here, but near enough for a visit, with a bit of traveling."

Alcey looked down at her hands, keeping herself from wringing them. She nodded.

Santee looked down at her, then moved closer to her, putting his arm along the back of the settle. "As I said, Alcey, I don't want to rush you. Would you like a while to consider what we've talked about?"

Her heart was racing, her hands gripped each other nervously, and she couldn't make them relax. She bit her lip, shaking her head.

He moved closer to her, putting his arm around her. "Will you marry me, then, Alcey?"

The musky scent of his buckskins, and the fresh, sunny scent that always hung about him surrounded her. And he was surrounding her, his arm resting around her shoulders as he bent over her. She swallowed and nodded. "Yes," she whispered.

The tips of his fingers gently touched her chin, lifting her face. She looked up at him. He bent lower, his blue eyes becoming blurred as they came closer to hers, and his lips touched hers. His arms enfolded her, closing around her with a firm, restrained pressure. Her breath caught in her throat, and her head swam as her heart pounded madly.

Then a golden, glowing warmth suffused her, a tingling that had been a potential but not actually anticipated, because it was a totally new reaction. Her arms seemed to move of their own accord as they lifted and slid around his neck. His arms tightened, one of his large, warm hands pressing against her back. The warmth became fiery within her, and she bit at his lips. He hesitated, not releasing himself, and she dug her fingernails into the back of his neck as she pushed herself against him. He lifted her and crushed her to him, kissing her hungrily.

"Pa?"

It was Simon, at the fence in front of the cabin. Santee lowered Alcey back to the settle. Alcey gasped for breath, feeling faint and dizzy with the heady throbbing enveloping her, and she leaned against his chest. His heart was beating rapidly, his breathing was heavy, and a tremor raced through his arms as he held her to him. He turned his head toward the door.

"What is it, son?"

"Grandma says she's making a pot of tea and cutting an apple pie."

Santee drew in a deep breath and released it in a soundless sigh. "Tell her I don't feel like any just now, son."

"Aye, all right, Pa."

Santee looked toward the doorway and listened, then he turned back to Alcey. He pulled her closer, bending over her and moving his lips over her eyes and forehead. "Perhaps I'd better go."

"Your mother will be scandalized if you don't, I suppose."

"And I have to get an early start in the morning."

"Where are you going?"

"To Cross Creek, to see about a farmstead."

Alcey nestled closer to him, touching his face with the tips of her fingers and his lips with hers. "How long will you be gone?"

His hands pressed against her back, and he moved his lips down her cheek to her throat. "No longer than need be. Two or three days, perhaps."

"Try to make it two. And if you're going to be gone for a time, you needn't leave this minute. Take me in there, Santee."

His lips covered hers again as he gathered her up in his arms, and he lifted her and carried her toward the bedroom.

# Part Four

# THE SETTLERS

# Chapter Twenty

The chill of the cold, soggy ground and of the night air along the creek penetrated Santee Collier's blanket, and his sleep was shallow, a light, restful doze. When a small animal moved in the brush a few yards away, he listened to it and identified it, then dozed again. Simon moved in his blanket on the other side of the fire and sighed as he settled himself again. Collier listened, then dozed again. Then a dog barked at the cabin up the hill from the creek, and Collier opened his eyes. The sky had partially cleared during the hour or so since he had last opened his eyes, and through the thin spring foliage of the trees overhead he could see several stars against the inky blackness of the sky. It was shortly before daybreak.

Collier sat up, took a stick from the pile of firewood and stirred the ashes in the fire, and pulled pieces of bark off the stick and dropped them on the hot coals. They smoked, then burst into flame. He tossed a handful of sticks on the fire, and leaned over and felt the buckskins draped over sticks pushed into the ground by the fire. They were almost dry. He pushed the blanket aside, stood up, and began dressing.

Simon sat up, stretching and yawning, and his blanket fell away from his bare shoulders and arms. At eighteen he was as tall as his father, and his shoulders and arms were beginning to fill out to the size of his father's. He climbed to his feet and began dressing. The dog at the cabin up the hill barked again, an excited yapping. A door slammed, and there was a distant whisper of a woman's voice talking to the dog. Simon stood still, looking toward the cabin and listening, then he began dressing more rapidly, shivering from the clammy touch of his buckskins, still damp from being soaked in the creek the night before. He picked up his rifle from the two forked sticks in the ground by his blanket, put it on the stack of pelts, and rolled up his blanket.

"I'll step up the hill and fetch the horses."

"Go ahead," Collier chuckled, piling more wood on the fire. "I won't deny you another look, but don't you try to corner her in the barn. Crawford's a good friend to us."

Simon grinned, gathering up his tomahawk and fighting knife, sliding them into the back of his belt as he stepped to the creek. He knelt and washed his face, then pulled his hair back and retied it with the leather thong as he walked back past the stacked packsaddles. The brittle limbs of a bush starting to sprout spring leaves whispered against his fringed buckskins and whipped back as he brushed past it, then his footsteps were inaudible as he walked through the trees in the darkness. Collier honed his skinning knife on his belt, sat on his heels by the creek, and began cutting off his beard and moustache, grasping handfuls and slicing the coarse hair off a quarter of an inch from his skin.

The gray, first light of dawn began filtering through the trees, and birds began stirring. Collier honed his knife again, took a small piece of mirror and chip of soap from a pack, and lathered his face and began shaving. A few minutes later the sound of the horses' hooves and their snorting and stamping in the chilly morning air carried through the trees, along with the murmur of conversation between Simon and Crawford as they came down the hill with the horses. Collier rinsed his face, feeling for stubble, then honed his knife again, and began scraping the stubble away, leaning close to the mirror propped in the fork of a bush. Simon and Crawford came through the trees with the horses, and Simon tied them to a tree as Crawford put a large, fire-blackened pannikin and kettle down by the fire.

"My woman sent you a bite, Santee. There's coffee, and some boiled beef and hominy bread."

"We're much obliged, Frank. Simon tells me she's just had another little one."

"About a month gone, now. It's a boy, and it's coming along good, thank God. We lost our last two before they were a week old, and it was a sore trial for us both times, especially her."

Collier nodded, rinsing his face again, and he buckled

his belt and put his skinning knife into the sheath at the side of his belt as he walked toward the fire. "Aye, we lost our third one, and Alcey took it hard. But we've three other healthy ones, not counting my boy Genesee and Simon here, so we're well off."

"You are indeed. Me and my woman passed the time of day with Alcey at the post in Cross Creek when we were down there last November, and she had the three little ones with her. That little Santee looks a handful, but he minds her well enough."

"She knows how to put a birch switch where it'll do the most good," Collier chuckled, gathering up his tomahawk and fighting knife and sliding them under his belt, and he glanced at Simon as he knelt by the fire. "I left the mirror and soap there, son."

Simon nodded, fingering the coarse black hair on his face as he walked toward the creek. Collier took a sip of the coffee from the pannikin, put it back on the edge of the hot coals, and lifted the lid off the kettle.

"This looks good, Frank. Have you had a bite?"

"Aye, that's all for you and Simon. It appears that you made a good catch last winter."

Collier nodded, taking a lump of beef and a piece of bread from the kettle. "We did well enough. We went to Kentucky again last winter."

"I've heard talk that Daniel Boone is taking some settlers there. Is that true, or is it just talk?"

"It's true enough," Collier said, chewing. "We crossed the Holston at Sycamore Shoals on the way back, and Boone, a man named Henderson, and several others were there negotiating with Chief Attakullaculla to buy all the land east of the mountains and to the reaches of the Kentucky and Cumberland rivers. That's Kentucky and a piece more, and they had the whole Cherokee Nation there talking about it. I talked to Boone, and he said he was going to start cutting a road from Long Island on the Holston on through to Cumberland Gap and beyond as soon as the treaty was signed."

"Henderson, you say? Oh, aye, that's this Transylvania Company we've been hearing about, then. I heard that Governor Martin said that Henderson and his company are nothing but a lot of pirates, with no Crown authority for what they're doing. And Governor Dunmore up in Virginia has said much the same, from what I hear."

Collier shrugged, taking another bite. "Dunmore's one to talk, what with all the trouble he stirred up trying to make himself a kingdom along the Ohio. He doesn't like to hear of a full pot that he doesn't have his hand in, and Martin fears that his purse will suffer if people move beyond where his tax collectors go. And bugger a lot of Crown authority, I say. I've never asked for any authority to go and do as I wished, and I'll not start now. If someone wants to stop me, he can get in my road and try."

Crawford laughed and nodded, tossing pieces of wood onto the fire. He warmed his hands over the fire and rubbed them together, looking at Collier. "What sort of land is there in Kentucky, Santee? Is it as good as everyone says?"

Collier took a drink from the pannikin and another bite, and he looked into the fire, chewing reflectively. "Better than you've ever seen in your life, Frank," he said quietly. "You can burn off a cane bottom, broadcast corn by hand and not touch it with a hoe, and reap no less than seven bushels an acre. I talked to a man who had been at Harrod's Fort in Kentucky, and that's what they'd been doing. Rivers full of fish, and forests full of game. And no quit rents or tax collectors. It's all you've heard and more."

"And you say the Transylvania Company has bought Kentucky, then? Despite what Martin, Dunmore, and the others say?"

Simon chuckled as he knelt by the fire, daubing with his sleeve at cuts on his face from shaving and taking a piece of bread and lump of beef from the kettle. Collier exchanged an amused smile with him, then looked at Crawford and shrugged. "They were negotiating with the Cherokees when I saw them, and I daresay they reached an agreement, because they had wagonloads of goods to trade. But I didn't see any Shawnees there, or others who might think they have something to say on the matter. There are several tribes who hunt in Kentucky."

"Then Henderson wants to talk to them as well, doesn't he?"

"I don't know as it would do him any good to try. The Shawnee are much like we are in that one lot will choose to go one way and bugger the rest, and other lots will do the same. And they're much like we are in that they'll shoot first and think about a treaty when they're out of bullets. As well as the Indians there are a lot of settlers coming down the Ohio and stopping along the Licking, the Falls, the Big Sandy, and other places. I'd hate to be the one to try to tell them that they're on land I bought from the Indians."

"Are they having a lot of trouble with the Indians?"

"More than they'd like. The man from Harrod's Fort I talked with is named Porter, and we met him crossing the Yadkin last autumn. He said that Harrod's Fort had been abandoned a few months before because of Indian trouble, but that was part of the stir that Dunmore caused. He said that they would probably go back with more people this year, and now that Dunmore has made a treaty with Chief Cornstalk, I'm sure they will. Ben Logan is also taking some people in this year, and then there's the ones that Boone will be taking in. As well as all those there are scattered settlers here and there who came down the Ohio. With all that many they should be able to help each other and weather any trouble that comes along."

Crawford nodded, stirring the fire with a stick, and he tossed the stick into the fire and sighed heavily. "Well, I don't mind telling you that I've thought about moving, Santee. It's come to the point that I'm not getting more than three or four bushels of corn an acre, and my tobacco doesn't amount to the tenth part of what it was when I bought this land. I'm having trouble paying my taxes and quit rents and still having something to eat through the winter."

Collier took another piece of bread from the kettle, nudged the kettle toward Simon, and picked up the pannikin. "You need to talk to my wife Alcey, Frank. I don't know what all she does or why she does it, but she's forever seeding in pasture where corn was the year before, planting winter cushaws where she wants to put potatoes the next year, and first one thing and another. And we have good crops, year after year."

"Well, the yield of my land isn't as great a problem as the increase in my taxes and quit rents. Have you thought about moving to Kentucky, Santee?"

Simon hesitated and glanced between his father and Crawford as he lifted the kettle and wiped up the grease from the bottom of it with a piece of bread. He looked back down at the kettle and continued sopping up the grease as Collier glanced at him. Collier took a drink from the pannikin and put it down by Simon, nodding. "I've thought about it, Frank. But if you've a mind to move to Kentucky, all you need do is ride up to Long Island and meet Boone's party. Simon here can write me out a letter to Boone, and I know him well enough that he'd take my recommendation on a man."

"I'm grateful for the offer, Santee, but if I'm going to venture my family's safety, then I'm going to be satisfied in my own mind that I've done all I can for them. I've heard of Boone and what he's done, but I know you. And I'd heard of you a good while before I met you. If you went to Kentucky, would you take a party with you?"

Collier looked into the fire, thinking, and slowly nodded. "If I moved, I would. But I wouldn't want it broadcast that I'm moving, when I don't know myself whether I am or not."

"Whatever's said over this fire will go no farther, Santee. You've no fear of a loose tongue in me."

Collier nodded again. "Then I'll be plain on the matter. I've studied about moving to Kentucky for odd's years, but what's been happening here of late has started me thinking more seriously about it. That's all I'd like to say on my intentions for the moment, other than the fact that I'm going to talk to Alcey about it. If I went, I'd want no less than thirty rifles in the party. And if I went, you'd be more than welcome to be a member of the party."

Crawford smiled gratefully. "It pleases me that I have your confidence, Santee, because I don't know a man whose opinion means more to me. When do you think you'll be making up your mind whether or not you'll go?"

Collier smiled and shrugged, shaking his head. "I've never brought up a matter to Alcey that she hasn't come back with fifty things concerning it that I should have thought of myself, Frank. I'll have to talk to her first, then I'll have a better idea of what's ahead of me."

"Aye, well, a man would be a fool to use one mind on a matter when two are readily available, and there's no question that Alcey has a rare head on her shoulders. My wife has been talking about going to Cross Creek for some things she wants as soon as the little one is fit to travel, and I need a few things myself. It could be that we'll be coming that way in a week or two."

"Then stop by the cabin, Frank. The least you'll have is supper and a place to rest, and we'll talk about this again. It could be that I'll know more about it then."

Crawford nodded, picking up the kettle and putting the pannikin in it as he rose. "I'll look forward to that, Santee. And I won't delay you any longer, because I know you want to be on the road and get on home." He put out his hand. "And you've my word that I'll keep a closed mouth on what we've discussed."

"That's best for now," Collier said, shaking hands with him. "We're grateful for the victuals, Frank."

"It was little enough, and you're more than welcome," he replied, turning to Simon. "I'll see you again in a few days, Simon."

"I'll be looking forward to it, Mr. Crawford," Simon said, shaking hands with him.

Crawford turned away from the fire, and the pannikin rattled in the kettle as he walked back through the trees. Collier began lifting the packsaddles from the stack and putting them in a row to load onto the horses, and Simon went for the horses and led them closer to the fire. They worked silently and rapidly, with the speed and ease of long practice, loading the horses, forming them into two strings of six, and putting out the fire. They mounted, checked the priming in their rifles, and Collier led the way out of the trees along the creek line.

The slope below the Crawford cabin was a grassy pasture dotted with stumps, and they rode diagonally across it, toward the wagon road that crossed the low hill a hundred yards in front of the cabin. Crawford came out of the cabin and walked around it toward the barn, lifting his arm and waving. Collier and Simon waved. A swath of land in front of the cabin and near the road had been freshly plowed, and a boy of ten or twelve and a girl of fifteen or sixteen were carrying rocks from it and piling them. The boy looked at Collier and Simon with an openmouthed gaze of awe, and the girl flushed and ducked her head as Collier nodded to her. Then Simon smiled at her, she turned crimson and grinned, and she picked up a large rock and hurried toward the rock pile with it. Collier glanced over his shoulder at Simon and chuckled. They turned onto the road, and Collier turned on his horse and looked back at Simon.

"There was one who's been cornered for a kiss if I ever saw one," he chuckled. "Now what did I tell you?"

"Not to corner her," Simon laughed. "But you didn't say what I was to do if I got cornered myself."

Collier laughed and nodded as he turned back around on his horse, settling his rifle across his arm. The sun was well above the horizon, and the overcast of the day before had broken up into large, fleecy clouds. The air was rapidly losing the chill of the spring night, and the surrounding territory was well settled and completely safe. Collier yawned and relaxed comfortably on his horse.

The road led up, down, and around low, rolling hills and farms, patches of forest, and occasional boggy thickets of briars. Tangled, scrubby growth stretched out on both sides of the road to the horizon. The horses were lean and weary from the hard winter and the trek, the ten pack horses were heavily loaded with large bales of pelts, and they plodded along at a slow walk, their heads drooping. Collier slumped on his horse, his eyes half-closed in relaxation bordering on dozing. People working in fields shaded their eyes with their hands to watch the horses pass, and occasionally someone waved. Collier roused himself to wave, then relaxed again.

When the sun reached its zenith, they turned off the road at a creek to water the horses and took handfuls of corn and jerked venison from a supply bag. They mounted again and rode back onto the road, eating the corn and venison. Collier finished his, then slumped on his horse again. The horses plodded along the road for another three hours, and their pace began gradually picking up. At the top of a rise in the road a low ridgeline became visible ahead. Collier sat up on his horse, yawning and stretching, and the horses increased their pace to a fast walk as they went down the slope and across the wide valley below the long ridge. Their heads lifted and their ears cocked forward, and they were almost trotting as they started up the rise. They reached the top of it, and Collier's horse angled to the side of the road and turned onto a narrow road branching off to the left without waiting for a tug on the reins.

The ridgeline was heavily forested, and the dense shade had a remaining touch of the chill of winter, the brush and smaller tress still bare and skeletal under the canopy of spring foliage on the larger trees. The road led along the peak of the ridge for a hundred yards, then diagonally down the right side of the ridge. The trees ended at a sharp line where they had been felled and left to season. The trunks were scattered about at odd angles in the grass that had taken root in the deep, rich mast where the sun had reached it. Some trees were trimmed of branches and others had dead, brittle branches still reaching up. Farther down the slope the trees had been dragged away, and the stumps were beginning to weather and rot.

The cabin was large, with a chimney on each end and a second story for bedrooms for the boys. Large outbuildings and stock pens were behind it, and towering white oaks were clustered around it for shade. The slope all around the cabin was fenced into large squares of pasturage and tilled area, from the creek to the line of trees at the top of the hill above the cabin. Smoke trickled from one of the chimneys, cattle and oxen grazed in the pastures, domestic ducks waddled in and out of the creek, chickens scratched in the dust around the cabin, and Collier's foster father sat on a bench in a patch of sunshine in front of the cabin, his crutch leaning against the end of the bench. Two hounds stirred beside the cabin and began baying in deep, ringing notes that rang through the valley. Two more dangerous dogs were kept cooped during the day in a pen at the side of the house, and they began baying and jumping at the sides of the pen. The horses splashed through the creek. Jared ran out of the cabin, whooping excitedly, then Santee and Shelby ran out. Nina limped outside, smiling radiantly. Alcey stood in the doorway.

Simon leaped off his horse and ran to Nina, and her wrinkled face was wreathed in a smile as she reached up to put her arms around him. Her hair was almost completely white, and she looked as if she had put on weight during the winter and was having trouble getting around. Santee had grown a little during the winter, and he was large for eight. Jared had definitely grown, and was very large for six. Shelby had shed his baby fat, and he was a sturdy boy of three. They crowded around Simon, shouting and pulling at him. Collier's foster father slumped on the bench, staring blankly into the distance and oblivious to the noise and excitement around him.

Alcey seemed more beautiful each spring—slender and lithe, her brown hair streaked with lines of sun-bleached yellow, her features soft and golden with her dark tan and flush of exuberant health. The girlish attractiveness of years before had turned into a far more appealing womanly beauty, and she had acquired a gracefulness and poise that set her apart from most other women. And she had also acquired self-confidence and independence that had combined with her pride to give her a charisma. She stood in the doorway with a half-smile, her sparkling blue eyes moving over him. He dismounted and walked toward her. She ran to him.

She was soft and warm in his arms, her lips were sweet under his, and the tips of her fingers caressed his face. He pulled her tightly to him, moving his lips down her smooth cheek and burying them in her throat. She made a sound of amusement, wriggling away from him. Her lips were damp and parted breathlessly, and her eyes shone more brightly as she glanced quickly at the children and looked back at him.

"It's good to have you home, love."

"It's good to be back home, Alcey. With you here it's always good to be back home."

Nina released Simon, patting his back and sniffling, and limped toward Collier to embrace him. Collier hugged her and kissed her and knelt and gathered the boys in his arms, patting them and ruffling their hair. Then he stepped to the bench where his foster father sat. The old man's white beard and hair were sparse and unruly, his pink scalp showing through his hair and his seamed, wrinkled face visible through his beard. His mouth was collapsed over his toothless gums, and he was thin and frail, the worn homespuns draped on his shrunken frame and his gnarled, splotched hands bony and resting slackly on his thighs. His eyes were still fixed on some distant place or time, bleary and unfocused.

"Pa, it's Santee. How are you?" The old man's eyes didn't flicker, and Collier leaned closer. "Pa, it's Santee!"

"He's all right, love," Alcey said cheerfully. "He's just gone for a minute, and he'll be back directly. He still takes his little spells of thinking about things or whatever it is, and there's nothing wrong with that."

"Aye, thinking about things," Nina chuckled, nodding. "He's all the same since Hannah's gone, Santee."

"He peed his breeches again last week," Jared giggled, and he and the other boys exploded into gales of laughter.

"You watch your mouth, Jared!" Alcey snapped, wheeling on him furiously. "You have respect when you talk about your grandpa, or I'll birch you and put you in the corner with Santee! And you get on back in there to that corner, Santee. First you can tell your pa what you did to get birched and put in a corner."

The boy looked at his mother resentfully, then looked down at the ground, moving his toes in the dirt. "I killed a chicken," he muttered.

"He killed my red rooster with his sling, that's what he did," Alcey said, frowning at the boy. "And he stays in the corner until he finishes eating that rooster. All right, you get on back in there and get in that corner. Jared, you and Shelby go get me some potatoes out of the root cellar, and get good ones that haven't sprouted or turned black." She looked back at Collier, smiling. "I expect you're about ready to eat something cooked at home, aren't you, love?"

"More than ready, but whatever you have on will suffice, Alcey. I don't want you cooking something big and going to a lot of work."

"It's no work to cook for you, love, and you and Simon both look like you've lost a bit of weight. Go ahead and take care of your horses, and I'll get supper on."

"All right, then. Where's Genesee?"

"He's up on the hill, hunting. He'll be down as soon as he catches sight of those horses. Or he'll be down directly in any event, because it's near time for supper."

Collier chuckled and nodded, walking back toward his horses. Simon led his horses toward the side of the cabin, and Collier took the reins on his horses and hesitated, looking at Alcey as she stepped into the doorway. She stopped in the doorway, looking at him. Her smile widened, then became brilliant, her white teeth shining and her eyes dancing.

"It's good to have you home, love."

"It's good to be home, Alcey."

She walked on into the cabin, and Collier turned his horses, leading them behind Simon's. Simon snapped his fingers and whistled at the dogs in the pen at the side of the cabin, and they snarled threateningly until they scented him and recognized him. All four of the dogs were large, powerful Black and Tan hounds, and they closely resembled their sire, the dog Alcey had owned when she and Collier married. All of them were fearless and would attack any person or animal on command, but the two in the pen were too apt to attack without command to be allowed to roam loose during the day, when a visitor might come to the cabin. The hounds looked at Collier as he passed the pen, and one of them wagged his tail halfheartedly as Collier snapped his fingers and spoke to them.

Collier looked around at the fences and buildings as he and Simon unloaded the horses and carried the pelts and packsaddles into a storage room at the side of the barn. There were signs of repairs that Genesee had made during the winter and the usual spring repairs were still waiting to be done—a few fence rails fallen down, a couple of doors on the barn sagging, loose shingles on the cabin and outbuildings, and other things—but it looked like it had been an easy winter and there had been no fires or other calamities. They turned the horses into a pen and began carrying corn to them, and a whoop rang out from the top of the hill. Genesee ran down the slope, shouting and waving.

At thirteen his movements still had something of the gangling awkwardness of a boy, but it was disappearing into smooth, economical coordination, and he had no difficulty bounding over the fences with the long rifle balanced in one hand. His powder horn and shot bag bounced at his side, a couple of rabbits swung from his belt, and a long pistol he had got during the winter was stuck under his belt. Alcey had relaxed another of her rules for his clothing during the winter. He was wearing buckskin moccasins and leggings as well as one of the fringed buckskin shirts Alcey had started making for him a couple of years before.

Only his breeches were of homespun, a single garment remaining until Alcey tacitly acknowledged him a man. He was tall, but he was smaller-boned than Simon had been at thirteen, and he was going to be more slender. His features were a shade darker than Simon's, a sharp contrast with his white teeth and blue eyes, with a strong similarity to Simon and the other boys. He and Simon greeted each other boisterously, hugging and slapping each other on the back, then he walked toward Collier, grinning. Collier put his arm around him affectionately, patting him.

"It's good to see you again, son. How is everything?"

"Everything's all right, Pa. Did you get a good catch?"

"Good enough. Where did you get your pistol?"

"I traded thirty-five coonskins for it at the post. The trader wanted fifty, but Ma talked him down to thirty-five. Here, have a look at it."

It was an old pistol, long and heavy and with a grip that slanted downward only slightly, but the brass fittings on the woodwork and the lock and barrel were in good condition, well greased and free of rust. Collier nodded, handing the pistol to Simon as he reached for it. "It looks a good one, son."

"It does and all," Simon said. "I wouldn't mind having one of these."

"Have a shot with it," Genesee said. "Shoot at that post over there."

Simon cocked the pistol and aimed at the post. The hammer dropped, the pan flashed, and the pistol fired with a crack. Splinters flew from the side of the post, and Simon lifted his eyebrows doubtfully as he lowered the pistol. "It wants to shoot to the right, doesn't it?"

"It does not!" Genesee snorted indignantly. "You pulled it to the right, clod! Here, hold my rifle, and I'll recharge it and show you how to shoot a bloody pistol."

"I'll leave you with it," Collier said. "But mind you don't shoot near any of the chickens. I'd hate to see you two birched and standing in a corner, at your ages."

They laughed as he turned away. He went to the door of the storage room, picked up the canvas bags of supplies, the blankets, and his rifle, and walked back around the cabin. The old man slowly turned his head and looked at

Collier as he came around the corner of the cabin. He blinked, smiling slightly. Collier walked past the door of the cabin to the bench.

"How are you, Pa?"

The question seemed to puzzle him. He looked up at Collier with a bemused expression, nodding uncertainly. "Well, my foot's plaguing me a bit, but no worse than yesterday."

"The weather's warming up now, and it'll probably get better right along. I've just returned from Kentucky, Pa."

The old man lifted his eyebrows in surprise. "Kentucky? You've just come from Kentucky? Well, that didn't take long, did it?"

Collier hesitated, then shrugged. "It took a few months, Pa."

The old man looked puzzled again, and he nodded vaguely, looking away.

"Do you want anything, Pa?"

The old man looked back up at him, musing, and shook his head. "I can't think of what it would be."

"Aye, well, I'll talk to you again directly, Pa."

"Aye, all right."

Collier went into the cabin and put his rifle in the rack by the door. Spicy, appetizing odors came from the pots and pans on the fireplace and hearth, and from a pork roast sizzling on the spit. One of the hounds was sprawled on the floor near the door, Santee was standing in a corner, and Nina and Alcey were bustling back and forth between the fireplace, cabinets, and table. Santee glanced around surreptitiously and looked back at the corner as Collier hung his powder horn and shot pouch on a peg at the side of the rifle rack and put his knives and tomahawk on a shelf over the rack. Alcey glanced over her shoulder with a smile as he carried the bags and blankets on into the room.

"Just put them over there by the corner, love, and I'll sort them out later. Nina mixed you a toddy, and it's over there on the hearth."

Collier leaned the bags against the wall, dropped the blankets on them, and walked toward the fireplace. "You'll find a pouch full of what that man over on the Clinch said was niter in one of the bags. It looks like niter to me, and if it is, there's a king's ransom of it in Kentucky. There are caves filled with it."

"Then it'll be good if it is, won't it? We'll try it out in the next day or two and see if it'll make gunpowder."

Collier nodded, picking up the large pewter cup on the hearth, and took a drink from it as he walked back toward the door. It was apple toddy, crushed dried apples blended with a potent mixture of water and rum, and spiced with ginger, cinnamon, and cloves. The hound rose stiffly with a groan and followed Collier as he walked back outside. The old man's eyes were closed, and he was dozing. Collier went to one of the large oaks in front of the cabin and sat down under it, leaning back against it.

The hound lay down by Collier with a deep sigh, and Collier absently patted the dog's head as he looked down the slope, a feeling of tranquil satisfaction settling over him. It was a quiet and peaceful late afternoon, the warm spring sunshine glinting on the ripples in the creek, and the birds and insects making a drowsy background to the sounds around the cabin—Simon and Genesee talking and laughing behind the cabin, Jared and Shelby arguing over a toy at the side of the cabin, and Nina and Alcey moving around inside the cabin. The warmth of the rum spread through Collier's limbs as he sipped the toddy, pondering about when to discuss the possibilities of moving to Kentucky with Alcey. It would be an upheaval of major proportions for her if they decided to go, and it seemed best to wait for a day or two before discussing it, until the furs had been disposed of and things had settled down to a routine.

Alcey came to the door and called, and Nina came out for the old man. There was a pleasant, cheerful confusion as everyone crowded around the table, the three boys scuffling, Alcey snapping her fingers at them, Simon and Genesee talking, and Nina seating the old man and pouring the buttermilk. The table was filled with food. There was pork roast, crisp from the fire and spiced with pepper and cloves, candied yams, smoked fish, cushaw dripping with butter, bowls of vegetables, pickled onions, cucumbers and cabbage, fried potatoes and onions, and corn bread. A bowl of hominy mush and pork boiled to a soft pulp was at the old man's place, and Santee's plate had a chicken drumstick and thigh on it. There was a bustle of passing dishes, and everyone began eating. Santee muttered something under his breath as he gnawed on the drumstick with an expression of distaste.

"What's that, Santee?" Alcey said.

"It's tough," he grumbled resentfully.

"Not half as tough as the back of my hand, and that's what you'll have in your mouth if you don't eat that and let it keep you quiet. You've only the rest of the breast to go, and you can have that for breakfast. Then you can leave the corner. And you can be thankful it wasn't a milk cow you knocked on the head with that sling."

Simon and Genesee guffawed, Jared and Shelby giggled, and Collier and Nina chuckled. The old man looked down at his bowl, spooning mush into his mouth and swallowing it. Collier smiled at Alcey as she glanced at him and looked back down at her plate, taking a bite.

"Did anything happen this past winter?"

She shook her head and shrugged. "It was easier than most. Santee fell off the barn and broke his arm less than a week after you left, but I put slats on it, it healed within a month, and it healed properly. Shelby got snakebit just before cold weather, but it was only a racer that bit him. And Jared was standing to eat and sleeping on his stomach for a while for not watching Shelby any better, so perhaps we won't have to worry about rattlesnakes until he's of a size to look after himself. Grandpa got a croup early in the winter, but we kept him in and wrapped up, and he got over it soon enough. Did you and Simon have any trouble?"

"No, it was an easy winter for us, Alcey. An easy winter and a good catch."

She smiled and nodded, taking another bite, then stopped chewing and glared at Santee and Jared as they began pushing at each other and arguing. The two boys looked at her, quietened, and began eating again. Collier smiled to himself, glancing between Alcey and the boys. The boys were high-spirited and inclined to be rowdy, but Alcey was a stern disciplinarian, and she controlled them easily. She had been the same way with Simon and Genesee, gradually relaxing her control as they became older, and her relationship with them was warm and loving, with them frequently seeking her advice and assistance on many things. She was more demanding with the boys than Collier's foster mother had been with him, quicker to punish and more severe in her punishment. But while his foster mother had been loving, she had been detached and unbiased in judgment of fault when trouble with others had arisen. Alcey was totally biased toward the boys, heated in her support of them against an outsider, regardless of who was right or wrong. In comparison with his foster mother Alcey was less affectionate and more loving.

Old Caleb mumbled something, rolling mush around in his mouth, and Collier leaned toward him. "What's that, Pa?"

He swallowed and licked his lips. "I wasn't worried about you."

"Worried? Worried about me? You mean on the trip? Oh, no, there wasn't any need to be worried, Pa."

The old man nodded, smiling toothlessly, and wheezed with laughter. "I told your ma it took longer to catch a girl than it did to collect a load of deerskins and furs, more especially one as comely as . . ." His smile faded and his voice trailed off into silence as he looked at Nina, then at Alcey. He looked at the boys, then back at Nina and Alcey in confusion. His bleary eyes had a lonely, lost look as they filled with tears. He lowered his head and began weeping quietly.

Jared made a sound of amusement in his throat, Santee smiled, and Shelby giggled. Simon and Genesee frowned at them, and Collier looked at them sternly, starting to say something. Alcey cut him off as she leaned toward them and looked at them narrowly, talking in a soft, steely tone.

"I've said for the last bloody time that you'll have respect for your grandpa. The next time I have to say it, it'll be said with a birch switch. And there'll be some who'll be blistered from the nape of their neck to their heels."

The hound lying near the hearth and the one lying inside the door got up and quietly walked out. The boys looked down at their plates contritely. The old man's sobs were loud in the quietness. Alcey looked at him, smiling gently. "Would you like a sip of rum, Grandpa?"

The old man looked at her, wiping at his eyes with the back of his gnarled, trembling hand, and nodded.

"Eat your supper, then, and I'll bring you a sip."

The old man sniffled and swallowed, wiping his eyes

again, and picked up his spoon and began eating. Alcey glared at the three boys coldly, then looked down at her plate and took a bite.

"The rum will go to his head, won't it?" said Collier.

She nodded and shrugged. "He gets confused on no more than a drop lately, but then he just goes to sleep. I know his foot must be a torment for him, although he doesn't often mention it, and I'm sure a sip of rum eases that as well. Here, have some more of this pork, love. And another piece of cushaw."

"I believe I will. During the past months I woke up at night dreaming of food like this, Alcey."

"Well, I just threw this together, and I'll set a proper good table tomorrow, after we get back from taking the furs in. We'll have chicken and dumplings, and perhaps a pie. I want to feed you and Simon up, because you both look a bit drawn this time."

She refilled his plate and put it back in front of him, then reached for Simon's plate. Simon and Genesee began talking about taking a couple of the hounds and going hunting for raccoon, and the old man finished his food and looked at Alcey expectantly. She got up from the table and poured water and rum into a cup. He sipped it, looking contented.

The light became soft and dim with sunset as they finished eating. Simon and Genesee took their rifles and left, whistling to the hounds. Nina took the old man to his room, then came back in and helped Alcey wash the dishes. Collier took a pipe from the mantel and filled it, and sat on his stool by the hearth and smoked. The three boys carried in firewood and water, then went to bed.

Alcey and Nina finished cleaning up, talking quietly, then Nina went to her room and Alcey took a towel and the pot of soap from the washstand and went outside. The cabin was settled for the night, and the rustle of the fire was a soft murmur in the stillness. Alcey came back in, her face shining and taut from being washed, and she put the soap and another towel on top of the washstand. Collier put his pipe back on the mantel, took the towel and soap, and went outside.

The two hounds were out of the pen, and one of them sniffed at Collier as he walked to the rain barrels at the side of the house. The sky was clear, and the stars and moon shone brightly. The distant baying of the other two hounds trailing game blended with the other sounds of the night. Collier stood on a rock by one of the rain barrels, undressed, and dipped water out of the barrel and bathed. The rock was still damp from the water Alcey had splashed over herself, and the fragrance of her body seemed to hang in the air. The night air was cool, and Collier shivered as he dried himself off and put his clothes back on.

Alcey was sitting on her stool by the fireplace, holding a pewter cup, and another cup was on the edge of the hearth in front of his stool. She had uncoiled and brushed her hair, and it lay over her shoulders and down her back. Collier picked up his cup of apple toddy and took a deep drink.

The silence between them was warm and companionable. Alcey looked into the fire, sipping her drink. When he finished his, she rose and carried the cups to the washstand. He followed her and put his arm around her shoulders as they walked toward their room.

# Chapter Twenty-one

The household was up well before daylight, and after a quick breakfast Collier, Simon, and Genesee carried in the pelts and hides while Alcey and Nina cleared the front room, built up the fire, and lit Betty lamps. Alcey had learned to judge pelts almost as expertly as Collier, and the strong, pungent odor of the pelts and skins filled the front room from the large bundles and loose furs littering the floor as Alcey and Collier examined and graded the beaver and otter pelts in the light from the fireplace and Betty lamps. Simon and Genesee went to milk the cows and feed the livestock, the old man sat by the hearth and looked on, Nina and the boys watched and moved pelts and skins about helpfully, and two of the hounds sat inside the door and sniffed curiously, the light shining in their eyes. Alcey and Collier separated beaver and otter pelts with prime fur and no grease burns or knife cuts, tied them into bundles of a dozen, and put the rough beaver and otter pelts into bales with skins bartered by weight—bear, wolf, raccoon, deer, and buffalo.

Daylight was starting to flood into the room as they finished. Simon and Genesee went to harness a span of oxen to the wagon and drive it around to the front of the cabin, and Alcey and Nina prepared food to take along on the trip to the trading post. Collier and the boys carried the pelts and skins outside, then loaded them into the wagon and helped the old man into the wagon as Alcey and Nina changed into clean dresses and arranged their hair. The sun was just above the horizon and beginning to warm the chill of the early spring night from the air as the wagon rumbled down the slope and splashed through the creek.

Events shortly after the purchase of the farmstead near Cross Creek had illustrated their complementary abilities

and had set a pattern in their marriage. The deed from the
dealer and the tax and quit rent assessments had established the size of the farmstead as seventy-five acres, but
land dealers had long been known as notorious cheats, and
officials had always been more than willing to collect tax
and quit rents on nonexistent land. Alcey had offered to
survey the land, her suggestion hesitant because she was
unsure of the prerogatives in their relationship, and Collier
had enthusiastically endorsed the idea. They had walked
the boundaries, Collier dragging the chain and Alcey taking measurements and making notes, and she had com-
puted the area at just over sixty-eight acres. The dealer had
been patronizing and sarcastic when they went to see him,
questioning the ability of any woman to survey land, and
confident that he had sufficient influence to win a lawsuit.
Then Collier had gone by himself and talked to the dealer
in private. The boundary of the farmstead had been extended onto land owned by the dealer, incorporating an
area of seven acres across the creek that had been the property line.

It was late morning when they reached the bustling community of Cross Creek. The streets were crowded with
drays and wagons, some up from or going to Wilmington,
and others from the local lumber mills or outlying farms.
And there were more people in the settlement than usual,
with a lot of men standing around in clusters and talking.
Acquaintances nodded to Collier, women along the street
and in wagons smiled and waved to Alcey and Nina, boys
shouted to the boys in the rear of the wagon, and Simon
ogled the young women. The clerk on the dock at the trading post went in for the owner when he saw the wagon
turning into the yard, knowing that there was going to be
some hard bargaining. The trader came out, jovial and
cheerful as he shook hands and began looking at the furs.

Upon Alcey's suggestion several years before they had
started separating and grading the pelts before delivering
them, and they made a much more impressive display
when graded and tied into neat bundles. Alcey had also
introduced a more aggressive bartering on the price for the
pelts and skins, demanding a proportionally higher price
according to how much of the total the trader insisted on
being taken as trade out of his post. The trader didn't want

to see the valuable pelts and hides taken to one of the other posts in town, and since Alcey had a good idea of how much the furs were worth, the trader's smile became more and more strained as they bargained. It was a process Collier enjoyed, knowing that he had been cheated many times in the past, and knowing that the trader was handicapped by his inability to calculate as rapidly as Alcey. The trader's smile was gone when the price was settled. Collier and the old man went inside with the trader for a drink of rum, and the others went around to the trading post.

The trader talked about a crowd that had collected in town earlier in the day. A man had been in town from the Wilmington branch of the Committee of Correspondence, a communication network between the colonies formed during the past three years for the purpose of exchanging views and disseminating information on resistance to British policies, and people had assembled to listen to him. Among other things the man had said that the first day of June was being suggested as a day of fasting and prayer, because that was the effective date of the Boston Port Act, a law passed by Parliament in reaction to an incident in which a group of Bostonians had boarded merchant ships in Boston harbor and dumped their cargoes of tea overboard.

Collier had always been galled by the fact that Parliament could pass laws affecting him while he had no recourse or control over the situation, because freedom to do as he wished had always been a basic tenet in his life. Alcey's attitudes were always formed at a more theoretical level than his, and she was inclined to quote Locke on inalienable rights of the human condition while Collier was more concerned on a less abstract plane. But they were in agreement in their resentment toward Parliament, as well as toward the North Carolina Assembly, which was dominated by tidewater aristocrats who pursued their own interests at the expense of those living in the hinterland. Alcey had been incensed by the Townshend Acts and gratified when they were repealed. Then she had been outraged by the Intolerable Acts passed by Parliament the year before and had started buying coffee instead of tea as a symbol of resistance against the duty on tea.

The trader was apprehensive about the effects of recent

events on his business, and specifically with the possibility
of an end to the bounty paid in England on naval stores,
which produced a lot of his profits. He was also concerned
with trade in general, because nonimportation agreements
had been proliferating among the shippers and importers at
the ports, and some of his stocks were becoming critically
low. But the trader was a merchant and disinclined to risk
creating animosity when it served no profitable end, and he
skirted around expressing any political views in event they
offended Collier. The old man rapidly got drunk on the
rum as Collier and the trader talked, slumping on his
chair and leaning against the wall. Collier finished his rum,
thanked the trader, then took the old man out to the wagon
and led the oxen around to the trading post.

The boys were crunching sweets, Simon and Genesee were
looking at a pistol, Nina was picking out some fabrics, and
Alcey was selecting food staples, a harassed clerk trying to
convince her that the tea in the store had been smuggled in
from Holland. Collier helped carry out a barrel of flour
and bags of sugar, salt, rice, and coffee, then he took Simon
with him to a tavern across the street from the trading post.
It was noisy, jammed with men who had been in the crowd
listening to the representative of the Committee of Correspondence from Wilmington, and there was a wide diver-
gence of views among the men in the tavern. Most of the
men seemed to have no strong commitment, grumbling to
an extent about Parliament but possibly to a greater extent
about the Assembly. The few who did have firm opinions
were sharply divided and arguing heatedly from diametri-
cally opposed standpoints. One side characterized recent
actions of Parliament as tyranny that had to be resisted,
and they were being called seditious fools by the other
side.

Most of the arguing centered around two tables, one
with several burly Scotch-Irish around it who kept toasting
the king and Parliament, and the other with a group of
artisans and farmers around it who toasted confusion to the
king and Parliament. The arguing occasionally became an
exchange of insults, each man trying to be louder and more
insulting than the last, and the barkeep kept crossing the
tavern and threatening the men at both tables with a bung
starter every time it appeared the arguments were about to

lead to blows. Collier and Simon stood at the counter and drank their rum, chuckling and observing the uproar. One of the Scotch-Irish was unwise enough to toast Governor Martin, and he was shouted down by most of the people in the tavern. Then a man at the other table toasted the colonists in Massachusetts. He was apparently newly arrived in North Carolina, because he referred to their actions as the first instance of direct confrontation with British authority. A roar of outrage rose in the tavern as men stormed vociferously about the boarding of HMS *Viper* in Wilmington harbor several years before. Duly chastened the man attempted to shift attention elsewhere by flinging a stinging insult at the other table, and it triggered a fight. The barkeep charged across the tavern as a wild melee erupted between the two tables, and other men leaped to his assistance, pulling flailing men apart and throwing them out the door.

Collier and Simon finished their rum, pushed through the surging crowd, and went back across the street. Alcey and Nina had finished picking out everything that was needed, and the old man was still snoring drunkenly in the wagon as Genesee helped the clerk load the last of the goods into the wagon. Santee was dusty, his shirt was torn, and he had a bloody nose and a black eye from a fight with another boy on the street, but he was triumphantly victorious from having whipped the boy. Everyone climbed into the wagon, and Collier turned it back toward the edge of the settlement. Nina opened the kettle of food, passed out bread and meat, filled cups from an urn of buttermilk and handed them around, and unsuccessfully tried to rouse the old man to eat his mush.

The sun beamed down from a clear sky, and the afternoon was warm. When they passed the last cabins and there was nothing to hold the interest of the three boys, they curled up among the goods and went to sleep. Simon and Genesee were weary from having hunted raccoons most of the night and arising early, and they pillowed their heads on bags and dozed. Collier felt restless, and he got down from the wagon and walked beside the oxen to hurry them along. Alcey and Nina chatted desultorily for a time, then Nina began dozing on the seat and Alcey stood up, gathered her skirt, and moved to the side of the wagon to jump down. Collier stepped back to the side of the wagon and lifted her down.

She smiled up at him as she shook her skirt straight and began walking along the road beside him. "That tavern you were in was a right place to go for a sip, wasn't it? Men were flying from it like hares from a burrow invaded by ferrets."

"Aye, they were," he laughed. "A man from the Committe of Correspondence in Wilmington was in the settlement earlier in the day, and what he'd had to say added to some rum caused a scuffle."

"Yes, I heard about him in the trading post, and the talk in there was heated enough without the rum." She looked down, taking a long step over a hole in the road, and sighed as she shook her head. "But it could be that we'll find no cause for amusement in such as this before too many more months have passed."

"Or it could be that we won't remember it. Things pass, Alcey."

She looked along the road, musing, and shook her head again. "The Stamp Act didn't. People sometimes reach a state of affairs where one side refuses to stop advancing and the other refuses to yield, the one becoming more demanding and the other more obstinate in refusal. There are crossroads where the choice cannot be changed once the path is chosen, and there are things that cannot be taken back, once said. Parliament and the king become ever more tyrannical, and some in the colonies become ever more rash. I fear for what comes next, love."

"You could be right. Some are talking about separating from England."

"And with good cause. The Massachusetts Government Act is the sheerest tyranny, taking away the right of people to elect their own representatives, and it could happen here next. I daresay Parliament had to do something about the destruction of the cargoes of tea in Boston, but the Boston Port Act was more ill-considered than the destruction of the tea. There are lawful means of dealing with such things, and a government that attempts to rule by edict rather than law is worse than no government at all. People here will have their rights, and he who would set his foot on their neck might have a care lest his toes be nipped."

"Well, if we did separate, we'd still have that lot of buggers in the Assembly to deal with. But at least they're where we can reach them. If a couple of scalps were lifted from amongst them, I daresay they'd have a thought for someone besides themselves and for something besides their purses."

"No doubt they would," Alcey laughed. "And there can be no question that the formation of the Regulars made them think. The Regulators were defeated, but their battle was won, to my way of thinking. Many of the cheating tax collectors, sheriffs, surveyors, and court clerks were replaced by more honest people. Well, we shall see what happens, love."

They walked up a long, low rise in the road in silence, the oxen trudging along beside them. A man on horseback came over the crest of the rise, riding toward them at a slow canter. He lifted his hat as he approached, Collier nodded, and Alcey plucked at her skirt in a gesture of a curtsy. Alcey walked a few steps ahead of the oxen as they reached the crest of the rise, and she snapped a twig off a sassafras tree. She broke it in two and handed Collier half of it as he caught up with her, and she smiled up at him as she walked beside him again.

"What do you have on your mind, love?"

He put the twig in the side of his mouth and began chewing it. "Have on my mind?"

She smiled fondly as she peeled the bark off the twig with her thumbnail, and she looked back up at him as she put the twig in her mouth and chewed it. "You've had something on your mind since you arrived home, and Simon and Genesee have been whispering like a pair of schoolgirls. What is it?"

"I should have known that Simon couldn't resist telling Genesee," he chuckled, opening the pouch on his belt and taking out an oilskin packet. "I thought I'd wait until things settled to talk to you, and I suppose this is as good a time as any."

Alcey took the packet and unfolded it, took out the sheet of paper. She read it, chewing the twig and moving it from one side of her mouth to the other, then nodded, her features neutral. "So the Transylvania Company will give you two thousand acres free and clear of quit rents and taxes if you will pilot twenty families to Kentucky, settle with them, and captain a fort for their protection."

"Aye. When Simon and I came back across the Holston, Henderson, Daniel Boone, and several others were there treating with the Cherokee to buy a lot of land. I talked to Boone, and he talked to Henderson and got that paper for me."

Alcey was silent for a long moment, looking at the paper again as they walked along the road by the oxen, then she folded it and put it back into the oilskin. "So you'd like to move to Kentucky, love?"

"I'd like us to think about it. Boone is cutting a road into Kentucky now, and he's taking in a group of settlers. James Harrod and Ben Logan are also taking in groups. There are a lot of settlers moving into Kentucky along the Ohio, and a lot already have. It won't be long until I'll be pressed to catch even a portion of the furs I caught this year, because Kentucky will be too settled. The land there is rich, Alcey, and there wouldn't be any taxes or quit rents. We could make ourselves a good living there with a lot less than two thousand acres."

She looked up at him quickly. "And give up going to hunt and trap each year?"

"If you could put up with me being about all the while. What do you think about it?"

"You've just given me ample cause to regard it favorably," she said, handing the packet back to him. "But I don't think you've a very valuable land grant there, love. I've read about this man Henderson and the Transylvania Company in the news sheets, and I'm sure I hardly need say that no Crown charter has been issued for this undertaking."

He nodded, putting the packet back into the pouch on his belt. "For all the difference it makes. I'm sure we'd have a good wait before we'd see the king sending soldiers to remove people from Kentucky, but it does go against that new law they passed, doesn't it?"

"Yes, the Quebec Act. And also the Royal Proclamation of 1763. But you're quite right in questioning what difference it makes. The Proclamation of 1763 didn't appear to unduly concern Governor Dunmore in his ventures along the Ohio. There is also the Watauga Association, which has had a number of settlements in violation of law for some years. Beyond that the news sheets have it that the board of trade is considering establishing a new colony west of Virginia to be called Vandalia. Considering that muddle one might as well do as one pleases. You say Henderson was treating with the Indians for the land? It appears that's hardly the end of the matter, or there would be no need for a fort, would there?"

Collier smiled wryly and nodded. "He was dealing with the Cherokee, and they're not the only ones involved. There'll be some trouble, like there was here years ago, but it'll pass. And as far as the Transylvania Company is concerned, I don't feel obliged one way or the other toward them. To my way of thinking I can move to Kentucky if I wish, and I can say it's mine as easily as they can. But Boone's involved with them, and he's as good a man as has ever walked. I'd like to keep his friendship, and I've no doubt that everyone in Kentucky will need to be friends with everyone else until all trouble with Indians has passed."

Alcey looked away, chewing the sassafras twig. They walked along the road in silence for several minutes as she pondered, then she looked up at him again. "How much trouble would you expect from Indians?"

"I think it would be on an order we'd be able to deal with, or I wouldn't suggest taking you. Indians haven't the stomach for the kind of fighting it takes to lay siege to a fort. There will be several forts there, and I'm sure there'll be enough men to form a good militia. And on that paper they say twenty families, but I wouldn't think of going with less than thirty rifles. Thirty good rifles in a sound fort could stand off hundreds of Indians."

"Well, I've heard many around here who are dissatisfied with things as they are and would as soon move elsewhere. If this Transylvania Company doesn't charge too much for land, I don't think it would be difficult to find thirty families to go."

"Nor do I and the charge is little enough. It's five guineas for five hundred acres to those who will clear and grow crops, but I don't know if they'd want taxes or how much quit rent there would be. In any event if I took people there, they could deal with the business themselves.

Frank Crawford brought up the subject to me when we stopped at his place on the way home, and I'd have the people soon enough if I put out word I was going. I didn't say yea or nay to Frank, by the way. He said that he would probably be bringing his family into Cross Creek within the next week or two, and he'd stop by to discuss it."

"How is his wife?"

"She and the little one are coming along very well. It's a boy."

A rivulet crossed the road at the bottom of the grade, turning several yards of the road into a swath of deep mud. Alcey lifted the hem of her skirt and walked along a thick, heavy footlog at the edge of the road as the oxen put their shoulders into the yoke and dragged the wagon through the mud. Collier waded through the mud beside them and urged them on. The wagon lurched through the mud and out onto solid ground, and Alcey hopped off the end of the log and began walking beside Collier again.

"What would we be able to take with us, love?"

"Not all that much, Alcey. I wouldn't trust wagons on the road that Boone is making, as few men as there are working on it and as hasty as it's being done, so we'd get another six or eight horses to go with the ones we have and take everything on pack horses. And we could drive the stock along. It would be slow, but there would be time to get there and put in something in the way of a crop this year."

"Grandpa and Nina wouldn't be able to walk."

"No, we'd have to put them on horses."

Alcey slowly nodded. Her expression was still neutral, but the normally cheerful line to her lips when her features were in repose was missing. She turned and looked at the wagon. "Genesee?"

Genesee sat up, blinking sleepily and rubbing his eyes. "Aye, Ma?"

"Run ahead and catch a good hen and get it ready to cook, dear. Scald it good before you pluck it, and singe the pinfeathers down."

Genesee hopped down, glanced around to see where they were as he yawned and stretched, then he stepped to the side of the road and broke into a swift trot, disappearing into the trees and brush. Alcey walked along beside Collier

for several more minutes in silence, then turned to the
wagon, gathering her skirt.

"Well, we have a lot to think about, don't we? Give me a
hand up, if you would, love."

Collier put his hands around her waist and lifted her,
and she stepped over the sideboard of the wagon. She sat
down on the seat, her lips pursed and her brows drawn in
thought, and Collier walked along beside the oxen again.

Alcey remained quiet and thoughtful when they got
home, and there was a pensive melancholy in her manner
that Collier could understand. The farmstead represented
an element of stability in his life, a point of return and
departure between trips, but it was the physical foundation
of her existence. Each log in the cabin had a meaning to
her, and her emotional investment in the farmstead was
deep. When he had returned home and found there had
been a fire on the roof of the cabin during the winter, to
him it had meant going over the temporary repairs, replacing burned ceiling boards and putting on seasoned shingles
in place of the boards Alcey had pegged over the gaping
hole. But to her it had meant a night of terror, of awaken-
ing in clouds of smoke and of fighting frantically to save
her family and her cabin. The cabin was their first home
together, the place where she had endured the pain of giving birth to four children, the place where she had endured
the agony of seeing one of her children sicken and die. To
her each of her possessions represented memories, each
piece of furniture and each of the things she had saved to
buy or had made was possessed of a lineage and history.

The others were subdued, perceiving that a matter of importance was under consideration, and the three boys were
less rowdy. Simon and Genesee were silent as they helped
carry the old man to his room and helped unload the
wagon into the pantry and back storage room. Collier
parked the wagon by the barn and turned the oxen into a
pasture, then went back to the cabin and sat by the hearth,
smoking his pipe. Simon and Genesee fed the stock, milked
the cows, and chopped firewood, then sat in the corner on
the other side of the fireplace, murmuring sleepily and dozing. When dinner was ready, Nina went to the old man's
room to try to rouse him to eat, and he ran her away from

his bed, cursing and trying to hit her with his crutch. The others gathered around the table.

After dinner Simon and Genesee left to go hunting again. The three boys carried in firewood and water, then went to bed. The old man hobbled in on his crutch, angrily demanding something to eat. He ate a bowl of mush as Alcey and Nina moved quietly around, cleaning up and washing dishes. Alcey gave the old man a cup of heavily watered rum, and he slumped on the bench at the table as he drank it. Nina helped him back into his room, then went to her room. The cabin was quiet as Alcey moved around with her soft footsteps, putting things away, then she went outside for her bath. She returned, and Collier went out.

The fire was blazing up when he came back in. Alcey was sitting on her stool with her cup of toddy, and his was on the hearth in front of his stool. He moved closer to the fire as he took a drink of his toddy. "The nights still have a chill to them, don't they?"

"They do and all, love. May I see your paper again?"

He took out the oilskin packet and handed it to her, and took another drink of his toddy, looking at her as she unfolded the paper and read it again. She studied it for several minutes, then she folded it back into the oilskin as she rose and put it on the mantel.

"I think it would be good to have the signature of another officer in the company on a letter agreeing to this matter, love. The company isn't properly chartered, but they're all we have at the moment and it's never too soon to begin assuring perfect title to land. I'll send off a letter to them tomorrow, addressing this matter and stating your intentions."

"You want to go, then?"

She smiled sadly and shook her head, taking a drink from her cup. "No. But I think it best, for the reasons you mentioned and for others as well. So it's done. Do you remember that I told you about my cousin Anthony Cosgrave who came to see me three years ago? He was thinking of finishing his active duty with the militia at the time, and it could be that this would interest him. I could write him, if you wish, because his experience with the militia would make him of value to the party. And he isn't the sort of man who would attempt to usurp your command."

"I'd hardly call it that," Collier chuckled. "But I'd be more than pleased to have him along."

"I'll write him, then. And it is a command, whatever you say, love. A command and a very heavy responsibility."

Collier shrugged, smiling whimsically and looking into the fire, then he looked at her. "I'm pleased that you settled your mind to go."

"I'm pleased that you're pleased, but you well know that I'd do as you wish in any event."

"And you well know that I'd not make you do something that was against your will."

She looked at him, a warm smile spreading over her face and becoming wider. Her cheeks flushed and her eyes twinkled as she rose, putting her hand on his shoulder. "Finish your toddy, love. It's late."

# Chapter Twenty-two

Late the following morning Alcey sent Genesee to the trading post to dispatch letters addressed to the Transylvania Company and her cousin, and Collier went to see a man named Ludlow, who lived on a small farm a few miles along the road. Ludlow had talked wistfully about his desire for better land and a larger farmstead when Collier had seen him in the trading post the year before, and he was an earnest, hardworking man in his early forties, with two teen-age sons and two small children. Collier found him in his fields, talked to him about going to Kentucky, and left him to think about it. During the afternoon two men who had heard Genesee talking in the trading post about going to Kentucky came to see Collier. They were both unmarried, both unemployed laborers without property and on borrowed horses, and neither of them had experience on the border or in the wilderness. Collier turned them down.

Simon and Genesee anticipated a time of relaxation and hunting before setting out for Kentucky, but a farmstead with standing crops was more valuable than a farmstead with fallow land, and Collier began breaking the ground to plant, with Simon and Genesee helping him. Ludlow came to see Collier, having decided to go and wanting information on preparations and things to take, and others came to see Collier as word began spreading. Most of them were the young and adventurous, and he turned them down. But a few seasoned, steady men came to him to discuss it and left to ponder and talk it over with their wives. A man named Patterson, who had a large family and had lived on the border, returned to tell Collier that he wanted to go. Then a man named Gillman, who had a family and had been in the militia, also wanted to go.

Crawford and his family came and spent the night, and

they left the next morning to go home and begin their preparations, then a man who was visiting relatives in the area came to see Collier. Massey was a large, congenial man in his late thirties, from Roanoke, married and with three children, and he had been in Lewis's force at Fort Pleasant where a decisive battle had ended Lord Dunmore's war. Collier was favorably impressed with Massey, who promised to write after he returned home and talked with his wife.

After the planting was completed, Collier began making preliminary preparations, heating scrap iron and fusing it into masses that could be packed on a horse, assembling hoops to make barrels, tubs, and buckets at the end of the trip, and going through his tools to see what new ones he needed. The niter he had brought from Kentucky produced a high-quality gunpowder, and he bought bags of brimstone to take along to make gunpowder. Genesee mentioned a female Bluetick hound that a neighboring farmer was going to dispose of because it was too vicious, and Collier sent Genesee for the dog and had it penned in a coop by the cabin. Two of the sows had pigs, and Collier picked out several to take along and started Simon and Genesee making crates for pigs, chickens, and ducks. Collier talked to his foster father during his more lucid moments, telling him that they were going to Kentucky. It finally became more or less rooted in the old man's memory, and at times he would be excited about it, at other times he would be morose, and yet other times he would forget what was happening and be confused by the conversation around him. Men continued coming to talk with Collier as word on what he was doing became widespread, and some came from as far away as the Yadkin and Wilmington. The list of families grew from ten to fifteen, then to twenty, and Collier told those from the outlying locations that the rendezvous would be Wolf Hills on the Holston Trace during the first week in May.

A thick letter from the Transylvania Company arrived at the trading post, and the trader sent a boy to the cabin with it. The letter confirmed the terms of the agreement with Collier and instructed him to settle near the headwaters of the Green River. A map was enclosed with the letter designating where he was to build a fort, and it also showed the location of Harrod's Fort on the Salt River, the place where Boone was going to build a fort south of the Kentucky River, and where Benjamin Logan would build a fort west of Dick's River. The letter also listed two families from Richmond who would be going with Collier, and asked him to designate a rendezvous. Collier hadn't anticipated that the company would add settlers to his party, and he didn't like having people in the party he hadn't met, but he had Alcey write a reply, giving the date and place of rendezvous and the instructions on preparations and things to bring that he had been giving the other people.

The list grew to thirty families, then thirty-two, and letters arrived from Massey and Alcey's cousin. Massey wanted to go, but Alcey's cousin couldn't. He had been promoted and remained in the Virginia Militia, but he had a married son, Anson Cosgrave, who did want to go. In addition he had a young recently widowed sister who wanted to leave the surroundings of her bereavement and make herself a life elsewhere. Rachel was twenty, and Alcey had never met her. Collier was even more disinclined toward unattached women than men, because they were less able to fend for themselves. But the woman was Alcey's cousin. He had her write replies to Massey and Cosgrave, giving them the date and place of the rendezvous and instructions on what to bring. A man named Elder came to see Collier about going, and Collier's initial impression was unfavorable. The man was in his fifties and looked somewhat weak and sickly. He had recently moved with his family from South Carolina and had very little stock and property, and it appeared that the man and his family might turn out to be a burden on the others. But Collier remembered that a man named Elder had married Ellen, Simon's mother, and during their conversation Elder mentioned that he'd had a brother killed by Indians on the Catawba. Collier told Elder he could join the party.

As the people in the vicinity of Cross Creek made their preparations to leave, the price of horses increased and the selection diminished because people were buying them for pack trains. Collier decided to buy his additional horses from Wilmington and to send Simon for them. He gave Simon instructions on selecting them and how much to pay. Land dealers in the area were busily visiting all those who were leaving and bartering for their farmsteads, most of them in collusion and paying very low prices for the land, and Alcey gave Simon a letter and money to have the farm advertised in the news sheets in Wilmington.

Most of the food staples and other supplies for the year were in the pantry and storeroom, bought at the time that the pelts and hides had been sold, and Collier and Alcey conferred over the other things they would need. Over the years Alcey had used the credit on pelts and hides and paper money to buy supplies, and she had hoarded all the gold and silver specie. It was buried in various spots around the barn, and when they dug it up and counted it, the total was well over a thousand guineas, an amount that surprised Collier. They made a trip to Cross Creek and bought the remainder of the supplies, goods, and tools they would need, and Collier bought a pistol for himself and one for Simon.

Another letter came from the Transylvania Company. It asked for a list of names and family members of the entire party, and it objected in a mildly indignant tone to Collier's instruction that all in the party possess sufficient pack horses to transport their belongings. The letter stated firmly that the road was adequate for wagons, and that Colonel Henderson was already enroute with a wagon train. Collier had Alcey write a reply, listing the entire party by name, and stating unequivocally that he would not have anyone in the party who brought wagons.

Collier was working on a pasture fence on the slope above the cabin on the afternoon Simon returned with the horses. He started walking down toward the cabin as he saw Simon ride out of the trees on the other side of the creek, leading a string of horses, then he stopped. There were only four horses following the one Simon was riding. Then another man came out of the trees, leading four more horses. The horses splashed through the creek, and Collier walked on down toward the cabin.

A voice among the hubbub of greetings and laughter in front of the cabin echoed across the years as Collier walked along the side of the cabin. It was that of Isaac Raines. Collier took longer strides, smiling with pleasure, then he stopped at the corner of the cabin, his smile fading. The last time Collier had seen Isaac had been when he and Alcey had been recently married and in the process of moving to Cross Creek, and Isaac had hardly looked his age. But the years since then had more than made up for years that had been light on him. And while Collier had heard that Isaac had been wounded in the leg and discharged from the militia when his right leg below his knee had been amputated, the wooden peg leg still took him by surprise, inconsistent with the Isaac of previous years. But it went with him well enough in his changed state. He was about fifty, but he looked older. The blonde hair had thinned and changed to a dirty white. His face was pouched and sagging, with several days' growth of white stubble on it. Most of his teeth were missing. His homespuns hung on him, his shoulders and arms were thin and shrunken, and his belly sagged.

His voice had changed, sounding weaker and with a hoarse rasp, and the hearty boom was gone from his laughter. He was bussing and hugging Alcey and Nina, then he exclaimed over Genesee and looked at the three boys, shifting his weight and balancing himself awkwardly on his foot and the peg leg as he leaned over to ruffle their hair. Collier fixed a smile of greeting on his face and walked toward the group.

Raines' smile faded slightly and became unsure and defensive as he turned, looking at Collier and extending his hand. "Well, well, here's old Santee, and not altered a whit. By God, there's no need to ask you how you are, Santee, and we've been hearing a lot about you down in Wilmington."

"Nothing to have me locked up for if I go down that way, I trust," Collier laughed, as they shook hands. "And you're looking hale and hearty and all, Isaac."

Raines looked more defensive as he shook his head. "Well, I cross a creek and get a look at myself now and then, so there's no need for you to . . . So you're going to Kentucky? I met Simon here when he was trading for his horses, and I told Martha that I thought I'd just meander up this way with him to give him a hand with the horses and to see you before you left."

"We're all more than pleased you did, Isaac, and the only thing that could have pleased us more would be if you'd brought Martha along."

"Well, we have this cow or two and a couple of horses to be looked after, so . . ." He looked at the old man on the bench in front of the cabin, and he smiled widely as he stumped toward the bench. "By God, here's old Caleb. Caleb, how are you?"

The old man was dozing, and Collier chuckled as he walked toward the bench with Raines. "He's a bit hard of hearing, Isaac, so you'll have to speak up."

"Aye, well, so am I, and he's older than I am," Raines laughed. "He has a right to be hard of hearing, doesn't he?" He leaned over in front of the old man. "Caleb! Caleb! Wake up, man!"

The old man jerked convulsively, and his eyes popped open. He looked up at Raines with a startled frown, then his eyes widened as they moved up and down Raines and a smile of recognition spread over his face. "Alvah! How are you, Alvah? And what did you do to your bloody leg?"

"No, it's Isaac, Caleb. Isaac! My dad's been gone these few years."

The old man's smile faded into an expression of disbelief, and he looked at Raines suspiciously as Raines took his limp hand and pumped it. "Oh, aye . . . well, how are you?"

"I'll do, Caleb, I'll do," Raines said, and he laughed boisterously. "I don't have but one foot to get cold, in any event. I was standing in the wrong place and got a ball through my leg."

"Oh, aye . . ."

Raines laughed heartily again, nodding. "But I'm glad I wasn't sitting there instead."

"Oh, aye . . ."

Raines' smile became strained, and he forced a chuckle. "If I'd been sitting there, I'd have got it through my chest instead, don't you see?"

"Oh, aye . . ."

The old man continued staring narrowly at Raines, unsmiling. Raines' smile became sickly, then it died away and he cleared his throat with an embarrassed sound, glancing at Collier. Collier put his hand on Raines' shoulder, turning him away from the old man. "He'll probably remember you directly, Isaac. I expect you're about ready for a sitdown after the ride, aren't you? Simon, did these nags walk all the way here, or did you have to carry some of them part of the way?"

"Carry?" Simon snorted, laughing. "This is as fine a lot of horses as can be bought in North Carolina."

"The boy can judge horses," Raines said, nodding in approval. "What's more, he can double a horse trader's tongue back down his throat and make him choke on it. He made you a good trade, Santee."

"Aye, they look like they'll do. Give him a hand with them, Genesee, and take Isaac's horse around with you. You're spending the night, aren't you, Isaac?"

"Well, if you wish."

"I'll hear nothing else. Do we have a sip of something about, Alcey?"

"Indeed we do," she replied, smiling at him and Raines as she walked toward the door. "Just step to the door where Grandpa won't see it, love, and I'll hand it out."

"Aye, it goes to his head," Collier chuckled, looking at Raines as he walked toward the door. "Go on and sit down by that tree over there, Isaac, and I'll fetch it."

Raines nodded, stumping heavily toward the tree. Nina followed Alcey in, Genesee and Simon led the horses around the corner of the cabin, looking at the horses and talking about them, and the three boys stood in a cluster by the door, gaping at Raines' wooden leg. Alcey handed two cups of rum out the door to Collier, and the three boys followed Collier toward the tree. Raines was sitting under the tree, wincing and rubbing his thigh above the peg leg, and he quickly stopped rubbing it and smiled congenially as Collier walked toward him. Collier handed him one of the cups and sat down by him.

"Here's your health, Isaac."

"Aye, and yours, Santee." He took a drink of the rum and sighed heavily as he wiped his mouth with the back of his hand. "That puts the breath back in a man, doesn't it? Well, so you're going to Kentucky, Santee."

"If I can ever get everything sorted out."

"And taking a good-sized party and all, I understand. Well, there'd be plenty more than willing to go with you, where they'd think again about going with someone else. The name of Santee Collier is well known, no bloody fear."

"I don't know so much about that, but it's a middling

good party. I have thirty-six families and a widowed cousin of Alcey's on the list."

"There aren't many who could get up a party half that size, no question about that." He took another drink of rum and sighed again. "You know, I never did get to see Kentucky, Santee, and now I never will. I was a fool to take that commission in the goddamned militia instead of keeping on hunting. If I'd had the sense you did, I'd be well off today, as you are. And I always did want to see Kentucky."

His tone was wistful, something more than a subtle hint, and he looked at Collier from the corners of his eyes and quickly looked away. He was asking to go. And he had obviously accompanied Simon from Wilmington in order to sound out the possibilities of going. If he had been anyone else, Collier wouldn't have considered it. But he couldn't refuse Raines. "Do you want to go, Isaac?"

"Me?" Raines snorted, frowning, then shook his head brusquely. "No, no, I'd be a burden, and this bloody wood leg . . . and I'm a bit old, I'm afraid. No, I didn't come up here for that, Santee. I only came to see you in event our paths don't cross again."

"Isaac, I'll pull that wood leg off there and brain you with it. You'd be no burden, and I'd have you in my party before anyone else, even if they had as many legs as a cockroach. Now do you want to go?"

Raines took a deep gulp of his rum, his hand shaking. He licked his lips and cleared his throat, and his voice broke as he started to speak. His eyes filled with tears and he pressed his lips together, his features twitching, and he took another noisy gulp of rum. The three boys were sitting on the ground a few feet away, gaping and listening breathlessly. Collier looked at them over the rim of his cup as he took a sip of rum. "You boys get around the cabin and find something to busy yourselves with."

They climbed to their feet and trotted toward the corner of the cabin, looking over their shoulders, and disappeared around the corner. Raines took another drink of rum and cleared his throat, and he wiped his eyes with the back of his hand. "Things have been going poorly for me lately, Santee," he said, in a strained whisper. "But I didn't mean to come here and inflict my troubles on you, or to—"

"We've been friends a long time, Isaac, and if there's something I can do to help you, I only wish you'd have let me know before. But if things have taken a turn against you, a good plot and a snug cabin in Kentucky will put them aright again. We could well use a man with your experience in the militia in our party. I was depending on having Alcey's cousin Anthony Cosgrave along, but he can't come."

Raines cleared his throat again and nodded, sniffling and drawing in a quick breath. "Cosgrave? Aye, I know him well. And while I won't say that I could fill even one of his boots, perhaps I could keep from being a burden, Santee. My youngest boy left and went up to Petersburg this past winter, and now it's just me and Martha there. And it's no goddamned good there anymore. Jobs are hard to find, they're trying to run all of us off the estuary because they want the land for something, and my taxes have got to where I can't . . . and I can get around well enough, Santee. You saw that, didn't you? And you see that little hole there near the bottom of my peg? Well, I have this slat with an iron cup on it, and I put it on the bottom of the peg and put a nail through the cup and that hole, and I can plow or walk through plowed ground without sinking into it. Walk just as if I had two feet, in fact. And I can turn my hand to any sort of task."

"Will you leave that, Isaac? Now do you have enough to buy what you'll need and to get horses for yourself and Martha as well as pack horses? If not, I can make you a loan."

"Oh, no, that won't be necessary, Santee. We've had some hard days, but we've kept something laid by. No, we have more than sufficient, but I'm very grateful all the same. Well, Simon said that you're forming up at Wolf Hills during the first week in May. If so I don't see that I'll have any difficulty at all."

"That's good, and we'd better go over what you'll need to bring along. Is your cup dry? Give it here and I'll get you another sip, and we can go over everything together."

"Well, perhaps just another drop, then."

There was something of the Isaac Raines of old in his eyes and smile as he handed the cup to Collier. But it was hardly more than a pathetic remnant, a ghostly and shadowy memory. Collier took the cup back to the cabin, and as Alcey refilled it he told her that Raines and his wife would be joining the party. Alcey silently nodded, her smile relieved and gratified.

Raines spent the night and left after breakfast the next morning, and Collier examined the horses Simon had brought back from Wilmington. They were all sound and healthy, none young enough to be difficult to control, but none of them old. He had Genesee and Simon bring all the horses into a pen by the barn, and he started a fire in the forge and began putting new shoes on them.

Alcey and Nina made waterproof oilskin bags and filled them with seeds, and made canvas bags for transporting fruit tree saplings. Genesee and Simon fastened crates together with straps and put them on the oxen's backs to accustom them to carrying the crates. A few crates were broken by the younger oxen's indignant buckling, but Genesee and Simon made more crates, and eventually all the oxen became accustomed to the crates, then to the pigs, chickens, and ducks in them. Collier made strong leather muzzles for all the more dangerous dogs, went over all the packsaddles and made repairs, and began loading his tools and equipment into packs on some of the saddles.

A man named Tuttle came from Wilmington to look at the farmstead in response to the advertisement in the news sheets. Alcey had arranged for assistance from some of the nearby people who were in the party going to Kentucky, and she dispatched Genesee in one direction and Simon in the other. Minutes later a man arrived on horseback and began silently looking the farm and buildings over with the attitude of a prospective buyer. Then a man and woman came in a wagon and began looking the place over. Tuttle came to the barn where Collier was working, and he gave Collier a cash deposit to hold the farmstead, agreeing to pay what Collier and Alcey had asked for the place.

Events moved rapidly as the final days approached. The fruit tree saplings were dug, put in bags, and tied into loads on packsaddles. Foodstuffs were loaded. Alcey and Nina packed things to be used along the way, arranging them so they would be conveniently accessible, and Simon and Genesee readied packsaddles to be loaded onto horses. When a buyer offered Elder a bonus price for immediate occupancy of his small farmstead, Collier told Elder that he and his family could make a temporary camp on the creek. They came one afternoon with their four thin horses and spindly cow and built an open-fronted shelter from timber lying about. The woman was a female counterpart of Elder, and their only child was a thin, lanky boy of ten. Then Tuttle arrived with his family and belongings in a wagon, and they moved into unused stalls in the barn.

On the last night Collier was wakeful for a time, because he could tell from Alcey's breathing that she wasn't asleep. He went to sleep, and when he awoke she still wasn't asleep. They got out of bed and began dressing, Alcey folding the bedding.

Tuttle and his two boys helped load the packsaddles on the horses and the crates of chickens, pigs, and ducks on the oxen in the predawn darkness. Alcey and Nina gathered last things to load on the horses, then they brought out a hasty breakfast and food in kettles to be eaten at noon. There was a stir in the darkness by the creek as the Elders readied their animals and moved along the road up the slope and through the trees to the main road. Alcey went in by herself to check the cabin a last time. The old man was sleepy, confused, frightened, and angry. He wanted to go back to his room, and he cursed furiously and hit out with his crutch at everyone who came near him. Collier took his crutch away from him and lifted him onto his horse, and he began weeping.

Dawn broke as Genesee and Simon turned the oxen and cattle out of the pen and drove them around the cabin. Collier took the lead rope on the first horse in one train and began leading the horses away from the cabin, whistling to the hounds. Alcey took the other train of horses and followed, and Genesee and Simon herded the cattle and oxen in behind the horses Alcey was leading. As Collier waded through the creek, he glanced around to make sure all the hounds were with him and all the dangerous ones were muzzled, then he looked back. The old man was humped over on his horse in the center of the train, still weeping. Nina looked comfortable on her horse in the center of Alcey's train. The oxen and cattle were herding well. The three boys were trotting along beside Alcey. Alcey was looking over her shoulder at the cabin. The Tuttles were moving their things into the cabin. Alcey turned back around and looked down at the ground, her shoulders slumped, her lips and chin trembling, and tears running down her cheeks.

A train of horses and cluster of stock moved along the road as Collier went up the slope and into the trees, then another moved along the road as he went through the trees. There was a din of noise, dogs barking, horses whinnying, cows lowing, pigs squealing, chickens squawking, ducks honking, and people shouting to each other. The sun was rising above the horizon as Collier turned onto the road. Three families and their animals were in sight on the road ahead of him, and two were in sight behind. They waved. Someone whooped and fired a rifle.

Collier looked back. The loads on the horses were riding well, none of the packsaddles leaning to either side. The old man had stopped weeping and was sitting up and looking around. The oxen and cattle were still herding well. Alcey was smiling radiantly, walking along with her free, lithe stride as she led the horses.

# Chapter Twenty-three

The horses began cropping the grass at the side of the road as Collier stopped, looking back and waving the others to the side of the road. The hounds sat down, looking at Collier and panting, then rose and followed as Collier dropped the halter rope and walked back to lift the old man down. Collier felt weary, but it was the weariness of frustration rather than fatigue. In retrospect the difficulties of protecting himself, a son, a string of horses, and a catch of pelts and hides in Indian country had been minor. Dealing with a large group of people comprised of individuals who became tired, ill, disgruntled, stubborn, disorderly, and illogical was a nightmare. He lifted the old man down from his horse and handed him his crutch.

"How are you feeling, Pa?"

The old man uttered a surly grunt, settling the crosspiece on the heavy, crude crutch under his arm. Collier walked along the line of horses toward the second string, and the old man hobbled along on his crutch, keeping up with Collier. Caleb's wiry constitution had produced reserves of energy and endurance that had surprised Collier, and what Collier had envisioned as a potential problem hadn't materialized. The old man had shrugged off cold spring rains, sleeping in a wet blanket on soggy ground, sparse and unappetizing food, and the wearinesss of the daily trek far better than many of the younger members in the party.

Alcey slid down from her horse, lifted Shelby down, and walked back toward Nina as she slid down from her horse. It was another tiresome conflict in Collier's mind. Enough of the supplies had been consumed to free a horse for Alcey to ride. Collier knew that he should buy more supplies before leaving the trace and the last source of supplies, and that he should allow Alcey and the smallest boy to walk.

But he also knew that he wouldn't. The extra margin of assurance of another two or three hundred pounds of supplies meant less to him than the indications of cumulative fatigue Alcey had been showing from the hardships of daylight-to-dusk travel, enduring the elements, looking after the boys, cooking, washing, and making a camp each night. It had taken a point-blank command to get her to ride instead of putting the other two boys on the horse. And she demonstrated her continuing resentment over the command by ostentatiously examining Jared's and Santee's moccasins before she opened the kettle and began passing out the food. The hounds gathered around, sniffing hopefully and whining impatiently. Collier took the corn bread and pork Alcey handed him, and he stared at her with a smile as he began eating, waiting for her smile. It came slowly and grudgingly, but it came. She tossed her head and sniffed, and pulled her tongue at him. Collier laughed, taking Simon's food, and he walked on along the line of horses, eating his.

The trains of horses stretched far back along the road, the horses cropping the grass and the people clustered around their kettles of cold food. Most of the people smiled, nodded, and spoke as he passed. Many of the greetings had an edge of reserve, because the majority were highly individualistic, resentful toward any authority even when they had placed themselves in the position of accepting some measure of control. It was a viewpoint that Collier could understand. Some of the greetings had more than an edge of reserve, because there had been a few problems. Several of the men had spent evenings loitering in taverns along the way until there had been a couple of late starts, and Collier had reprimanded the men and stopped the practice. Some of the people had expected to stop when someone became ill. The more devout had expected to stop and rest on Sundays. A number of people had been unwilling to enure themselves to the sparse and monotonous food necessitated by travel and had started killing their chickens and dipping into vital food reserves until Collier had stopped them. Collier's hounds had killed a few other dogs and bitten a few people. And there had been other things.

There were cold glances from some of the groups. Loftus had a sixteen-year-old daughter who had derived pleasure

from provoking fights between youths. The girl's mother
had intruded into the conversation between Collier and
Loftus, her attitude more or less explaining the origin of
her daughter's conduct, and Collier had threatened to
thrash her. Billingsley, a large, swaggering man in his late
twenties, had shown a tendency to make himself too pleasant to some of the other men's wives, and he had whipped
a couple of men who had become angry. He had declined
Collier's invitation to fight with his choice of fists, knife
and tomahawk, or firearms. And he had stopped making
himself so congenial to the women at large. Billingsley
looked away with a stony expression as Collier passed. His
wife, a somewhat plain but pleasant and hardworking
woman a few years older than him, glanced up at Collier
with a timid and surreptitious smile.

A lot of the people remained affable, and the initial im-
pressions of some of them had been misleading. Patterson,
a garrulous, strong-willed man who had been one of the
most enthusiastic tipplers in the taverns, immediately
stopped drinking when Collier talked to him. He had
seemed a potential troublemaker, but he had become one
of the most cooperative men in the party, always strongly
endorsing any decision Collier made. The Elders had
turned out to be one of the hardiest families in the party,
and they hadn't touched their packs of supplies. The quiet,
thin boy snared rabbits at night and knocked squirrels from
trees with his sling during the day, and the woman pulled
young poke shoots and grubbed up other edible plants and
roots along the way. They looked thin, weak, and sickly,
precisely the way they had looked while camping on the
creek below the cabin, while the days of travel had made a
difference in other people who looked stronger and health-
ier.

There were the usual small difficulties. Turner lifted his
hand and called out through a mouthful of food as Collier
passed. "Say, Mr. Collier, one of my horses has thrown a
shoe."

"Pad it up with some rags or leather or something. We'll
be in Wolf Hills by dark, and there'll be a forge there so we
can check all the shoes on the horses."

"I'm having trouble with this one packsaddle again,"

Parsons said as Collier passed. "She's coming all to pieces on me now."

"Make a sling out of some ropes and hang the load on the horse's back, then, or get someone to give you a hand and carry part of it. There'll be tree forks to make a new one in Wolf Hills."

All the cattle and oxen were in a herd at the rear of the line of pack trains. During the first day of travel it had become obvious that the logical way to drive the cattle was in a single herd, with youths in the group as drovers. Collier had put Simon in charge of the herd and youths. And there had been problems. Two animals had strayed and become lost at night, while the boys posted to watch them had dozed off. While camped near Clayton the herd had broken into a cornfield and ruined it, necessitating taking up a collection to pay the farmer for the damage before he summoned the authorities. After a couple of scathing reprimands from Collier Simon started using his fists to enforce his orders. A couple of the parents had objected, and Collier had overruled the objections while watching Simon to make sure he didn't become overbearing. He hadn't, regarding his responsibility for the herd with something of the distaste and grim resignation with which Collier viewed his responsibility for the entire party. The youths had quickly become more conscientious, and Simon had relaxed his stern control and gradually stimulated a sort of camaraderie among them.

Collier gave Simon his food, and he began eating. The cattle had spread out on both sides of the road and were grazing, and the youths were trotting back and forth, going along the line to get their food from their families and eating it as they returned to the herd. Simon nodded toward one of the oxen, talking through a mouthful of food.

"We almost lost a pig this morning. They broke a hole in the side of one of the crates, and one of them was hanging halfway out of it. I patched it up with some twigs for now."

"Is that our chickens with that hen on top of the crate?"

"Aye, she hurt her comb one way or another, and the others were pecking her to death. I took her out and tied her there for now, and I suppose we can make a basket or something to keep her by herself until her comb heals."

Collier nodded, glancing around at the youths. "Which

one of these boys can take over your job with the herd when we're beyond Wolf Hills?"

Simon grinned, stuffing another bite of food into his mouth. "That's a question that's pleasant to my ears."

"It should be no surprise. You know I'll need you to protect the party when we're in Indian territory, not bothering with kine."

"I'm still glad to hear it." He looked around and shrugged. "Genesee could do it."

"He's going to be leading the horses I'm leading now."

"Barton, then," Simon said, nodding toward a heavyset youth a few yards away. "He knows stock, and he has a good head. And he'll be able to leather anyone who needs it, if it comes to that. But it probably won't, because he gets along with everyone and everyone knows now that it can happen."

Collier nodded, turning away. "I'll talk to him tomorrow, then."

"Are you and I going to be together after Wolf Hills, Pa?"

"No, I'll have all those who know what they're doing in Indian territory scattered along the sides of the column, eight or ten rods off the road, and I'll be out in front."

Simon nodded, taking another bite of his food and looking around at the cattle and youths as he turned away, and Collier walked back along the road. Most of the people had finished eating and were resting, and they stirred as Collier passed, preparing to start out again. Alcey had finished feeding the hounds, and she was putting the muzzles back on those that wore them. Nina, the old man, and the three boys got up from where they were sitting at the side of the road. Collier helped Nina onto her horse, and Alcey slowly and deliberately looked at Santee's and Jared's moccasins again as Collier walked along the train of horses and waited on her to help her onto her horse. He lifted her on and surreptitiously pinched her thigh, and she clicked her tongue and looked away with a flushed smile as he lifted Shelby onto the horse in front of her. The old man waited by his horse, and Collier lifted him onto it, walked along the train of horses to the first one, and led the horses onto the road. The other horse trains were moving onto the road, and Simon and the youths were herding the cattle together and starting them along the road. Collier turned back around and walked along the road, the hounds trotting in front of him as he led the horses.

Spring arrived later in the mountains than on the coastal plain and Piedmont to the east, and the trees still weren't in full foliage. The mountains along each side of the long, wide valley had a lingering touch of winter blackness diluting the bright green of new foliage, and the air near the roiling Holston River, swollen in its spring flood, was damp and chilly. Large farms were scattered along the road and on the other side of the river. Narrow, rutted tracks led off the road and back into the foothills, where squares of cleared and cultivated land dotted the gentle slopes. People working in the fields stopped to look at the long column of horses and herd of livestock, and those near the road frequently walked over to find out where the group was going and to ask the latest news of the world outside the valley.

Farmsteads were always older and more closely spaced near the settlements, the newer and more distant ones having been cleared as the area had become settled and safe. The previous day the farms visible from the road had indicated that Wolf Hills was near by their signs of having been established years before—old weathered fences pieced with new rails and old cabins built in the shape of blockhouses. As the afternoon wore on, the stretches of forest along the road diminished and the farmsteads were those that had been tilled for many years. Some of them had newer cabins located near piles of charred timbers and shattered stubs of chimneys overgrown with weeds, where cabins had been burned in raids of years before.

The road curved away from the river toward the foothills, circling around a flat floodplain covered with cane, in a series of gentle swells on the edge of the foothills. As Collier reached the top of a rise, he saw two horses by the road where it crossed the peak of a long ridge a mile ahead. A man stood up from where he had been sitting in the grass by the horses, then another man stood. The two men leaped on their horses and raced toward the column at a pounding run, waving their rifles. Puffs of smoke came from the rifles, then the crack of the rifles echoed along the road as the whoops of the men became audible. It was Raines and Massey.

They reined up as they approached Collier, their horses panting and stamping and making Collier's horses prance restively, and they turned to ride along the road beside Collier. "By God, I knew you'd be here today, Santee!" Raines crowed triumphantly. "And you've won me a gallon of rum on a wager!"

"Then you can split it with me," Collier laughed. "How many people have arrived?"

"Eleven families, including one that came in late last night."

"Well, we're short one, then, but there are two more days before the week is out. How are you, Massey?"

"I couldn't be better, seeing this. It appears you've set out to settle Kentucky in one great go, by God. Did you ever see the likes of this, Isaac?"

"I told you that Santee Collier doesn't do things by halves! Santee, the trader has a space set up along the river for everyone to camp, and there's firewood and everything. And he pens horses and kine for tuppence a day, which includes all the fodder they can eat."

"We'll have a day or two of that, then. Our stock can use feeding up before we go on through."

"I thought so. Here, Massey, why don't you go tell the trader that they're on the last stretch? He can have everything ready for their stock."

"Aye, I'll do that," Massey said, kicking his horse. "I'll see you at the camp, Santee."

Collier nodded and waved as he rode away, and he turned to Raines. "Is there any word of Boone or others on the trace to Cumberland Gap?"

"We've had no word from Boone, or none that I've heard. A man named Calk was through here with a dozen men three weeks ago, heading for Kentucky, and Ben Logan and a group of ten or twelve left out of here two weeks ago. And we got word that Henderson and a party of fifty left Long Island along Boone's trail a week ago." He hesitated, then shrugged. "And we heard that Henderson has wagons with him, Santee."

"I heard that too. And he might have a ship with him, but getting it there is another matter. That's not a wagon road, and that's why I said no wagons, Isaac."

Raines looked away and coughed uncomfortably, shrug-

ging again. "Well, you have some, Santee. Two families
who came in from Virginia have wagons with them."

"Then they've got as far as they're going," Collier replied. "I had Alcey write that company twice to tell them I
wouldn't take wagons, and I'm not going to."

"Aye, well . . . well, I'll get on back here and speak to
Caleb and Alcey. And I'll cheer your people up a bit and
let them know they're almost there."

"Do that, Isaac. Simon's back there in charge of the cattle. Tell him about the pens and where they are when you
get back there, if you would."

Raines nodded, turning his horse and greeting the old
man cheerfully. Caleb muttered in reply, and Raines
moved on back to Alcey and began talking with her. When
Collier reached the top of the long ridge, he saw the settlement two miles ahead, a dozen cabins and the sprawling
complex of a trader's post on a wide bend in the river.

Massey rode out from the trading post and walked his
horses along beside Collier, pointing out the place along
the edge of the river where the trader wanted the party to
camp. The trader's men were bustling around the stock
pens, a few Indians and people from the cabins were looking curiously as the party approached along the road, and
people were moving around canvas shelters and open-
fronted pole and sod shelters on one end of the camping
place. Four large wagons were parked behind two of the
canvas shelters.

Collier turned off the road as he neared the trading post
and led the horses past the stock pens toward the edge of
the river, looking back to see if the cattle were going into
the pens smoothly. He glimpsed them starting in, then his
line of vision was blocked as the column dissolved into disorder, people hurrying to pick out their spots along the
riverbank. Collier whistled to the hounds and called them
closer as he crossed the cleared space to the edge of the
river, trains of horses hurrying along on both sides of him,
and he stopped at the edge of the high bank and walked
back to lift the old man down. A young couple ran up to
Alcey and greeted her excitedly as she dismounted. The
man's frock coat, knee breeches, and tricorn were dusty
and rumpled from travel, and his shirt and stockings were
wrinkled and muddy. The woman's bright, frilly calico

dress also showed signs of travel. Collier lifted the old man down and started to walk toward Alcey and the young couple, then another woman came through the crowd. She joined the couple talking to Alcey, and Collier stopped, looking at her.

Her face was averted, and all he could see was her bright red hair and her slender figure in her calico dress. Memories from years before returned with stunning force. Memories of Ellen. Then the woman turned as she smiled and talked to Alcey. Her features were different, but there still seemed to be some resemblance to Ellen, and Collier attributed it to the woman's red hair and impatiently pushed the thought out of his mind as he walked along the horses. The few times the subject of Simon's mother had been remotely approached between him and Alcey, she had made it clear that her standards of morality and propriety didn't allow for youth or any other excuse as an alibi for fathering illegitimate children, and it was one of the few closed subjects between them.

Alcey turned to him as he approached. "Love, I'd like you to meet my cousin Anson Cosgrave and his wife Mary. And this is my cousin Rachel." To them she said, "This is my husband, Santee Collier."

The man looked affable, with a boyish grin, and he lifted his hat and bowed as he spoke. His wife was pretty, and she dropped her eyes demurely as she bobbed in a curtsy. Rachel was a year or two younger than them, very pretty but less shy than Mary, her green eyes level and frank as she curtsied. The memories of Ellen were safely buried again as Collier smiled and spoke to them.

"I'm pleased to meet all of you. None of those wagons over there belong to you, do they?"

"No indeed, sir," Anson said. "Three of them belong to a man named Selwyn, and one belongs to Monroe over there. We brought only horses, as you instructed. And I'd like to take this opportunity to express our gratitude that you graciously consented to allow us along."

"I'm more than pleased to have you along. Did you have an easy enough journey thus far?"

"Nothing beyond fatigue that a day's rest cured, thank you. Our son had a congestion for a day or two, but he's recovered from it."

"And I've left him napping in our little shelter," Mary said. "I must rush back to him, because he's surely awakened."

"Stay for a moment and meet the rest of my family, dear," Alcey said, her smile pleasant but one of firm control over a younger relative. "This is Mr. Bledsoe, my husband's foster father, and I'll ask you to excuse his difficulty in hearing and his fatigue from the journey. This is Nina, and here are my sons Santee, Jared, and Shelby. There, that's done, and if you wish, you could . . . oh, here are Genesee and Simon. Lads, step on over here and meet my cousins."

They were carrying the crates of chickens, ducks, and pigs, Genesee following Simon and struggling with the crates he was carrying. Simon stopped, looking at Rachel with a dumbfounded grin. Genesee ran into Simon with his crates, Simon stumbled, and Genesee put his crates down and stepped forward. Simon continued staring at Rachel with a grin. And Rachel looked back at Simon with a wide, frank smile. There was a momentary stiff silence, then Genesee chuckled with amusement, and Collier smothered his smile as Alcey frowned with aggravation at Simon, breaking the silence.

"My dears, this is Genesee and this is Simon, my husband's sons. Lads, this is my cousin Anson Cosgrave and his wife Mary, and this is my cousin Rachel. Mercy, Simon, have you been riding in a crate with pigs to keep from walking? Your shirt is a shame. Mary, if you fear all this noise might be upsetting your little one, you could see to him and all of you could return for a chat and a cup of coffee when we've settled in."

"That's very kind of you," Mary replied. "Anson was making me a box for a crib, and when it's done we'll bring the baby over so you can have a look at him."

"Yes, I'd like that very much. We'll see you again directly, then."

Mary took Anson's arm, and the three moved away, smiling. Simon continued gazing at Rachel with an infatuated grin, and she smiled at him as she followed Anson and Mary. They disappeared into the mass of horses and people, and Alcey turned on Simon in irritation.

"Simon, what on earth possessed you to so take leave of

your senses? Did I labor in vain in my attempts to instruct you in—"

"Don't be hard on the lad, Alcey," Collier chuckled. "He's eighteen. All right, let's get these packs—"

"Eighteen?" Alcey barked, turning to Collier. "Is that reason to have the manners of some lout of a hod carrier? I'll not have him shaming me and displaying such—"

"You're right, Alcey, you're right," Collier said loudly. "Simon, you have a mind to what your ma says and you act as you bloody should, or I'll have a word with you. Now let's get the packs off these horses. Santee, go get some firewood. Jared, collect those hounds and tie them, and watch Shelby. Alcey, you pick out where you want your fire and everything, and we'll get it set up for you."

Alcey turned away, still fuming. Genesee and Simon began taking the packsaddles off the horses, Genesee chuckling with amusement and Simon craning his neck in the direction Rachel had gone to see if he could catch a glimpse of her. Collier pulled the crates of chickens, ducks, and pigs into a row, and he nudged Simon with a warning frown. Simon nodded, turning glumly and looking at the horse he was unloading.

The noisy confusion on all sides diminished as people got their horses unloaded and led them away to the stock pens. Collier, Simon, and Genesee stacked the loaded packsaddles, Collier sent Genesee to find poles to make a shelter, and he and Simon led the horses toward the pens. A group of men had collected at the rear of the pens, listening and muttering to each other as Raines and another man argued heatedly. It was about the wagons. Raines broke off as he saw Collier approaching, and he beckoned.

"Santee, here a minute, if you would. We'd like to have a word with you on the matter of wagons."

"Aye, we would and all," a man in the group said resentfully. "I didn't spend all my bloody money for horses to have them as pets."

"Nor did I," another man growled. "I could have bought wagons for less than horses, and bloody wagons carry more and don't eat fodder."

Other men grumbled as Collier walked toward the group, leading his horses behind him. The man Raines had been arguing with was a tall, arrogant-looking man of forty or so, in a frock coat, waistcoat, and knee breeches that were neat and clean, a contrast with the group in sweaty, dirty homespuns and buckskins. His stance was posed, his hand cocked on his waist, and he had an expression of bored, lofty amusement. He lifted his hand slowly and touched the peak of his tricorn, looking at Collier.

"Selwyn," he drawled. "At your service."

The man's bearing was aggravating, and his neatly groomed appearance indicated he had either slaves or bound servants with him to see to his belongings. Collier looked at him in silence for a long moment. Selwyn blinked, his aplomb beginning to fade. Collier nodded cooly. "It appears that you either didn't receive or didn't heed my advice regarding wagons. The road we'll be traveling isn't a wagon road."

"I beg to differ. I have it on good authority that it is a wagon road, and—"

"You have the word of a company clerk in Richmond, if you call that good authority. I have the word of the man who made the road—Boone. It isn't a wagon road."

"But not a week gone Colonel Henderson set out on the road, and he had wagons with him."

"And no doubt we'll be finding those wagons or what's left of them well before we reach Kentucky. Henderson can do as he wishes, but there'll be no wagons in my party."

Selwyn looked concerned, then he shrugged and smiled sardonically. "I must say that's a strange tone for a man to take in reference to his employer, but that's neither here nor there. Regardless of what you say, I believe that Colonel Henderson and his—"

"Well, is it a bloody wagon road, or is it not?" Billingsley demanded angrily, pushing to the front of the group of men. "Have I wasted all my bloody money buying goddamned horses?"

"Aye, who knows what it is?" another man shouted. "Who in the bloody hell has seen it?"

Collier's temper flared as a babble of angry grumbling broke out among the men. "It's a goddamned trail!" he barked, glaring around him. "When I talked to Boone, he said he'd be on the Kentucky River within three weeks of starting out, and he was going to try to make it within two. Neither Boone and his party nor any other lot short of a goddamned army of thousands can make a wagon road from Long Island to the Kentucky River within two weeks. Have any of you seen Cumberland Gap? Then I'll tell you about Cumberland Gap. It would take fifty men a month or longer to cut a wagon road through there alone, and it's not the hardest place on the trail by a long way." The men subsided, looking at him in silence, and he looked back at Selwyn. "And as far as Henderson being my employer, I don't have an employer and I never have had."

Selwyn's arrogance had gone, and he was frowning with alarm. "Well, I anticipated difficulty along the way, and I have eight servants with me to carry my baggage over difficult places and even disassemble the wagons and carry them, if necessary. Surely that will—"

"They'd be carrying it all on their backs from Martin's Station or before," Collier said shortly, shaking his head. "I'll not have the whole party held up because you failed to do as you were advised. Those wagons aren't leaving with my party, and they won't leave behind it, either. I'll not have the whole party bothering with your wagons to keep from abandoning you in Indian country, so I'll take an ax and knock the spokes out of the wheels if you try to leave behind the party with them." He looked around at the men again. "Now does anyone have any more questions?"

The men murmured negatively, shaking their heads. Collier looked at Billingsley stonily. "Do you have anything else to say, Billingsley?"

Billingsley turned away, scowling defensively and shaking his head. Collier glanced around as he tugged on the halter rope and led his horses on toward the pens. "Pass it around that I want a meeting of all men in front of the trading post at daybreak tomorrow, and everyone's to bring his rifle so I can have a look at it."

"But what am I to do?" Selwyn asked in an agitated tone. "I've invested heavily in this, and I can hardly turn around and—"

"You'd do well to try to find some horses," Collier interrupted him brusquely. "Beyond that I've no more advice for you."

A hubbub of conversation broke out as Collier and Simon led the horses away, Raines expounding triumphantly about the wagons. The trader was at the gate in front of the pens, watching a clerk counting the animals going through the gate and making notes on owners' names, and he greeted Collier expansively, inviting him into the trading post for a drink of rum. Collier sent Simon to help Genesee make camp, and went inside with the trader. The trader was buoyantly enthusiastic about the opening of the trail into Kentucky, envisioning a flood of settlers coming along the Holston Trace. Collier talked with him about it, made arrangements with him to use his forge to reshoe horses, then left and walked back around the pens toward the camping area.

The long shadows of sunset were stretching across the trampled clearing between the trading post and the edge of the river. People were working on shelters along the riverbank, and a haze of smoke from the campfires was drifting out over the river. The barking of dogs blended with the clamor of chickens, pigs, and ducks in crates. Children ran about and played behind the shelters, and their shrieks and laughter sounded bright and cheerful. A short, heavyset man in a frock coat, knee breeches, and tricorn was walking along behind the shelters, and he stopped, looked at Collier, then hurried toward him.

He puffed breathlessly as he approached Collier, lifting his tricorn. "Mr. Collier? I'm George Monroe."

His manner was courteous, and he had a worried smile on his round, friendly face. Collier stopped, nodding amiably. "I'm pleased to meet you."

"And I'm pleased to meet you, Mr. Collier, but I'm a bit undone, I fear. I had assurance that I could travel by wagon to our land, and now I find I can't. And I'm at a loss as to how to proceed. I've all my worldly goods in that wagon there, and I came in company with Selwyn on the understanding that his servants would help with my wagon if the way became difficult. But now . . ." He sighed heavily, shrugging.

"Do you have any money left?"

"Well, a bit. My family and my wife's father helped us, and I still have a few guineas."

"Some of these settlers back along the road here would probably be willing to buy your wagon, because wagons are scarce and expensive here, and the trader here has some extra horses. You could sell your wagon and buy some horses."

Monroe stroked his chin, his lips pursed in thought, and slowly nodded. "I'll speak with my Meg about it, and perhaps I could make some such arrangements in time. I wouldn't presume to ask you to delay leaving until I could see to it."

"You will have ample time. I understand I'm still short one family, and it'll be a day or two before everyone has seen to shoeing their horses and all. Talk to your wife, and I'll go with you when you talk to the trader and see that he doesn't try to rob you."

"That's very kind of you, Mr. Collier, very kind indeed. I'll go speak to my wife, then, and I'll have another word with you about it later."

Collier nodded, and Monroe lifted his hat again, walking hurriedly toward the wagons. Simon and Genesee had a open-fronted shelter almost completed, and they were putting boughs on top of it and weighting them down with sticks. Raines stumped around the shelter, waving a gallon jug as he whooped and beckoned Collier, and Collier laughed and waved as he walked toward the shelter. Smoke was rising from in front of the shelter, and Alcey and Nina were moving around the fire. Martha Raines was sitting by the fire. She looked older, and as though her health might be failing.

And Rachel was sitting by the fire, talking animatedly with Alcey, Nina, and Martha. Simon was fumbling with the boughs and sticks as he put them on the shelter, looking across the edge of it at Rachel. She turned her head occasionally as she talked, glancing toward Simon.

# Chapter Twenty-four

The line of footprints left barely discernible spots where the thick bed of leaves had been disturbed. The leaves from the previous autumn were pressed down and stirred occasionally to show the grayish edges that had fallen in prior years. Collier followed the trail as it went up a steep slope. The wind had eddied around the foot of a large rock, scouring the leaves away and baring the ground, and Collier knelt by the spot of bare ground and looked at the light footprint in the center of it. The straight line of a patch on the bottom of the moccasin that had made the footprint exended across the soft impression in the dirt. There had been old Indian signs all along both sides of the trail from Wolf Hills, and the previous day he had found fresh footprints made by an Indian paralleling the column of people, horses, and cattle along the trail. The footprints he had found on bare dirt had shown a patch on the bottom of one of the Indian's moccasins.

The distant clamor of noise from the column jarred with the quiet of the forest. The sun was setting, and the noises from the column were those of settling for the night. The same thing had happened the day before. During the day the Indian had paralleled the column at a distance farther from the trail than Collier went in his sweeps along both sides. In late afternoon the Indian had closed on the trail, found a clearing and made an accurate guess that the column would stop there for the night, then had left at right angles to the trail.

It was worrisome. A single scout would indicate a very small party of Indians, but the rest of the party could have gone for reinforcements, leaving a single scout to shadow the column. It was more worrisome because of developments in Kentucky. Since leaving Wolf Hills the group had been meeting men straggling back along the trail, and the stories they told had dampened the mood of the group. Boone's party had been attacked by Indians, two men had been killed, and another seriously wounded. Harrod had come down the Ohio with a large party several weeks before, and a number of them had been killed during an Indian attack. Several of the men coming back along the trail had been in Henderson's party and had left it to return to Virginia.

It was late, and it would be both futile and dangerous to follow the footprints farther. Collier sat under a tree and listened to the quiet sounds of the forest around him and the distant noises from the trail as the people made camp for the night. Axes rang against wood, cattle lowed and horses whinnied, and a strong odor of woodsmoke carried through the trees. The air became cold with the penetrating chill of spring in the deep mountains as darkness fell and the warmth of the day dissipated. The moon rose, and hazy, misty fog hung a few feet above the ground. Collier rose and silently made his way back down the slope toward the trail.

He crossed the trail, went up the slope on the opposite side, and made a wide circuit around the campsite, well beyond the perimeter of the sentries around it. The sounds of the forest were normal, and the noise from the campsite rapidly died away as the people ate and settled for the night, weary from struggling along the arduous trail through the mountains. Collier came back down the slope to the trail again, then moved quietly along it. He heard a slight rustle ahead of him, and he pursed his lips and whistled, mimicking a night bird.

"Santee?" Raines said quietly.

Collier walked on and stopped by the tree Raines was leaning against. "I found fresh signs again, not an hour old. The same as yesterday."

Raines sighed heavily, shifting his weight on his wooden leg. "What do you think it means?"

"I wish I knew. Is everything all right?"

"Aye. The guards are all out, and what they've been hearing from those coming back from the Gap will keep them awake. Today was easy compared to that stretch across the Clinch."

"We're through the worst of the mountains now. We'll

pass Martin's Station tomorrow, and we should make the Gap in another two or three days."

"Are we going to stop at Martin's Station?"

"No need to, because we'll be there early in the day, with hours left for traveling. Well, I'll go get a bite."

"Aye, all right. I have my blanket with me, and I'm going to stop here for the night."

"I'll see you in the morning, then."

"Aye, all right, Santee."

Collier walked on along the trail to the clearing. It was a hundred feet in diameter, with the horses picketed along a rope on one end and the cattle in a rope and pole corral on the other, watched over by a half dozen boys holding their blankets around them. The people were scattered out around the clearing, their belongings stacked close by. Many were rolled in their blankets by the glowing embers of their fires, and a few were talking quietly. Monroe and his wife were sitting by their fire, their two children in blankets beside them, and they looked up and nodded, their round, smiling faces shining in the flickering light of their fire. They were cheerful, congenial people, knowing little about the forest, animals, firearms, and other essential things, but they were eager to learn. Collier was glad he had helped Monroe arrange his affairs so he could come along. And he was glad he had left Selwyn behind.

The hounds were scattered around the fire, and the three boys and the old man were in their blankets. Alcey, Nina, Simon, and Genesee were sitting by the fire. And Rachel was there too, as she frequently was. Collier nodded to them as he put his rifle down and took the top off the kettle by the fire.

"It is necessary that we speak with you, Santee," Alcey said in a low, firm, acid tone.

Collier looked up, taking a piece of bread and meat from the kettle and suddenly observing the tension in the atmosphere around the fire. Genesee's eyes were dancing with humor. Nina's features were carefully neutral as she looked at the fire and probed it with a stick. Simon and Rachel were looking down, both of them flushed and extremely ill at ease. Alcey was enraged. Collier nodded, taking a bite of the bread and meat. "All right, then."

Alcey rose, motioning toward a tree. "Over here."

Collier nodded, standing. Simon cleared his throat with an embarrassed sound, looking toward Collier and dropping his eyes as he stood up. Rachel rose, her eyes on the ground. Collier followed Alcey toward the tree, Simon and Rachel behind him. Alcey stood in the dark shadow folding her arms, the firelight dimly illuminating her face. Her lips were a thin, prim line. Collier took another bite and looked at her questioningly. She glanced at Simon and Rachel.

"I found Simon and Rachel in the trees in a most improper situation," Alcey said in a low, acrimonious tone. "*Most* improper."

Collier stopped chewing. He looked from Alcey to Simon and Rachel, struggling with his almost uncontrollable urge to burst into laughter, then he swallowed and sighed heavily, trying to make his voice stern. "Well, bloody hell. What have you to say for yourselves?"

Simon shrugged and moved his hands in a helpless gesture. Rachel cleared her throat as though she were going to say something, then she abruptly buried her face in her hands and began weeping quietly. Simon looked at her in consternation. He lifted his hand as though he were going to pat Rachel's shoulder, then he dropped it as Alcey leaned toward him, glaring at him. "It was my fault," he blurted.

Collier nodded, taking another bite and glancing at Alcey from the corner of his eye. From her expression she expected him to do something. And he wasn't sure what to do. "Well, now," he said firmly, "it doesn't do away with it to own fault, does it?"

Simon looked at Rachel in an agony of dismay as she continued weeping, then he faced Collier. "We're going to get married."

Alcey stiffened and made a sound of surprise. Rachel stopped weeping as a strained grin spread across Simon's face as he looked at her and nodded. She cleared her throat and wiped her eyes with the back of her hand. Collier swallowed, sucked his teeth reflectively as he thought about it, then casually took another bite.

"Aye, very well, then."

"Now just a moment," Alcey said quickly in a cautious

tone, frowning thoughtfully. She bit her lip, glancing at the boy and girl. "We can't be precipitous on such a . . . Have you and Simon discussed this, Rachel?"

Rachel made a noncommittal sound in her throat, still looking down at the ground and wiping her eyes with her hands.

"But we want to, don't we?" Simon said hopefully.

A faint shamefaced smile playing around her lips, she shrugged and nodded.

Alcey sighed musingly, then motioned toward the fire. "Well, we can discuss this, and . . . you go back to the fire. Your father and I will talk about this."

Collier put the rest of his food in his mouth as they turned and walked away, and he looked down at Alcey as he chewed. "It's the proper way out of this, isn't it?"

Alcey was silent for a moment, her eyes following Simon and Rachel as they walked back toward the fire. "Yes, but there's something about this that . . . In any event how are they to be properly married out here in the wilderness?"

"Joe Martin is a justice of the peace, and we'll be at his station tomorrow. We can have it done and be on our way in less than half an hour."

"Half an hour?" Alcey said indignantly. "If it's to be done, it'll be done properly, and you may be assured of that! Half an hour indeed!"

Collier swallowed and sucked his teeth, thinking, then nodded. "Perhaps we could lay over, then, and feed the stock up, rest, and get an early start toward the Gap."

Alcey was silent for a moment, then she sighed heavily. "I'm still not satisfied that they . . ."

Her voice faded. Collier waited for her to finish the comment, but she looked away into the darkness. "Satisfied about what? This has been the cure for what we have here for as long as the sun has been rising and setting."

Alcey looked up at him, her brows drawn in thought. She started to ask something, hesitated and changed her mind. Then she shrugged. "Perhaps so, love."

"No perhaps about it," he chuckled, moving closer to her and patting her hip. "Otherwise you'd have to keep them tied or in sight all the time."

"Stop that!" she snapped, slapping at his hand and mov-

ing away from him as she tried to keep a smile from forming. "Simon has too bloody much of his father in him, and
there's the problem."

"If he had more, he'd wait and try to find one as pretty
as mine instead of settling for Rachel, even though she's
pretty enough. Talk to them, then, and see if they can leave
each other alone for the night. I'll get on out into the trees,
and I'll see you in the morning."

"There'll be no misunderstanding about tonight, no
fear," Alcey said grimly, following him toward the fire. "I'll
see to that."

Simon and Rachel glanced up as Collier and Alcey returned to the fire. Collier picked up his rifle and blanket,
checked the priming in his rifle and pistol, and snapped his
fingers at one of the muzzled hounds. The other dogs
stirred and started to get up, and Collier waved them back
as he walked away from the fire. He picked his way
through the people and piles of belongings to the side of the
clearing, the hound following him, and walked quietly into
the trees. A sentry turned, hearing the hound trotting
through the leaves. Collier walked past the sentry and on
up the slope above the clearing for a hundred yards, then
he sat down under a tree, put his weapons beside him, and
snapped his fingers. The hound moved closer, and Collier
took the muzzle off the dog, pulled his blanket around himself, and lay down. The hound lay down beside him, listening, then curled up and went to sleep.

At first light Collier made a circuit of the slopes above
the clearing, then put the muzzle on the hound and went
back into the clearing. People were moving about, women
cooking, and men readying their belongings to load their
horses. Word about Simon and Rachel getting married had
spread through the group, and the mood was lighter among
the people than it had been since leaving Wolf Hills, joking
and laughter replacing the grim silence of fear of Indians
and endurance of the privations of the trek. They shouted
jocular comments and bawdy suggestions and advice, making Simon grin bashfully and Rachel flush in embarrassment.

The clearing became a mass of confusion as the men got
their horses and began loading them, then the disorder began resolving itself as Raines rode out at the head of his

train of horses, Genesee following him and leading a train, and Alcey and the others falling in behind. The flank guards moved out into the forest on each side of the trail and began floundering along through the trees and brush, and the cattle lowed as the youths stirred them into motion. The slow pace set for the column by the lumbering oxen and the pandemonium of the column in motion along the trail went against Collier's most fundamental instincts for moving rapidly and silently through the forest, but the volume of noise was in itself a safety factor, a warning of a force of rifles too large and dangerous for anything less than a large, well-armed war party to attack.

The rugged, stony Clinch highlands were behind, with their tortuous grades and precipices with creeks and rivers rumbling in the depths below. The trail was a path through the densely forested valleys, a path that had been laid down through the centuries by buffalo in their wandering between grasslands. It curved gently, following the line of least effort along the contours of the land, and Collier walked along it a hundred yards ahead of the column until it was all in motion and moving along at its normal pace. Then Collier began trotting rapidly along the trail, pulling away from the column.

The noise of the column diminished, then faded behind, and he continued trotting along the trail at a pace that swiftly covered miles. The sun rose above the peaks of the tall mountains towering over the valley, and the air began warming. The trail crossed a creek, Collier stopped and drank, then he splashed through the creek and trotted on along the trail. Another creek crossed the trail farther along, and joined the other one a few yards off to the left as it gurgled and splashed over large stones. A third creek crossed the trail, and the noise of the rushing water became a loud, steady murmur. The trail opened out into a clearing ahead, and Collier slowed to a walk.

Part of the clearing was a wide gravel bar by a bend in the creek, and the forest had been cut back from the gravel bar to provide a clear field for rifle fire and space to grow vegetables around the buildings in the center of the clearing. There was a trading post, with its stock pens, warehouse, barn, and other outbuildings, a large building that had been recently constructed, and four cabins. What had been three other cabins were heaps of charred timbers and the ruins of chimneys, and all the buildings except the new one showed signs of repairs from the damage done when they had been abandoned during Indian raids the year before. Three men were sitting on a split-log bench by the door of the trading post, and one of them rose as Collier stepped into the clearing. He whooped with delighted laughter, walking rapidly toward Collier with long strides and extending his hand.

"By God! Santee, it's been a hell of a time, hasn't it? How are you?"

"I'll do, Joe," Collier replied as they shook hands. "It appears you're doing well enough here."

"Oh, I'm about to get things put right again. Henderson said he thought you might be coming through with a party."

"I've forty-two families coming along a couple of hours behind me."

"Forty-two?" Martin exclaimed. "By God, Henderson said he thought you might have as many as twenty, but . . . Come on over, Santee. Come on over, and let's sit down and talk."

Collier nodded as they walked toward the trading post. "Can you accommodate our stock for the night?"

"With no trouble at all. The Indians left me a full crib of fodder to come back to, and I got more off Henderson when he came through. He had bloody wagons with him, with everything you can imagine in them."

"Aye, I saw where his men had taken them apart and carried them and the loads over Clinch, and I saw where the trail had been widened along."

"Well, you won't see any more of it," Martin chuckled. "The wagons and most of what were in them are in that building right there. Boone told him not to bring wagons."

"He should have listened. There were two families with wagons waiting on me when I got to Wolf Hills, and one of them is still there, as far as I know. The other man found himself some horses. Joe, you're a justice of the peace, aren't you?"

"Aye, I am and all."

"Then I've a chore for you. My boy Simon needs wedding to a young widow in my party."

"Simon's going to be wed?" Martin crowed, slapping Collier's shoulder and laughing hilariously. "By God, I'll do it right and proper, then."

"Aye, my wife wants it proper. The party will be here shortly, and I had in mind having the wedding about sundown, after everyone's had a chance to clean up and rest. And we have a fiddler in the party, so we can have a bit of merriment after the wedding."

"A fiddler?" Martin said in delight. "By God, I'll put my suit on, then, and we'll make this a really proper wedding. And I have this empty cabin out here where Simon and his bride can spend the night."

"I'm sure they'll be grateful for the bed, but I doubt if anything will happen that hasn't," Collier said dryly.

"I'm not shocked, considering who Simon's pa is," Martin chuckled. They stopped in front of the trading post, and he motioned toward the two men on the bench. "This is Freeman and Barber. They were with Henderson, and now they're on their way back to Virginia. This is Santee Collier, the man I was telling you about."

"If you're taking people to Kentucky, you're taking them to their death," one of the men grumbled darkly. "There's naught but flaming Indians up there."

Both of the men were ragged and ill-kempt, with sullen, disgruntled attitudes, and they both looked like men who had spent all their life in a town or settlement. Collier ignored the comment, looking at Martin. "Have you seen any Indians about?"

"No, that treaty Henderson made with the Cherokee seems to be holding, but whether or not we'll see any Shawnee later in the year is another thing. The only Indians I've even seen are those who hunt and trap with Rafe Siler. He's been here for a few days, camped over there in the trees.

"Siler? I thought he hunted and trapped along the Mississippi."

"He does, but he's down on his luck and he ended up over here some way or other."

"Some Indians are over there in the trees?" one of the men on the bench growled belligerently. "By God, if I still had my rifle, I'd shift their arses soon enough!"

"You'd get shifted," Martin chuckled. "You want to

leave dealing with Indians to those who know something about them."

"And you want to watch your goddamned mouth as well," a quiet, steely voice said from the corner of the building. "Your scalp will stay a lot tighter on your head."

Collier turned. A tall, lean, leathery man was leaning on his rifle by the corner, looking bleakly at the two men on the bench. His buckskins had once been a light color and richly decorated with beads and porcupine quills, but they were worn, sweaty, and greasy, with patches and sewn places where they had been torn. His face was craggy, his nose twisted to one side from being broken, and the scars on his face were almost hidden by his dark tan. He was of indeterminate age, but the grizzled stubble on his face and the lank, greasy hair hanging from under his fur cap was streaked with gray. And he was a woodsman. The open space between the side of the building and the trees was covered with deep, dried grass between the stumps, which was normally noisy to walk through, but Collier hadn't heard him approaching. His cold blue eyes moved to Collier.

"You'll be Santee Collier, I expect. I've heard of you. I'm Rafe Siler."

"Aye, I've heard of you," Collier said, stepping toward him. "I heard you hunted and trapped the foot of the Cumberland and along the Mississippi."

Siler's thin lips relaxed in a wintry smile as they shook hands. "I had some bad luck and ended up over this way."

"Well, that's the kind of thing that can happen to any of us."

"I expect so."

The two men on the bench rose, looking at Martin. "We'll be on our way, then. What's the charge?"

"Ninepence apiece, but you appear more in need of it than me. Leave it for now, and if you're ever back this way you can pay me then."

One of the men grunted sarcastically and started to make a comment, then he glanced at Siler cautiously and changed his mind. They picked up bundles from beside the bench and walked toward the trail. Martin chuckled wryly and shook his head as they walked away, then he turned to Collier. "Santee, I'll leave you to talk to Rafe while I go see to the pens and things. Is tuppence a head for feeding the stock too much? I'll throw in a bottle of rum for the fiddling, and I'll do the marrying for free."

"That sounds more than fair, Joe."

"I'll go rouse some of my louts and see to it, then."

Collier nodded and looked back at Siler as Martin walked away. "How is the trapping along the Mississippi?"

Siler was looking at Collier musingly, and he shrugged. "Better than most. We could go over to my fire and have a rest, if you want to."

His tone was cautious, making the offer of hospitality less than a friendly overture in event it was rejected. Collier felt an instinctive liking and affinity for the tall, quiet man, and his ragged state stirred sympathy. Collier nodded, cradling his rifle across his arm, and they walked toward the trees. Siler walked with a long, loose stride and the habitually soft steps that had been too quiet for Collier to hear as he had approached the building, and his rifle contrasted with his appearance, an expensive weapon that had been cared for lovingly, the barrel and lock well greased, with silver inlay on the stock, a silver lid on the patch box, and silver thimbles for the ramrod.

"We met some Cherokee. My wife and her people are Creek, and I expect you know that a Cherokee would rather take a Creek scalp than a white one. We lost might near five hundred pelts, all my traps, eight horses, and our supplies."

"I've been lucky and I've never lost my catch or horses, but it's been luck because it can happen to anyone. But you have your scalp, and as long as you have that, you can get the rest of it again."

Siler grunted and nodded as they walked into the trees. "I wouldn't have that if it had been a war party. It was a hunting party, and there must have been fifty of the buggers."

They walked into a small clearing where the underbrush had been cut down in a circle a few feet wide. Four adult Indians and three children were around the fire in front of a small, open-fronted shelter. An old man was lying on a blanket, his shoulder wrapped in a poultice held in place by bark and vine bandages. Two were women, one with a child that was half white, and the other with two children that were full Indian. The younger brave was in his early twenties and had scars of battle on his face and lean, sinewy chest and shoulders, some of them fresh. They were all ragged, thin, and hungry-looking, and they had a few belongings, a couple of bundles wrapped in blankets in the shelter, a battered musket on the blanket by the old man, and a bow and arrows by the younger brave. The children moved closer to the women, looking at Collier apprehensively, and the adults looked at Collier with wary, guarded willingness to be friendly.

"This here is Kelotha, my wife. That's Shepeshe, her brother, and that's Metotha, his wife. And this is Chethake, my wife's pa. Peletheke, my wife's other brother, is out trying to find a rabbit or something. He's not much more than a lad."

Collier nodded to the women and stepped around the fire, leaning over the old man and extending his hand. The old man's seamed, wrinkled face creased in a cautious smile as he weakly lifted his good arm to shake hands. "Are you hurt bad, Chethake?"

"He's not too bad," Siler said as the old man looked at him. "The ball didn't hit a bone and I got it out without too much trouble, but it takes a while for old ones to heal."

Collier turned to the younger brave. He rose to shake hands with Collier, smiling tentatively. His moccasins and leggings were worn and patched, and Collier glanced at them as they shook hands. "You understand long knife talk, Shepeshe?"

"Understand little," Shepeshe replied in a heavy accent, his smile widening. "You talk slow, I understand little."

Collier lifted his foot and tapped the bottom of his moccasin, then pointed at Shepeshe's feet. "You let me see. You let me see moccasin."

Shepeshe looked politely puzzled, then his eyes widened in understanding and he burst into laughter as he said something in Creek. He lifted his right foot and pointed to the patch on the bottom of his moccasin, a patch in the pattern that Collier had seen in the tracks of the Indian shadowing the party. "You got good eye," he laughed. "You got Indian eye."

"He caught you, did he, Shepeshe?" Siler laughed. "By God, you do have good eyes, Santee, because Shepeshe doesn't leave much of a trail. I had him track you for the past couple of days, because I wanted to know when you'd be here. Come on and sit down."

Collier stepped back around the fire and put his rifle to one side as he sat down. "Why did you want to know when I was going to be here?"

Siler sat down, leaning his elbows on his knees and sliently looking at the dead ashes of the fire for a long moment, then he glanced at Collier as he picked up a stick and stirred the ashes. "Somebody said that you used to be married to a woman who was half Indian."

"Aye, my first wife was half Delaware."

Siler nodded, absently breaking bits off the stick and tossing them onto the ashes. "Going by that I thought you might be a man who wouldn't shy away from an Indian just because he's an Indian, and you wouldn't start eyeing his scalp unless he was looking yours over."

"You thought right. I've had trouble with Indians, but I've never caused it beyond being and doing where and what they thought I shouldn't be. And I don't hold all Indians at fault for the trouble I've had, no more than I hold all whites at fault for trouble I've had with whites."

Siler nodded again. "Well, you see the shape we're in. I have three or four charges of powder in my horn, and Chethake there has less than that. After we were attacked, we worked our way over in this direction, and I intended to work on down through the mountains to get back home to Georgia. But there are a lot of Cherokee between here and Georgia, there are a lot of settlers who'd take my wife's and boy's scalp to be doing it, and we don't have the horses and supplies to move fast and quiet. Martin told me that you might be coming along, so I stopped to talk to you. Now I figured that you'd have more farmers and town people than woodsmen in your party, and from what Shepeshe tells me, I figured right."

"You did. Henderson's party was eating their cattle all along the way, and we'd be doing the same but for my boys Simon and Genesee, and two or three others."

"Well, and I thought about the fact that you're going to be in Shawnee country before long. And from what I've heard, they're causing everyone plenty of trouble in Kentucky. So I figured that maybe you could use a couple of hunters and scouts. If it would be worth some supplies to you, we could go along with you, do some hunting and scouting, help with the fort, and do whatever else comes along. And maybe we could even settle with you for a while to grow ourselves some corn, collect a few hides, and work ourselves into better shape than we are now. I've been living on rabbit for so long that I think my ears are growing, and it's been so long since I've had a pinch of salt on my victuals that I've forgotten what it tastes like."

Collier scratched the stubble on his face, thinking. The Indians looked at him with silent, rapt interest. The shreds of wood on the hot ashes smoked, then a flame began licking up. Siler peeled dried bark off another piece of wood and dropped it onto the flame, then put the piece of wood on the fire and leaned his elbows on his knees again, looking at the fire and waiting for a reaction from Collier. "It's something to think about, Rafe," Collier said carefully.

"It takes some thought," Siler said, nodding. "While you're thinking, bear in mind that I know these people here. I've been hunting and trapping with Chethake for better than fifteen years, and he's as good a man as I've met, Indian or white. I've been hunting and trapping with Shepeshe here since he wasn't much more than a lad, and he's just like his pa. And Peletheke will be too. They're as honest as any who have ever walked, and they care less for rum than most Indians, and a sight less than I do. I've made my life with these people and I don't regret it, because they've been better to me than whites ever were. But I can understand that you have a responsibility for the people in your charge, and that you have to give ample thought to everything concerning them."

"It's more of a chore than I thought it would be, or I might not have taken it on," Collier chuckled ruefully. "Well, I'll think about it, but however I decide, I'll see you right on some supplies."

Siler shook his head firmly, picking up his rifle and gathering himself to rise. "We'll earn what we have. If it were winter and we were starving it would be another thing, but we're not in such straits. You think it over, and we'll talk about it some more. I'm going to see if we can get a few rabbits or something, and I want to get Peletheke back in here before your party gets here and someone mistakes him for a hostile."

"That would be wise," Collier replied, picking up his rifle and standing. "As soon as the party gets here, I'll spread the word around that your people are here. And I'll be talking to you again when I've considered what we've discussed."

Siler nodded amiably, cradling his rifle across his arm and walking away from the fire. Shepeshe gathered up his bow and arrows, smiling and nodding to Collier, and followed Siler. The three children gazed up at Collier fearfully as they huddled against their mothers, thin and drawn with hunger. The women's eyes reflected numb, patient endurance. The wrinkles on Chehake's face creased into the lines of a smile again as he nodded to Collier.

Collier walked back toward the trading post, pondering. He felt an instinctive trust for Siler and the Indians, and if he had been alone, he would have unhesitatingly joined up with them. But he wasn't alone. The advantages in having two additional and highly skilled scouts and hunters were obvious. But the danger of someone in the party shooting one of the Indians by mistake was also obvious. As he walked out of the trees, a distant whisper of sound from the party moving along the trail was audible, and he walked toward the trail.

# Chapter Twenty-five

When darkness fell, the clearing around the log buildings was alive with laughter, conversation, and sounds of merriment. The pale illumination of the full moon was dimmed by the ruddy light of the roaring bonfires and resin torches in the open space by the trading post, and the chill of the misty fog rising from the creek was dispelled by the warmth of the flames. Simon and Rachel sat on stools by the long deal table of food the women had prepared, enduring the raillery of people gathered around the table. The fiddler stood on a stump and sawed on his instrument as he called sets for a reel, and couples swirled in the rapid steps of the dance as others clapped their hands and whooped and whistled. Bottles of rum made their rounds, the dancing became more energetic, the banter directed at Simon and Rachel became more pointed, and the gathering became more noisy. Simon and Rachel were conducted to the cabin by laughing couples, the dancing began again, and youths shivareed Simon and Rachel in the cabin, pounding on the door and beating on kettles outside the bedroom window. Siler and the Indians sat in a silent, straight row in the dim light at the edge of the trees and watched, the old man with his blanket pulled around him and leaning against a tree for support.

The people strived to cling to the fleeting moments of their enjoyment and the respite from their fears and the privations of the trek. Sparks flew high into the air as more logs were thrown onto the bonfires, fresh torches blazed, and the fiddler's instrument wailed and shrieked in rhythm to his hoarse voice as he called sets again. Then the food and rum were gone, and the fiddler was drunk. The torches sputtered out, and the bonfires died into beds of embers.

The blanched, ghostly light of the moon claimed the clearing, making stark, dark, stationary shadows to replace the leaping shapes of the dancers in the firelight. Veils of misty fog from the creek invaded the clearing with their frigid touch. The gathering quietly broke up. Collier had made a decision, and he carried salt, rice, beans, peas, corn, gunpowder, and shot to where Siler and the Indians were camped.

Most of the people in the group were suspicious and distrustful of the Indians at first. Then the trail went through dark, dense stretches so thickly forested that dead trees leaned in the limbs of adjacent trees to rot, and a few more men came back along the trail with stories of terror. Everyone had fresh venison every day, everyone slept more soundly at night, and they willingly contributed from their supplies for Siler and the Creeks and rearranged loads to free a horse to carry the supplies and Chethake. Friendship rapidly developed between Genesee and the sixteen-year-old Peletheke, and between Simon and Shepeshe.

The trail entered Powell's Valley, a long valley with an insurmountable mountain wall rising on the right, and Siler and Shepeshe ranged ahead to check Cumberland Gap. Collier led the column on a long day of forced march along the last stretch of the valley and through the Gap, a deep saddle between sheer walls, and the people in the group whooped, shouted, and fired off their rifles as they entered the portal into Kentucky. They camped on a marshy bottom in Yellow Creek Valley, just north of the Gap, and the next day they moved on along the trail to Cumberland Ford.

The river was in its spring flood, a yellow, swollen torrent, and they rafted the women, children, and supplies across, swam the horses and cattle across, and camped for a day to dry and repack loads that had been soaked. The trail no longer followed those trampled by generations of buffalo as it went north. It was a path laboriously chopped out by Boone and his men and trampled down by Henderson's party and others, stretching across broken hills densely covered with trees and brush, and down through swamps covered by immense canebrakes. The horses were thin and weary, and they struggled under their heavy loads as they stumbled through sinkholes. The cattle were lean and hungry, and they tried to slip away into the canebrakes to graze. Chilly spring rains fell, many campsites were in swampy bottoms, and sickness became widespread among the people.

Collier sent Siler and Shepeshe ahead to search for the best route from Boone's trail to the headwaters of the Green River, and by the time the party reached the point to turn west off Boone's path Siler and Shepeshe had already cut the trail. It led for a short distance through brush and cane thickets, then the tangled growth opened out into rolling hills covered with alternating stretches of stands of towering trees and lush, fertile meadows.

The map Collier received from the Transylvania Company was less than accurate and had few details, and Siler and Shepeshe had picked out a good site for a fort. A wide sweep of gently inclined meadow stretched down from a hill crowned with a dense stand of trees, with several springs dotting the meadow and two creeks joining below the meadow. The group camped by the creek for the night, and four families were gone the next morning.

The lack of any indication of hostile Indians had eased the fears of many in the group, and the sight of the boundless stretches of thick forest and rich land made them eager to begin planting their crops and building their cabins. Collier called a meeting and offered to have Alcey immediately begin surveying tracts for those who would work on the fort. Five men refused to have anything to do with a fort; they took their families and belongings and left. Several others wavered, inclined to believe Collier's and Siler's warnings about Indians but afraid of losing choice selections of land to those who went ahead, and there was general disagreement over how much work and effort were required. Collier insisted on having a large fort with all the necessities to allow the entire group to live in it until there were enough settlers in the area to give a degree of assurance against Indian attacks, so several of those who were wavering, left.

Twenty-two families remained when Alcey began surveying land and work began on the fort. A few of the men and women cleared and plowed land along the creek to plant corn and vegetables for the group. Axes rang against the trees in the forest on top of the hill, towering trees toppled, and oxen dragged them down to the meadow. The men topped and trimmed the trees into sixteen-foot lengths, then joined them in sections to form walls. Small bands of buffalo roamed within a few miles of the activity for several days, then began moving farther away as Siler, Shepeshe, and Simon hunted them to provide food. Deer and turkeys darted through the forest on the first day trees were being cut, then disappeared.

Four more families, impatient with waiting for the fort to be completed before they started work on their farms, departed. Boone rode in from his settlement on the Kentucky River to inform Collier of a meeting of delegates from all the settlements at the end of May, and he sympathized with Collier over his difficulty in getting full cooperation on building a fort. Boone described his settlement as still only a rectangle of cabins without the palisade walls he wanted for protection, and he had been unable to get the people in his party to do as much as Collier had accomplished.

Two of the corner blockhouses were completed, blocky structures with overhanging second floors to give a clear field for rifle fire when the walls were in place, then the blockhouses were joined by a long wall. Game in the immediate area became very scarce, and some of the men who had moved away from the creek began stopping Siler, Shepeshe, and Simon on their way to hunt game, trying to barter with them for venison or buffalo. They refused, under orders from Collier to provide game only to the families at the creek and working on the fort.

Collier laid out the lines for the rest of the fort, and work on it continued slowly. The fort would cover just over an acre in area, with the corn and vegetable fields on the creek just within rifle range from the walls, and the walls well out of rifle range of the forest at the top of the meadow. The interior of the fort began taking shape when Collier, Simon, Raines, Siler, Cosgrave, and others began building cabins against the wall between the blockhouses. Collier called a meeting to elect delegates to send to the meeting at Boonesboro, sending word to all the people who had moved away from the creek about the meeting, and they elected him, Raines, Monroe, and Massey as delegates.

Boonesboro was a cluster of cabins on a meadow by the Kentucky, many of them unfinished and open-fronted, and there were no women at the settlement. The meeting was comprised of delegates from Boonesboro, Harrod's Fort, Logan's Station, Boiling Springs, and Collier's Fort, and lasted for two days. Monroe, whose brother had been a burgess in the Virginia legislature, led the delegation from Collier's Fort in the debates and deliberations of the first meeting of the Transylvania legislature. Laws were enacted that provided for the punishment of criminals, and banned profane language and breaking the Sabbath. Collier had with him the surveys that Alcey had completed, and Henderson confirmed Collier's two-thousand-acre tract and several others. He refused to approve several for settlers who hadn't yet paid the company for the land, and Collier pledged his land as security to get them approved. Henderson opened and closed the meeting with speeches, and there were ominous hints in his speeches that the Transylvania Company proposed to charge substantial quit rents on all the land sold to settlers.

When Collier and the others returned, the work on the fort had moved rapidly ahead. Several of the families who had moved away from the creek had been dipping heavily into the supplies of foodstuffs they had brought with them, and they had moved back to the creek to get game. Genesee and Peletheke had joined Siler, Shepeshe, and Simon in hunting, in order to provide enough game for the families returning to the creek. There had also been a couple of minor Indian scares, and the bland innocence of the hunters on the subject indicated that they had thought of a ruse to stimulate interest in getting the fort completed. Another blockhouse had been completed, a short wall was in place, and the timbers for the fourth blockhouse were ready to assemble.

A few others decided to live in the fort for a time, and the long and short walls were filled with cabins except for the spaces where the gates would go. The work on the fort and the plowing of new ground had resulted in damaged and

broken plowshares, chains, and axes, and a former black-
smith set up a shop by his cabin. A weaver and a harness-
maker followed his example, and the fort took on the appearance and atmosphere of a town, with a constant
murmur of activity, children running and playing, dogs
barking, clothes hanging on lines, and people visiting back
and forth in the evenings after dinner.

Arguments developed, and Collier found himself called
upon to mediate. A chicken or a pig would be claimed by
two families, someone would be accused of fouling the
spring, and others would consider themselves slighted in
the division of game meat. A more serious dispute arose
when the vegetables along the creek began to mature.
Those who had remained at the creek all the time demanded a larger share because of the labor they had invested, and those who had been gone for varying times and
returned claimed need. But the vegetables matured rapidly in
the rich, well-watered soil along the creeek, particularly
those that had been planted by the Indian women and
fertilized with pieces of fish from the creek. The fort was
nearing completion and didn't require as many men to
work on it, and Collier resolved the problem by releasing
more of the men to plow and plant more land along the
creek.

The second long wall was completed, and Collier had
pens for all the stock built outside the wall, with a gate so
the stock could be driven inside if the fort came under attack. The last blockhouse was completed, the second short
wall went up, and the gates were assembled and readied to
hang. On the morning the gates were hung a celebration
developed spontaneously. Raines hobbled off to his cabin
and returned with a bottle of rum, then another man went
for a bottle. Alcey and some of the other women had made
a canvas flag with a large letter C in the center of it, and
several men dragged in a long pole to mount the flag in the
corner of the fort. They raised the pole, the flag fluttered in
the breeze, and men whooped, fired their rifles, and drank
toasts to the christening of Fort Colliersville. The fiddler
brought out his instrument and began sawing out a tune,
and couples began dancing.

By afternoon a buffalo calf was roasting over a pit in the

center of the fort, all the people had joined in the merriment, and women had put on their best dresses and badgered the men into shaving and cleaning up. A corner of the long, wide expanse of trampled earth enclosed by the tall walls was filled with dancing couples. Others stood in clusters, laughing and talking, and children chased each other back and forth through the adults. The youths drove the cattle and horses in from grazing and put them in the pens, and as word of the celebration spread, people began arriving from the outlying farms to join the music and dancing and to stake a claim on the fort in time of need.

The fort was almost deserted the morning after the celebration, the people gone to their tracts of land to lay prominent boundary markers, girdle trees so they would die and season, and make other preparations for building on their land. Collier's two thousand acres included the upper edge of the meadow above the fort, the forested hill where timber had been cut for the fort and cabins, and stretched down across meadows and creeks on the other side of the hill. He had given no more than passing notice and thought to it, but he had glanced over it numerous times when going through the forest to pick out trees, and while working with the men cutting trees and dragging them out with oxen. He had considered building a cabin on top of the hill, overlooking the fort.

Collier and Alcey talked about it as they walked up through the meadow to the hill. The idea of building the cabin there appealed to Alcey, and there were several springs on the hill and various good locations for a cabin. Near the bluff overlooking the meadow was a flat outcropping of rock, and it appeared that it would take little effort to remove the soil from the rock so it could be used as a foundation. There was a large spring near the outcropping of rock, and for some reason the thought of using the living rock on the hill as the foundation for the cabin delighted Alcey. She looked at the spring and talked about where she would want the springhouse, paced off the dimensions of the cabin on the soil covering the rock, and pointed out trees she would want left around the cabin for shade.

As Collier and Alcey walked back down through the meadow toward the fort, a rider came along the creek to-

ward the fort at a slow canter. He was a man Collier hadn't
seen before, tall, heavyset, and with bright red hair, and he
rode with an erect posture, his shoulders back and his chest
thrust out. The horse splashed through the creek, circled
around the corn and vegetable fields, and cantered up the
meadow toward the fort. The man circled the fort on his
horse, looking at the blockhouses and at the walls with an
almost proprietary air, then he rode through the gate and
disappeared into the fort.

He was standing in front of their cabin and talking to
Nina as Collier and Alcey walked through the gate, with
the old man slumped and dozing on the bench by the cabin
door and the three boys standing in the doorway behind
Nina and gaping. Nina saw Collier and Alcey approaching
and said something to the man, pointing. The man glanced
at Collier and Alcey, smiled as he touched his tricorn, and
folded his hands behind his back, waiting for Collier and
Alcey.

The man's eyes were dark and deep-set, and he had
strong, bold features. He stood with his feet apart and his
shoulders back, stiffly erect and military in bearing, and he
had an aura of authority about him. As Collier and Alcey
approached, he smiled politely and bowed slightly as he
touched his hat. "Mr. Santee Collier? I am Captain George
Rogers Clark, at your service."

"I'm pleased to meet you. This is my wife Alcey."

"I am delighted to meet you, Mistress Collier."

"And I you, Captain Clark. Would you care to step in
for some refreshment?"

"I'd be delighted, and I thank you for the invitation." He
stepped to the corner of the cabin, tied his horse, and
walked back toward the door, looking around the fort. "I
must say that I've never seen a more substantial Fort, Mr.
Collier. You could teach military engineers how to con-
struct a fort."

"I like to see to the safety of my wife and family. And
the people with me, of course."

"You've done that, and more. We'd be well off if every
fort in Kentucky was a fraction as sturdy. Those blockhouses are most excellent in every respect, and I see you
have a water supply within the walls. With a good supply

of powder and shot, this fort could withstand any force."

"Any that didn't have cannon, and I've heard of no Indians armed with cannon."

Clark pursed his lips and nodded thoughtfully, looking around again, then took off his tricorn as he walked through the doorway. "I've heard a lot about you, Mr. Collier, much of which is hard to believe. But in meeting you and seeing what you've done here, more of it becomes easier to believe."

"The credit for what you see here properly belongs to others," Collier replied, motioning Clark toward the table. "There are a lot of good people in the party I brought here. And I've heard a great deal about you, Captain Clark. You've spent a good while in the Virginia Militia, haven't you? My wife has a kinsman in the Virginia Militia—Major Cosgrave."

"Anthony Cosgrave?" Clark said as he put his hat on the table and sat down across from Collier. "Aye, we're very good friends, and he's a fine officer."

"Have you seen Anthony of late, Captain Clark?" Alcey asked, carrying cups and a bottle of rum to the table. "He has many relations among us here. His son is here and his young sister is married to our son Simon, and they would appreciate word of him, as I would, of course."

Clark shook his head. "No, it's been a year or more since I saw him last, and I've just come from Virginia. But I didn't see or hear of him while I was there." His expression became solemn as he pursed his lips, looking at Collier. "I bring back news of the utmost import, Mr. Collier. I stopped by here to tell you so you may inform your people, then I'm on to the north to spread the word to the other settlements. Shots have been exchanged with the British. General Gage sent a force from Boston to Concord to take military supplies colonials had stored there, and there was an engagement at Lexington in which both sides suffered losses. There was another engagement at Concord, and our forces harried the British back to Boston, killing some two hundred."

The room was quiet. Alcey stood holding the cups and bottle, looking at Collier. Nina knelt by the fireplace, peering over her shoulder. The three boys by the door were silent. Clark's horse stamped outside and a fly buzzed in the room, the noises sounding loud in the stillness. Collier sighed, looking out the door at a woman carrying washing into her cabin across the fort, and shrugged. "Well, the fat's in the fire, isn't it? Not that it's any great surprise." He turned to Alcey. "I suppose we'll have to think about what we're going to do, Alcey."

"Going to do, Mr. Collier?" Clark said. "What do you mean?"

"I mean if there's a call to arms, I won't be skulking off on the other side of the mountains from the fighting. If we're to win the British, we'll need every rifle."

"Indeed we will, but where, Mr. Collier? Now it could be that this exchange of fire will bring the king and Parliament to their senses. Or it could be that we'll have war. And if it be war, remember the British forts on the Ohio. Remember that the tribes north of the Ohio have treaties with the British. If we leave Kentucky, then our frontier will be the Holston and the Shenandoah. With Indians armed by the British pressing us, then perhaps our frontier will be the Yadkin. And then perhaps we'll be pressed into the sea. But if we stop here, then our frontier is here. And I didn't come here to escape the fighting, Mr. Collier. I came to sound the call to arms. The call to arms for Kentuckians to ready themselves to defend Kentucky."

Collier looked at Alcey, pondering. Her features were expressionless, but he knew she wanted to stay. Since their arrival she had expressed a deep satisfaction with the place, and she wouldn't want to leave it. She stepped to the table and put the cups down. The cork squeaked as she pulled it out of the bottle, and the rum gurgled and splashed as she poured it into the cups. She slid one of the cups in front of him and one in front of Clark. She folded her arms as she turned back to Collier, her features still expressionless. Collier looked out the door at the fort again, musing, then nodded.

"Aye, I'm a Kentuckian. And I'll stop here."

Clark smiled widely, lifting his cup. "Here's your health, Mr. Collier. And Kentucky."

Alcey was smiling radiantly. Nina smiled, glancing up.

Jared murmured a question, pulling at Santee's arm, and Santee shrugged him off impatiently, looking at the adults. Collier nodded, lifting his cup.

"Your health, Captain Clark. And Kentucky."

# Part Five

# THE KENTUCKIANS

# Chapter Twenty-six

The metallic clangor of the alarm shattered the quiet stillness of the afternoon. Alcey turned away from the window-frame she was smoothing with a plane, snapped her fingers at Shelby and motioned him to her, and began rapidly gathering up the food basket, water bottle, and tools, her face tense and gray. Collier dropped his ax and ran through the doorway of the cabin framework to the edge of the stone foundation, Simon following him. Two horses were by the north gate of the fort, and Siler and one of the Creeks were standing by them and talking with Raines. Collier scanned the horizon. Trees blocked most of the view, but a grayish spot of smoke was visible against the foliage of the rollings hills to the north. Simon pointed to it.

"That'll be the Elder place."

Collier nodded, turning and trotting back into the cabin framework. "You bring your ma and the boy down to the fort. I'll get on down there and see what it is."

Simon nodded, hastily gathering up tools. Alcey looked at Collier with a strained smile as he patted her shoulder, and he ran toward the side of the cabin framework, carrying his rifle under his arm and pushing his pistol, knife, and tomahawk into his belt. He climbed through a window-frame and ran through the trees to the horses. They shied away from him, and he seized the halter rope on one of them, jerked the horse around as he bent to untie the hobbles on its forelegs, and leaped astride, drumming his heels against its sides.

The horse trotted cautiously and stiffly through the rocks, brush, and trees to the edge of the forest, then broke into a run down the meadow. A dozen or more riders were in sight along the creek, racing toward the fort. The cattle and horses belonging to those still living in the fort were at the far end of the meadow, a mile away, and Santee, Jared, and the other boys were herding them together and driving them toward the fort. The Ludlow and Turner cabins were down the creek from the fort, and the women from the cabins were leading their children and driving their stock toward the fort. The Indian with Siler and Raines was Shepeshe, and Peletheke and Genesee came into sight far down the creek as Collier neared the fort. They were leaning over their horses' necks and lashing them, overtaking and passing other riders.

"There's been an attack over at the McCready and Elder places!" Raines shouted as Collier reined up. "They're all dead!"

"How many Indians?"

"A dozen or fifteen," Siler replied. "Shawnee. But I've an idea they were advance scouts, because they weren't in any kind of a hurry. I sent Peletheke and Genesee to make a sweep to the north to see if there were any more, and from the looks of the way they're riding in, they must have found some."

"Hunters or war party?"

"War party. I told all the people along Laurel Creek about it as we came back this way, but I didn't tarry around to tell anyone else."

Collier nodded, looking around and controlling his prancing horse. Rachel, Siler's wife, and Shepeshe's wife were drumming hammers against a long bar of iron suspended on a rope just inside the gate, and the clamor of the alarm was deafening by the gate. Simon's horse came out of the edge of the trees above the meadow, Alcey and Shelby on the horse with Simon, their arms filled with tools, baskets, and other things that had been taken up on the hill for a day of working on the cabin. The hounds were milling around the gate, baying and snapping at each other, aroused by the flurry of excitement. Other men reined up, dodging the hounds and shouting questions, and Raines and Siler told them what had happened. Peletheke and Genesee approached at a dead run, their horses splashing and plunging through the creek, racing toward the fort.

"Big war party!" Genesee shouted as they reined in their gasping horses. "Fifty or more! They attacked that settle-

ment up by Buffalo Slough, and some of the people got
away and are coming this way!"

"They should have bloody heeded you, Santee," Raines
said. "The sods wouldn't listen to you."

Collier nodded, looking at Genesee. "How many are
coming this way?"

"We saw three men and two women who had little ones
with them, but there might be more. One of the men took a
shot at us, and we went well around them."

Collier nodded. "You were right, Rafe, and they'll probably be on down this way as soon as they're finished at
Buffalo Slough, so we'd better get everyone in and fort up.
Shepeshe, you and Peletheke get in the fort and stay in it.
Genesee, get your goddamned shirt and hat on so you
won't get shot at again, and when Simon gets here, you two
ride south to the Fields' place and warn everyone along the
way. From the Fields' place, circle around to the west as
far as Alder Creek, warn everyone along the way, and
come on back in. Siler, take Parsons, Hood, and Givens
there, and ride out and bring in those people from Buffalo
Slough. Take some horses with you so you can get them
back here in a hurry. Henry, you and Allen come with me,
and we'll warn the people north of Alder Creek. Isaac,
have all the stock put in the outside pens for now as people
drive it in, and tell Alcey to pen these hounds so they won't
get riled up and start attacking people. Genesee, take the
muzzle off that hound Seth there, and hold the rest of them
until I get away with him."

The group of men began breaking up, Siler mounting his
horse and three men following him as he rode around the
fort toward the horses being driven in, and two men following Collier as he nudged his horse with his heels and
snapped his fingers at one of the hounds as Genesee struggled with the dog, taking the heavy muzzle off its head.
Collier checked the priming in his rifle and pistol and motioned the hound ahead of him as he kicked his horse and
urged it into a swift trot.

The enervating clamor of the alarm faded behind him as
he rode through the creek and across a wide stretch of
meadow that extended into the forested slope on the other
side of the creek. People alerted by the alarm were coming

out of the trees on each side of the meadow, not knowing
the degree of urgency of the situation, assuming the worst,
hurrying frantically. Women herded their children and carried babies, prized kettles, quilts, and other household articles they particularly valued. Men led horses loaded with
irreplaceable tools, bags of food, and other things hurriedly
piled on them. Children carried clothes, cats, and fowl.
Collier sent Henry and Allen on a sweep along the sides of
the meadow to tell the men there was time to bring in all
their livestock, and the two men fell in behind him again as
they entered the forest and rode west.

The sound of the alarm became fainter, then inaudible as
the horses' hooves thudded in a swift canter. The hound
ran a hundred feet ahead and ranged from side to side,
sniffing along the ground, and Collier scanned the shadows
in the trees as he rode along. The trees ended at the top of
a long, gradual slope, and there was another wide meadow
with a patch of cane in a marshy bottom in the center of it,
two cabins on one side, and one on the other. Collier
looked back at the men, motioning one toward the two
cabins and the other toward the single cabin. The men
kicked their horses into a run. Children were playing in
front of the cabin, dogs barked at the riders, and men in the
fields began running toward their cabins. Women ran out as
the riders pounded up in front of them, shouting, then the
people began scurrying about. The hound tore through the
patch of cane, flushing three squealing hogs from it, and
ran out the other side, sniffing along the ground. Collier
circled around the cane, scanning the edge of the trees, and
motioned the hound ahead of him. The hound ran into the
trees, and Henry and Allen fell in behind Collier again and
pulled their horses back to a canter and they rode into the
trees.

At Alder Creek they turned north and worked back and
forth through the rolling hills, warning the people in their
cabins. A woman at a cabin near the north end of their
sweep was heavily pregnant, and Collier left Henry to assist
the family in getting to the fort and rode on with Allen.
There were two more cabins, then only the Elder and
McCready cabins were left.

A haze of woodsmoke hung in the trees, becoming
thicker as they approached the clearing where the Elder

cabin was located, and Collier reined his horse back to a walk, holding his rifle ready. He reined up in the shadows at the edge of the trees, and his horse hung its head and panted heavily. The house and barn had burned down, and billowing clouds of smoke were rising from the ashes and rubble. Three bodies were sprawled on the bare, trampled ground in front of the cabin. A span of oxen was yoked and hooked to a plow in a field by the cabin. One ox was collapsed on the ground, and the other was leaning sideward from the heavy weight on the yoke. Crows were hopping around the bodies. The hound ran back and forth, sniffing along the ground, sliding to a stop occasionally to scent carefully. The dog worked around all the remains of the outbuildings, then along the edge of the trees around the clearing. Collier touched his heels to his horse's sides and rode out of the shadow of the trees.

The crows flew up, crying angrily. The three had been scalped, and the woman's dress was pulled up and a thick, charred firebrand had been thrust into her vagina. Her thin, wrinkled face was frozen into a twisted, grotesque mask of agony. Allen dismounted from his horse and vomited. Collier rode out of the heavy smoke coming from the ashes of the cabin, looking at the ground which was marked with unshod hoofprints. Fruit tree saplings along the edge of the plowed ground by the cabin were trampled down, and Collier dismounted by one that was still standing. His horse was nervous from the odors of death hanging in the air, and it tossed its head and stamped skittishly, rolling its eyes. Collier pulled the horse closer to the sapling and tied it. Allen led his horse over by Collier's.

"See if you can find a mattock and shovel or something."

Allen's face was blanched, and his hands trembled violently as he tied his horse to the sapling. He turned his head aside and spat, and wiped his mouth with the back of his hand. "Do we have time to bury them?"

"We'll take time."

Allen walked along the edge of the plowed ground toward the remains of the small outbuildings behind the rubble of the cabin. The hound trotted past Collier, pausing and sniffing a spot noisily, then ran on. The ox still standing had an arrow in the side of its chest, it breathed with a loud, hoarse, wheezing sound, blood running from its nostrils. Its feet were splayed apart and its legs were quivering with effort as it struggled to stay on its feet and support the heavy weight of the downed ox pulling on the yoke. Collier took out his tomahawk as he walked across the plowed soil to the ox. It looked at him with dull, glazed eyes. He chopped it between the eyes, jerked the tomahawk out of its skull, and chopped it again as it went down. The hound trotted by, hesitated and sniffed at the oxen, and ran on. Allen walked back along the edge of the plowed ground with a mattock and two shovels.

"I'll dig the hole if you'll pull them over here."

Collier wiped his tomahawk on the ground and pushed it back under his belt as he walked toward the bodies. Allen began digging. Collier bent over the woman's body and jerked the firebrand out, threw it away, and balanced his rifle in his right hand as he took the collar of the woman's dress in his free hand and dragged the body toward Allen. He dropped the body by the edge of the plowed ground and walked back, and he hesitated and looked again at the boy as he started to take the collar of the man's shirt. The boy's eyes were closed, a sign of unconsciousness rather than death. Collier knelt by the boy, putting his hand on his chest and glancing over him. The back of the boy's head was dented slightly from a blow with the flat side of a tomahawk, and the naked bone where the boy had been scalped gleamed in the sunlight. His heart was beating, and he was breathing shallowly. Collier held his rifle in one hand, gathered the boy up in his arms, and carried him toward the horses.

"This lad is still alive. We'll take him back with us and see if we can do anything for him."

Allen glanced at the boy and averted his face, slamming the mattock into the ground and ripping up clods of dirt. Tears were running down his cheeks, and his breath came in ragged pants. "What kind of swining, fucking savages are they to do this to people who never harmed anyone or anything?"

"You take a hold of yourself, Allen. This is no time or place to let your feelings run amuck."

Allen nodded, wiping his face with his sleeve, and he dropped the mattock, snatched up a shovel, and threw loose dirt out of the hole. Collier dragged the man's body to the edge of the plowed ground and dropped it by the woman's. The hound trotted by, sniffed at the bodies, and ran on. Rocks that had been cleared from the plowed ground were piled a few yards away, and Collier carried several of them and dropped them in a pile by the hole. When the hole was four feet deep, Collier motioned Allen out of it, rolled the bodies into it, then put his rifle down by his feet and took the other shovel to help Allen fill the hole. They filled it, put the rocks on the mound, and picked up their weapons and walked toward the horses.

"You carry the lad."

Allen nodded, untying his horse with shaking fingers, and he mounted. Collier lifted the boy's limp body up to him, untied his horse and mounted, and whistled to the hound. The hound ran from the other side of the clearing, and trotted ahead of the horses as Collier motioned. Crows flew down and gathered around the oxen as Collier and Allen rode away.

The woodsmoke was dense in the trees as they rode toward the McCready cabin, limiting visibility to a few yards, and Collier held the pace back to a rapid walk, with the hound ranging a hundred feet ahead. He reined up at the edge of the clearing where the cabin was located and waited while the hound checked it. The house and barn were still burning, smoke boiling from them. Dead animals were lying in the stock pen behind the cabin, but there were no bodies in sight. The hound was more intent, finding fresher scent, but nothing else. Collier rode across the clearing, Allen following him. More of the open space around the cabin and outbuildings came into sight as he crossed the clearing, and still he didn't see any bodies. His horse shied from the flames and heat of the burning cabin, and he tightened the reins and kicked the horse with his heels, riding around the cabin. A team of oxen, a milk cow, and three horses were dead in the pens, but there were no bodies.

"Where do you think they are?"

Collier shrugged. "They could have tied them in the cabin or barn before they fired them, or they might have taken them prisoner." He nodded toward the hound sniffing closely around the east side of the clearing. "Seth is finding a heavy trail over there, so they probably took them prisoner and left off in that direction to rejoin the main party. If they hadn't had prisoners, they would've attacked another cabin or two south of here."

"The McCreadys would be better off dead than prisoners of that bloody lot."

"No doubt about that," Collier replied. He reined his horse around, whistling to the hound. "Let's get on back to the fort."

Allen pulled the boy closer, turning his horse. The hound ran back across the clearing, and Collier motioned him ahead as he rode toward the trees. Collier urged his horse to a canter as they rode back into the trees, turning to the south.

The trees flashed by, and dappled spots of sunshine penetrating the screen of foliage above flicked across Collier's face. The hound scampered through piles of leaves and scattered them, ranging from side to side with a long, effortless lope. The bright gleam of the sun shining down on a clearing broke through the trees ahead, and Collier slowed to a trot. He waved the hound ahead to check the clearing, pulling his horse back to a walk, then urged the horse to a canter to cross the clearing as the hound came back out of the trees on the other side. Collier's horse began panting heavily, he reined back to let the horse catch its breath, then urged it to a canter again.

The fort was a seething mass of activity, people streaming into it, women hurrying their children along, and men herding their stock into the pen on the long side of the fort nearest the creek. A haze of woodsmoke hung over the fort from fires inside it, and the heads of men standing on the firing scaffolds inside the walls were visible between the sharp points of the palisades. The hound was panting heavily and Collier's horse was gasping for breath, and Collier slowed his horse to a walk as he approached the creek. The hound leaped into the creek, lapping up water and swimming across. Collier's horse waded through the creek, scrambled up the bank on the other side, and trudged toward the fort.

Raines was standing at the gate, his rifle cradled across his arm, waving the people in and watching the edge of the trees on the hill above the meadow. He nodded and waved as Collier and Allen approached. "They're about all here, Santee. Who's that you have there?"

"The Elder lad. He's been scalped but he's still alive. Did all the riders get back?"

"Aye, they're all back. And Rafe and his men brought in five men and three women from that lot over at Buffalo Slough, as well as several little ones."

Collier nodded, riding into the fort. It was pandemonium, the hounds cooped in the large pen by the gate baying and snarling, families in clusters by their piled belongings along all the open stretches of walls, dogs barking and children running back and forth, babies crying, men standing around in groups and talking loudly, and other men shouting to each other on the firing scaffolding. A dog charged up and barked at the hound with Collier, and the hound lunged, snarling. Genesee ran from a cluster of people and seized the hound, pulling it off the dog, and he dodged its snapping teeth and dragged it toward the pen as the dog stumbled away, yelping shrilly. The group from Buffalo Slough were gathered by the wall inside the gate, and three of the men walked toward Collier as he dismounted.

"Did you see any of them out there, Mr. Collier?"

"No. How many people did you lose?"

"Forbes, his wife and his four little ones, Johnson and his wife, Ted Reynolds, his wife and two little ones, Abe Clinton, and his wife and three little ones. They attacked their cabins first, and we got out and around the Slough to come over this way."

"They'll be here soon enough," another man said. "We saw two of the buggers while we were on the way over here, and I took a shot at them. I believe I winged one of them."

"No, you didn't. And you're bloody lucky you didn't. You saw one of the Creeks who live here and my boy Genesee over there, and if you'd winged one of them, I'd hang your scalp on my belt."

The man flushed hotly, looking at Genesee and glancing up at Shepeshe, Peletheke, and Chethake on the scaffolding. "Well, I wouldn't go to shoot your boy, but it appears to me that we've goddamned Indians enough outside without having them inside as well."

"If you don't like the way we conduct our goddamned affairs here, then you can goddamned well be gone!" Collier snapped angrily. "And if you cause any trouble with any of those Creeks, you'll deal with me! And you'll wish you were dealing with the Shawnee again instead!"

"He didn't mean to offend," the first man said placatingly. "We've just come through a miserable bad time, seeing our friends killed and barely escaping with our own lives, and we—"

"And you brought it on yourselves. I told you that you needed a blockhouse, and I didn't ride over there to talk to you because I had time to spare or needed to exercise my horse. And you had a goddamned good laugh at me for my trouble. There's no man walking who won't have my hand when he's in need or victuals from my table when he's hungry, but I'm bloody loath to help those who won't shift for themselves. And it's certain that I won't listen to talk about those Creeks from someone who's not worth the tenth part of any of them. Is that woman over there ailing?"

The man turned and looked at the woman, nodding. "Aye, she's a few months in a delicate condition, and she fell a time or two when we—"

"Take her down to the third cabin there and have Susannah Cox look after her. If you need powder and shot, speak to Isaac Raines about it. He's the one with the wood leg."

"Aye, well, we're certainly grateful, Mr. Collier."

Collier nodded, turning away. Genesee was walking toward him from the dog pen, looking at his torn sleeve and a bite on the side of his hand. Collier took the Elder boy from Allen, Genesee took the horses and led them toward the stock pen inside the fort, and Allen walked toward his wife and children huddled against the wall on the other side of the fort.

People looked with horrified fascination at the boy's head as Collier carried him toward his cabin. The old man was on the bench outside the cabin door, watching the seething activity with a blank lack of understanding. The interior of the cabin was stifling, the fire roaring and Alcey, Nina, Rachel, and Mary Cosgrave melting lead, casting bullets, and cutting patches. The three boys were in a corner, greasing cloth to make patches. The women looked at the boy Collier was carrying with blanched faces, and the boys stared, round-eyed. Collier put his rifle down against the wall, shoved a stool over to the door with his foot, and sat down.

"Fetch me a leather awl, Alcey."

Alcey dropped a bullet mold as she got to her feet and went to a shelf in the corner. Collier arranged the boy's limp form in a sitting position on the floor in front of the stool, and clamped the boy's head between his knees. Alcey crossed the room and handed Collier the leather awl, and he put the sharp tip of the awl on the edge of the scalped spot on the boy's head and rotated the awl between his palms, driving the tip into the bone. A tiny drop of pinkish fluid appeared around the tip of the awl, and Collier lifted it, moved the tip an eighth of an inch along the edge of the scalped spot, and began drilling another hole. Mary Cosgrave fainted, and Nina and Rachel lifted her and took her outside. Alcey watched Collier, her face drawn and gray.

"Will he live?"

"I don't know, Alcey. This is a bad knock on his head here, and it would kill most people. But it didn't kill him right away, so perhaps he has a chance. This you see leaking out of his skull from these holes will dry and make a scab, and skin will grow under the scab. But flies will have to be kept off his head. One maggot in his head will kill him."

"We'll keep the flies off. I've seen what you're doing now, so do you want me to do it while you're seeing to other things?"

"No, it'll be a while before I'm needed."

She turned away, looking at the boys in the corner. They were still gaping at the Elder boy. Alcey snapped her fingers and pointed, and the three boys began greasing the cloth again, looking surreptitiously at the injured boy. Nina and Rachel came back in, and the three women sat on the floor in front of the fireplace again, casting bullets and cutting patches. Mary Cosgrave came back, averting her face as she passed Collier, and joined the other women.

Raines stumped up to the doorway and looked at the boy's head, then at Collier. "Some of the men say they've seen movements in the trees at the top of the hill."

"Get everyone away from the west side of the fort. Bring

the stock into the pen inside the fort, put some men around the pen with rifles, and have the water buckets filled."

Raines nodded and stumped away. Collier continued drilling the tiny holes in the boy's skull. The pinkish fluid formed into a shiny layer over the portion of the bone that had been drilled. The boy's limbs twitched occasionally. He urinated, and it puddled under his legs and around Collier's feet. The odor was strong in the sweltering heat of the cabin. Collier wiped sweat from his face with his sleeve and began drilling another hole.

Alcey crossed the cabin and took Collier's shot pouch and powder horn, carried them to the table and filled them, then returned and hung them around his neck, knelt by his rifle, and opened the patch box and pushed a handful of patches into it. Genesee and Simon came to the door and handed in their shot pouches and powder horns, and Alcey filled them and handed them back with handfuls of patches. Collier finished the last row of holes in the boy's skull, picked him up, and carried him into a bedroom. Alcey followed him in.

"If they use so many fire arrows that it gets away from us and you have to leave the cabin, try to keep from getting dirt on his head."

"Very well, love."

She knelt by the bed and fanned her hand at a fly that buzzed around. Collier started to turn away, then he leaned over her and patted her shoulder as he kissed her. She smiled up at him wanly, touching his face with the tips of her fingers, and looked back at the boy's head, fanning her hand at the fly. Collier went back into the front room, picked up his rifle, and went outside.

It was much quieter, and the atmosphere of tension in the fort was almost palpable. The old man was dozing on the bench by the door. The women and children huddled against the cabins and wall on the east side of the fort were silent except for babies and a few of the smaller children crying. Dogs were sitting in the shade and panting, and the hounds in the pen had calmed and stopped baying. Most of the men were crowded onto the scaffolding on the east side or looking through loopholes in the wall at ground level, murmuring to each other. Simon, Genesee, Siler, Cosgrave, and the three Creeks were together at the end of the scaffolding by a blockhouse, and Collier climbed a ladder to the scaffolding and walked along it to them. They shuffled, making room for him at the wall.

"They're up there," Siler murmured, nodding toward the hill.

Collier nodded, checking the priming in his rifle, and glanced around. Everyone was away from the west side of the fort, the stock was crowded into the interior pen, men were near the pen with rifles, and full water buckets were spaced along the scaffolding. Collier rested his rifle between two of the palisades and leaned against the wall, watching the edge of the forest above the meadow.

The afternoon sun was warm. The stock in the pen shuffled and moved, a cow occasionally lowing softly or a horse snorting when they were crowded too closely by another animal, and the scaffolding squeaked and swayed as men moved around, talking quietly and watching the hill. Minutes dragged by. An hour passed, and the light became softer as the sun began inclining to the west.

Collier saw furtive movements in the trees at the top of the hill, and they became more frequent and less furtive. A thin haze of smoke became visible in the trees, and it rapidly thickened into clouds. Simon and Genesee looked at Collier, and Collier shrugged. It was the framework of his cabin burning. And it was the third time he had built the framework and it had burned. A thin, distant whisper of sound from the top of the hill became audible, a voice rising and falling in shrill intonations, the haranguing of braves by their war leader.

"Plukemenoti," Chethake murmured.

"Chief Pluggy?" Siler said, looking at him, then looked at Collier. "We have us a right one up there, then. And without a doubt they've just had their powder horns and shot pouches filled in Detroit."

Collier silently nodded. The smoke billowed up, and flames became visible. The haranguing of the chief continued, then it was drowned in the chanting voices of dozens of braves. The sound grew louder, and movements among the trees became visible. More children among those huddled below the scaffolding began crying with fright as they heard the chanting, and men moved nervously on the scaffolding. Collier lifted his rifle and shook it, jumping up and down as he threw his head back and bellowed a war whoop. Siler, Simon, Genesee, and the Creeks began shrieking wildly, jumping up and down and shaking their rifles and tomahawks. The scaffolding bounced violently and a deafening roar rose as all the men began shouting and whooping at the top of their voices. The hounds in the pen exploded into a frenzy, baying and flinging themselves at the sides of the pen. Animals in the pen surged about, alarmed cows and horses adding their lowing and whinnying to the uproar.

A widely spaced line of Indians ran out of the trees and raced down toward the fort, arrows notched in their bows and smoke from burning resin streaming back from the tips of the arrows. A surging movement raced through the men on the scaffolding as they shouldered their rifles. Collier picked out an Indian and lifted the bead high above the tiny form zigzagging down the meadow. Rifles began cracking along the scaffolding, and the acrid odor of burned gunpowder floated past. The line stopped, and the Indians flexed their bows, lifting them for maximum elevation. The rifle fire became a drumming rattle, smoke boiled along the top of the wall, and Collier squeezed his trigger.

The arrows left thin trails of smoke in the air as they arced toward the fort. One of the Indians staggered and stumbled, and other Indians took his arms as the line ran back up the meadow to the trees. Collier began reloading. The arrows pattered and thudded into the meadow on the east side of the fort. Two slammed into the open space in the center of the fort. One went into the west wall of the fort, and flames sputtered around it and went out. One went into the roof of a cabin below the scaffolding, the resin splattered over the shingles around it, and flames leaped up. A man on the scaffolding threw a bucket of water onto the flames, extinguishing them. Another line of Indians ran out of the trees and raced down toward the fort, smoke whipping back from the tips of the arrows notched in their bows. Collier shouldered his rifle.

The lines of Indians began coming farther down the slope, and the rifle fire directed at them was more effective, wounding and knocking down one or two in each line. And their aim with their arrows was more accurate, burning arrows thudding into the roofs of the cabins and occasionally going into the stock pen and making some animal bellow

and thrash wildly about until a rifle stilled it. Another line
stopped, and Simon fell against Collier as he squeezed his
trigger, spoiling his aim. He glared at Simon irritably, then
looked around him. The old man was leaning on his crutch
and holding his rifle, shot pouch, and powder horn as he
shouldered Simon. His eyes were clear and focused, and he
had a purposeful expression on his face.

"Move your arse over and give a body some room, Santee."

"I'm Simon, Grandpa," Simon chuckled.

"Well, move, whoever in the bloody hell you are! Move
your arse over and give a body some flaming room!"

Simon laughed, looking at Collier and edging closer to
him. Collier nodded and laughed as he moved over and
began reloading his rifle. The old man loaded his rifle,
rested the barrel between two of the palisades, and propped
himself comfortably on his crutch, looking up at the hill. A
line of Indians ran out of the trees. The old man took careful aim and fired.

The lines of Indians with fire arrows began coming at
more rapid intervals, approaching closer, and arrows
rained down on the fort. A fire on the roof of a cabin began blazing out of control, and Raines assembled women
into a bucket brigade to extinguish it. Spots all over the
outside of the east wall and the inside of the west wall
smoldered around arrows stuck into them, smoking arrows littered the trampled ground in the center of the fort,
and the animals in the pen kicked and bucked frantically,
trampling numerous dead animals underfoot. Lines of Indians with rifles began alternating with the ones with the fire
arrows, and rifle balls slammed into the palisades. A line of
Indians with rifles ran far down the meadow, a withering
fire from the scaffolding and ground-level loopholes cut
down four of them, and two men stumbled and fell on the
scaffolding.

A dozen Indians ran down and gathered up wounded
and dead, rifle balls kicking up dust around them, then
they went back into the trees. There was silence for several
minutes, then loud chanting and whoops began ringing out
from the top of the hill. Chethake murmured something.
Siler nodded as he lowered his rifle, and he glanced at the
setting sun and looked at Collier.

"It looks like they have a bellyful for now. What do you think?"

"It looks that way."

Siler looked up at the sky. "We'll have a good, bright moon, but they'll probably be back after it sets. And again in the morning." He lifted an arm and pointed toward the top of the hill. "They'll come back when the rising sun is right there and in our eyes, like that last lot did. And maybe they'll have some ladders, like that last lot."

Collier nodded. "We'll man the blockhouses in the morning."

"Aye, that'll stop them. Or most of them, and we can have our knives and tomahawks sharp for the rest."

Collier nodded again, glancing at Simon and Genesee. "Let's go get a bite to eat. Help your grandpa down the ladder."

They pulled at the old man's arms, urging him toward the ladder, and Collier walked along the scaffolding and climbed down. The atmosphere of tension was gone, people were moving about, and a hum of conversation and laughter was developing. Children ran about in the center of the fort, collecting the arrows. Four men with wounds were being attended by women. Raines was stumping about and shouting orders, directing men who were dragging dead cows out of the pen and bringing out baskets of potatoes, corn, and vegetables from one of the blockhouses.

The cabin was noisy and congested, one of the women from Buffalo Slough and her children crowded into it with friends of Alcey's and Nina's from outlying cabins. Collier gave Alcey his shot pouch and powder horn to refill, and took a candle into the bedroom to look at the Elder boy. He was still alive, and the fluid seeping from the holes in his skull was forming into a crust as Nina sat by the bed and fanned the top of his head with a woven cane fan. Alcey handed Collier his shot pouch and powder horn when he went back into the front room, and she cut a piece from a buffalo roast on the spit and put it on a piece of bread for him. Genesee and Simon brought in the old man as Collier stood by the door and ate, and the old man sat at the table and ate his mush, talking about the battle in a loud voice. The situation had summoned his endless reserves of vitality again, peril bringing a keen awareness of his surroundings. But even as he talked, he was already confusing this battle with others, Simon with Collier, the time with past years, and the crowd in the cabin with gatherings of distant times. Simon, Genesee, and the women exchanged amused glances as they nodded and agreed with the old man.

The fort was filled with smoke from cooking fires as people roasted potatoes, corn, and thick cuts of the cattle that had been killed. Collier stood on the scaffolding as darkness fell, looking at the glow of fires on top of the hill and listening to the Indians chanting and whooping. The sounds the Indians were making had no apparent effect on the people in the fort, because the atmosphere was relaxed and cheerful. The battle had gone heavily in favor of the fort, some damage and four minor wounds compared to a dozen or fifteen wounded among the Indians, some probably serious and a few possibly mortal. It was the fourth major attack the fort had withstood. None of them had been the same, and all of them had created doubts and apprehension before battle was joined, particularly since McClelland's Station on the east fork of the Kentucky River had fallen.

There had also been minor skirmishes, roving hunting parties or war parties of a half dozen braves or so, more intent on stealing invaluable horses than on taking scalps, with one or two isolated cabins coming under attack and a relief party rushing out from the fort. Each attack had brought its toll of casualties. Only two had been killed defending the fort, because the fort was strong. But several had been killed in outlying cabins. And the casualties in a larger sense included those who gave up and formed bands to trek back along the trail to Virginia and North Carolina. While the population in the vicinity of the fort had increased from people moving closer as the fort gained something of a reputation for impregnability, the population as a whole in Kentucky had decreased during the past months. So the effect of a minor wound suffered by a man was the same as a mortal wound, as far as the population in Kentucky was concerned, when that minor wound became the deciding factor that made a man gather his family and belongings and leave.

The moon shone brightly down on the meadow, the fires in the fort died down, other men moved around on the scaffolding and talked in quiet voices, and Simon, Genessee, Siler, and the Creeks stood silently around Collier as he looked up at the hill and pondered. Plukemenoti was the chief who had led the battle against McClelland's Station when it had fallen. He was known to be both resourceful and savage in his attacks. There was no question in Collier's mind that the fort would withstand the coming attacks. But if the Indians got close enough under cover of darkness to put burning resin under the foot of the wall, or if they brought scaling ladders at daybreak, there would be casualties in the fort. And perhaps more people leaving to return to Virginia or North Carolina.

"I could take a few men out into the meadow when the moon sets," Siler murmured. "We could give them a little surprise when they start down this way. Or I could take Shepeshe and we could carry a couple of blunderbusses up there and remind them we're down here."

"There's a bloody good idea," Genesee said excitedly. "I could go too and take—"

"No," Collier said. "Our best course is to let them take the risks and pay the cost of taking risks. But it galls me as much as anyone to stand and await their pleasure."

He glanced around, musing, then looked back at the pen inside the north gate where the hounds were cooped. When outsiders were going to be in the fort, it was essential that the dogs be securely locked up, because the only predictable thing about them was that they were dangerous. But all the people who depended upon the fort for protection avoided the hounds and were tolerant about their viciousness, because they were valuable. When going to the assistance of outlying cabins under attack, Collier always took some of them along. They would fearlessly attack Indians, and in a couple of instances when the Indians had detected the relief party coming and had tried to set up an ambush, the hounds had broken up the ambush. They were all young, because older ones had been killed by Indians or in fighting among themselves, and about half of them had to be kept muzzled. None of them was particularly friendly, the Creeks had to be particularly cautious around them, and while Alcey was better at controlling them than anyone else, her control was only marginal when they were excited. And when they were fully aroused, no one could control them.

If the hounds could be made to attack the Indians in their camp, it would enhance the reputation of the fort. Such things were the stuff of legend, talked about around fireplaces in settlements and discussed at councils in the Indian villages. A fort with a prickly, dangerous reputation was more likely to be avoided by Indians and to attract settlers, both of which were worthwhile objectives in Collier's mind as he looked up the hill and listened to the Indians chanting. He turned away from the wall.

"We'll cast the hounds on them, and that'll stir them a bit. Genesee, go fetch your ma to the north gate. Simon, get some torches and rawhide thongs. Rafe, you come along and leave the Indians here."

"Cast the hounds?" Siler chortled. "By God! Now there's an idea!"

"It is and all," Simon laughed. "When those hounds get loose, then they'll—"

"Come along and let's get to it," Collier interrupted impatiently, walking along the scaffolding. "Perhaps it'll work, and perhaps it won't."

He climbed down the ladder and walked toward the north gate with Siler. A couple of other men followed, chuckling and talking with Siler, and people around the glowing embers of fires looked up sleepily as they passed. The hounds stirred in the pen as Collier approached it. They had settled down from their earlier excitement, and the more aggressive of the hounds began prowling along the sides of the pen, growling and nosing at the thick, heavy bars in the pen through the thick leather muzzles on them. The other men gathered at the side of the pen, and the other hounds rose, stretched, and nosed at the bars.

Simon brought blazing pitch torches, planted them in the ground, and began untangling a handful of rawhide thongs. More men gathered around, and several of the hounds began growling threateningly, their eyes shining and their bared teeth gleaming in the light of the torches. Alcey and Genesee crossed the fort, and Alcey's features were set in lines of grim resignation. She loved the hounds. Collier shrugged apologetically as he put his hand on her shoulder.

"It doesn't set well with me either, Alcey."

"Let's do it and be done with it. But Daisy and Jill can't go."

"No, I didn't plan on casting them. Call them out and we'll tie them up."

Alcey walked toward the pen. The hounds crowded to the front of the pen as Alcey knelt by the door, snapping her fingers and talking to them. She got one of the pregnant bitches by the door, then opened it a crack and began pulling the hound out. The other hounds pushed at the door, a couple of them bayed, and Collier took the hound's head and forelegs and pulled her out as Alcey closed the door. The hound struggled in Collier's arms, beginning to growl. A man stepped forward helpfully, then snatched his hand back with a startled oath as the hound snapped it. Simon tied the hound's legs together with a thong, the hound got his sleeve and tore a long rent in it, and he jerked his sleeve out of the hound's mouth and helped Collier carrying her to one side.

The other nine hounds began stirring more and baying at the people around the pen as Collier pulled out the other pregnant bitch, a long, lanky dog with a distended belly and eyes that gleamed with a ferocious, feral light behind her leather muzzle. Simon tied her, then Collier and Alcey began reaching between the bars and taking the muzzles off the other hounds. Another man reached between the bars and jerked his hand back with an exclamation of pain and surprise, blood streaming from his hand. Other men laughed at him and speculated about what the hounds would do to the Indians. Collier pulled at the thongs on the muzzles with quick, careful tugs, snatching his hands back as the hounds became more aroused and snapped at him more often.

Collier finished loosening a muzzle enough for a hound to shake it off, watched as Alcey untied the last muzzle, then stepped away from the pen, motioning the men back. "Everyone get back on the other side of the torches. These hounds will empty this fort if they decide to loiter about here when they're riled, so we don't want anything to attract their notice. We want them to go straight out the gate. Siler, you and Simon take down the bar and get ready to open one side of the gate. You help them, Genesee. Everyone get well back. All right, Alcey, stir them up."

The men moved back to the edge of the light of the torches, watching. Siler, Simon, and Genesee lifted the heavy bar down from the gate and pulled one side of the gate ajar, ready to open it. Alcey looked at Collier with a dejected expression, sighing heavily, then she turned to the pen and began clapping her hands together and shouting at the hounds.

"Seek, Jip! Seek! Seek! Seek, Belle! Seek, Seth! Seek, Blue! Seek, Dock! Seek, Moll! Seek! Seek! Seek, Drum! Seek! Seek!"

Her voice was drowned in the outburst of baying that swelled to a roar as the hounds rapidly became aroused. They raced around inside the pen in a boiling mass, their anger and excitement continuing to mount as they searched for a way out and something to attack, and they began flinging themselves at the sides of the pen and gnashing their teeth at the bars. Alcey stood by the door of the pen, holding the wooden pin on the latch and watching Collier. The hounds became frenzied, and they began fighting among themselves, making the pen shudder violently as they fell against the sides of it. Collier motioned to the three at the gate, and they dragged the side of the gate open, getting behind it as they pulled it back against the wall of the fort. Collier motioned to Alcey. She jerked the pin out of the latch, shouting at the hounds and waving them toward the gate.

Two hounds exploded from the pen as the door opened a crack, and the door flew off the pen and slid across the ground. The hounds swerved from side to side, then streaked through the gate and out into the darkness as Alcey waved and shouted. Four more hounds burst out of the pen, splintering a bar at the side of the door, and they shot through the gate. Two hounds rolled out of the pen in a mass of snapping, snarling fury, fighting each other, and more hounds tore out of the pen and ran over the top of them, racing toward the gate. The last hound ran out of the pen and veered toward Genesee as he looked around the edge of the gate. Genesee leaped for a crossmember on the gate, pulling himself up. The hound leaped for him and tore the leg on his buckskins open. A chorus of frantic baying erupted outside the fort as the hounds scented the trails of the Indians in the meadow and burst into the ringing

peals of hot trail. The two fighting hounds untangled themselves and raced through the gate. The hound attacking
Genesee hesitated, looked at the gate, and ran out.

· Collier ran to the ladder and climbed it to the scaffolding. The hounds were dark shadows against the meadow in
the bright moonlight, streaking up through the meadow
and baying excitedly. The chanting of the Indians at the
top of the hill became ragged and faded as the baying of
the hounds approached the top of the hill, taking on a
more heated note. A ferocious snarl of a hound attacking
and a shrill, startled scream of pain rang out, then another
Indian shrieked in pain and fright. Pandemonium broke
out on the hill. Rifles cracked, and a bedlam of hoarse
shouts and screams blended with the snarls, baying, and
occasional yelps of pain from the hounds. A horse uttered a
penetrating whinny of terror. Other horses squealed, and
there was a heavy drumming of hooves coming down the
hill in the direction of the fort.

"They flushed their horses!" Siler howled with delight,
pounding Collier's shoulder. "By God, they flushed their
horses! They'd rather lose their scalps than their goddamned horses!"

Collier laughed and nodded, and he turned and cupped
his hands around his mouth, shouting. "All rifles to the
firing line! Shoot any horse you can get a bead on! Let
them walk back to the Ohio! And let them think again
before they attack us!"

Men whooped, scrambling up the ladder and running
back and forth along the scaffold. Dark shadows swept
across the meadow, and rifles cracked along the scaffold.
Horses screamed and floundered to the ground in the
meadow. More panic-stricken horses ran blindly back and
forth on the hill and down through the meadow. A cluster
of six or eight charged past the fort, and blazing rifle fire
cut them down. The continuing uproar on top of the hill
was almost drowned in the sound of the rifle fire on the
scaffold, then the horses began scattering wider and avoiding the fort. The sounds of the Indians battling the hounds
faded, and enraged Indians began running down through
the meadow firing blindly at the fort. Men on the scaffold
returned a blistering fire, shooting at the pan flashes in the
meadow.

The people in the fort were gleeful over the success of the ploy, howling with joyous laughter. Collier had Raines bring out rum and summon the fiddler, and couples began dancing and singing in one corner of the fort, increasing the chagrin of the Indians as they heard the lighthearted sounds of celebration. A sporadic fire continued between men on the scaffold and furious Indians in the meadow, then it died away. The people in the fort became weary, the singing and dancing diminished, then stopped. Alcey stood by the gate and whistled for the hounds, and Simon, Genesee, and Raines waited with her to open the gate a crack and guard it with rifles when a hound crawled to the gate and whined. Four returned, all of them severely wounded, and she took them to the cabin to doctor their wounds.

Silence hung over the fort and meadow as the sky lightened and dawn broke. Collier counted thirty-eight horses in the meadow, some of them wounded and standing shakily with their heads drooping, and others twitching on the ground. The bodies of three Indians who had been killed during the exchange of gunfire during the night were sprawled on the meadow. Two hounds that had died trying to crawl back to the fort were a few yards from the gate.

The rifle fire killing the wounded horses within range drew no reaction from the top of the hill. Collier took a fast horse and rode across the meadow at a full run, shooting more of the wounded horses and riding closer to the trees, yet there was no rifle fire nor arrows from the trees. He rode into the trees. There were more dead and wounded horses, the bodies of two more hounds that had been hacked with tomahawks, the remains of fires and the cinders of the framework of the cabin, and many pools of blood where the hounds had fought. The Indians had left, heading north toward the Ohio, most of them walking.

# Chapter Twenty-seven

Collier turned and looked at the door as he heard Raines approaching, talking and laughing heartily with another man who had a deep, booming voice. Then he recognized Clark's voice. They stopped in front of the door, and Clark looked in, taking off his hat and rapping the doorframe with his knuckles.

"Well, here he is himself. The one who trains hounds to be better Indian fighters than any man who ever carried a rifle."

Collier laughed as he walked toward the door. "Aye, but I can't break them from fighting everyone else, myself included. How are you, Major Clark?"

"I'm well, and I'll beg to correct you. It's Lieutenant Colonel Clark now."

"Is it indeed? And well deserved, moreover. My congratulations, Colonel Clark."

"Thank you very much. How are you, Alcey? As though anyone so pretty could be in other than the bloom of health."

"La, you do have a sweet turn of phrase, Colonel Clark. I am well, and you have my congratulations as well. Have you dined, or would you care for a sip?"

"I had nothing nearly so tasty as what you put on a table, but it sufficed. And I'll have a sip, but first I'd like to finish with the congratulations." He opened the leather pouch slung from his shoulder on a strap, thumbed through papers in it, and took out one and handed it to her. "Have a look at that, if you would."

Alcey took the paper, unfolding it and turning it to the late afternoon sunlight coming through the door. Her eyes opened wide, and she turned to Collier with a delighted smile. "You've been commissioned, love! You're a captain now!"

Raines laughed heartily as he stepped closer to Collier and slapped him on the shoulder. "And about bloody time and all! Captain Collier, by God! I like the sound of that!"

Collier chuckled and shrugged. "Well, it's something to put on my tombstone. Was your hand in this, Colonel Clark?"

"I had a word to say on it, but it was like a cup of water in a river. Fort Colliersville is well known, and you're well known, Captain Collier."

"As he should be," Alcey said, smiling proudly. "I'll put your commission away and fetch that sip. Will you have one, Isaac?"

He shook his head, turning back to the door. "I'll have one later. I want to let everyone know that we have a captain commanding our fort."

"I'll give you something else to tell them," Clark said. "You can let them know that Burgoyne surrendered to Gates at Saratoga last October. That'll cheer them up some."

"Burgoyne's been defeated?" Raines said, looking back with a wide smile, and he nodded as he stumped out the door. "By God, that'll cheer them up more than some. I'll let them know."

"So Burgoyne surrendered," Collier said, waving Clark toward the table. "It's past time we were having some good news to go with the bad. Have you just come from Virginia, then?"

"Aye, I had some conferring to do," Clark replied vaguely, walking toward the table, and he looked at the boy slumped on the stool by the hearth. "Is that lad ill?"

"That's the Elder lad. He was knocked on the head and scalped in that last big raid we had last year. We managed to keep him alive, but he's not much more than alive."

"Timothy is doing very well indeed," Alcey said firmly as she put cups on the table and poured rum into them. "He's a sweet lad, and he's improving every day. And if I construe Colonel Clark's look correctly, he wants a private word, so I'll leave you gentlemen to your rum and take Timothy for a walk down to Simon's cabin."

Clark put his hat on the table and sat down, smiling at

her. "Nothing gives me more pleasure than your company, Mistress Collier, but affairs of the militia intrude upon my personal desires."

"And with such a silver tongue, you'll doubtless be a brigadier when we see you next," Alcey chuckled, crossing the room to the hearth. She adjusted the knitted wool skull-cap on the boy's head and took his hand. "Come along, Timothy, and I'll take you for a nice walk. Come along, dear."

The boy looked up at her dully, then slowly gathered himself and stood. He followed her with his shuffling, faltering gait as she led him to the door, his head bobbing as he looked blankly down at the floor. Clark watched them as they went out the door, then he shook his head as he took a drink from his cup. "Bloody hell . . . "

"Aye, he's a pitiful lad. That knock on the head took away most of his sense, and he sits about and looks at the floor all the time. But as Alcey said, he's improving. He used to foul himself like a baby, but she got him out of that."

Clark grunted and nodded, taking another drink of rum, and looked at the bedroom doorways. "Are we alone?"

"My pa's in the bedroom asleep. Everyone else is at my boy Simon's cabin. His wife Rachel was taken bad."

"Not serious, I hope."

"She was in a delicate way and lost it. This is the second time it's happened. She's a sturdy-looking girl, but she can't seem to carry properly."

Clark nodded again. "Well, I trust she'll recover in good order." He took another drink of rum, glanced at the doorway, and looked back at Collier and spoke in a quiet voice. "I'm calling you to active duty."

"That was bloody quick, wasn't it?" Collier chuckled. "And how much more active can I get? I'm forever taking men and running off this way and that when there's a raid."

"I want you to form a company of twenty-five men, together with their horses, weapons, and other equipment. You'll be gone for several months."

Collier was lifting his cup, and he put it back down. "Are we going to the east?"

Clark shook his head, glancing at the door again. "No. As I said, I've just come from conferring, and I had talks with several people, including the governor. Several things came from that, not all of which I can tell you, and what I do tell you must remain between us. Now it's no secret that the British are actively inciting the Indians against us, giving them weapons and buying scalps. The time has arrived for us to be done with hiding in our forts and enduring attacks. The time has arrived for us to take the battle to the enemy."

"Across the Ohio?"

"Across the Ohio, and into the villages and the forts. But the forts first, because that's where the weapons and the money for scalps come from. Furthermore the Spanish are offering support. If we can free the Ohio to the Mississippi of British control and travel at will on the Mississippi, we'll have a supply line all the way from New Orleans to Fort Pitt. A supply line is vitally needed in the east."

"What forts will we be attacking first?"

"I can't tell you that," Clark said, shaking his head. "I've told you what I have so you'll see the necessity of picking twenty-five of your best men, rather than leaving all the best men here to defend the fort, and that's all I can tell you for now. I have men coming from the Holston and from other settlements here in Kentucky, and I'm bringing men from the east, so it will be a substantial force. You're to meet Simon Kenton at Drennon's Lick at the end of May, and he'll know where to lead you. But he won't know as much as you about where we'll be going from there, and there's no need for you to tell him. Or anyone else."

Collier nodded. "The end of May gives us little time to see about our plowing, planting, and other things we have to do."

"It gives me little time for what I've to do, as well. I'm just on my way to the Monongahela, I'm still raising men, and I've yet to draw my stores. But we have a hard chore ahead of us, and we'll need an early start on it. The end of May at Drennon's Lick, Captain Collier."

Collier nodded again, taking a drink from his cup. "I'll be there, and with my men."

Clark smiled with satisfaction, emptying his cup, and

shook his head and rose as Collier reached for the bottle to pour more into it. "No, I must be on my way, and with a clear head for traveling through the night."

"Aye, you've apparently a good deal of traveling ahead of you," Collier replied, rising and walking toward the door with him. "Shall I ask Alcey to put you up something to eat along the way?"

"I'm grateful, but I have victuals in my saddlebags. Give your daughter-in-law my best wishes and hopes for a speedy recovery."

"Aye, I will."

They went outside and walked toward the gate, and Raines came along the line of cabins with several men. They crowded around, congratulating Collier and talking with Clark about the war in the east, and Clark chatted amiably with them as he continued walking toward the gate with his long, impatient stride. He disengaged himself cordially at the gate, shaking hands with the men, and mounted his horse and rode away. Collier walked back toward his cabin, pondering about what he had to do.

Twenty-five to thirty men was the usual number he had taken with him in response to calls for assistance from other settlements under siege, but the duration of such trips had been only a few days. In picking the men to take along, there was a balance to be achieved between assuring adequate protection of the fort while the men were gone, and taking along men who would be equal to what was required of them. And in picking the men to take to join Clark's force, the judgment factors were even more critical. The men would be gone for months, so those left at the fort had to be capable of both defending the fort and providing relief parties if other settlements came under attack. At the same time the men picked to go had to be dependable. Fighting in Kentucky was demanding, but there were forts, farms, and settlements in Kentucky, numerous places of refuge. North of the Ohio there was only a wilderness occupied by hostile Indians and dotted with forts manned by British regulars and French militia loyal to the British.

At one time it would have been difficult to find twenty-five men in the fort and among the outlying cabins who were capable of effective fighting even in Kentucky. And at one time many of the men in the fort and among the outlying cabins would have gathered their belongings and families and gone back along the trail, if ordered to ready themselves for an absence of months to fight. But that time was in the distant past, in events if not in years. All the men had become skilled, crafty fighters in Indian warfare. Those who would leave had left, and those who had remained were determined to remain.

But men who lived in isolated cabins and had no sons thirteen or over to do the work and provide protection in their father's absence were automatically eliminated, as were men who lived in isolated cabins and whose wives were pregnant. There were other factors to consider, aside from the various degrees of skill in fighting. Raines had to stay, both because of his wooden leg and because he was second in command of the fort. All the Creeks had to stay, even though they would have been Collier's first choice to take deep into hostile territory, because Clark was assembling his force from various places, Collier didn't know the men, and too many whites didn't trust any Indian. Siler, Simon, and Genesee were the best hunters and fighters in the entire group, and one of them had to stay to assist Raines and lead hunters in providing game. The older men wouldn't take orders from Genesee, and since Rachel was ill, it made sense to take Siler and Genesee, leaving Simon.

Collier discussed it with Alcey, and their only point of disagreement was on Genesee. Her motherly protectiveness toward him kept her from seeing him as a man, but he was sixteen and Collier kept him on the list to go. As Collier picked the other men and notified them, a rumor developed that they were going to the east to join the Continental forces in North Carolina. Collier did nothing to discourage the rumor, and women discussed the lists they were giving their husbands of things to bring back with them. Raines suggested that the men chosen be given instructions in rifle drill and marching, but Collier vetoed the suggestion, disliking rifle drill and marching himself, as most of the men did, and regarding it as a useless irritant that took the men away from things they had to do. Those who weren't going helped those who were in their early plowing and planting, and Collier met with the men and went over what they were to take with them, limiting them to essentials they could carry with them on their horses.

Raines also suggested a feast before the men left, and a more or less ceremonial departure, and Collier accepted the suggestion. He saw the value in giving the men selected to go a sense of self-importance, because it seemed likely that there would be other trips of long duration.

The feast and celebration was held on the night before the departure, and all the families from the outlying cabins came to the fort. Rum was in short supply, because all supplies from the east had become both scarce and extremely expensive. But a lay preacher named Thomas Holt had recently moved from Harrodsburg and built a cabin along the creek from the fort. He provided spiritual sustenance of two sorts, having brought with him distilling equipment with which he made a fiery, powerful whiskey from corn. Holt contributed several gallons of whiskey, a fat doe was roasted over a firepit in the center of the fort, and there was dancing and singing until late at night.

The fort bustled with activity in the predawn darkness as the men prepared to leave. Horses stamped, dogs barked, children ran back and forth, and women wept. As dawn began breaking, the men lined up with their horses. Holt prayed, his eyes bleary and his voice hoarse from freely imbibing of his produce the night before. Then there were farewells, and the men mounted and rode through the gate, the others following and waving. The double column of men filed along behind Collier in something approaching military order until they were over the first rise and the fort was out of sight, then the column broke up, some men fanning out to hunt game and the others riding in a cluster around Collier and discussing the trip.

Trails had developed between all the forts and settlements, many of them suitable for travel by wagon, and they had an easy ride to Harrodsburg. They found that a group had left Harrodsburg the day before, and they made a forced march the following day and caught up with part of them. There had been an argument among the Harrodsburg men about where to stop and camp. Part of them had gone on, and Collier and the combined group caught up with them the next day, finding them where they had stopped to dry and smoke two deer they had killed. The man Harrod had put in charge of the group had accepted the assignment under duress, and the men had a meeting and elected Collier their officer. Collier didn't know most of the men and didn't want to be responsible for more than his twenty-five men, but his group wanted a share of the venison, and his accepting the post appeared to be a condition for sharing. He tentatively agreed, contingent upon Clark's approval.

Kenton was at the tiny settlement of Drennon's Lick when Collier and the men arrived. Two groups that had come by separate routes from the Holston were also there, and the entire encampment was embroiled in arguments of one kind or another. The officer in charge of one group of Holston men had resigned his post and refused to have anything to do with the men, and those in the other group refused to obey any orders given by their officer. Kenton had just arrived from Fort Pitt with six men, each of them bringing a large canoe, and he had instructions from Clark to take the entire group from Drennon's Lick to Corn Island just above the Falls of the Ohio by canoe. One group of the men from the Holston had come on horses, and they refused to leave their horses at Drennon's Lick. Collier's men and those from Harrodsburg also loudly refused to leave their horses when they found out about the arrangements.

There were almost a hundred men in the combined groups. Kenton was smiling, nonchalant, and amiable, answering any question he could, willing to discuss or speculate on any matter, and refusing to be drawn into an argument over anything. Collier discussed the impasse with Kenton, searching for some solution, but Kenton had no suggestions and he regarded the group as a more or less typical assembly of an army of frontiersmen, all individualists, all highly skilled and deadly warriors, and all exceedingly poor soldiers. Kenton knew only that Clark had told him to take the men to Corn Island, and he was content to wait until they were ready to go or until Clark came looking for them.

A solution offered itself when the Holston men whose officer had resigned met and elected Collier their officer. At first Collier adamantly refused to be responsible for any more men. Then Kenton came as close as he would to making a suggestion, referring to the fact that the group of Holston men who wanted him to be their officer were also

the ones who were mounted, and it would be possible for
Collier to lead all the mounted men overland to the Falls.
The impasse would be resolved, because the other Holston
men had agreed to go by canoe with Kenton and talk with
Clark about finding them another officer when he arrived
at the Falls. Collier thought about it, then agreed to do it if
the officer who had resigned would act as lieutenant. The
man considered it, then accepted when the men met and
agreed to obey orders relayed through him by Collier. The
encampment began breaking up.

The south shore of the upper Ohio was relatively free of
Indians, and the force Collier was leading was of a strength
that only the largest of war parties would challenge, but
Collier demanded disciplined order in the march along the
river. And the men obeyed implicitly, accustomed to moving stealthily through the wilderness as a matter of habit,
and recognizing that their safety was involved. Frequent
travelers along the river had made a trail of sorts along
some stretches, and Collier moved the column along at a
walk, with Genesee and Siler on foot ahead of the column,
and scouts out on the flank on the side opposite the river.
They got organized and enroute late on the first day, moving only a short distance, and by the second day a routine
had developed and they moved steadily down the river all
day, stopping only for a short rest and food at noon. During the noon halt on the third day Genesee came running
back along the trail to talk to Collier. He and Siler had
found two large canoes sunk in the edge of the river and
concealed with brush.

Collier left the main body of men where they were and
went forward with Genesee and Siler to look. A half mile
farther along the river a creek ran through a deep rocky
ravine to the river, and the canoes were sunk and weighted
down with rocks in the shallow water at the mouth of the
creek. Collier moved cautiously about, walking in deep turf
and on rocks to keep from leaving footprints, and examined the ravine and canoes. The brush covering the canoes
was brittle, cut several weeks before, and ensuing rains had
washed away any signs of footprints or hooftracks. Collier
took Genesee and Siler back along the trail, ordered all the
fires extinguished, and moved the men a mile back along
the trail to confer.

The canoes had obviously been left by a raiding party of a dozen to twenty Indians that had come across the river, and the situation offered an opportunity to set up an ambush. The possibility of dealing a swift, devastating blow at a party spreading terror and death among the small settlements and isolated cabins in Kentucky was appealing, and for the first time, Collier perceived an advantage in commanding a large body of men. The men enthusiastically supported the idea, many of them chafing because they had come to fight and all they had done thus far was travel and argue. But there was no way of knowing when the Indians would return to the canoes. Collier wasn't sure when Clark would be at the Falls, but it was reasonable to assume that he would be there within a few days, and it was a certainty that he would be expecting to find his army there when he arrived. And Collier had some doubts about exposing part of Clark's army to casualties before Clark had even seen the men. But the idea of ambushing the Indians was so appealing to the men that there were indications that Collier would be leaving with only twenty-five men if he ruled against the ambush. Clark would then be waiting for a part of his army, and the men could suffer heavy casualties if they weren't effectively deployed and controlled during the ambush.

After long and heated discussion the men agreed to wait four days for the Indians, then destroy the canoes and go on if the Indians hadn't returned. They had passed a grassy valley two miles back along the trail, and Collier sent ten men with all the horses back to the valley, with strict orders to light no fires and to keep a close watch over the horses. Then he divided the remainder of the men into two groups to deploy along the sides of the ravine. He picked a stretch of several yards where the ravine was deep and had steep sides, and he positioned the men in the deep brush and trees several feet back from the edge of the ravine. Siler joined him where the trail crossed the ravine near the river. They carefully erased the traces left by the half of the men who had crossed the trail, then Siler took up his post on one side of the ravine, Collier took his place on the other side, and Genesee went to the head of the ravine to begin his vigil of watching for the Indians.

It began raining, and Collier saw the men willingly and

stoically endure conditions that would have shattered the
discipline of the most rigorously trained line soldiers. They
sat motionless, carefully keeping the locks of their rifles dry
in wrappings of oilskin. Darkness fell, and the only sound
was the patter of rain and the quiet sounds of the forest as
the hours of the night dragged by. When gray daylight
came, the men were huddled in their soggy blankets. They
munched kernels of corn and pieces of jerky, and went
without water while listening to the creek gurgling a few
feet from them. When they had to relieve themselves, they
silently crept away to dig small holes deeper in the brush
so the area around the ravine wouldn't become saturated
with the odors of humans, then they returned and sat motionless in their blankets. Darkness fell again, and it continued raining.

The dark hours of the night slowly dragged by, and another dawn came, a soft drizzle still falling. Collier felt
numb and dazed, and his body was stiff from sitting motionless on the wet ground. He almost dozed at times, then
realized he was starting to go to sleep and opened his eyes
wide, shrugging off the leaden drowsiness by force of will.
A wind stirred and it stopped raining for a few hours, then
it began again. A lower limb on a clump of brush moved a
few feet from him, and he was suddenly looking at Genesee, his young, smooth face drawn with fatigue but his eyes
dancing with triumph. Genesee pointed at the ravine, then
moved his hand rapidly in Indian sign language gestures:
signals for a man walking, a scout, the number three, attack, and negative. Collier nodded. Genesee silently disappeared. Collier cautiously moved his legs, easing the stiffness from them, then got on his hands and knees, crawled
to the edge of the ravine, and clicked his tongue. A moment passed, then Siler leaned sideward from behind a
clump of brush on the other side of the ravine. Collier re-
peated the signals that Genesee had made. Siler nodded
and disappeared behind the brush, and Collier crawled
back where he had been.

The three scouts moved silently along the ravine, the
tops of their heads intermittently visible as they straightened up and looked up at the edges of the ravine. It took
them several minutes to work their way along the ravine to
the trail that crossed it, and two of them examined the trail

as the other one went to check on the canoes. Then all three moved silently back along the ravine. Collier got to his knees again and crawled along the ravine, pointing out a place of concealment on the edge of the ravine to each man. They crept toward them, their bearded faces lined and weary, and their eyes shining. The limbs on the brush on the other side of the ravine trembled occasionally as Siler moved his men into position. Collier crawled back to his place, and Genesee slipped through the brush and knelt by him, lifting his fingers rapidly and indicating eighteen. Collier nodded, pointing out a firing position for Genesee to take.

Horses' hooves clattered on the rocks in the ravine, the sound rapidly becoming louder. The first Indian came into sight, riding a horse and leading two. The second one was leading a single horse. They continued around the bend in the ravine. Collier counted them on his fingers, and the first one was well past him when the fifteenth came into view. All of them were riding horses, and most of them were leading one or two. Many of the horses were loaded with large bundles of looted belongings. Three more came into sight. Collier took careful aim at the eighteenth Indian and squeezed the trigger.

The Indian was slapped backward off the horse, his arms flopping limply. The roaring fusillade of rifle fire that rippled along the sides of the ravine following Collier's shot was deafening, and the ravine was filled with boiling clouds of gunpowder smoke. Indians shrieked and shouted, horses whinnied and plunged, and the men along the sides of the ravine bellowed war whoops. Collier saw an Indian near the end of the line wheeling his horse around, and he jerked out his pistol, cocked it, and fired. The Indian slipped off his horse. A stunning blow slammed into the side of Collier's head, knocking him to the ground. His mind reeled groggily, and Genesee's face swam around in front of his eyes. The awareness that he had been hit cut through the numbing fog in Collier's mind, bringing keen alertness, and he sat up and felt his head as Genesee pulled at him, looking at him with a terrified expression. A rifle ball had grazed his left temple and clipped off the tip of his left ear. He nodded reassuringly to Genesee, snatching out his fighting knife and tomahawk as he climbed to his feet and gathered himself to leap down into the ravine. Then he relaxed. It was all over.

It took most of the rest of the day to collect the panic-stricken horses and gather up the weapons and loot the Indians had been carrying. Four of the horses had been seriously wounded in the rifle fire and had to be shot, and Collier put the twelve scalps the Indians had been carrying in a pouch to turn over to Clark. They rejoined the men guarding the horses, built roaring fires to warm themselves and dry their blankets, and cooked a hot meal. Haggling broke out over how to divide the horses and other spoils of battle, and Collier suggested dividing everything into three lots that would be parceled out to his men, the men from the Holston, and the men from Harrodsburg. The size of the lots was to be determined by the relative size of each group.

His suggestion was accepted and worked smoothly with the horses, because the numbers involved worked out evenly, but it was more complicated on the other property. The rifles the Indians had been carrying were of varying condition and value, and their loot from raids included furs and hides, blankets, kettles, and other household articles, tools, and miscellaneous single items of a kind. With several men wanting them haggling broke out again. Collier's head was throbbing painfully, and the problems of command were beginning to weigh heavily. He picked out one of the larger men who was arguing loudest, and offered to fight him with fists, knife and tomahawk, or firearms. The haggling stopped, and the men agreed to accept Collier's division of all the property.

The worrisome thought that Clark might already be at the Falls and impatiently awaiting the arrival of the rest of the men nagged at Collier as they continued along the river. But when Corn Island came into sight, the only indication of the presence of people was a smudge of smoke from campfires hanging above the thick foliage. Then canoes put out from the upper point of the island and the men in them shouted greetings over the roar of the river as they fought the current, and the men with Collier raced their horses back and forth along the bank and bellowed war whoops and scalp whoops.

The proximity of the island to the long white rapids of

the Falls made the horses nervous about getting into the water, and after the canoes ferried all the weapons and supplies to the island, more men came over to help force the horses into the water and swim them across. The men on the island had killed a young elk, and there was a noisy reunion and a feast. The men who had been with Collier told about the ambush and displayed their booty. Kenton and his men left with the canoes, going back upstream. Collier organized work parties to build pens for the horses and a shelter to store the weapons and loot captured in the ambush; and the men on the island settled down to a lazy routine of fishing, floating rafts over to the shore to hunt, and bickering around their campfires.

Clark arrived three days later with four large wooden boats carrying supplies he had picked up at Fort Pitt and crewed by men he had raised on the Monongahela. He was accompanied by twenty settlers in other boats who had joined his flotilla for protection while coming downstream. He was surprised to find the large herd of horses on the island, pleased by the news of the ambush and the auspicious prelude it provided for the expedition. He immediately began taking control over the men, organizing them into squads and companies, assigning responsibilities, and organizing work parties to build cabins for the settlers staying on the island. And the reasons for Clark's choice of Corn Island became clear when he confiscated all rafts and ordered that no more be built, then called the men together and told them they were going to take Fort Kaskaskia. The idea of fewer than two hundred men venturing deep into the midst of thousands of enemy with the objective of capturing a fort and settlement gave pause to the most intrepid. But with no rafts or canoes it was difficult to desert from an island in a river and reach the shore with a dry rifle and gunpowder.

It seemed to Collier that convincing the men to go was a more ambitious undertaking than the expedition itself. While the men from his fort were willing to go if he was, the others had more reservations. But the audacity of the undertaking appealed to a lot of the men, and the aura of command and natural leadership that Clark possessed was much in evidence. He had a shrewd knowledge of human nature and he knew frontiersmen, and he manipulated the men expertly, always choosing the right instant for an explosive fit of temper, a cold glare, a silent sarcastic smile, or a comradely slap on the shoulder. Some few men from the Holston resisted Clark's persuasive personality, and they secretly built a raft and escaped in the night. Clark sent runners who bypassed them and spread the word among the cabins and small settlements as far south as Harrodsburg that deserters had fled from his army. The deserters were treated with scorn and contempt when they began showing up, and were even denied food and shelter—the right of any traveler on the frontier. They began straggling back.

Of the two hundred men, uncomfortably close to half of them had elected Collier as their officer. He ended up with the more manageable number of fifty—the men from his fort and a group from the Holston. The other company commanders were Captain Helm, a man of sixty with a calm, judicious manner and a fondness for apple toddy; Captain Nolen, a young, aggressive man with something of Clark's leadership ability; and Captain Vail, an experienced militia officer Clark had brought from the Monongahela. The entire group went ashore and practiced maneuvering as a unit, and the companies took turns practicing rowing the large boats up and down the river above the Falls. During the training and preparations Collier made arrangements with the settlers on the island to care for the horses and look after the property captured during the ambush, in exchange for five horses.

Clark had frequent conferences with the company commanders, during which, it quickly became evident that the expedition against Kaskaskia was anything but a rash undertaking. Preparations had begun over a year before, when Clark had sent scouts along the Kaskaskia River to pose as hunters and gather information. The fort was manned by a large contingent of French militia and commanded by a French officer in the British service. While it was well armed, it was somewhat in need of repair. And it had been chosen as an objective at high levels in the Continental government for several reasons. A victory in the west was needed to bolster morale among the Continental forces and civilians. Kaskaskia was a fort that could possibly be taken with a force of a size that wouldn't drain off vitally needed soldiers and large amounts of supplies from the east, as long as total surprise was achieved before the attack. The Mississippi had to be opened to get supplies from New Orleans to Fort Pitt. And most of all a Continental victory against the British with no forces north of the Ohio would set the northern Continental boundary at the Ohio.

The boats were loaded and launched at daybreak on a morning in late June, rowed for a distance upstream to come back downstream with good speed and negotiate the channel through the Falls. Just as the boats were going through the rapids, the early morning light began fading and twilight fell, the dark shadow of an eclipse covering the sun. Some men stared up at the sun in superstitious fear and others began praying, and Collier bellowed at them at the top of his voice as his boat began losing speed and headway in the channel. The men threw their weight against the two-man oars again, and the boat shot safely on through the channel. Full daylight gradually returned, but many of the men construed the period of darkness as some sort of evil omen. Collier wasn't sure what had happened, but Genesee knew about eclipses and told him and the men. Some of the men remained unconvinced, regarding Genesee's explanation as fanciful and preferring the more familiar supernatural explanations for what went on around them. They muttered morosely as they pulled on their oars.

The broad belt of the river twisted and turned, and there was a different view around every curve, broad floodplains covered with cane becoming high, muddy banks, and craggy, rocky peaks crowned with gnarled, weathered trees overhanging the water changing to long stretches of dense, deep forest, all of it untouched, unspoiled, an uninhabited wilderness. The boats sped along during the day as the men heaved on the oars, and they slowed at night, men in the bow watching for snags in the moonlight and a few men pulling on the oars to maintain headway while others dozed. At the mouth of the Tennessee, they camped on an island for a day to rest and cook hot meals, then set out downstream again for Fort Massac.

Fort Massac was an abandoned French fort, and below

Massac the river was heavily patrolled by Indians allied to the British to intercept supplies coming upriver from New Orleans. The river was also patrolled upriver from Massac by enemy scouts, but Clark speculated hopefully that there would be no alarm at Kaskaskia if enemy scouts had spotted the boats, because Massac was far upstream from the point where a party would land to go overland to Kaskaskia. And the thoroughness of Clark's planning and the detailed information he had gleaned about the area from his scouts became evident again when they reached Massac, because there was an old, overgrown trail between Massac and Kaskaskia. Clark ordered the boats pulled out of the water and hidden, and for the men to cache all equipment and supplies except weapons and a small pouch of corn and jerky for each man. While they were preparing to start out for Kaskaskia, William Linn, one of the men who had been with Kenton with the canoes, came downriver in a canoe with an express dispatch for Clark from Fort Pitt. France had signed an alliance with America.

But Versailles was a long way from Kaskaskia. The French in the Americas had lived under British rule peacefully and profitably for thirteen years, and there might reasonably be some skepticism toward such news when delivered by a tiny military expeditionary force penetrating far into hostile territory. Clark deployed the men in single file so they would leave little sign of their passage and not bring hostile Indians in behind them, and they traveled rapidly toward the northwest, rationing their corn and jerky and resting a few hours each night in cold camps. The corn and jerky began giving out on the third day, and the men supplemented their dwindling food with dewberries, blackberries, and raspberries along the way. Fat bear and deer crossing the trail were a temptation, and Clark had the company commanders constantly caution the men against firing a rifle. The corn and jerky were gone by the fifth day, and it was difficult to get the men past the well-laden briar patches.

On the afternoon of the sixth day, the men slipped into a thicket on the edge of the floodplain along the Kaskaskia River, across the river from the settlement and fort, and Collier lay in the edge of the trees with Clark and the other company commanders as Clark examined the settlement and fort with a small telescope. There were no Indians camped along the river, and the activity in the settlement and around the fort appeared normal, the gates of the fort open and people moving about on their affairs. So the commander of the fort was either unaware of their presence, or he had set a trap.

The floodplain narrowed farther up the river, and there were four cabins on high ground a half mile away, with several small boats pulled up on the riverbank in front of them. Clark took a stick and drew lines on the ground, outlining the battle plan. When darkness fell, they would advance up the floodplain to the cabins, take the occupants hostage, and seize boats to ferry the men across the river. Nolen's men would take the settlement, confiscate all weapons, and make the occupants stay in their houses. Vail's men would block all roads leading out of the settlement. Helm's men would surround the fort. Collier's men would seize the fort, preferably by overpowering guards. There would be no gunfire, no wanton killing, no taking of scalps, no molestation of women, and no seizure of private property. Clark finished, and Collier went back to tell his men. They listened, their eyes bleary and their unshaven faces lined with fatigue. Then they lay back down and grumbled about their hunger as they slapped at flies and mosquitoes.

Darkness fell, and the deep grass on the floodplain looked white in the bright moonlight. Nolen's men moved out of the trees in two dark, twisting lines against the grass as they ran toward the cabins. Collier motioned as he ran out of the trees, and his men followed him. The grass whipped at his legs, and the ground became muddy underfoot. He lifted his rifle and powder horn over his head as he began running through puddles in the grass. The men stumbled, cursed, and panted hoarsely behind him, their running footsteps sounding loud in the darkness. Dogs barked ahead, then one yelped loudly as Nolen's men disappeared into the shadows around the cabins. Men's heads and shoulders were momentarily silhouetted against the yellow squares of the windows. A door slammed, and a woman screamed in fright. Collier reached the shorter grass near the front of the cabins, and he slowed, motioning his men toward the bare, trampled space between the cabins and the riverbank.

The men collapsed in two ragged lines, gasping for breath, and Collier panted as he moved along the line, counting them. One was missing, then Genesee came from behind one of the cabins, dragging a large basket of fresh, unshucked corn, his teeth shining in the moonlight. The men leaped for the corn, and Genesee handed Collier an ear as he began shucking one. Collier jerked the shucks back and bit into the corn, the fresh kernels sweet and milky.

Clark's voice had a dangerous, threatening note as he questioned men in the cabins; then he came out and talked to Collier and the other company commanders. As far as the people in the cabins knew, the fort wasn't under any state of increased alert, and most of the militiamen were married and would be in their houses in the settlement. Nolen's men lined up at the bank and started going across in the boats, the oars rattling and squeaking in the locks, and Collier grouped his men as the line of Nolen's men became shorter. Children from the cabins brought baskets of raw carrots, radishes, and turnips freshly pulled from the gardens and with dirt still clinging to them, and the men snatched them from the baskets and ate hungrily. Collier got into a boat with a couple of his men and the last of Nolen's, rowed across to the clump of trees a few yards from the settlement where Nolen's men were gathered, then sent the boat back. The boats worked back and forth, and more men crowded around Collier as they hopped out of boats and ran onto the bank, munching vegetables. Then Helm's men began coming across.

The fort was on the other side of the settlement on a high point on the riverbank, and Collier led his men toward it in the shadow of the bank, slipping and sliding in the mud at the edge of the water. The weathered palisade walls gleamed in the bright moonlight. Cannon gunports in the blockhouses were shuttered, and Collier saw no heads above the palisades. He climbed the bank in front of the fort and trotted toward it, waving his men forward on each side of him. The wide double gate in front and the small postern gate beside it were closed and locked for the night.

Dogs barked in the settlement. Collier put his eye to a crack in the postern gate. There was a gleam of lights inside the fort. He motioned Genesee forward. Genesee handed his rifle to a man, hopped lightly onto Collier's shoulders, then strained to reach the top of the palisades. Collier gripped Genesee's feet and lifted him. Genesee stretched higher, then pulled his legs up and silently disappeared over the palisades.

The bar inside the door clanked with a wooden sound, and the door squeaked open. Genesee pointed to the scaffold on each long side of the fort. Collier looked, saw the sentries, and nodded. He pointed to the ladders, the sentries dozing on the scaffolds, and the blockhouses as his men slipped silently through the doorway. A long barrack building was on the left side of the fort, the commander's house was in the rear, and a warehouse and several small buildings were on the right. Windows were lighted in the commander's house and in one end of the warehouse. Collier sent Siler with several men toward the barrack, Clark took two men and ran toward the commander's house, and Collier took four men toward the warehouse. Timbers on the scaffold squeaked as the men swarmed up the ladders and ran along them. A surprised sentry uttered a muffled shout as he was seized. The barking of dogs in the settlement outside the fort was loud. A door rattled in one of the blockhouses. Collier jerked open the door by the lighted window in the warehouse and ran in. It was the armory. A lamp was burning on a table, and a man was asleep at the table, his head on his arms. Another sat in a corner asleep. He leaped up, and Genesee pushed him into the corner, his tomahawk lifted threateningly. The man at the table jumped up, and Collier threw him back against the wall, his knife at the man's throat.

Muffled sounds became louder, and the tense quietness dissolved into a swelling volume of noise. Doors slammed, men barked commands, and startled shouts rang out in the barrack. Collier and Genesee pulled the two men outside. Siler and his group were pushing sleepy, disheveled men out of the barrack, and others were dragging sentries down the ladders. The main gate groaned open, and Helm's men rushed in, whooping. The door of the commander's house stood open, and light shone out. Torches began blazing.

Collier shouted at his men to collect the prisoners in the center of the fort. They huddled together, their arms over their heads, looking at each other in numb shock. The barking of dogs in the settlement became frenzied as Nolen's men began a noisy house-to-house search for weapons. Kaskaskia had been taken.

# Chapter Twenty-eight

An atmosphere of terror hung over Kaskaskia, one of the supply points from which Indian war parties had been dispatched into Kentucky. And now it was in the grips of a tattered, unshaven horde of avenging frontiersmen who had appeared out of the night. The fate of inhabitants of Kentucky settlements captured by Indians was well known in Kaskaskia, and Collier watched the developments as Clark used his skill in dealing with people.

The vicar general of Louisiana was in the settlement, and he and a deputation of leading villagers came to see Clark. Clark received them cordially, expressed insulted astonishment over their fears of rape, torture, and murder, and informed them of the alliance between France and the United States of America. Overjoyed the priest and leading villagers undertook to exercise their authority in implementing the alliance at a local level. Militia officers signed an oath of allegiance to the United States. A detail of militia accompanied Nolen to Cahokia, fifty miles to the north, and the militia there signed the oath of allegiance.

Lieutenant Governor Abbott, commander at Vincennes, had gone to Detroit and left a French militia officer in command, and the priest went to Vincennes to plead the American cause and save the citizenry and militia the miseries of war. He returned with the oath of allegiance signed by the militia officers, and Clark dispatched Helm with twenty-five men to take command of Vincennes. The merchants of Kaskaskia summoned the chiefs of the Kaskaskia, Peoria, and Mechegame Indians to a treaty council with Clark. Clark dispatched an express messenger with the news of the capture of Kaskaskia, Cahokia, and Vincennes. A bateaux came up the Kaskaskia from Corn Island, bringing news of the outside world. The Continental Army had been defeated at Monmouth. There had been Indian massacres on the Susquehanna in Pennsylvania and in the Cherry Valley of New York. Daniel Boone and twenty-eight men boiling down salt on the Licking River in Kentucky had been taken prisoner by a party of Shawnees led by Chief Blackfish.

The armory in the fort at Kaskaskia was used to store weapons belonging to the villagers and militia between the time the fort was captured and the oaths of allegiance were signed, and it was well stocked with ammunition and spare weapons provided from the British stores depot at Detroit. Clark kept the armory and the supply warehouse securely locked and guarded, but Collier and the other officers had the keys from time to time in the process of storing and returning seized weapons. And in looking around inside the armory Collier found nine swivel cannon and swivels, all neatly wrapped in heavily greased canvas covers.

Guard duty was rotated between companies. Collier had possession of the keys for only short periods and rarely at night. The cannon tubes weighed almost two hundred pounds each and the swivels were heavy, bulky, and difficult to conceal. It took quick reaction and coordination between Collier and the men from his fort when all the circumstances became aligned and it was possible to slip one of the heavy tubes or a swivel out of the armory and fort without being seen. But a month after the fort had been captured two of the cannon and swivels to mount them had been quietly slipped out of the fort and buried in the forest a mile down the river.

Replacements for men due to be released from active service were slow in arriving, coming up the river in bateaux and boats in groups of five to ten. Clark was anxious to keep up as much show of strength as possible during his negotiations with the Indians, and he talked Collier into remaining and keeping his men at Kaskaskia for an extra month. In late August Clark released Collier and his men, giving them the use of two boats due to be returned to Corn Island. They loaded into the boats, floated down to where the cannon and swivels were buried, dug them up and put them in the boats, then continued on downstream.

The men from the Holston and Harrodsburg had been released before, and they had taken more than their share

of the captured horses from Corn Island. But they had left
the bulk of the weapons and other property, and there were
plenty of spare horses to carry the things that had been
captured in the ambush, as well as the cannon and swivels.
Collier and his men used the boats to ferry all their belongings to the south shore of the river, left the boats at the
island and swam the horses across, then loaded the horses
and started south.

The fort had undergone two major attacks while they
had been gone. The east wall had been damaged by fire
and was being repaired. Two families in outlying cabins
had been killed as a preliminary to one of the attacks, and
four men from the Holston that Collier had met on the
expedition to Kaskaskia were moving their families into
the area. The cabin that Collier had started once more on
the hill again had been burned. Boone had escaped from the
Shawnee. Peletheke had gone to the Creek tribal grounds
in Georgia and returned with a wife, and he had brought
back his wife's two brothers and their families.

And Collier's foster father had died. Collier had been
expecting it in a way, because the old man had been almost
eighty. But in another way it came as a raw, agonizing
shock. Someone he had instinctively expected to be there
always was gone, leaving a vast, hollow emptiness. Even
when standing and looking at the roughly hewn and
crudely carved headstone in the cemetery by the fort, it
was difficult to accept the fact that the old man was gone.
An age had ended. The final, long, finely inscribed page in
a lengthy chapter had turned.

There was another raid a week after Collier and the
other men returned. The swivel cannon were mounted on
the east wall of the fort, and both cannon fired once,
smothering the east wall of the fort in a huge cloud of gunpowder smoke that slowly drifted away and sprayed the
meadow with a hail of bits of broken pewter and pieces of
scrap iron. Of the twelve Indians visible in the meadow,
eight were killed or wounded. The Indians left.

Some of the crops at the cabins had been destroyed during the raids in the summer, but those along the creek and
under the protection of the fort were untouched, the harvest was bountiful, and there was a surplus of food. Collier
led heavily armed groups to the Licking River for salt and

to the caves for niter to make gunpowder. Then he led a party to the relief of Holcomb Station when it was besieged by Indians. By the time the trees began turning and the weather was cool, most of the people from Holcomb Station had moved to the vicinity of Fort Colliersville.

The Indian raids were more sporadic and the raiding parties smaller as the weather turned cold, and they diminished more after the first snowfall. Word arrived that the Virginia legislature had voided the land claims of the Transylvania Company, but that settlers' claims would be let stand upon proper application and registration at the land office in Harrodsburg, and Alcey prepared the original survey reports and claims again. Collier sent Genesee to Harrodsburg with the claims, and Genesee returned with a letter given him by an express messenger he met in Harrodsburg. It was from Clark, calling Collier and a company of twenty-five men to active duty, and ordering them to report to Kaskaskia with all possible speed.

The story of the ambush and the expedition had been told and retold, and Collier was inundated with volunteers. He picked thirty-five men, leaving Simon and taking Genesee again, and he took along two extra men to bring back the horses from the Falls. The headquarters for Clark's operations had been moved from Corn Island to a tiny fort on the south side of the river, and there were other men gathering in response to summonses from Clark when Collier and his men arrived. Several of the men were from Kentucky and a number from the Holston and Clinch. While Collier knew some of them casually and a few of them well, they all seemed to know him well, shaking his hand and addressing him familiarly. They immediately elected him their officer. There were enough to man a large boat waiting at the fort, and they set out down the river.

The trip down the Ohio was slow and tedious, the boat putting into the shore each night because of the danger of hitting a snag and capsizing during the dark, overcast nights. And the trip up the swollen Kaskaskia was toilsome, putting into the shore each night because of exhaustion from fighting the current. When they reached Fort Kaskaskia, Clark was waiting impatiently for Collier. He had missed the two cannon at the fort and had heard about the sudden appearance of two cannon at Fort Colliersville, but other matters were uppermost on his mind. He now held the rank of colonel, and Collier had been promoted to major. And Lieutenant Colonel Hamilton, a British line officer, had brought a force of British regulars from Detroit and retaken Vincennes.

A French trader who had been at Vincennes when Hamilton captured it had come to Kaskaskia. Clark had interrogated him and obtained extensive information, all of an alarming nature. The force Hamilton had brought with him was large and well equipped, and Hamilton was having repairs made to the fort and more cannon emplacements built. He was openly boasting about a spring offensive against Kaskaskia and Cahokia, and was sending out messages to the tribes to assemble in the spring for that purpose.

Clark proposed to preempt Hamilton's attack by a daring cross-country march, and the element of surprise was almost assured. The winter weather had moderated, but it was virtually impossible to march a force through the boggy prairies between Kaskaskia and Vincennes in winter, a trackless waste of ice and half-frozen mud. And the element of surprise would be an issue in the outcome only as far as the walls of the fort. British regulars didn't sleep while on sentry duty, and forts weren't taken by surreptitious entry when manned by British regulars.

A part of the force against Hamilton was to be amphibious. Clark had secured a large boat from the Mississippi and converted it into a dreadnaught, with a crew of forty to row and man rifles behind high bulwarks, and a battery of six cannon—two four-pounders and four swivels. The boat was christened the *Willing* in honor of a captain who had braved a gauntlet of Indians along the Ohio to ferry military stores from New Orleans to Fort Pitt. It was to slip down the Kaskaskia, along the Ohio, then up the Wabash to support the attack on Fort Sackville at Vincennes. The boat left the day after Collier and his men arrived, with the entire populations of Kaskaskia, Cahokia, and the surrounding areas present and in a wild uproar of martial fever and jubilation as the boat slipped away down the river, exchanging thunderous cannon salutes with the fort. Clearly the waves of the Kaskaskia, Ohio, and Wabash were ruled by Clark, not Britannia.

It appeared to Collier that the waste of priceless gunpowder in salutes and possibly much of the reason behind commissioning the *Willing* was to inspire confidence in Clark's undertaking and promote a state of morale that would increase the chance of success. If so, it worked, because the French raised a company of volunteers to accompany Clark. But the frontiersmen needed no more inspiration than to know that they were marching against Hamilton, known throughout Kentucky County as "The Hair-Buying General" because of his generous gifts to raiding parties returning from Kentucky with scalps.

Clark's wily cunning in dealing with men had never been more in evidence, and he relaxed discipline almost entirely during the first days of the march. The force of less than two hundred men and the pack animals were allowed to spread out in confusion, his only orders that everyone keep pace and keep moving in the same direction, and that no officer mount a horse and ride under any circumstances. Marching through the winter rain and slogging through the mud all day, then camping on wet ground and sleeping in soaked blankets was exhausting, but the men were allowed to fire at game at will, because the distance from Fort Sackville was much too far for rifle fire to make any difference. The men had a feast each night around roaring fires, Clark organized Indian dancing and other entertainment, and stumbling through knee-deep mud or wading through water up to the armpits and holding rifles and powder horns high overhead was less of a hardship and more of a contest to the men when they were looking forward to the feast and entertainment at the end of the day.

When they reached the Little-Wabash, greater difficulties beset them. Rain had been so heavy that the Little Wabash and the Wabash were both far out of their banks and were flowing together across the three-mile stretch that normally separated them, and there was a stretch of water five miles wide ahead of the men. In a private conference with company commanders Clark confided that he wanted the Little Wabash behind the men so there would be no thought of turning back if morale faltered, but he wanted to keep the Wabash between his force and Vincennes for as long as possible in event Hamilton received warning from a scout and tried to send out a force from the fort. A raft was built and floated out to find the shallow water between the two river channels. It was three to five feet deep, with only a moderate current. A platform was built in the trees in the shallow water, the supplies and weapons were rafted to the platform. Horses swam over, and the men marched upstream between the two rivers, with guides out in front with poles to mark a trail. They camped in water for two nights, climbing into trees to sleep, then they reached higher ground, where there were occasionally soggy knolls to camp on.

At the point where they were to meet the *Willing* and be ferried across the Wabash, the boat wasn't in sight. Rather than let the men settle down to await a boat that might have met with an accident and never arrive, Clark went out with a small party to try to find the *Willing* and keep the men moving upstream. They were well within the range of hunting and scouting parties from Vincennes, all shooting at game was forbidden, and they ate carefully rationed food from their supplies. When the food supplies were gone, they ate the horses that had been carrying them.

Two weeks after leaving Kaskaskia they were nine miles below Vincennes and within sound of the morning cannon at Fort Sackville. There was still no sign of the *Willing*, and Clark started the men building canoes. They built two and found another one floating down the river, and spent a day crossing the river. Several of the French among the group had friends and relatives in Vincennes, and when a camp was set up a mile from the fort and settlement, Clark sent them to the settlement with a message for all civilians to keep off the streets and in their homes. The men went out during late afternoon and returned just after dark with the reassuring news that the fort hadn't been alerted. When Clark moved the men forward under cover of darkness and into the settlement, the friends and relatives of the French in the group had hot food waiting.

Fort Sackville was securely locked for the night and totally isolated from the settlement, which seethed with activity as the men ate and made preparations for the attack. A crucial point in Clark's plan was to convince Hamilton that he was being assaulted by a large force, and he positioned the men around the fort carefully. Collier and his company had the side near the church, and he put his men around it and behind the churchyard fence. A single platoon of

Clark's men began firing and jeering at the sentries in the fort, and a bustling stir of activity began in the fort. Then all of the men poured a blistering fusillade of rifle fire at the walls of the fort, and the noise inside increased to an uproar.

A three-pound cannon opened up on the church, then was immediately silenced when Collier had all his men direct their fire at the gunport, driving the matrosses away from the cannon. Fires inside the fort silhouetted men inside as they passed cracks where some of the palisades hadn't been lined on the inside with heavy boards, and the fires were quickly extinguished as Collier's men easily picked off men inside the fort from a distance of thirty yards. Clark sent an order to alternate between firing as rapidly as possible and to cease firing entirely to give the impression of toying with those inside, and he sent a few men into the streets of the settlement to create a commotion. The men in the settlement whooped, shouted, and laughed, giving the impression that there was a large force besieging the fort, with men on the firing line being continually relieved by fresh men. Collier's men fired and ceased firing, and jeered and cursed at those inside, promising them death by torture and inviting Hamilton to come out and buy some scalps.

People in the settlement informed Clark that a hunting and scouting party of a dozen men and an officer had gone out during the day, and Clark had scouts posted outside the settlement to listen for their return. When the scouts reported that the party was slipping back along the river in the darkness, Clark had the rifle fire around the fort diminished, then stopped. Scouts continued reporting the progress of the returning party as they crept toward the fort to try to get in, and the party came through the settlement toward the church. Clark came to Collier and told him to pull his men back, let the party pass and allow them to get into the fort, then to jeer and shout as they climbed in and give the impression that the force outside was so large that another dozen men inside was of no consequence.

Collier pulled his men back to give the returning party a wide path. The frozen silence around the fort was emphasized by the noise of the men still whooping, shouting, and laughing in the settlement, and the muffled sounds of the men creeping past the church was loud in the stillness. They reached the wall of the fort, whispered sibilantly with those inside, and a few minutes later there was a sound of men scrambling up ropes. Collier and the men around him began shouting and firing their rifles into the air. Men behind a cabin at one side of the church threw torches which landed under the wall, lighting the men frantically climbing the ropes. A rifle cracked by Collier and one of the men fell heavily to the ground at his rope parted. Genesee smiled apologetically and shrugged as Collier looked at him. Five ropes were still dangling when all the men were over the wall, lighted by the flickering flames of the torches, and Collier's men cut them in two with rifle fire.

Cold, gray dawn broke. Some of Collier's men lay with their rifles aimed at loopholes in the walls of the fort, and when the loophole darkened from a rifleman peering through it, they fired. Others fired intermittently at cracks where palisades weren't lined with boards, making a deadly crossfire of rifle balls sing through the fort. Clark sent a detachment of men to approach the fort under cover of the riverbank, and they began ostentatiously digging and throwing dirt into the river, as though tunneling under a corner of the fort and mining it with gunpowder. Men watched the river hopefully for the *Willing* to come and batter the fort with cannon.

During late morning a white flag waved at the postern gate of the fort. The sign of peace, truce, and surrender on the frontier was an uplifted rifle butt, so one of Collier's men shot the stick holding the flag in two, thinking it was a taunt. Other rifles fired holes in the flag as it fell. Clark bellowed angrily, and the firing stopped. Another flag waved at the gate. Captain Helm, a paroled prisoner of Hamilton's since Hamilton had retaken the fort, came out and talked with Clark. Clark refused Hamilton's terms, sent Helm back in, and the firing started again.

Helm had befriended a group of Kickapoo Indians while he held the fort, and they came to watch the battle, share the whiskey the men were passing around, point out targets, and take occasional shots at the fort themselves. They also brought the information that a party of Shawnees back from raiding in Kentucky was on the way up the river.

Clark dispatched an officer and part of a company to ambush the Indians, and they returned during the afternoon with a bag of scalps the Indians had been carrying, eight fresh Indian scalps, and four prisoners. All firing on both sides stopped as the four prisoners were seated on the ground by the river in full view of the fort, tied back-to-back. The officer who had led the ambush tomahawked the prisoners, and the men dragged them to the river and threw them in. When Helm again waved a truce flag, Clark and Hamilton met at the gate to discuss terms of surrender. The garrison marched out and stacked their arms, and Clark marched his men in as Hamilton stared in shocked disbelief at the small, tattered force that had taken the fort from him.

The *Willing* finally arrived and took Hamilton and other prisoners downriver to be moved across Kentucky to Virginia. Clark released all French militia who had been in the fort and allowed them to return home to Detroit, taking copies of the alliance between France and the United States with them, and Fort Sackville became Fort Patrick Henry. With the first dispatches that came in from Virginia news of promotions and commissions were received. Collier was promoted to lieutenant colonel, Siler was commissioned a captain, Raines was recalled in his commission as a captain, and Simon and Genesee were commissioned lieutenants.

Clark wanted to mount a campaign against Detroit and undertake other operations to secure the territory north of the Ohio and reduce Indian raids on the frontier, and he left Collier in command of Fort Patrick Henry and went to Virginia to discuss his plans. The problems facing Collier were diminished when the military government of the area was ended upon the arrival of a county lieutenant of the new Virginia County of Illinois, but the administration of the fort and military affairs were difficult and frustrating. When the weather began turning warm, most of the men chafed to return home and replacements began arriving, so Collier released the men who had come with him, keeping only Genesee to read and write for him. Letters came from Alcey, long and chatty, with good news and bad. The victories in the west had brought new settlers from the east, particularly from areas plagued by bands of raiders belonging to neither the British nor the Continental forces. New settlements were springing up—Bryan's, Grant's, Ruddle's, Estill's, a town called Lexington, and others. Some of the land claims by the settlers around Colliersville were being challenged. Collier's claim for two thousand acres had been rejected outright, and his basic claim for five hundred acres was being questioned. The land clerk of Kentucky County was Horace Selwyn, the man Collier had refused to bring to Kentucky because he'd had wagons with him.

In late summer Collier found out that Raines had been killed during an Indian raid, and he had Genesee write a letter to him to Siler, asking him to take command of Fort Colliersville. He also had a letter written to Clark, asking that he be relieved so he could return home. It was several weeks before he received a terse reply that he couldn't be relieved. Clark was busy raising men to strengthen the defenses of Fort Nelson at the Falls and to build a new fort at the mouth of the Ohio to be called Fort Jefferson, and he was also planning several schemes to retaliate against the Indians raiding in Kentucky. Several replacements for men being relieved at Fort Patrick Henry came from the area of Colliersville, and they told Collier that everything was well at the fort and with his family. Simon, Siler, and other men had started rebuilding Collier's cabin on the hill above the fort once more, and they had plowed and planted some of his land on the other side of the hill for Alcey during the summer.

The new year brought news that Clinton had taken Savannah, and shortly afterward he took Charleston. Cahokia was attacked by a party of Delaware led by the British, and Clark took a force up from the Ohio to relieve Cahokia. Shortly afterward Captain Henry Bird led a large party of Shawnees across the Ohio and attacked Ruddle's Station and Martin's Station with artillery. A number of the settlers in the stations were massacred, and the remainder were led into captivity north of the Ohio. Clark went to Kentucky, drafted a large number of new settlers and land speculators into the militia, confiscated military stores and collected volunteers, and took an army of almost a thousand men north of the Ohio in a retaliatory raid through Indian villages, burning, killing, and destroying crops.

Alcey mentioned in letters that Rachel was pregnant

again. She had miscarried several times and Collier had little hope that she would carry this baby to full term, but subsequent letters from Alcey reported that Rachel's pregnancy was progressing satisfactorily. Collier hoped to return home before cold weather, and when the news indicated that the Indian activity had ebbed and there might be men available to replace him, he had Genesee write another letter to Clark, asking to be relieved. Clark replied that he would be relieved in the spring of the following year.

There was a single letter from Alcey during the winter, and everything was well. The reputation of Fort Colliersville had spread among Indians as well as settlers, because the number of settlers in the area was still increasing and there had been no Indian attacks in the area for months. The cabin on the hill was almost completed, and Rachel's pregnancy was still progressing well.

Lieutenant Colonel Hunter relieved Collier in early spring and brought a short letter from Alcey. Rachel's baby had been born and was doing well, but Rachel had weakened and died shortly after the birth. Simon had taken a relief party to Grant's Station when it came under attack and had been killed during the battle.

# Chapter Twenty-nine

The soft breeze sweeping along the narrow road carried a strong odor of woodsmoke from the direction of the fort and settlement, and the horses lifted their heads and began walking more rapidly. Collier's horse started to break into a canter, and he tightened the reins and held the horse to a walk. Genesee's horse sidled and bobbed its head as it fought the bit, then it also settled to a walk again. Genesee leaned over and patted his horse's neck, then he sat back in the saddle and looked at Collier, chuckling.

"For a while I thought you were going to scalp the bastard."

Collier frowned, then he smiled slightly and nodded. "So did he, I believe. And I might yet, by God. He'll not do me out of what's mine. Or rather he'll not do me out of what I want to leave to you boys."

Genesee started to say something, stopped himself and thought again, then he shrugged. "Well, don't worry about me, Pa. You know, I've been thinking about going over to take a look at the Missouri country."

His tone was cautious, not wanting to cause a disagreement. Collier looked at him. "How long have you been mulling that over in your mind?"

"Oh, it's just something I've thought about. And for a while I suppose. But I haven't wanted to just up and leave. There are things to be done, and Simon isn't here anymore."

His tone was even more cautious in mentioning Simon. Everyone knew it wasn't a subject Collier liked to discuss. After more than a year it was still painful. And in addition to the torment of the loss of a son he had loved deeply, there was a gnawing question that wouldn't go away. In talking to others who had been there, it was clear that Simon had ridden into an ambush. A very transparent ambush. Collier wondered what he had said or failed to say that had led Simon into disregarding what should have been obvious warnings of an ambush. Collier wondered if he had been careless or seemingly foolhardy in Simon's presence at some time or other, and if Simon had related that action to the warnings he should have perceived. Simon's training had been his father's responsibility, and Simon's death pointed unswervingly toward the fact that at some time or other he had failed in that responsibility. In addition to the agony of loss he felt guilty. And he now wondered if there was something that he should have told or showed Genesee that he hadn't, or if there was something he had said or done around Genesee that he shouldn't have.

"You're your own man, Genesee. You're nineteen years old, and if you want to go to Missouri country, it's up to you."

"I'd never go and not have things right here. And I'd never go without your blessing."

"Things are all right enough here, and you have my blessing, lad. But when and if you go, don't think so much of what's behind you. A man who looks behind himself sees his arse. I've no idea where I came from, and I credit that in large measure as being what brought me here. You'd do well to fix the same idea in your mind. I'm plain enough for you to see as your father, but neither of us knows where I came from. And as far as your mother goes, I can't even remember her father's last name."

"Gireaux. Ma has it written down in that old Bible and among all the papers she's always writing on."

"That's right, I remember now. Regardless, you'd do well to remember what I say. When you go, leave it all behind you."

"There's no great rush, in any event, Pa. You were talking about breaking some new land, and that'll keep us busy for a while."

"It could as easily keep those other three busy and give them something more to do than hunt raccoon all night and sleep all day."

Genesee laughed and nodded. "They like their hunting, don't they? But I like to hear a hound on a hot trail myself, as far as that goes. But do you think there's any point in breaking new land when we're not so sure about the claim? I'm loath to work very hard at breaking land for someone else to plant. And those papers Selwyn had might as well be in some other language. Ma might be able to read them, but I couldn't make head nor tail of them."

"She's too near her time to be riding around on a horse, or we would have taken her along. And I'll probably take her up a while after she's had the baby, because she has a lot of friends in Harrodsburg and she's been wanting to see them. But I'm not worried about the land, lad. Some bastard might need to worry about his scalp, but I'm not worried about the land."

Genesee's smile faded. "A lot of people are having trouble about land, aren't they? Colonel Boone is, I understand."

"He is. I was talking to him when I was up at Lexington last month, and he mentioned it. He sells a piece of land he's proved, then something goes wrong with the title and he has to sell another piece to pay back the money and to pay lawyers. Then something is wrong with the title on that one, and he gets further behind all the time. The same thing has happened to General Clark, and more. They're even trying to make him pay for some of the supplies he ordered for the forts during the war, which is small thanks to a man who put our northern border on the Great Lakes instead of the Ohio River."

"Small thanks indeed, and people soon forget, don't they? A lot of things have changed since the war ended, not least among which is this pack of land speculators who rushed in here. They're the cause of most of the trouble over land."

"Them and the lawyers. Lawyers can't get any fees until they go to court on something, so they stir up things to go to court on. I'll take hostile Indians over goddamned lawyers any day. Hostile Indians only want a man's scalp, not his whole hide."

Genesee smiled wryly and nodded, holding his horse back as it again tried to break into a canter. The road curved around a shoulder in the hill on the left, and the fort came into sight. The months of relative calm and the drift of most Indian attacks to north of the Ohio and south of the Cumberland had resulted in a changing aspect in the fort, and it was more the centerpiece of a growing settlement than a fort, its timbers weathered and showing signs of rot, burned spots on the walls fading into the mottled color of the rest of the timbers, and deep grass grown up around the open gates. Cabins were outside the west wall where the stock pens had once been, a small church was on the south end in front of the cemetery, a grove of young fruit trees was on the east side of the fort, and there were other obstacles to a clear field for rifle fire and places of concealment near the walls that would have been prohibited before. A dozen families of Creek Indians lived in the fort and had garden patches and stock pens along the creek. Other cabins in the fort had been taken over by repair and small manufacturing and mercantile shops. Shepeshe and several other men were standing near the north gate of the fort. Collier and Genesee waved as they turned onto the road leading up through the meadow to the cabin.

Simon and the others who had worked on the cabin had cut down more trees around it than Collier liked, but there were still two large oaks in front, and several oaks, maples, and birches around the sides and behind it. It was large—a front room, kitchen, and bedrooms off a hallway downstairs, and more bedrooms upstairs. The windows had glass in them, and there was a rock chimney on each end. Despite a size that gave Collier a vague impression of ostentation, the cabin seemed comfortable and homey to him, mostly because Alcey liked it. Three of the hounds were sprawled on the porch, and chickens were scratching in the dirt around the cabin.

Genesee reached for Collier's reins as they dismounted. "I'll take him to the pens for you, Pa."

"All right, then. When you're through, come on in and we'll find a sip of something and talk over that new ground we're going to break."

Genesee nodded, leading the horses toward the pens, and the chickens in front of the porch scattered as Collier walked toward them. The hounds looked at him and thumped their tails on the porch. There was a murmur of voices in the front room, Alcey's and those of two men, and the room was dim after the sunlight outside as he walked inside. Collier put his rifle in the rack, nodding to

the two men as they rose from the settle. Then he blinked
and looked closer. Alcey rose from the other settle and
walked toward him, smoothing her apron over her swollen
stomach with a habitual motion.

"Love, we have visitors. This is my son Jude and his
associate, Mr. Josiah Farnsworth. Jude, Mr. Farnsworth,
this is my husband, Colonel Santee Collier."

At first glance it was like seeing Jubal years before. His
breeches, waistcoat, shirt, cravat, and stockings were meticulously neat and clean, his hand was limp, damp, and soft,
and his bow and murmur of greeting were superciliously
polite. The other man was about forty, dressed the same,
and looked like a weasel.

"How's your pa, then?"

"His health is not the best, sir, but he endures. And he
asked me to convey his wishes that you fare well and enjoy
good health."

"He did? Well, when you see him again, you can tell him
that I do. And give him my best."

"Jude and Mr. Farnsworth are here looking into land
transactions, love," Alcey said, her smile and tone anxious.

"Are you now?" Collier put his pistol, knife, and tomahawk on the rack and shrugged indifferently as he walked
toward the settle where Alcey had been sitting. "You've
ample company, then, even if it's not the sort of company
I'd choose for myself. We have four land speculators for
each and every farmer coming through the Gap or down
the Ohio."

There was a short, stiff silence. Alcey cleared her throat
nervously, smoothing her apron over her stomach, and sat
down on the settle by Collier. The two men glanced at each
other as they stepped back to the other settle and sat down.
Jude crossed his legs, smiling blandly. "We're not precisely
land speculators, sir. And while we're not averse to looking
at farming land and such, we'd mostly like to investigate
the area of the niter caves, to the south of here. Also we
have options on some of the land along the Cumberland
that was granted to soldiers in the late war, and we'd like
to have a look at that before we go further with the matter."

Collier nodded, folding his arms and looking out the
window. "Then you might have a thought for your scalp.

It's been awhile since we've had any trouble with Indians
around here, but there's still plenty to be found. And the
Cumberland is one of the places to find it."

"Yes, that's what we understand," Farnsworth said. "It
appears that we could have an end to it once and for all,
doesn't it?"

"I hold that most of the blame can be laid at our own
door. And I'll not try to tell you your business, but you're
wasting your time looking at the land around the niter
caves. Most of it is fit for nothing but growing briars and
weeds."

The two men glanced at each other again as Alcey stirred
on the settle, smoothing her apron. Jude's smile was wider
as he looked back at Collier. "Well, we're more interested
in the niter caves than in the land around them."

It took a moment for Collier to understand his meaning.
Then it became clear. He had always regarded the niter in
the caves as something on the order of water in a creek or
fish in a river, there for everyone to take when they had a
need. It hadn't occurred to him that someone might lay
claim to the land, fence off the caves, and then mine the
niter and sell it. But Judal had always been the sort of
individual who would think of a way to do something like
that, and then do it. Collier looked out the window again.

The silence began stretching out. Alcey cleared her
throat, smiling at Jude. "Are you primarily engaged in
property transactions now, Jude?"

"No, I wouldn't say primarily, Mama, even though I've
been putting much of my effort into property dealings of
late. Father and I are still engaged in shipping and trading,
and we've done some dealing in property around Wilmington since the war. That's how I came to know Josiah here,
and we decided to look into this venture together. And Father stands ready to invest in it, of course." He looked at
Collier again. "Father did mention that we might possibly
prevail upon you to obtain for us the services of a guide."

"Yes, we've been discussing it," Alcey said quickly, looking at Collier. "I thought that Genesee might be able to go
with them."

Collier shrugged. "You can ask him. I can't speak for
Genesee."

"We would, of course, make appropriate compensation,"

Farnsworth said. "And from our conversation with your good wife, it appears that we might be of some small service to you. We understand that you're having difficulty in perfecting the title to your property here. That being a matter in which we are well versed we could undertake to resolve that for you."

Collier felt irritated over Alcey's discussing their personal affairs with the two men. He glanced at her, then at Farnsworth. "I believe resolving it will amount to lifting some bastard's scalp, and that's a matter in which I'm not unversed. A bugger named Shively who I've never seen or heard of before said that he bought title to land that overlaps mine."

There seemed to be some silent communication between Farnsworth and Jude as they looked at each other. Farnsworth lifted his eyebrows thoughtfully and stroked his chin. "Yes, I daresay we might be able to clear it up. You say you've never heard of this man before? Has he made an offer to buy your property?"

"No, and what do you mean? Do you know him?"

"I think I know of him," Farnsworth replied, and he looked at Jude again. "Isn't he one of those who were in that business on the Lees River?"

"I'm sure I've heard the name," Jude murmured musingly. "And I believe that's where I heard it."

Farnsworth nodded, looking back at Collier. "Yes, if I'm not mistaken, he is one of several who represent certain . . . ah, principals. These principals advance funds, and their representatives use the funds to purchase property and challenge titles in court. Ordinarily one of these representatives will challenge a title and offer the challenged party a sum of money for the property, and the offer is frequently taken by those who are ready to move on elsewhere or who wish to avoid litigation. And it is usually taken sooner or later, because few can afford protracted litigation. But our names aren't unknown to these people. And if this matter is what it seems to be, it will be dropped when our names become involved."

"That seems a very dishonest thing," Alcey said indignantly. "I'd classify that as common thievery, or worse."

The two men exchanged a glance once more, and their smiles seemed sardonically amused and patronizing. "I certainly wouldn't want to attempt to defend the ethics of the means," Jude chuckled. "But this sort of thing does happen, Mama. We've found it before."

Collier hadn't understood all the ramifications of the explanation, but it was clear that he had been the target of some kind of trickery. A gnawing anger seethed within him, and he didn't like Jude's and Farnsworth's faintly amused, offhand attitude about the matter. "Well, I've only finished dealing with the county land clerk on this land, and I thought he was as much of a twister as anyone would ever meet. But it appears I was wrong. Still when I find this bugger Shively, I believe I'll be able to see to him easily enough."

"And another would take his place," Farnsworth replied nonchalantly. "Even if one tracked the matter back to the company funding him, one would have only an office manager and clerk. The principals themselves are well concealed. And ordinarily there is also some connivance on the part of land clerks, so perhaps your dealings with him weren't entirely concluded. The wedge they usually use is an old claim that was rejected as imperfect, and they have it brought into consideration again. Or sometimes they use faulty surveys. In order to do any of this they must have the run of the land records, which they get from land clerks."

"Well, perhaps we can see an end to the difficulty if you'll see what you can do," Alcey said, standing. "Would you care for a sip of toddy, Jude? Supper will be done directly, and a toddy might be good now."

"Yes, thank you, Mama."

"And you, Mr. Farnsworth?"

"Yes, thank you very much."

"I'll make them and see how supper is coming along, then. You'll have one as well, won't you, love?"

It had taken her a long time to get around to asking him. And the way she had turned the problem on the land title over to Jude and Farnsworth was vastly irritating. Collier silently nodded. Alcey smiled anxiously, smoothing her apron over her stomach and moving heavily toward the kitchen door, then she hesitated and turned to the front door. "Oh, here's Genesee. Dear, I'd like you to meet my son Jude, and his associate, Mr. Josiah Farnsworth."

At other times and to other people she had introduced Genesee as her son. The omission was glaring. Genesee looked strong, handsome, and healthy in comparison to Jude's and Farnsworth's pallid, sickly, unwholesome appearance, stepping lithely forward to shake hands with them as they stumbled and shuffled stiffly in their heavy, clumsy shoes. But his smile was far too quick and too wide. There was no reason why he had to exert himself to be friendly with them. Collier felt aggravated at him.

"Genesee, dear, Jude and Mr. Farnsworth need a guide to conduct them to the niter caves and along the Cumberland to look at some land. In return they've very graciously offered to deal with the difficulty we've experienced on the property here. They'll need a guide for about a month or so."

"And in addition there will be compensation for your time, of course," Jude said.

"Pay, do you mean?" Genesee chuckled, shaking his head. "No, no need for that. We're family, aren't we? And a month more or less is little enough to me."

"There's a good lad," Alcey said gratefully, patting Genesee's shoulder as Jude and Farnsworth smiled in satisfaction. "Go ahead and sit down and talk, dear. I'm just going to check on supper and make a toddy for everyone."

Collier looked out the window, and on the edge of his vision he saw Alcey looking at him as she went into the kitchen. Genesee had been very quick to claim kinship with Jude. And in everyone's rush to help Jude and Farnsworth the fact that Genesee was to help in plowing some new ground had been overlooked.

"You're familiar with the niter caves, then?" Jude asked.

"Oh, aye, I've been there any number of times for niter to cure meat and make gunpowder."

"And with the Cumberland?"

"Not as much as with the niter caves, but I'm sure I could find my way around anywhere along it."

"Where would you say most of the niter caves are located?"

"In the hills east of Spruce Flats, I'd say. What do you think, Pa?"

Collier shrugged as he rose and walked toward the hallway. "You know as much about it as I do, Genesee. I'm going to have a look in on my granddaughter."

Collier glanced through the kitchen doorway. Nina was mixing something in a bowl at the table, and Alcey was preparing cups of toddy on the washstand. Timothy Elder huddled on his stool by the hearth, his frail, lanky body folded up and his knitted wool skullcap pulled down on his head as he stared blankly at the fire. Sweat was standing on his face, but he preferred to stay inside and be near Alcey rather than outside where it was cool. Over the years Alcey had patiently worked with him and taught him to carry in wood and water, believing that the boy derived satisfaction from doing something useful. But it was difficult for Collier to tell if he did. What the boy was thinking—or even if he was thinking—was always hidden behind a blank, total lack of expression except when something frightened him. Alcey glanced over her shoulder to say something to Nina, and saw Collier through the doorway and smiled quickly.

"Are you going to have a look in on little Sheila, love? If you do, please be quiet, because she's asleep."

Collier nodded, and he walked along the hallway to the baby's room. Peletheke's wife was in a chair in the corner with her baby in her arms, silently rocking back and forth. Collier nodded to her, quietly closing the door, and crossed the room to the cradle under the window.

In a way the baby was a small remnant of Simon, something of him left behind, a contact with him even though he was gone. But beyond that she was priceless because of herself. A grandparent's pride aside she was an exceptionally beautiful child. Instead of the formlessness of many very small children's faces, her features were clear and distinct, delicately shaped, with finely contoured lips and nose, and enormous eyes.

Rachel's miscarriages had made it seem unlikely that she would ever have a healthy baby, but Sheila was strong and sturdy, as though she had sapped the life force from her mother in leaving her body. She was larger than Nepanna's baby, even though it was a month older and a boy. There had been something of a problem for a time, because Sheila had greedily devoured Nepanna's milk and tried to take most of it away from Nepanna's baby, then the problem had been resolved when Sheila had started eating frumenty and pap earlier than usual. She was a strong, healthy, beautiful baby.

But her fine, thin hair stirring in the gentle breeze coming in the window was far lighter in color than the lightest blonde, a shimmering, silvery white. And despite her healthy constitution, her skin was stark white. The tiny, beautifully shaped lips were colorless. It took a close look to find the minute fingernails, as lacking in color as the fingers. Her eyes were the palest blue, looking huge in her small face. They were almost the color of the eyes of the blind, even though her vision appeared to be normal.

The albinoism had become more distinct during the past months. It was bothersome only because it automatically fell into the classification of a birth defect. And it was a subject everyone tacitly avoided. The only time it had been mentioned in Collier's presence was when Shelby had ventured a remark on it with boyishly gauche directness, and Alcey had replied sharply. But in a way it seemed to enhance the baby's delicate beauty, giving it an angelic quality.

She didn't cry nearly as much as other babies, and far less than the boys had. And while still a baby she already seemed to be developing a personality. At times there appeared to be intelligence behind the large, hazy blue eyes. In moments of anger and frustration Collier always found it soothing to be around her. It was different from the parental pride and satisfaction he had always found in his sons, not necessarily more intense, but love of a different quality. They had been lusty, brawny children. She was a small, precious jewel.

Her eyelids opened. The enormous, icy-blue eyes looked up at him for a long moment, seeming to study his face. Her breathing was more shallow for a few seconds and her lips moved as she swallowed, then she closed her eyes again and her breathing became deeper as she went back to sleep. He turned and walked quietly out of the room, closing the door softly behind him.

Genesee was laughing and talking with Jude and Farnsworth when Collier returned to the front room, and his cup of toddy was on the table by the settle. And his resentment returned. He had been fighting battles over the land title for years, first one difficult, frustrating problem surfac-

ing, then another. It made him appear a helpless fool for
Jude and Farnsworth to casually announce that they could
resolve the latest problem simply by having their names
connected with it. And if what they said was true, a more
appropriate solution would be to track down Shively and
the men behind him and put a knife to their throats. But
things had changed. Battles were fought with sheaves of papers rather than with rifle, knife, and tomahawk. That
opened the door to the dishonest who could twist things on
the sheaves of papers to their own devious ends. And he
couldn't even read the sheaves of papers. So in a way he was
a helpless fool.

Jude and Farnsworth had mincing, fussy ways about
them. Their tones and expressions were patronizing, and
they crossed their legs like women when they sat. Genesee's self-respect appeared to have deserted him, considering the lengths to which he went to be friendly with the
two, laughing at their attempts at humor and agreeing with
what they said.

Alcey was worse. She had always been a proud, confident, self-reliant woman, facing the world with a level look
from her blue eyes. The warm, loving relationship between
her and Simon and that remained between her and Genesee had always included a healthy measure of respect from
them. The three boys laughed, played, and joked with her,
but they also obeyed her implicitly and never ventured to
try her temper. Of the people who had known her most
had liked her, many had loved her, and all had respected
her.

But to Collier she appeared almost servile toward Jude.
At dinner she struggled to think of things to talk about
with him, trying to ingratiate herself with him. And he
seemed almost contemptuous toward her. Alcey kept forcing things on him to eat, hanging on every word he said.
The three boys were childishly silly, rattling on to Jude
about the hounds and raccoons when it was obvious that he
knew nothing about the subject and wasn't interested. After
dinner Alcey struggled upstairs to see to rooms for Jude
and Farnsworth, rushing about and endangering herself
and the baby she was carrying. And Jude was like his father, regarding all that was done for him with bland
aplomb, as no more than his due.

Jude and Farnsworth retired early to get an early start the following morning, and their servant came from the barn and sat in the kitchen door to eat. Some settlers in the area had slaves and Alcey had always been acidly straightforward with them in her attitudes regarding slavery, but she appeared to have forgotten her attitudes for the moment. The servant went upstairs to get Jude's and Farnsworth's shoes and clothes to clean them, and Alcey and Nina helped him, laughing and talking with him. Collier took his pipe and went outside to get out of the noise and confusion, and he sat on the chopping block and smoked. The hounds were trailing a mile or two up the creek. It sounded like the boys had cast the hounds near the pastures, when Collier had told them not to because of people's complaints about the hounds frightening their stock.

Love made it easy to overlook things that would be objectionable in another, and there had been few times when anything had come between him and Alcey. And he couldn't remember a time when there had been anything that couldn't be resolved by discussion and compromise. But the multitude of causes for resentment and dissatisfaction he felt evaded formulation into specific and concrete terms even in his mind, and the only things he could think of that could be put into words were trite. As they lay in bed, her breathing indicated that she was lying awake. The silence between them rang with tension as she waited for him to say something. And he couldn't think of anything to say. After a long time the distant sound of the hounds trailing changed to the frenzy of the pack gathered where the game had gone to tree. Later the boys came home, laughing and talking outside the cabin and entering quietly to go to bed.

Any friction between him and Alcey always made him sleep poorly. And it always made him feel out of step with everything around him, with what would be minor nuisances at other times becoming cause for rage. When he arose in the early morning darkness, Alcey was already up, and rushing about again, jeopardizing herself and the baby. The cabin felt congested with people and activity, even though the boys were still in bed from hunting late, as they frequently were. At breakfast Alcey cautioned Jude at length about the dangers of the Indians along the Cumber-

land. It didn't appear to occur to her that Genesee was
going as well.

Collier went to feed the stock as Genesee began gathering
up his things. Genesee had bagged some supplies the night
before, and he carried them to the barn and sorted them
out to load them on a couple of packhorses. The servant
came back from the cabin, burping and rubbing his stomach contentedly, and he saddled Jude's and Farnsworth's
horses and led them to the cabin. Collier finished feeding
the stock and helped Genesee load the packsaddles and tie
the bags down firmly. Genesee was oddly cheerful and
seemed to be looking forward to the trip, humming and
whistling as they loaded the horses.

They finished loading the horses, and Genesee led his
horse over to them, gathered the reins and halter ropes together, and put out his hand to Collier. "I'll see you in a
few weeks, Pa."

Collier nodded glumly, shaking hands. "You watch yourself. Being out with people who know nothing about Indians or the forest is like having a copperhead in your blanket."

"I'll be all right. In any event we're going by Harrodsburg first for them to look at some records or something.
And while we're there, I'll make sure they see to the title
on the land and get that cleared up. Then we're going
down by Spruce Flats and over to the Barren River, and
from there we'll go on down to the Cumberland. It should
be easy enough, and they know they'll have to listen to me
while we're in the forest."

"They know it here, but they might forget it when they
get there. Both of them think a lot of themselves, and
they're apt to be slow to listen. That Jude is the image of
his father, and while he was always sly enough in his
sneaking, scurvy way, the sod would never listen to anyone
about anything. You do what you have to do, and you get
yourself back here safe and sound. And if it comes down to
protecting them with your life, bugger the sons of bitches.
Just have something to tell your ma so she won't be upset
with you."

Genesee laughed and shook his head. "It won't come to
that, and I'm sure they'll listen. And Jude is all right, you

know. He has his ways and they aren't ours, but he's pleasant enough."

"Pleasant enough?" Collier barked in sudden, furious anger. "How in the goddamned hell do you get that he's pleasant enough when—" He broke off, choking back the torrent of words. Genesee recoiled, looking at him with a startled expression. Collier didn't want to part from Genesee with angry words and a misunderstanding between them, and Genesee was still very much a congenial and straightforward boy, with a lot yet to learn about devious and untrustworthy people. He controlled himself, forced a smile, and put his hand on Genesee's shoulder. "Well, it's neither here nor there. Just look after yourself, lad. The world has armies of people like that pair, but it only has one like you."

Genesee relaxed, smiling. "I'll be careful, Pa. You don't have to worry about me."

They led the horses to the cabin, where Jude and Farnsworth were standing on the porch talking with Alcey and Nina. From the conversation they intended to return to the cabin and stay for a day or two after the trip, which was almost reason to temper the anticipation of Genesee's return. There was a bustle of leavetaking, Jude and Farnsworth shook hands with Collier again, then the line of horses moved off down the road across the meadow, Alcey and Nina waving. Collier lifted his hand and waved to Genesee.

The cow was bawling in the barn. The three boys were still in bed, and Alcey and Nina went back into the cabin and talked quietly as they moved around in the kitchen. It appeared that no one was going to milk the cow unless Collier did, so he took a bucket and went to the barn. Four of the hounds were sprawled in the early morning sunshine by the barn, tired from their chase the night before. They lifted their heads as Collier passed, then stretched out again with heavy sighs and dozed off, twitching their skin at flies hovering around them. Collier milked the cow and took the milk to the springhouse, musing about the new ground to be plowed and thinking irritably about the boys still being in bed. They stayed in bed until Alcey made them get up, and of late she had been letting them sleep until well after sunrise.

Collier became aggravated as he thought about it. He
went back along the path to the cabin, then up the steps
and along the hallway to the end rooms where the boys
slept. He pushed the door of Santee's room open and
looked inside. Santee's clothes were in a pile on the floor,
and he was snoring soundly in his bed, the blanket
wrapped around him and only a bare foot visible.

"Santee!"

Santee's arms and legs flailed convulsively as he struggled to untangle himself from the blanket, and he sat up
with a sleepy, startled expression, pushing his hair out of
his face. "What is it, Pa?"

"It's well past sunrise, that's what it is. Get your arse out
of that bed and down to the barn. We're going to break
some new ground."

Santee yawned and nodded, scratching his head and
pushing the cover aside. "I thought the cabin was on fire."

"You'll think your arse is on fire if you keep on lying
abed of the morning," Collier replied, turning away from
the door and walking back along the hallway. He went
down the steps, then turned. "And get Jared and Shelby
down to the barn with you. They can carry rocks."

"Yes, sir. I'll have them down just as soon as we get a
bite!"

"You'll forget having a bite, and you'll get them and
yourself down there now!" Collier shouted at the top of his
voice.

Santee's quick, affirmative yelp was almost drowned in
the explosion of noise triggered in the kitchen by Collier's
thunderous bellow, Nepanna's baby bursting into frightened screaming, a pan clattering as it was dropped, and the
crash of a bucket hitting the floor. Collier turned and
looked through the kitchen doorway. Timothy had been
carrying a bucket of water through the back door, and water had inundated the kitchen floor. The thin, drawn face
under the wool skullcap was transfixed with terror as he
stumbled back out the door. Alcey rushed to him, pushing
the bucket out of the way with her foot, and followed him
outside. She put her arms around him, and murmured to
him soothingly. He put his head on her shoulder, his fingers digging into her back as he clutched her, his terrified
eyes still riveted on Collier. Nina stooped painfully and be-

gan gathering up the panful of potatoes she had dropped. Nepanna walked back and forth with her baby, rocking it in her arms and murmuring to it. Collier turned and went out the front door.

Nothing went right. The ground along the creek was wet, and it clung to the plow. The plowshare felt dull. The grass was deep and thick, and the sod layer was tough. The plow kept binding on large rocks, and Santee seemed incapable of leading the oxen in a straight line across the contour of land sloping up from the creek. Jared and Shelby began talking and laughing about their hunt the night before as they piled rocks. Their chatter became more and more irritating to Collier, and he finally shouted to Santee to stop the oxen. He glared at the two boys.

"You two get your mind on what you're doing before I thrash the pair of you!"

Jared, always the most outspoken one of the three, replied resentfully, "We're watching what we're doing, Pa."

"You're stumbling around like a pair of fools, that's what you're doing! Are you trying to get snakebit? Get a stick and turn those rocks over before you pick them up!"

They began looking around for sticks, then glanced toward the cabin. Alcey was walking down the slope, carrying a large pan covered with a cloth. She looked at Collier with a placid, pleasant smile as she approached.

"I brought a bite for the boys, love. They should have something in their stomach when they're working in the sun."

The three boys looked at Collier. He nodded, wiping his face with his sleeve. "Go ahead, then. And don't be all day about it."

"I put a cup on the wall by the springhouse," Alcey said, handing the pan to Santee. "Dip yourselves some buttermilk from the brown crock just inside the springhouse door."

"All right, Ma. Do you want us to unhitch the oxen, Pa?"

"You'll wait awhile before you see me let my oxen stand in the sun while you're sitting in the shade and stuffing your face. Lead them up and tie them by the trough, where they can get a drink."

Santee handed the pan to Jared and unfastened the clevis

between the plow and doubletree, and Shelby took the lead rope. The boys walked up the slope, leading the oxen behind them. Alcey pushed a wisp of hair back from the side of her face as she looked at the furrows along the creek. "This has the look of good land, love. If it's this rich on up the hill where it'll be drier, we might try some tobacco on it."

"It might grow tobacco higher up."

Alcey smiled vaguely and nodded, pushing at her hair as the gentle breeze tugged at it, and started to turn away. Then she hesitated and looked back at him, her smile fading as her eyes searched his face. She was silent for a moment, then she spoke in a soft, placating tone. "Is it because I love Jude that you're angry with me, then? The fact that I love him doesn't mean that I love you and the boys a whit less, you know. Nothing can change that, love."

The smoldering anger within him abruptly became fiery, a seething rage, and he shook his head brusquely, looking away. "He's your son, and I'd be the last to deny you the right of loving your own child. But knowing you as I do, I'm at a loss as to how you can find love for him when he treats you like dirt under his feet, much as that scheming bugger of a father of his did."

Alcey blanched and recoiled, an appalled expression on her face. "But he treated me well," she said, shaking her head rapidly. "He's had little affection, poor soul, and he finds it difficult to express affection the way our boys do, but he certainly didn't treat me . . ." Her voice faded, and her eyes filled with tears as her lips began trembling. "He loves me!"

Collier's anger suddenly drained away, leaving a hollow, leaden depression. And as he looked at her, her swollen body shaking with sobs, her beautiful face twisted, and tears running down her cheeks, he felt wrenching guilt and sorrow for having been deliberately cruel to her. He put his arms around her, pulling her to him. "God, Alcey," he sighed heavily. "I wish I could bite my scurvy tongue off for saying that. It isn't true, and I didn't mean it. And I don't know why I said it."

She hesitated, then leaned against him and put her head against his chest, wiping her eyes with her hands. "He does love me."

"Of course he does. Who in the bloody hell could meet you and not love you? And moreover, a son. I know he loves you, and I know he must be sorry that he's never come to see you before. But he couldn't be a part as sorry as I am right now for what I said."

She drew in a deep, shuddering breath, looking up at him, then smiled tremulously and shrugged. "It's done and past, so let's leave it, love."

"No, it'll never be past for me, the way I feel, and I'll never say anything like that again to you, Alcey. And I'll not leave it until you forgive me."

Her smile was warm as she blinked the tears from her eyes, and she lifted her hand and touched his cheek. "I forgive you, and gladly, love. I owe you much, and I'd forgive that and much more. Will you walk back with me?"

"Aye, I will," he said, putting his arm around her shoulders and turning her toward the cabin. "You shouldn't be climbing up and down out here and carrying things, and I'll help you back up to the path. And I don't know how it is that you owe me anything. Between us I've always been the one who owed you, not the other way around."

Alcey wiped her eyes with the back of her hand, looking down at the grass as they walked through it. "Yes, I know that's how you feel, love, because that's the way you've acted every day of our marriage. And that's why I owe you, you see."

"What do you mean?"

She started to reply, then shrugged and shook her head. "Nothing, love." She smiled up at him, then looked away, sighing. "You know, I wish there had been some way I could have forewarned you that Jude was here so you wouldn't have had it thrust upon you so suddenly. I knew it would be difficult for you, because you've always been a bit jealous of our sons. So considering he's Jubal's son and you and Jubal never—"

"Jealous of our sons?" he said in astonishment, stopping and looking down at her. He backed away a step as he looked at her, then he burst into boisterous laughter, shaking his head. "How in God's name can a man be jealous of his own sons, Alcey? No, I don't know what I've said or done to make you think that, but it's not the case at all."

She smiled at him, then nodded and looked away. "Very well, love."

He laughed again, putting his arm back around her shoulders and walking her toward the cabin again. "Don't give me your sly look," he chuckled. "I can see that you think otherwise, but you're wrong. A man can't be jealous of his own sons, Alcey."

"Then I was wrong, and it isn't important in any event, love. Rafe had a hog break a leg this morning, and he butchered it and sent us a nice lot of backbone and ribs. We'll have that and some of the new potatoes for supper."

The change of subject had been quick and transparent. And a hint of the knowing smile hovered around her lips as he looked down at her. He chuckled and patted her shoulder fondly as he leaned down and kissed her.

He left her on the path from the barn to the cabin, and walked back down to the creek. An oppressive burden had been lifted from his mind. The strain between him and Alcey was gone, and the day had changed. The sun was bright and sparkling, the caroling of the birds was lively and cheerful, and the creek gurgled merrily. The air had a warm, vibrant feel. Even the fact that Jude and Farnsworth were dealing with the problem on the land title rankled less, because it seemed appropriate to send weasels to deal with rats. The boys brought the oxen back down, and there was an intense pleasure in working with his sons around him, the three of them strong, muscular boys, looking very much alike with their black hair and blue eyes, but individuals and all different from each other. Santee was the congenial one, usually amiable, smiling, and eager to please. Jared had a quicker temper, and he always said what was on his mind. Shelby was the quiet one, with a slower but more vicious temper that might be dangerous in time. Where Santee and Jared would strike back in retaliation, Shelby took time to find a stick or stone to strike back with. And in time the stick or stone might be a knife or rifle. A quality they all shared was self-respect, and it took Collier a while of laughing and joking with them to break through their aloof and polite reserve. Then he did, and they laughed and joked with him.

Everything went right. There were fewer large rocks on up the slope from the creek, and the plow easily tore through the sod and bared the rich, fertile earth with its warm odor and soft, damp feel. Jared and Shelby talked and laughed as they rolled and carried rocks, and Santee exchanged comments with them when he passed them, leading the oxen back and forth along the edge of the widening plowed strip. Collier guided the plow, and the deeply satisfying feel of the plowshare rolling the earth open vibrated in the handles of the plow as the oxen put their massive strength against the yoke.

By sunset the swath of freshly plowed soil extended well up the slope from the creek, and the oxen were sweaty and weary as they drank at the trough and went to their fodder to eat. Collier was tired, the relaxed, gratifying fatigue that was combined with a feeling of accomplishment. He was also hungry, and dinner was rich, spicy, and delicious— pork backbones and ribs, new potatoes, vegetables, and corn bread. The quiet joy of the family group around the table provided a sustenance that was even more essential, and the satisfaction was more intense because of the renewed harmony between him and Alcey. The boys were tired and hungry as well, but at dinner they shrugged off their weariness with the boundless reserves of energy of youth, and began talking about taking the hounds and going hunting for raccoons.

The boys left after dinner, whistling and calling the hounds. Alcey and Nina washed dishes and cleaned up the kitchen, Timothy sat on his stool on one side of the hearth and Collier sat on the other, and Nepanna bathed Sheila and her own baby to get them ready to go to bed. Collier held Sheila for a few minutes, and she lay in his arms and looked up at him gravely with her massive, pale blue, strangely wise eyes.

Collier went out and bathed, and when he came in, Alcey was mixing him a cup of toddy. The others had gone to their rooms, and the kitchen had the quiet atmosphere of the end of a day. He filled his pipe and sat on his stool again, and Alcey gave him the cup, took out her writing box and the old Bible, and sat on her stool in front of the hearth. Collier puffed on his pipe and sipped his toddy, looking at the writing box. Simon had made it for her. It was large and fit across her thighs to give her a smooth surface for writing, the lid was hinged and had a recess for her inkwell, and there was a hasp and a large padlock on the box. Alcey lifted the lid and took out several sheets of paper she had filled with her small, neat lines of writing. She looked through them, rustling them softly, then put them back in the box and opened the old Bible.

"You got a good stretch of that new ground broken today, love."

"It'll do for a day's work. The boys put their backs into it as well. They're good workers when they set their mind to something.

"They're three lazybones," Alcey chuckled fondly. "The only thing they can stir themselves on is running my hounds to death. She looked up from the Bible, her smile fading. "Rafe's boy Uriah said that Indians killed a man over by Alder Creek yesterday. Do you think it might be a good idea to keep the boys in for a while?"

Collier shook his head, puffing on his pipe. "I'd hate to be the Indian that tried to bother those boys as long as they have those hounds with them. And a lot of killing that's blamed on Indians is done by robbers for what a man has in his pockets. Who was killed?"

"Uriah didn't know the man's name. He said it was someone new. Someone his father didn't know."

Collier nodded, taking a drink from his cup, and he puffed on his pipe again. The distant baying of the hounds blended with the chirping of crickets coming through the open door. "It sounds like they've struck a hot trail."

Alcey turned her head, listening, then looked back down at the Bible. "Yes, they're running full out, aren't they?"

"Aye, they are. What are you going to do with all you're writing about the family, Alcey? Pass it along to the boys?"

"No fear of that," she laughed. "Those louts would use it to light a fire. No, if one of them marries a smart girl who has her wits about her, then she'll get it. If not, I'll light a fire with it myself."

"You might give it to little Sheila when the time comes. She could add onto it, if that's what you have in mind. And I'm sure she'd have more interest in it than a daughter-in-law, because it concerns her and hers directly."

"I'm a daughter-in-law, you know."

"No, not the way most are. You were as much a daughter to Ma and Pa as Jubal and I were sons, and more so in the case of Jubal, I believe. And there are few daughters who'd look after their pa in his old age the way you did mine."

"I did what I could, and I treasured their love, God knows." She turned the pages in the Bible and nodded. "Perhaps it would be better for Sheila to have all this, not that it's so precious because I did it, but because I do think it's something worth keeping and passing along. Your mother and father toiled all their lives, and that deserved to be written down so others will know about it. You did far more for this country than most, and that had to be put down the way it happened." She turned to the first page in the Bible and looked at it. On one side of the page under Frieda Kohler's name, Jubal Collier and Alcey Martin Collier were listed, with Jude underneath. The other side of the page had several names listed. Santee Collier with a blank space at one side, and Simon underneath. Santee Collier and Aimee Gireaux Collier, with Genesee underneath. Santee Collier and Alcey Martin Collier, with Santee, Jared, and Shelby underneath. Below Simon's name, Rachel Cosgrave Collier had been written in, with Sheila underneath. Alcey looked back up from the Bible, smiling at Collier. "But there's a part I'm missing, and it would be of interest to Sheila."

"What's that?"

"We've never discussed who Simon's mother was."

Collier's smile faded. He looked at Alcey unsurely, moving on his stool, then looked at the fire and shrugged. "It's neither here nor there. And I've never mentioned it, because I'm well aware of how women are about things like that. Not that I'd hold it against you for not wanting it waved about in your face, mind. Well, I think you're right about that new ground being good soil for tobacco, but it's late in the year for thinking about tobacco, isn't it?"

"Yes, we could plant it in corn this year, and then think about it again for next year," she replied absently, looking at him musingly, then she chuckled dryly. "Women aren't nearly as put out on things of that nature as men are. And you may be assured that I'm well aware of what a rogue you are."

"Not half as much as you make me out to be," he said,

laughing uncomfortably. "We've more than enough corn in the ground already, haven't we?"

"We could find a good market for it in Lexington if we have more than we need." She looked back down at the Bible, waiting, then looked at Collier again. "Well, who was she, love?"

He drew in a deep breath and released it in a sigh, shrugging, and picked up his cup. "Ellen Harnett was her name, and she lived on the Catawba. Her husband was a trapper and he got killed, then she married a man named Elder. They were both killed during an Indian raid, and I went by there and fetched Simon to Wilmington." He took a drink from his cup, put it down on the hearth, and looked at Alcey. She was frowning with intense concentration, and her frown was changing to an expression of dismay as the color drained from her face. He leaned toward her. "Are you all right, Alcey?"

She made a sound in her throat, looking into the fire, her eyes wide with horror and her face blanched.

"What is it, Alcey?" he said in concern, leaning over and taking her arm. "Are you all right?"

She nodded absently, then blinked and glanced at him, nodding again. "Yes."

"Well, what is it? What's wrong, Alcey?"

She cleared her throat and straightened up on her stool, glancing at him again and smiling weakly as she nodded. "Yes . . . yes, I'm all right."

"But what made you go that way? What's wrong, Alcey?"

She pushed at her hair, drawing in a deep breath and collecting herself, then touched her stomach. "Perhaps it was the baby shifting."

"The baby shifting? That's never made you go that way before. You looked like you were about to . . . here, have a sip of this toddy."

"No, it wouldn't be good for the baby, love. And I'm all right now. It was just a passing thing."

"Well, I'm not surprised, the way you've been running about these past two days. You're going to have to look after yourself better. Are you sure you're all right?"

"Yes, I'm quite all right now, love."

Collier sat back on his stool, looking at her with a concerned frown and puffing on his pipe. Alcey looked down at the Bible for a long moment, pondering, then she closed it and put it on the edge of the hearth. She opened the writing box again, taking out the sheaf of papers. There was a half-filled sheet on Simon, Rachel, and Sheila, and she separated it, then opened the box and took out her quill, knife, and inkwell. She sharpened the quill, opened the inkwell and dipped the quill, and began writing about Ellen Cosgrave, Rachel's older sister and Simon's mother. She now knew the reason for Sheila's birth defect—a kinship she wished to hide but must record.

A faint whimper of a baby crying came along the hall, then stopped. Collier looked toward the hallway, listening, then reached for his cup. "That'll be Nepanna's baby."

"Yes, little Sheila rarely cries at night. I wish I could say the same about those three I had."

Collier chuckled and nodded. "She is a good baby. I only wish Pa could have been alive when she was born. He always wanted a girl in the family named after my ma."

"Yes, it's too bad he didn't live a while longer so he could have seen her. But he had a good life, love, and he's gone to his reward."

"Aye. If that one you're carrying is a girl, what do you want to name it?"

"Frieda."

Her tone was a statement of intention, not a suggestion. Before they had always discussed names for the children, and while he had always deferred to her choices, there had been discussion. And he didn't particularly like the name. It had a foreign sound. "What made you think of that name, Alcey?"

"Don't you like it, love?"

He thought, then smiled and shrugged, puffing on his pipe. "It's all the same to me, if that's your choice. You're the one having it, and if that's what you'd like to call it, then I won't argue."

"That's what I'd like, if it's a girl."

Alcey looked back down at the paper, dipping the quill again. It made a soft scratching sound as she wrote. Collier picked up his cup to take a drink, then looked at the doorway. The baying of the hounds was a velvet sound in the night, taking on the triumphant rhythm and tone of victory as the pack gathered where the game had gone to tree. "It didn't take them long to put him up, did it?"

Alcey looked at the door, listening, then looked back down at the paper. "No, it didn't, love."

"Those are good hounds."

"Yes, they're good hounds, love. They run a good race."

# THE SUPERCHILLER THAT GOES BEYOND THE SHOCKING, SHEER TERROR OF *THE BOYS FROM BRAZIL*

# THE AXMANN AGENDA

## MIKE PETTIT

1944: Lebensborn—a sinister scheme and a dread arm of the SS that stormed across Europe killing, raping, destroying and stealing the children.
NOW: Victory—a small, mysteriously wealthy organization of simple, hard-working Americans—is linked to a sudden rush of deaths.

Behind the grass-roots patriotism of Victory does the evil of Lebensborn live on? Is there a link between Victory and the Odessa fortune—the largest and most lethal economic weapon the world has ever known? *The Axmann Agenda*—it may be unstoppable!

**A Dell Book**          **$2.50    (10152-2)**

At your local bookstore or use this handy coupon for ordering: